SAY GOOD-BYE TO THE HOMEWORLD. . . .

"My Khans," Osis began, speaking in the low, rumbling tone of a Smoke Jaguar. "I come to you with grave news.

"You are all aware that the Inner Sphere, claiming the aegis of the Star League, has attacked our holdings in the Occupation Zone. But that is of no consequence. Though they have made a few initial gains, I assure you, my Khans, that the Smoke Jaguar will soon turn and rip out the throat of his tormentor. Then they will feel the wrath of the Jaguar. We shall punish these foolish barbarians for daring to make such an obscene claim to the throne of the Star League.

"But, my Khans, a new threat has arisen, one that was not to be expected. I waited to bring you this news until I could confirm it for myself. Now it is confirmed, and it is news that might mean disaster for all of the Clans, not just the Smoke Jaguar. . . ."

CAMERON STAR

BATTLETECH®

Twilight of the Clans VI:
SHADOWS OF WAR

Thomas S. Gressman

A Roc Book

ROC
Published by the Penguin Group
Penguin Putnam Inc., 375 Hudson Street,
New York, New York 10014, U.S.A.
Penguin Books Ltd, 27 Wrights Lane,
London W8 5TZ, England
Penguin Books Australia Ltd, Ringwood,
Victoria, Australia
Penguin Books Canada Ltd, 10 Alcorn Avenue,
Toronto, Ontario, Canada M4V 3B2
Penguin Books (N.Z.) Ltd, 182–190 Wairau Road,
Auckland 10, New Zealand

Penguin Books Ltd, Registered Offices:
Harmondsworth, Middlesex, England

First published by Roc, an imprint of Dutton NAL,
a member of Penguin Putnam Inc.

First Printing, September, 1998
10 9 8 7 6 5 4 3 2 1

Series Editor: Donna Ippolito
Cover art by Bruce Jensen
Mechanical Drawings: Duane Loose and the FASA art department

ROC REGISTERED TRADEMARK—MARCA REGISTRADA

BATTLETECH, FASA, and the distinctive BATTLETECH and FASA logos are trademarks of the FASA Corporation, 1100 W. Cermak, Suite B305, Chicago, IL 60608.

Printed in the United States of America

For Brenda

Thanks once again to all those who contributed their time, encouragement, and expertise to the creation of this story. Thanks to Donna Ippolito, who kept the fire lit under me, and made me be the best I could. My gratitude to those experts too numerous to mention here who contributed their knowledge of things dark and esoteric. Any errors in these pages are mine alone. Thanks again to Brenda for all her patience. And, as always, thank You, Lord.

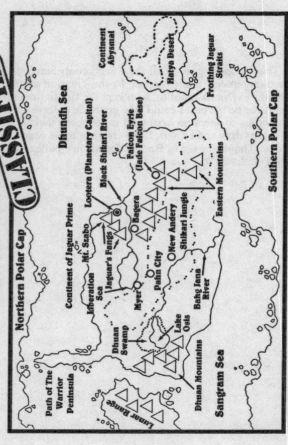

MAP OF HUNTRESS

CLASSIFIED

Northern Polar Cap

Path of The Warrior Peninsula

Dhuan Swamp

Liberation Sea

Continent of Jaguar Prime

Mt. Szabo

Jaguar's Fangs

Myer

Bajera

Pahn City

Lootera (Planetary Capital)

Black Shikari River

Dhundh Sea

Continent Abysmal

Hatya Desert

Falcon Eyrie (Jade Falcon Base)

Frothing Jaguar Straits

ONew Andery

Shikari Jungle

Bahg Jana River

Eastern Mountains

Lunar Range

Lake Oats

Dhuan Mountains

Sangram Sea

Southern Polar Cap

Prologue

The year is 3060.

Task Force Serpent, a massive invasion force drawn from across the Inner Sphere, has been sent far behind enemy lines to strike at the Clan Smoke Jaguar homeworld of Huntress. Their mission is twofold: attack and seize Huntress and obliterate the Smoke Jaguars' war-making capability. At last, after nearly a year's voyage through the uncharted vastness of space, they have arrived.

But even before Operation Serpent could come within striking range of Huntress, its original leader, Marshal Morgan Hasek-Davion, was assassinated. Command of the task force passed to General Ariana Winston, commander of the elite Eridani Light Horse mercenary brigade. Under her skilled direction, Serpent launched an historic assault, seizing the Clan homeworld. Against all odds, it seemed that the operation might well defy all conventional military wisdom, and be the proverbial walkover.

But, as in all military operations, many things can go wrong and no force commander can prevent them all. Inner Sphere troops control the world of Huntress, but Winston fears the Jaguar garrison may have managed to send out a call for reinforcements before they fell.

Now, as her force carries out the second half of their mission, the destruction of the Smoke Jaguars' future ability to make war, none of them is aware of the new threat bearing down on them.

Grand Council Chamber, Hall of the Khans
Warrior Quarter, Strana Mechty
Kerensky Cluster, Clan Space
13 March 3060

IlKhan Lincoln Osis looked around the ancient chamber from beneath the onyx-inlaid, silver-chased mask concealing his features. His manner and bearing proclaimed the strength and pride of his warrior's spirit, though he hated the thought of what he was about to do.

The Khans of all the Clans had gathered in the council chamber at his command. Most had laid aside their ceremonial masks, as would he once he took his seat at the head of the council. Only Vladimir Ward of the Wolves and Marthe Pryde of the Jade Falcons retained their masks, almost, but not quite, openly mocking him as Khan of the Khans.

No matter, Osis told himself. *Once the business at hand is done with, I will turn on those two foolish weaklings and strangle the life out of them.*

With his back as straight as a 'Mech's driver rod, Osis strode to the ilKhan's place. He was a huge man, his size and muscular bulk the crowning glory of the genetic engineering program that had created him. Such a formidable build was necessary to control the sophisticated Elemental battle armor for which he had been bred and trained. Out of that massive suit of powered armor, Osis somehow seemed even larger. His ebon skin and the impressive layers of muscle gave him the appearance of a dangerous predatory animal.

For a moment he surveyed the other Khans coldly through the thin sapphire lenses set into his mask's eye-slits. The deep blue wafers simulated the ice-blue eyes of a smoke jaguar, while at the same time having a slightly telescopic effect on the mask-wearer's vision. To Osis, it seemed that the mask gave him the ability to see into the other Khans' souls, and he did not like what he saw.

The Grand Council Chamber was the seat of Clan political power. It was here in this large, echoing room that the decision to finally invade the Inner Sphere had been made. A subtle feeling of centuries and immense power suffused the very walls of the chamber. The Khans of all the Clans sat in carved granite seats behind broad marble-topped tables in the places prescribed for them. Originally, Osis knew, there had been twenty such tables, one for each of the Clans.

Behind each desk there hung an archaic cloth banner, hand-embroidered by some member of the laborer caste, displaying the symbol of the Clan represented by the Khan and saKhan who sat beneath the banner. Each of the polished mahogany tables held, concealed in their surfaces, a wide array of data retrieval and display equipment.

Now there were only sixteen places. Three of the missing Clans—Widowmaker, Mongoose, and Burrock—had been Absorbed by larger, more powerful Clans. The fourth, the Not-Named Clan, had been wiped out in a bloody Trial of Annihilation because of the taint of a lust for power. As those Clans vanished for all time, their seats were left empty as a grim reminder to the surviving Clans of the price of failure or weakness. Indeed, Clan Burrock had only recently been Absorbed by Clan Star Adder in the midst of the preparations for a renewed invasion of the Inner Sphere.

A thrill of anger rumbled in Osis' chest as he turned his gaze upon Severen Leroux and Lucien Carns, respectively the Khan and saKhan of the Nova Cats. To his mind, many of the Smoke Jaguars' troubles had begun two years before, when his Clan's best and brightest, the Tau Galaxy, was destroyed by two Clusters of the Nova Cats' Sigma Galaxy on the planet called Wildcat. Now, there were rumors of the Nova Cats laying down their arms before the Inner Sphere invasion force, sometimes without even the pretense of a fight. Osis had long suspected the Cats of weakness, with their reliance on mysticism and belief in dreams and portents. Even in the wake of the destruction of Tau Galaxy, Osis would not have believed any Clansman capable of the kind of duplicity in which the Nova Cats now seemed to be engaged.

I will deal with the Nova Cats in their turn, Osis promised himself.

Directly opposite the chamber's sole entryway stood another table. It was here that Kael Pershaw was installed as Loremaster.

With a low growl, Osis lifted the mask, revealing his own features at last. He felt his face go hot with anger when he saw Vlad and Marthe slowly—intentionally so, he was sure—removing their own vizards. It took an effort of his will, but Osis was able to push his anger aside and just as deliberately took his seat.

For the moment, my Khans, but only for the moment.

"Hear my words, Khans of the Clans," rang out the voice of the Loremaster. "I am Kael Pershaw, and I serve as Loremaster for this gathering of the Grand Council. I hereby convene this conclave under the provisions of the Martial Code, as laid down by Nicholas Kerensky. Because we exist in a state of war, all matters shall be conducted according to its provisions."

"Seyla," the Khans intoned solemnly in unison.

Pershaw nodded to Osis, then resumed his seat. Slowly, deliberately, Osis stood. He knew that a predator must move just that way until the precise moment to pounce.

"My Khans," he began, speaking in the low, rumbling tone of a Smoke Jaguar. "I come to you with grave news.

"You are all aware that the Inner Sphere, claiming the aegis of the Star League, has attacked our holdings in the Occupation Zone. Were it not for the delay caused by the Trial of Absorption against Clan Burrock, we would have renewed the Crusade before now, and forestalled the Inner Sphere attack."

He waved his hand in contempt. "But that is of no consequence. Though they have made a few initial gains, I assure you, my Khans, that the Smoke Jaguar will soon turn and rip out the throat of his tormentor. Then they will feel the wrath of the Jaguar, and learn the folly of their hubris. The sacred banner of the Star League can fly over Terra only when the descendants of the Kerenskys return to Terra. We shall punish these foolish barbarians for daring to make such an obscene claim to the throne of the Star League.

"But, my Khans, a new threat has arisen, one that was not to be expected. I waited to bring you this news until I could confirm it for myself. Well, now it is confirmed, and it is news that might well mean disaster for all of the Clans, not just the Smoke Jaguars. I have received and confirmed reports that a task force, bearing the Cameron Star of the Star League, and claiming to act under the direction of the First Lord, has arrived at Huntress.

"Even now, these barbarians are attacking the homeworld of Clan Smoke Jaguar. Reports state that they have seized Mount Szabo and our genetic repository. Such a thing has never happened in all the long history of the Clans. One of our homeworlds has been seized and the legacy of many thousands of warriors is being threatened by freebirth barbarians from the Inner Sphere.

"I call upon you, my Khans, to rise in the defense of your ilKhan. Most of the strength of the Jaguar is in the Inner Sphere, fighting to retain what we have won through lawful conquest. I have no force here on Strana Mechty, save my command Star of Elementals, the warriors of the Jaguar's Den, and the command Trinary of Shroud Keshik.

All the rest of my forces are in the Occupation Zone. I have committed even the bulk of my naval reserve forces to the defense of my Clan's holdings, keeping back only the *Streaking Mist,* my personal command ship.

"I have called you here today, my Khans, to ask that you stand with me, lend me your strength, aid me in my righteous quest to drive the invader from my homeworld and purge this blot upon the honor not only of the Smoke Jaguar, but of the Clans as a whole."

As he spoke Lincoln Osis suppressed a shudder of revulsion at the idea of his homeworld being defiled by the presence of Inner Sphere troops. He also hated the idea of having to come before the Grand Council asking the Khans of the other Clans for help in defending Huntress, but he had no real choice. He knew that the two Galaxies of troops garrisoning that planet were little more than useless solahma or warriors who had proved themselves unworthy of the front lines. Also present were a few sibkos of new, unblooded warriors about to test out from training, but Huntress was not defended by front-line OmniMechs any more than by front-line warriors. The garrisons were equipped principally with second-line machines or even Inner Sphere 'Mechs taken as *isorla.* The cadets, their instructors, and the solahma units stood little chance of throwing the invaders back. To retake Huntress, he would need help, and the only help immediately available would have to come from the other Clans.

For a long moment there was silence. Then Severen Leroux, Khan of the Nova Cats, spoke in low, hushed tones, as though to himself.

"It is as it has been foreseen. The Jaguar will pass through the flames. Will he come out again? I cannot say."

"I want none of your fortune-telling, Khan of the Nova Cats," Osis growled. "What I need is your strength."

"IlKhan, are we to understand that the Inner Sphere, these barely jump-capable barbarians, have somehow found their way to Huntress? To one of the Kerensky Cluster worlds?" Khan Bjorn Jorgensson of the Ghost Bears spoke slowly and deliberately. "That is not possible. No one is privy to the complete route of the Exodus Road, not even our own ship captains who command the ships that take us to and from the Inner Sphere. How can you expect us to believe that the Inner Sphere has discovered the key to a secret so long hidden?

"We are all well aware that the Successor States, believing that in unity they might find the strength to reclaim some of their conquered territory, have joined together under the banner of the Star League, and for that they will be punished in due time. But, how can we credit your story of an invasion of Huntress?"

"It is true, Khan Bjorn Jorgensson." Marthe Pryde stood, but she was not looking at Jorgensson. She fixed Osis with a green-eyed stare that perfectly matched the empty gaze of the lifeless Falcon mask upon which her fingers now rested. Her voice fairly dripped with satisfaction.

"As you are all well aware, long before the start of the Crusade, ilKhan Leo Showers gifted the Jade Falcons with a piece of Huntress. He allowed us to establish a small presence there, a research station in the Eastern Mountains of the planet. We call it Falcon Eyrie."

Marthe grinned wickedly as she reached into one of her uniform's breast pockets. When she pulled her hand out, she was holding a small datachip. Slipping the device into the reader unit set into the council table's polished mahogany top, Marthe touched a control, and a strong baritone voice filled the room.

"Khan Marthe Pryde," the voice said. "I, Star Colonel Nikolai Icaza, salute you from Falcon Eyrie on Huntress.

"My Khan, I bring you unfortunate news. Eight standard days ago, a large war fleet jumped in from hyperspace, arriving at the Huntress zenith point. At first we were unable to discern the identity of the new arrivals, except that we believed them to be Clan vessels on their way to or from the Occupation Zone. As you are certainly well aware, the Smoke Jaguars have been moving many ships into and out of their holdings in the Inner Sphere."

Osis gasped in surprise. He knew of Falcon Eyrie, of course. What he didn't know was that the Falcons were using the small base to keep track of his Clan's ship movements. Osis narrowed his eyes as he gazed at Marthe Pryde. What else had the Jade Falcons learned from their little enclave on Huntress? Unfortunately, that too would have to wait.

"It took us some hours," the recording continued, "to discern the true identity of the newly arrived vessels. It was not until we intercepted coded transmissions between the Smoke Jaguar ships lying at the Huntress jump points and Galaxy Commander Russou Howell's command center that we were able to identify the newcomers.

"My Khan, the incoming war fleet hails from the Inner Sphere.

"According to our best intelligence analysis, the fleet consists of no fewer than five WarShips and ten transport-type JumpShips, although there may be more. As you are aware, our sensor and tracking facilities here are severely limited. Whatever the composition of the war fleet, it was sufficient to transport at least forty combat DropShips into the system.

"Huntress is now under heavy assault by the forces of the Inner Sphere. Radio intercepts suggest that the commander of the task force is General Ariana Winston, of the Eridani Light Horse. We have intercepted transmissions from the Kathil Uhlans, the Com Guards, and the Lyran Guards as well.

"As of this moment, Falcon Eyrie is not under attack, although our sensors have detected a body of armed men skulking in the rocks north of our perimeter fences. We believe them to be Inner Sphere reconnaissance troops, sent to keep this installation under surveillance.

"For now, we seem to be safe from attack, and will hold ourselves apart from any involvement in what seems to be an affair concerning the Smoke Jaguars only. If you have any instructions to the contrary, I await them.

"I remain Star Colonel Nikolai Icaza, at Falcon Eyrie, Huntress."

For a few moments there was stunned silence in the council chamber. Then, the solemn gathering erupted into outcries, curses, and protests, the whole conclave threatening to dissolve in a storm of arguments and shouted recriminations.

"Khan Marthe, how long have you known of this?" Lynn McKenna, Khan of the Snow Ravens, barked at her.

"Why have you not brought this to the attention of the Council before this?" That from Khan Ian Hawker of Clan Diamond Shark.

"Fifteen starships cannot carry all that number of troops. Your garrison forces should be able to defeat them, ilKhan. Do you mean to suggest that if we do not aid you Huntress must fall?" demanded Bjorn Jorgensson.

Osis winced at the Ghost Bear Khan's estimate of his garrison's capabilities. He had purposely kept the size and nature of his garrison force a secret until now. Had the other Clans learned that Huntress was defended by mere solahma troops who were, by Clan standards, ill-equipped, he would have risked a Trial of Possession. Osis also knew that approximately a Galaxy-sized body of troops, under Galaxy Commander Hang Mehta, was on its way to Huntress, but he did not know precisely where that fleet was right now. He had ordered Mehta and what was left of her decimated force in the Occupation Zone to withdraw and return to Huntress for refit and reorganization. That was further information he had not revealed to his fellow Khans.

Now he was paying the price for those secrets.

"The Ice Hellions have only limited forces, ilKhan," snapped Asa Taney, Khan of the Hellions. His words sounded like the angry, staccato bark of his Clan's totem. "What if we do give you our support, and the barbarians prove stronger than you suppose? What if they make a drive on Hector or another of our worlds? The forces we do have are sufficient only to defend our own holdings, not to launch an offensive to retake the Smoke Jaguar homeworld for them."

A murmur of agreement rose from the Khans of the smaller, less powerful Clans.

"IlKhan, you speak as though the loss of Huntress to

these barbarians is a foregone conclusion," said Marthe Pryde. "Have you so little faith in the strength of your Clan? Perhaps another Trial of Absorption is in order."

"I agree with Khan Asa Taney," Perigard Zalman of the Steel Vipers said. "The Smoke Jaguars are an Invading Clan. As such, they should be powerful enough to protect themselves without asking the other Clans for help. Why should we weaken ourselves in the defense of another Clan? Thus far only the Smoke Jaguars have been targeted by the Inner Sphere. If we waste our strength retaking Huntress, how long will we have to wait for enough trained warriors to renew the Crusade? We have already been delayed once so the Star Adders could add to their strength and holdings. Should we delay again because the Smoke Jaguars haven't the strength to hold on to what is theirs?"

"It is not true, Khan Perigard Zalman, that only the Smoke Jaguars have been attacked," Osis snarled. "The Nova Cats have suffered the loss of several worlds in the Occupation Zone."

"That is true, ilKhan," Severen Leroux said quietly. "But our losses have not been as grievous as yours. We have seen the future, and have embraced it. The limb that will not bend will be broken."

Only Vlad Ward sat silent, thoughtfully running a callused forefinger along his scarred jaw.

"Order! Order!" Osis was shouting. "Let us have order here, my Khans."

Gradually the tumult died away.

"This is what I have been trying to tell you," Osis snarled. "And now you have confirmation. Independent confirmation.

"Now is the time to act in concert. If we do not destroy this blight, this outrage, it will turn to devour more of the homeworlds when it has finished with Huntress. You must lend me your strength. Give me whatever military assets you can spare. Your personal guards, your training cadres—it matters not to me. Only lend me your strength, and I will crush these barbarians into dust. Then, there will be honor to spare for all of the Clans."

"A very pretty speech, ilKhan." Vlad Ward seemed to be suppressing a smile as he finally began to speak. "But what proof have we that these barbarians will, as you say, 'turn and devour more worlds'? I well know the strength of the Jaguar on Huntress. Khan Marthe's man says that the barbarians arrived in, what, forty DropShips? Even assuming that this estimate is accurate, how many 'Mechs could they be carrying? Five hundred at the most. IlKhan, are you telling us that your garrison on Huntress cannot deal with five regiments of Inner Sphere troops? Why, during the Crusade, there were times when half as many Jaguars destroyed half again as many barbarians in a single day."

Khan Jorgensson rose to speak. "While I cannot confirm Khan Vladimir Ward's estimate of the size of the invasion force, nor the capability of the Huntress garrison, I do agree with Khan Marthe's commander on Huntress. This seems to be a matter between the Inner Sphere and the Smoke Jaguars, and only the Smoke Jaguars. Let the rest of the Clans not insert ourselves in this matter, but allow the Smoke Jaguars the honor of defending their own homeworld. If they triumph, as I am certain they will, then all the more honor to them. If the unthinkable happens, if Huntress falls to the forces of the Inner Sphere, then perhaps Lincoln Osis is not fit to be the ilKhan of the Clans after all."

"Are you all mad?" Osis roared, leaping to his feet. "Can you not see the danger to us all?"

"It appears to me that there is danger only to your Clan's homeworld, *quiaff*?" Marthe Pryde snapped. "The rest of us are under no threat from these *surats*."

"IlKhan," Severen Leroux said quietly. "There is a proposition before this conclave. You are honor-bound to call for a vote."

"Very well, my Khans." Osis straightened his spine, determined to abide by the decision of the Council like the trueborn warrior he was. In that moment, he was no longer certain whether he would accept the aid of the other Khans even if they voted to help him. "I call for the vote."

Osis flopped angrily into his seat as Kael Pershaw stood to take his place.

"As Loremaster, I now call the vote." Pershaw's voice was deep and solemn. "The vote shall be by voice. You shall say yea if you are in favor of aiding Clan Smoke Jaguar in the defense of Huntress. If you oppose such action, you shall say nay.

"Khan Ian Hawker of the Diamond Sharks, how say you?"

"I say, nay, Loremaster." So too did saKhan Barbara Sennet.

"Khan Bjorn Jorgensson of the Ghost Bears, how say you?"

"The Ghost Bears say, 'nay,' Loremaster," the big man replied, seconded by saKhan Aletha Kabrinski.

One by one, the votes were cast. As the Clan in question, the Smoke Jaguars did not vote. One by one, thirty death knells were sounded for Clan Smoke Jaguar. The entire Grand Council, every Khan of the Clans, had voted against sending any aid to Huntress.

"Very well, my Khans," Osis snarled once the final vote had been cast. "I shall go to Huntress myself, taking with me only my personal guard. I shall destroy the filthy *surats* who have dared profane my homeworld with their unclean feet. And then I shall come back for you."

Snatching up his mask, ilKhan Lincoln Osis stormed out of the chamber without even first dismissing the Council.

2

Warrior Sector
Near the center of Lootera, Huntress
Kerensky Cluster, Clan Space
14 March 3060

Good God, General Ariana Winston said to herself, appalled at the sight that lay before her. *We meant to show the Jags the true horror of war. I don't think we really understood it ourselves.*

All around her stood the blackened ruins of the stark gray buildings that once had housed various branches of the government of Clan Smoke Jaguar. According to the intelligence briefings she had received, Lootera, the capital city of the planet called Huntress, hadn't been that much to look at when it was intact. But, in the wake of the destruction wrought against the military and governmental facilities by the troopers of Task Force Serpent, the Warrior's Sector of the city was taking on the aspect of a ghost town. Many of the buildings housing the Jaguars' militocracy had been gutted by fire. Black soot stained the outer curtain-walls above the now glassless windows, showing where flames had so recently devoured their contents. Winston was amazed to see that most of the ravaged structures had not collapsed, a tribute, she supposed, to the solid nature of the simple Clan designs. Though she could not see it from her location in the center of the battered city, General Winston knew that the devastation taking place in the planet's main space port just to the south of Lootera was even greater than the destruction taking place in the city itself. The spaceport was almost exclusively a military installation and was therefore a primary target for her demolition crews.

The Whitting Conference had set three objectives for Task Force Serpent, of which she was now commander. The first was to destroy the military forces defending the Smoke Jaguar homeworld of Huntress. Having accomplished that, the Inner Sphere troops were to destroy that Clan's ability to make war in the future. Their third mission objective would be accomplished by completing the first two. Serpent was to drive home, in an unmistakable fashion, the fact that warfare was an essentially terrible thing, and not a series of ritualized "Trials" or wargames, as the Clan culture tended to view it.

Winston remembered well the old proverb: "It is well that war is so horrible, else we should grow too fond of it." The aphorism was part of the tradition the Eridani Light Horse held so dear. Unfortunately, it was a sentiment that the Clans, as a whole, had forgotten. For that reason, they seemed to have grown inordinately fond of what was essentially an ugly, dirty business that should be avoided at all costs.

She had elected to take a tour of inspection of the Jaguar capital partly out of a sense of duty. As task force commander, she had the responsibility to make sure that the Conference's orders were being carried out. Mostly, her visit to the ugly gray city was born out of curiosity.

Winston had been a mercenary soldier all of her adult life. During that time she had fought in numerous campaigns. In most cases, the enemy wasn't all that different from her employer, or the Light Horse itself. Though there had been substantial cultural differences, these had been balanced by some common frame of reference with the enemy. She had seen how they lived, where they worked, shared some common values. In many cases, the enemy piloted machines identical to her own.

With the Clans none of those common bonds existed. Few citizens of the Inner Sphere had ever seen one of the Clan homeworlds. Those who had, like Phelan Kell, said very little about what they saw and experienced during their sojourn with the Clans. For Winston, and the men and women of Task Force Serpent, this was their first close look at the society behind the implacable invaders of the Inner Sphere.

Ariana Winston had seen cities laid out in an austere fashion before. Many of the towns she had seen on other worlds had been so constructed, but in a manner that showed a certain simple elegance. In a jarring counter-point, Lootera, and indeed most of the large cities on Huntress, were spartan, almost harsh in their design. Square, gray buildings with opaque windows lined narrow streets that could have been laid out with a laser, so straight did they run.

Only the Warrior's Sector provided any relief to the dull, unimaginative plan of the city. There, wide avenues were lined by gray pillars, creating an almost Roman appearance. The widest and grandest of these broad streets ran laser straight, to the northern edge of the city, where it ended at a circular fountain dedicated to General Aleksandr Kerensky.

Kerensky had been the last and greatest of the Star League generals. Almost three hundred years ago, he led the Star League armada out of the Inner Sphere, in hopes of saving mankind from destroying itself. After traveling across the vast, uncharted expanse of space, the armada found and settled a number of inhabitable systems. Later the General's son, Nicholas, reformed his father's followers into what would eventually become the Clans.

Winston had become familiar with the fountain, almost to the point of boredom, for it stood in the center of the Field of Heroes. The wide stone parade ground was lined with now-ruined statues of BattleMechs, each dedicated to great deeds performed by some long-ago Jaguar warrior.

Beyond the fountain at the base of Mount Szabo crouched a low, massive pyramidal structure. The monumental edifice housed the Smoke Jaguars' genetic repository, a facility dedicated to nothing else but the preservation of the DNA of the Clan's bloodnamed warriors.

Winston walked along the empty streets, marveling at the coldly efficient destruction her troops had wrought upon the Warrior's Sector. Anything having to do with the Jaguar war machine had been ransacked by her troops, who had searched for the tiniest bit of intelligence which might be useful against its former owners. Then the engineers had moved in, setting incendiary and destructive charges to wreck the once proud structures. Fine gray dust blown from the wrecked buildings coated her black-skinned face and short curly hair. Wind-borne ash stung her eyes. Both were a testament to the ruthless efficiency of her troops. What could not be salvaged had been blown up or burned.

As she rounded a corner, Winston caught sight of a low-slung Blizzard hover transport, bearing the prancing black stallion insignia of the Eridani Light Horse, as well as the blood red 50 of the Fiftieth Heavy Cavalry Battalion. An armored infantryman standing vigilantly at the foot of the vehicle's open ramp saluted casually as he caught sight of his commanding General.

Following the Light Horse's seizure of Lootera, Major Kent Fairfax, the Fiftieth's commanding officer, moved his infantry units into the city, assigning them as military policemen. According to Fairfax, his MPs were there as much to ensure that no member of the Task Force molested any of the Jaguar civilians, as to prevent the Jags from causing problems for their new, and temporary, masters.

Winston would have doubted the seriousness of any other officer, had he come to her with such a statement. But the Fiftieth Heavy Cavalry, called "the Bloody Half Hundred," were dedicated to the protection of all noncombatants, especially those of the Eridani Light Horse. With the members of the Fiftieth on guard, she could rest assured that the civilian population of Lootera would be treated fairly. It was a matter of comfort to her that Paul Masters' dire prediction that the members of Task Force Serpent might degenerate into a rioting mob when the order for destruction came had proven groundless. The troops were conducting themselves with restraint. Even in the age of BattleMechs and starships, the concept of total war was foreign to most soldiers, and, in a way, that was good.

A bit farther down the street, Winston saw a less gentle reminder that the Jaguar capital was a city occupied by a hostile force. A gray and green *Watchman* stood like a ten-meter-tall sentry in the middle of the road. The soot-stained facades of Clan buildings, including one that had until recently housed the planet's secondary command, communication, and control center seemed to glower hatefully at the Light Horse war machine. The BattleMech had been stationed in the square as a precaution against any attempt to retake the C3 facility.

BattleMechs were the lords of the battlefield, or so ran the conventional wisdom. Towering as much as twelve meters high, and weighing as much as one hundred tons, they could carry as much armor and firepower as a battalion of conventional tanks. Until the coming of the Clans, with their advanced technology, the Inner Sphere had thought their 'Mechs to be the final word in military power. They had been wrong.

When the invaders swept in from the coreward Periphery, they brought with them machines so advanced as to seem apparitions from the pages of science fiction. They moved faster, hit harder and absorbed more punishment than any two of their Inner Sphere counterparts. Called OmniMechs, each machine could be specially configured with the right mix of weapons and ammunition to fit a particular mission. Stopping them had proved to be nearly impossible. The Clans' stated goal had been the capture of Terra, the birthplace of all mankind. Their long-range goal was the reestablishment of the Star League, that near mythical time of relative peace, prosperity, and technological advancement that was spoken of in the same reverent tones as Arthur's Camelot.

Only the intervention of ComStar, the secretive, semi-mystical order of technopreservationists, who had pre-served a secret army of 'Mechs, all boasting long-lost Star League technology, had brought the Clan invasion to a halt, and that only for a time.

Seven years had gone by when the leaders of the Inner Sphere, against all expectations, banded together to re-form the Star League, and to carry the fight to the Clans. Aided by data gathered by ROM, ComStar's intelligence branch, and augmented by a shadowy figure known only as Trent, who was said to be a defector from the Smoke Jaguar Clan, the leaders of the great houses decided to launch a pair of massive counter-strikes against the Clans. The goal was to wipe out one entire Clan, at once reinforc-ing the Inner Sphere's claim to the mantle of the Star Lea-gue, and convincing the surviving Clans that the League meant business.

The primary thrust of this counterstrike was called Opera-tion Bulldog and was aimed at driving the Smoke Jaguars out of the Draconis Combine, while Task Force Serpent slipped quietly around the Jaguar's flank to attack his home-world and destroy his ability to make and support war.

As she stood looking up at the tall, square-shouldered 'Mech, Winston wondered about the progress of Operation Bulldog. Time, distance, and the need for secrecy dictated that Task Force Serpent remain out of contact with its In-ner Sphere counterpart. If all was going according to plan, Bulldog, led by Prince Victor Steiner-Davion, would be driving the Jaguars from the coreward sections of the Combine by now. But, Winston had small hope of that. No military operation ever went according to plan.

A sharp, electronic buzz sounded in her ear, yanking her out of her silent reverie. She started at the abruptness of the noise. Feeling the burn of embarrassment in her cheeks, she glanced around the square, hoping that no one saw her surprised jump. With her left hand, she swung the boom microphone of her headband-mounted field communicator in front of her lips.

"Winston."

"General, this is the comm center. I have a report from Colonel Masters." The technician's voice was surprisingly clear. Usually, the headset communicators were so full of static that it was difficult to make out what was being said. "He asked me to tell you that he is almost finished dismantling the New Andery training facility."

"Acknowledged, comm center," Winston replied. "Did he say how long he'll need to finish up?"

"Yes, ma'am. About twelve hours or so." The communications tech paused. "Colonel Masters also says that most of his damaged 'Mechs are back on line, and he should be up to fighting strength in a couple of days."

"Hmm," Winston grunted to herself, then asked, "have we gotten any reports of guerrilla or partisan activity at any of our AOs?"

"Stand by," the tech replied. "I'll check."

For several long moments, the line was silent. Winston was beginning to wonder if the communicator clipped to the back of her fatigue cap had failed. Then, the tech's voice buzzed in her ear once again.

"General, all Areas of Operation report all secure. All unit commanders have deployed pickets, and have sent out recon patrols, as per your orders. Looks like everything's pretty quiet."

Winston ignored the tech's editorial comment.

"Have the AO commanders report in at two-hour intervals. Even if there's nothing to report, I want to know about it." Winston's clipped orders gave vent to the uneasy feeling she'd been carrying around in her guts all day. "Remind them that a number of Clan warriors, including Galaxy Commander Russou Howell, the Huntress garrison commander, are still unaccounted for. *And* we don't know if the garrison got off a shout for help. I want to get this job over and done with quick. I don't want to get bogged down in fighting partisans or guerrillas, only to have a Jag relief force jump down our throats."

* * *

Many kilometers to the southwest, in the yard of a steel-making plant near the city of Myer, General Andrew Redburn, commander of the Kathil Uhlans and Ariana Winston's second in command, sat silent and alone on the clawed foot of his gold-accented black *Daishi.* The massive, one-hundred-ton 'Mech was not an Inner Sphere design. One of the heaviest OmniMechs used by the Clans, the 'Mech had been captured during the invasion by the Federated Commonwealth. Neither was the *Daishi,* whose name in Japanese meant "Great Death," the 'Mech in which Redburn had begun. His *Atlas* had been broken out of its bay aboard the Uhlans' DropShip *Dauntless* and given to another FedCom MechWarrior, whose machine had been shot from beneath him during the initial assault on Huntress. The huge, bird-like *Daishi* had once belonged to the Marshal of the Armies of the Federated Commonwealth, Morgan Hasek-Davion.

Morgan had been Task Force Serpent's original commander. Selected because he was a brilliant strategist and superb battlefield commander, not to mention being possessed of the devil's own luck, Morgan was the cousin of the Prince of the Federated Commonwealth, Victor Steiner-Davion. He had also been Redburn's best and oldest friend.

Morgan had worked and fought and argued with each of the various, and wildly individual, leaders of the units that made up the task force, until Serpent was a single integrated whole. He led the task force through its first engagement with the Clans, a naval battle against the Ghost Bears in an unnamed system, later dubbed "Trafalgar" by the men and women of the task force. He had resolved internal problems arising from the disposition of prisoners with a minimum of strife, and had won the admiration and respect, not to mention the affection and love, of the nearly fifty-five thousand men and women involved in the long-strike operation.

Someone hadn't loved Morgan, though. Shortly after the victory at Trafalgar, a man known as Lucas Penrose had sneaked into the Marshal's stateroom aboard the *Invisible Truth* and placed a fast-acting, deadly poison in a whiskey bottle. Morgan died, very likely without even realizing it.

The recollection of his best friend's death left Redburn with the feeling of an ice-cold hand clutching at his heart. He had yet to fully recover from the deep-seated feelings of grief and loss. While he was fighting, planning an offensive, or dealing with any of the hundred problems that face a senior military officer daily, Redburn could push the emotions aside. But, when he was alone, the sadness came flooding back.

Redburn had but two regrets where Morgan was concerned. The first was that he'd never had the chance to tell him goodbye, and the second was that he hadn't killed Morgan's killer himself.

Equal parts luck and diligence, the components of any successful investigation, had turned up discrepancies in Penrose's files. Those discrepancies led General Winston, Commodore Alain Beresick, the ComStar fleet commander, and Major Michael Ryan, the commander of the Draconis Elite Strike Teams assigned to Serpent, to want to question Penrose. Apparently believing himself discovered, Penrose killed his guards, and tried to escape. No one quite understood that. If Penrose was the assassin, why didn't he have a more substantial fall-back plan? Ryan had supposed that, being a professional, Penrose may have so believed in his cover and his alibis that he didn't need an escape plan.

Whatever his motives, Penrose had tried to coerce Winston into giving him a JumpShip and accompanying him as a hostage while he made his escape. Again through good fortune, Winston discovered Penrose's threat was a bluff, and, in the ensuing brawl on the *Invisible Truth*'s number one grav deck, killed the assassin with a well-placed pistol shot.

Redburn didn't begrudge Ariana Winston the satisfaction of killing Penrose. He actually envied her. Destroying the man who had killed his best friend would have brought some sense of closure to the matter. As it was now, Penrose had died without leaving any clues as to who had hired him and why. The conspiracy mavens in the Inner Sphere press would have a field day when the events surrounding Morgan's death became known. Some, he feared, would even blame Prince Victor for ordering the death of his own cousin.

Redburn snorted derisively at the thought. Morgan loved Victor, and the Prince returned that affection. Victor would no more have Morgan killed than Redburn himself would.

A distant thump shook him out of his meditation. He started up from his metal seat, fearing that the Jaguars had launched a counterattack, then relaxed again. The thick billow of oily black smoke coming from the far side of the steel mill compound revealed the source of the noise. A lance of heavy and assault BattleMechs had been ordered to raze the facility, using their heavy combat lasers and particle cannons. The jarring sound, more felt than heard, was the result of parts of a huge Bessemer-type converter being blasted into molten gobbets of liquid metal by the wrecking crew's weapons.

Before the actual destruction process had begun, Redburn, like most of the rest of Serpent's commanders, hadn't a clear idea what was involved in wrecking a planet's entire war-making capability. Not only did military bases, command centers, training facilities, and arms manufacturing plants have to be razed to the ground. All the industry that might be used to support, repair, or resurrect any of those installations had to be wiped out as well. That meant all specialty steel fabricators, chemical plants, POL refineries, and even some plastics manufacturers had to be destroyed.

The task force engineers used up all of the explosives they'd brought with them, plus whatever they could salvage from the Jaguars, and still it wasn't enough. To facilitate the obliteration of the planet's heavy industry, Winston ordered all BattleMechs mounting energy weapons to help in the destruction. Ballistic weapons, such as autocannons and missile launchers, would have been far more efficient, because the damage from high-explosive warheads was more generalized than the tight, pinpoint impacts of energy weapons, but ammunition was in short supply and couldn't be spared. In some places, infantrymen with sledgehammers and cutting torches were destroying lighter pieces of equipment.

There were a number of protests, claiming that the soldiers of the task force were warriors, not vandals, but, in the end, the General's orders were carried out.

Redburn sighed heavily and got to his feet. The destruction of the steel mill was almost complete. It was time to move on to the next target.

I just want to be done with this, he told himself. *I just want to be done with this and go home.*

3

Black Shikari Jungle, East of Pahn City
Huntress
Kerensky Cluster, Clan Space
15 March 3060

"In the name of Aleksandr Kerensky, you screeching *stravag* idiot," Galaxy commander Russou Howell cursed. "What do you mean, 'the barbarians are destroying Pahn City'?"

"Exactly what I said, Galaxy Commander." The warrior, a blonde female wearing the red and gold collar flashes of a Star Commander, snapped back. She was unimpressed by her superior's outburst. "I saw it with my own eyes. The barbarians are dismantling the factory complex, as though they mean to ship it back to the Inner Sphere piece by piece. Whatever they cannot carry off, they are piling up in one of the large storehouses. It is my belief that they mean to destroy whatever they cannot take with them."

Though she was technically solahama, a dishonored warrior long past her prime, Star Commander Tonia still had a warrior's pride. She considered it her duty to carry out any task assigned to her without question, and to the fullest extent of her abilities.

At Howell's command, she had taken the remnants of

her Reconnaissance Star to within a few hundred meters of the smoking, battle-scarred factory complex. There, she watched as heavily armed infantrymen, wearing camouflaged fatigues accented by strips of dull maroon and gray tartan, supervised as technician and laborer castemen carried bits and pieces of the factory complex's equipment out of the compound. Salvage and repair crews swarmed over the shot-riddled, flame-scarred hulks of ruined Battle-Mechs. Looking more like large, bipedal ants, the technicians cannibalized serviceable parts from some shot-up machines to repair others.

Tonia was familiar with the process, having gone through it herself just twenty hours ago. The battered *Javelin* she had piloted on her reconnaissance mission to Pahn City was an old Inner Sphere design, but one that had been upgraded in the years following the Great Crusade to liberate Terra. She had been a part of that Crusade, a proud member of the Sixth Jaguar Dragoons. She had taken part in the vicious fighting on Yamarovka, when the Dragoons' OmniMechs tore through the defending Inner Sphere machines, securing the planet in a matter of hours. She'd also participated in the first combat drop onto Tukayyid the Accursed. Gravely wounded in that battle, she had been denied the solace of a warrior's death along with her comrades, who sold their lives for glory in the blood-soaked Dinju Pass.

Because she had been one of few survivors of the Sixth Dragoons, Tonia had been judged by her Clan as somehow flawed. Declared solahma, she had been ordered back to Huntress for "reassignment," where she would live out her days in shameful, miserable uselessness.

In the glory days of her youth, she had proudly commanded a *Timber Wolf,* one of the Jaguars' most powerful OmniMechs. Now, here on Huntress, she had to suffer the indignity and disgrace of piloting a crude Inner Sphere machine taken as *isorla* from the Draconis Combine, from the very barbarians she had hoped to conquer. It mattered not to her that the thirty-ton 'Mech had been updated with the latest technology available to the Combine. Compared to her *Timber Wolf,* the *Javelin* was a child's toy.

When the barbarians launched their cowardly sneak attack on Huntress, the Jaguar's lair, she had thought to expunge ten years' worth of shame by grinding the invaders into the mud beneath her 'Mech's armored feet. But, the fortunes of battle had again conspired against her. In the initial clash with the Knights of the Inner Sphere, her *Javelin* had been crippled by a savage volley of PPC and autocannon fire. It had ripped through the light 'Mech's torso, shattering the power plant and forcing her to eject. Again she was wounded and taken out of the fight early. By the time she dragged herself back into the predesignated rally point, the battle was over, and the order had been given to withdraw.

In the wake of the calamitous battle, several wounded pilots, whose 'Mechs had fared better than they had, were removed from combat status and their machines stripped out to make a few, fully functional units. Tonia had been assigned to one of these. Slapped together from the salvaged parts of three Inner Sphere designs, her armored mount was basically a forty-ton *Hermes II,* but many of the machine's vital components, including the rapid-fire class 5 autocannon mounted in its chest, had been salvaged from the other two units. As a result the hybrid machine was balky, and occasionally developed a limp in its right leg.

Still and all, it was a BattleMech, and she was a MechWarrior. When Galaxy Commander Russou Howell ordered her to take the ad hoc reconnaissance Star to learn what the invaders were doing at Pahn City, the joy of battle began to rise in her veins once again. The surveillance had taken most of the day. Her Star had slipped back into the Jaguar bivouac well after dark, and it was now after midnight.

"How are their sentries disposed?" Howell barked, turning the electronic mapbox toward her.

"They have a few infantrymen standing guard on the

compound itself, here, here and here," she replied, indicating different spots along the perimeter of the factory complex. "There are nine BattleMechs that I saw within the compound, and they seemed to be powered up and ready to move on a moment's notice. In addition, there is at least a full Cluster's worth of combat-capable machines in there too. I believe there may be as much as a full Galaxy of troops defending the factory."

"Freebirth." Howell drew the profanity out into a hiss. "I had hoped to raid the factory to get ammunition and materiel that would allow us to keep fighting. We are but one jump from Strana Mechty. It cannot be that no one is aware that Huntress has been invaded. We must keep fighting until reinforcements arrive."

"Galaxy Commander," Tonia said, gently taking the mapbox out of her superior's hands. "If it is a supply raid you are planning, may I suggest this?" After manipulating a few controls, she passed the device back to Howell.

"The invaders seem to be the Northwind Highlanders. They have grounded their DropShips five kilometers away from the factory complex, presumably to keep them out of the fighting should we muster a counterattack. I realize that we have but three Trinaries worth of 'Mechs and Elementals at our disposal, but I suggest we divide our force and launch two simultaneous attacks. The first, and smallest, force would attack their DropShips. That would draw at least some of their 'Mechs away from the factory. Then the larger force could move against the remaining barbarians, eliminate whatever holding force they leave at the complex, and seize the supplies we need."

For a few moments, Howell said nothing. He stared at the mapbox, with his arms folded across his chest. His eyes flickered across the glowing screen, as though he were mentally calculating distances, response times, possible troop movement, and the like. Finally he looked up.

"Very well, Star Commander Tonia. We will undertake your plan." Howell waved another solahma officer closer, indicating that he should look at the mapbox. "Star Captain Cyrus, you will lead the diversionary attack on the

Highlander landing zone. I will give you one Trinary's worth of 'Mechs. You are to overrun any security force the barbarians may have left on guard ships and attack the grounded DropShips directly. Inflict as much damage as you can. If we can cripple or destroy some of those *savashri* freebirth vessels, so much the better. You must give the Highlanders the impression that they are under full attack and are in danger of losing *all* of their ships. They must be convinced to pull the bulk of their force away from the factory, leaving it vulnerable to our attack.

"I will command the main attack myself, with the remaining two Trinaries. Star Commander Tonia, you will lead the way."

Tonia felt a pride swelling in her chest that she had not known in many years. The Galaxy Commander had not only accepted her plan wholesale, but had assigned her to the point of the entire attack.

"When the Highlanders move to counterattack at the landing zone, we will move in," Howell continued. "Once the facility is in our hands, technicians, Elementals, and any dismounted MechWarriors will seize whatever transports there may be at the complex, load them with supplies, and withdraw. We will carry off as much materiel as we can and destroy the rest."

Howell rose, dusted off the seat of his uniform trousers, and addressed the warriors gathered around him.

"Remember, all of you, this is a supply raid. We are desperately short on ammunition for our autocannons and missile launchers. You are free to use your energy weapons as much as your heat sinks will permit, but fire your ballistic weapons sparingly. Now, go and brief your warriors. We will move out in thirty minutes."

Tonia, like the rest of the officers around her, saluted crisply and turned away. Now, at last, she would be able to strike a blow against the barbarians that would hurt. Now, in some small measure at least, she would be revenged for the years of indignity she had suffered, bearing the label of solahma like the brand of Cain. Now her honor would be restored.

* * *

From her position, half-concealed beneath a vine-covered tree, Tonia watched as a quartet of medium BattleMechs patrolled just outside the torn and broken fence surrounding the Pahn City factory complex. Just over three hundred meters away, the tall, humanoid machines moved slowly, as though they were armored giants out to take the late night air. The rest of the compound was dark and silent. Tactical doctrine said that the best time for a surprise attack was between the hours of oh-three-hundred and oh-five-hundred. That was the time when the average human's physiological and mental cycles were at their lowest ebb. Tonia glanced at the *Hermes II*'s chronograph. Its pale green numbers read 0356. In a few moments, Star Captain Cyrus would be launching his attack, and then . . .

Suddenly lights snapped on inside the factory complex, followed by a whirlwind of movement. In the ghostly green and black world of her 'Mech's thermal imaging system, Tonia saw the figures of men and women dashing around the compound. Heat bloomed in the power plants of the invaders' BattleMechs, as their pilots brought the machines to deadly life. Despite the rising tide of impatience Tonia felt, she held her position. She was under orders not to launch the attack until Galaxy Commander Russou Howell gave the command.

In a rush, dozens of the enemy BattleMechs bolted from the compound, heading eastward toward the DropShip landing zone, shaking the ground with the impact of their running feet.

A click sounded in her ear, signaling an incoming message.

"Stand fast, Star Commander," Galaxy Commander Russou Howell ordered, over a secure laser-based communication link. "Give them enough time to get out of the immediate area."

Before Tonia could acknowledge the order, Howell broke the link.

Quickly, the drum-roll thuds of the enemy's running feet faded into the night, and still the order to attack didn't come. Only a dozen or so enemy 'Mechs could be seen within the complex. Tonia selected the nearest of them, an ugly, handless machine called a *Whitworth* by its Inner Sphere designers. That would be her first target.

Her eyes flicked between her tactical display, the spectral image of the enemy 'Mech on her main viewscreen, and the chronograph. Minutes ticked by, and still the order to attack didn't come. Tonia released the joysticks that controlled her 'Mech's movement and targeting, and wiped off sweat on the rough nylon of her cooling vest.

"Star Commander Tonia, you may attack." Howell's order, although anticipated, was so sudden that, when it came, Tonia jumped.

"Aff, Galaxy Commander."

Tonia punched the control that would bring her targeting computer on line. Instantly a red cross hairs snapped into existence on the main viewscreen. A slight flick of the left joystick, and the targeting reticle came to rest over the *Whitworth*'s boxy torso. Tonia paused for a half a breath, allowing the computer an extra five seconds to chew on the firing solution, and then caressed the trigger.

A lance of flame three meters long spat from the *Hermes II*'s chest, as the rapid-fire autocannon sent a long stream of orange glowing tracers ripping into the *Whitworth*'s belly.

All around her, the jungle seemed to explode. Lances of laser fire and jagged bolts of man-made lightning from particle projection cannons clawed out of the darkness to swat at the Highlander 'Mechs.

Tonia saw the *Whitworth* reel from her sudden, unexpected assault, but she knew the forty-ton machine was tougher than that. She heard the hollow clank as a new cassette of armor-piercing shells dropped into the Imperator Ultra autocannon's breech mechanism. The "ready" indicator on the weapons status display flashed green. Again she turned the gun at the Highlander 'Mech, which was starting to turn to face the surprise attack. Small explosions danced across the *Whitworth*'s left arm and torso, leaving holes in the tough armor protecting the 'Mech's portside missile launcher.

This time, the enemy warrior was not taken by surprise, nor did he stagger under the assault. Instead, he turned to face the onslaught. A sharp, whooping tone ripped at Tonia's ear, indicating that the enemy had locked his weapons onto her 'Mech. Yellow-white flame erupted from the box-like launchers affixed to the *Whitworth*'s shoulders, as twenty long-range missiles, guided by sophisticated Artemis fire-control systems, roared through the night air, eager to savage her already abused 'Mech.

Fortune smiled on Star Commander Tonia. One volley of missiles fell short, scattering metal shards and clods of dirt for several meters. The other flight of missiles struck her *Hermes II* in the right leg, cratering the thin armor protecting that limb.

Snarling like an enraged jaguar, Tonia burst from the cover of the creeper-wrapped tree and charged at the Highlander 'Mech. Another twin volley of missiles reached out to splinter torso and leg armor, while a lance of coherent light flashed past her cockpit so close that she could have lit a candle off of it. Less than a hundred meters from her enemy, Tonia skidded to a stop. Lifting her 'Mech's arms, she savaged the *Whitworth* with a stuttering blast of pulse laser fire that widened and deepened the gaps her cannon shells had opened in the enemy's plastron.

Before the barbarian could recover, Tonia poured another burst of laser energy into the badly damaged machine, adding a third volley of precious autocannon shells to the mix. Then, she unleashed the *Hermes II*'s most fearful weapon. Raw, liquid fire vomited from her 'Mech's left arm to envelop the *Whitworth*'s head in dark orange flames and black oily smoke. Sweat burst forth from her skin as heat flooded into her cockpit.

The Jaguar warrior knew that a flamer did little real damage to an enemy 'Mech, and often the amount of waste heat generated by the weapon was not worth its use. But, as a psychological weapon, only an inferno launcher surpassed the flamer.

The *Whitworth*'s head split open and a bright column of rocket exhaust carried the Highlander pilot clear of his damaged machine. Tonia's ploy had worked. She had tricked the experienced enemy warrior into panicking by first savaging his 'Mech with autocannon and laser volleys, and then following up with a brutal attack using the weapon that all men feared—fire.

All around her, the Jaguar warriors were sweeping the Highlanders' security 'Mechs from the field. Elementals and a few of the boldest dismounted 'MechWarriors had already charged into the compound to seize hovertrucks previously loaded with vital supplies by the Northwind Highlanders. The captured vehicles raced toward the safety and shelter of the thick jungle.

With the joy of battle singing in her blood, Tonia swung her much-abused *Hermes II* in a quarter-circle, seeking a new opponent.

Two hours later, Tonia was descending the chain ladder hanging from her 'Mech's torso. Careless of the skin she lost on the rough steel, she slid the last few meters to the ground. Elation filled her heart. Now, no matter what happened to her, she had proved that she was not a worthless has-been merely because the fortunes of war had allowed her to survive to the advanced age of thirty-nine. Her Star had spearheaded a successful raid on an installation held by an enemy of greater strength, a raid that she had helped plan and execute.

The materiel taken in the attack would allow the forces under Galaxy Commander Russou Howell to continue fighting until reinforcements arrived. Even if they did not, and Tonia died in battle, she would die happily, for, in her own eyes at least, she was once again a warrior.

There was no such elation within the Pahn City factory complex. Colonel William MacLeod, commander of the Northwind Highlanders, paced silently through the battle-scarred compound. Captain Oran Jones stood in the shadows of a broken wall, watching the Colonel as he stalked red-raced through the wreckage. MacLeod ignored the junior officer. He had left Jones, along with a company of

'Mechs from Third Battalion, in charge of the compound, while the rest of the regiment left to protect their Drop-Ships. No sooner had they engaged the Smoke Jaguar forces attacking the landing zone than a second, larger force moved against the complex.

As soon as he learned of the attack on the factory, MacLeod ordered the balance of his Third Battalion to turn about and reinforce Jones' Company. By the time the reinforcements arrived, the fighting was over. Shortly thereafter, the Jags attacking the DropShips broke off and withdrew into the night.

On the surface of it, little damage had been done to either the DropShips or to the 'Mechs of Jones' Company. MacLeod had been inclined to put the attack down to a well-planned harassment by survivors of the Huntress garrison. When he learned the truth of what had happened at the factory during his absence, the Colonel's Highland temper boiled over. In colorful, profanity-laced Gaelic, he gave the Captain the dressing-down of his young life.

"Then, of all the knot-headed stupidity," MacLeod bellowed into Jones' face, as the younger man stood at rigid attention, his eyes fixed in what is known as the "thousand-meter stare" adopted by enlisted men and junior officers during a royal chewing-out. "You let the *sassanach* get their bloody hands on enough bloody supplies to fight a guerrilla war for a bloody month, and you don't bloody pursue them! What in the name of all that's holy were you thinkin' of?"

"Colonel, sir I . . ." Jones tried to defend himself, but MacLeod wasn't having any of it.

"Shut up, laddie. I'll tell you when you can talk."

"Uh, Colonel?" a voice spoke in quiet, polite tones from the shadows.

"What is it, Captain Campbell?" MacLeod barked.

Captain Neil Campbell, the powerfully built, red-haired commander of the Northwind Highlanders' Royal Black Watch Company, stepped into the light.

"Sir, I couldn't help overhearin'. Come to that, I think yer bein' a bit too hard on the lad. After all, the rest of us went harin' off into the night, chasin' a lot o' wastrels who shouted at us from the dark."

"What?" MacLeod hissed.

Campbell merely cocked his head as if he hadn't heard. "We all fell for it, same as he did." He grinned, saluted, and walked away, whistling *The Skye Boat Song*.

For a moment, MacLeod's face so darkened with blood that Jones feared his commander was going into apoplexy.

"Baarragh," he growled and spun on his heel, leaving Jones standing at attention by the shattered wall. As Captain Campbell had so eloquently reminded MacLeod, he had been completely taken in by the Jaguars' diversionary attack. So conditioned was he by the conventional military wisdom that said "protect your DropShips at all costs," that he had moved the bulk of his force away from his primary objective, leaving the factory complex open to a Jaguar attack.

It took several minutes' pacing for MacLeod to get his temper under control. When he did he shook his head and laughed ruefully to himself. Stepping up to Captain Jones, MacLeod looked the younger man square in the eye.

"Captain Campbell was absolutely right," he said. "We were all fooled by the Jags tonight. I owe you an apology, Captain."

"No, sir," Jones answered, taking MacLeod's offered hand. "There's nothing to forgive. Like you said, we all fell for it."

"Aye. Well, one thing's for sure." MacLeod shook his head again. "I don't reckon we've seen the last of those Smoke Jaguars."

===== 4 =====

Eridani Light Horse Command Post
Mount Szabo, Lootera
Huntress
Kerensky Cluster, Clan Space
15 March 3060

"**V**ery well, Colonel, understood." General Ariana Winston passed the communication headset back to a technician, and leaned her elbows wearily on the edge of the mobile HQ truck's holotable. The message from Colonel MacLeod, telling her that the Highlanders had been attacked by a Jaguar raiding party, had been disturbing enough in its own right. There was no need for her sense of foreboding to make it any worse. A few days earlier, after the planet Huntress had been declared secure, she had instructed the officers under her command to make every effort to locate and capture a number of Clan commanders who had not been accounted for. They had not been found among the bondsmen, the Clan term for prisoners that Task Force Serpent had adopted for its own use, nor had their bodies been identified by graves registration.

Though she realized that in any military engagement, there would be a certain number of MIAs, the number and rank of the Jaguar officers who were missing in action bothered her. She knew that the warriors of Clan Smoke Jaguar were perhaps the most aggressive and tenacious of all the Clans. She understood that surrender and retreat were not parts of the Smoke Jaguar doctrine of war. Still, she couldn't shake the ominous feeling that at least some of those officers had led a portion of their men into the wilderness, from whence they could fight a guerrilla campaign against Task Force Serpent. That is precisely the course of action she would have taken if the roles had been reversed.

It was this apparent synchronicity of thought that bothered her. The Jags, and indeed all the Clans, were supposed to be up-front warriors. Everything that she had ever seen or heard of their battle tactics said that they were not given to partisan-type tactics, instead relying almost exclusively on the lightning attack and the aggressive defense. Now, here they were, executing a night-time raid on a captured facility, not to liberate it, but to seize the supplies that would allow them to keep on fighting. Not only that, but they had employed a diversion, a deceptive ruse of which she had not believed the Clanners capable.

Most of the troops onplanet were solahma, she mused. *Maybe being dishonored somehow frees them up to be more creative in their tactics.*

Another thought came on the heels of the first.

Why are they holding out? As far as they know we're here to stay. They can't possibly believe they can win. They can't possibly think a rag-tag bunch of survivors and diehards equipped with second-line 'Mechs and whatever equipment they stole from the Inner Sphere can kick this entire task force offplanet. Can they?

No, it's got to be something else. It could be sheer, stubborn pride, but it doesn't feel like that. I hope I'm wrong, but I've got this really awful feeling that they're waiting on reinforcements. The after-action reports say that it isn't likely the Jags got off a call for help, but we can't be sure.

"Corporal," she called aloud to the communications technician manning the mobile HQ's radio console. "Hot up the net. I want to talk to all of the unit commanders."

"Right away, Gen'ral." The tech began twiddling knobs and punching buttons to bring up the task force's broadband radio net. With any such communication system, even encrypted, there was a chance that the enemy would be able to intercept the message and gain potentially valuable intelligence. That was a risk she was going to have to take. In fact, if the Jags were able to intercept and decode the transmissions, that might work in her favor.

After several minutes of fiddling with controls and muttering into his boom-mounted headset microphone, the tech turned in his chair and gave Winston a thumbs-up, indicating that the communications net had been established and that all of her regimental commanders were on line and awaiting her message.

"Attention all commands, this is Dancer. It is possible that you have all heard by now that Dundee was attacked early this morning by a force of 'Sierra Jays' of approximately regimental strength." The message was going out using the task force's standard encryption, but Winston still felt it necessary to use code names wherever possible. If the Jags were able to intercept and decode the message, the lack of such circular references would immediately make the transmission suspect. At least, it would if she were the one intercepting the message. Thus, she was "Dancer," MacLeod was "Dundee," and the Smoke Jaguars were the "Sierra Jays."

"Thus, I am issuing the following order," she continued. "All commands are to tighten local security measures. Your last mission objective orders are to be completed as rapidly as safety permits. All area commanders are instructed to send out combat patrols to locate and capture or eliminate any hostiles who might have escaped from the initial invasion.

"All commands, respond and acknowledge."

"Dancer, this is Lion." General Andrew Redburn of the Kathil Uhlans was the first to answer. "Lion acknowledges and will comply."

"Dancer, Paladin acknowledges. Will comply." Paladin was Colonel Paul Masters of the Knights of the Inner

Sphere. There was a note of reluctance in the Knight Commander's voice. He had never been happy with what Winston had referred to as the "last mission objective order," the decision of the Whitting Conference and the renewed Star League Council that any industry or facility that the Jags might use in the future to rebuild their war machine be razed to the ground.

Masters had argued against that particular course of action all the way from Tharkad, where the conference had been held, to Defiance, where the task force was assembled and trained, to Huntress, where the plan was even now being implemented. In the end, he had to give in. The destruction of the Jaguar war machine was part of his mission, and he was honor-bound to carry out that mission. Only the fact that the mission orders stated that casualties among the Jaguar civilians were to be avoided at all costs softened the affront to Masters' knightly code enough to allow him to carry out the Council's directives.

One by one the rest of the commanders checked in, ending with Marshal Sharon Bryan, the commander of the elite Eleventh Lyran Guards. Though she was still, technically, the leader of the Guards, a badly broken arm, suffered when an exploding ammunition magazine forced her to eject from her *Banshee,* made it necessary for Bryan to pass field command to her subordinate, Colonel Timothy Rice.

Rice was an able commander in many ways Bryan's equal, but he lacked one character trait that Winston found comforting and Bryan annoying. Though a Lyran patriot, Rice was not the rabid Steiner loyalist that Sharon Bryan was.

When Bryan's curt, "Gauntlet to Dancer, wilco" had faded from her headset, Winston spoke again.

"All commands, this is Dancer. All right, get cracking. I want to get this business over and done with as soon as possible. Keep me posted on your progress. With any kind of luck, we can finish trashing the Jags' war machine and be to hell and gone away from here before any reinforcements show up.

"Dancer out."

Slipping the headset from her matted hair, Winston looked out the open door of the mobile HQ van.

Maybe, just maybe we can pull this off without having to fight again, she thought, adding a fervent prayer. *Oh God, I hope I'm right.*

5

***Delta Galaxy Flagship* Korat**
Zenith Jump Point, Huntress System
Kerensky Cluster, Clan Space
19 March 3060

Time and space distorted, seeming to twist the deck beneath Galaxy Commander Hang Mehta's feet into a Mobius strip of lurching steel. A barrage of light and sound more fierce than any artillery fire she had ever experienced battered at her senses. Then, as abruptly as it had begun, the nearly physical assault on her senses ended, leaving in its place a lingering roil of nausea deep in her guts.

Mehta ignored the rising in her craw, the normal after-effect of a hyperspace jump, and turned her attention to the holotank that dominated the *Korat*'s bridge. Ghostly images of the Smoke Jaguar fleet were still fading into existence as other starships emerged at the Huntress zenith jump point. So far as she knew, the *Korat*, a *Liberator* Class cruiser, was the largest Clan WarShip to escape from the Inner Sphere forces that had invaded the worlds of the Smoke Jaguar Occupation Zone.

"Freebirth!" she spat, the profanity rising more from a general sense of frustration than from anger at any specific target.

Those her Clan and her culture counted as no more than *surats*, the basest of creatures, had done the unthinkable. They had united under a common banner, and had forced a Clan, *her Clan*, to pull back from the Inner Sphere. Mehta had lived through it, and still she could barely comprehend it. It gave her a little comfort to know that Delta Galaxy— *her* Galaxy, the Cloud Rangers—had been one of the few Smoke Jaguar units to mount a counter-offensive against the Inner Sphere barbarians. Were it not for the confusion stemming from the hastily planned counterattack, she would have been with Delta Galaxy's Command Trinary when it made its suicidal combat drop into Pesht. Instead, she and the Nineteenth Striker Cluster were caught on Matamoros and decimated by the Second Night Stalkers and the Ryuken-Yon. Only by sheer luck had she escaped death or capture at the hands of the Inner Sphere freebirths.

The barbarians had built an alliance, uniting their petty, squabbling states into a single avenging force. They had planned, organized, and launched a major offensive against the Smoke Jaguar Occupation Zone. They had driven the pride of her Clan before them like chaff in a hurricane. Eventually, ilKhan Lincoln Osis had ordered the shattered remnants of his forces to pull back from the Inner Sphere. They were to return to Huntress, where they might reorganize and re-equip their battered remnants in preparation for a return to the Occupation Zone. Only the knowledge that she was returning to the Kerensky Cluster at the orders of her ilKhan saved any shred of Hang Mehta's warrior pride.

The greatest insult of all was the idea that the Inner Sphere force claimed that they were acting under the banner of a united Star League. The very notion of the filthy *stravags* claiming the sacred aegis of the Star League filled Mehta's heart with a burning anger that could only be extinguished in the blood of her enemies.

She trembled with rage as she remembered the savage fighting on Matamoros, where her command Star had been broken and smashed by troops of the Draconis Combine wearing the Cameron Star next to their own filthy Kurita dragon. She remembered how one after another of her 'Mechs fell to the cowardly traps set for them by the Night Stalkers. Her right arm and ribs still pained her, a legacy of the death-black *Hatamoto-chi* that had first poured PPC and missile fire into her already damaged *Timber Wolf,* then stepped in close and smashed its cockpit into a mass of tangled wreckage. It was only by sheer luck that Mehta survived the destruction of her 'Mech, and a small miracle that she was not permanently injured. It was a major miracle that she was found and pulled from the *Timber Wolf*'s wreckage by a withdrawing Point of Elementals.

Her shattered right arm was still immobilized by a thick plastic cast, and her second-degree burns and broken ribs were nearly healed, but Galaxy Commander Hang Mehta could not say the same thing for her spirit. Following the debacle on Matamoros, she had not been able to join her warriors in their assault on Pesht. Many of them had died honorably while she lay wounded and helpless in a sick bay bunk. Mehta's Jaguar heart burned for the chance to return to the Inner Sphere, to track down the cowardly Combine freebirth who had wounded her, and to wash out the stain of her dishonor in the *surat*'s blood.

The barbarians had not been satisfied with the near destruction of the Cloud Rangers. Even as the shattered remnants of her command Trinary was withdrawing from the accursed Matamoros system, they were harried all the way to the jump point by Combine aerospace fighters. Then, in perhaps the most shocking of all the indignities she had been forced to endure, three of her precious DropShips and the *Lola III* destroyer *Griffin* were obliterated by a fleet of Inner Sphere WarShips. Mehta remembered the surprise she had felt, even through the curtain of shock and pain-killers, at the realization that her force was being attacked by more WarShips than she would have believed existed in the entire Inner Sphere. Only the *Korat* and two *Vincent Mk 42* corvettes, the *Ripper* and the *Azov,* along with a small number of transport JumpShips, had made it out. Mehta counted herself lucky to have escaped with even the barest fraction of her command still intact.

That will all be mended, she promised herself. *In time, the Cloud Rangers will be rebuilt. Then we shall return to the Inner Sphere and teach those filthy freebirths the meaning of defeat.*

The warriors currently under her command had been thrown together from the survivors of many units. Some of these, like the 2nd Jaguar Guards and the 267th Battle Cluster, belonged to front-line Galaxies like Delta. Others, the survivors of the 17th and 143rd Garrison Clusters, were less experienced warriors who had been stationed in the Occupation Zone after the Truce of Tukayyid.

Hang Mehta had contacted the ilKhan immediately upon arriving in Clan space. She had been fully intending to make a proud report of how she had taken the broken remnants of the Jaguar occupation force and, over the nine months of the journey from the Inner Sphere to the homeworlds, smelted and forged them into a single, combat-ready weapon. Lincoln Osis had cut her off, almost in mid-boast. She still refused to fully believe what he had told her.

"Galaxy Commander Hang Mehta," the ilKhan had replied. "You are directed to proceed at once to Huntress. I have received reports of an Inner Sphere invasion fleet that is even now attacking the Jaguar homeworld. You will go to Huntress and wipe the invaders from the face of that planet. Not a single one of those foul *surats* must be allowed to survive."

Mehta knew that the ilKhan would not lie, and certainly could not be mistaken about such an unthinkable event as an Inner Sphere invasion of Huntress. Still her mind could scarcely grasp that the freebirth barbarians could find their way undetected to the Kerensky Cluster with sufficient forces to invade one of the homeworlds.

She looked at the images of her tiny fleet as they slowly swung and rolled into position to recharge their jump drives. With a pang of irritation she noticed that one of the destroyers had not yet begun to maneuver into a position from which to deploy its jump sail, the dead-black, kilometer-wide, but silk-thin disk designed to capture solar energy for use in charging the starship's massive jump drives.

Something is not right, Mehta realized, and the thought shook her to her core. *That is* not *one of my ships.*

"Enlarge that vessel," she snarled, pointing at the finger-long image. Instantly the holographic projection expanded until it was as long as her arm. The thimble-shaped ship was not one of the WarShips that had jumped into Huntress with her, nor was it a Smoke Jaguar vessel of any kind.

"Galaxy Commander, computer-image analysis indicates that the target vessel is *not* a Clan WarShip." The sensor operator hesitated as though fearful of Mehta's wrath. "Analysis suggests that it is a Federated Commonwealth *Fox* Class corvette."

Mehta showed no trace of anger. Instead she peered closely at the insubstantial WarShip hovering a meter and a half above the bridge deck. The short, stubby vessel bore the arrogant insignia of a clenched fist against a golden sunburst, the symbol of the Federated Commonwealth. Below this brazen display of insolence and strength was emblazoned the word "Antrim." For long seconds, Mehta was unable to move or speak, so stunned was she to find an Inner Sphere WarShip here in the very den of the Smoke Jaguar.

What the ilKhan said was true! The reality of the situation hit her like a Gauss slug. *The barbarians have found their way to Huntress!*

"Galaxy Commander, the computer confirms that the target vessel is a *Fox* Class corvette. Her maneuvering drives are coming to life, and I believe she is bringing her weapons systems on line. Scanners now also detect at least eight more intruder vessels, at least half of which may be WarShips." The technician's voice trailed off.

"There is more," Mehta said, turning to glare at the pale-faced sensor operator. "What is it?"

"Galaxy Commander, the nearest target vessel bears the markings of both the Federated Commonwealth and the Cameron Star. The Star League Defense Force has gotten here ahead of us."

"That is not possible," Mehta hissed, sounding more like an angry Steel Viper than a Jaguar.

"Galaxy Commander, I am picking up a shore-to-ship message. It is being broadcast in the clear." The young woman manning the communication console paused for a moment, studying her instruments intently. "It seems to be originating from Huntress."

"Let me hear it."

The tech responded to Mehta's command by punching a series of controls on her panel. A rough voice, made even rougher by the crackle and squeal characteristic of long-range space communications, broke from the overhead bridge speakers.

". . . al Winston asked that you be informed that the Eridani Light Horse has almost completed 'Mech repairs."

The Eridani Light Horse! Mehta knew that name, every Clan warrior did. She also knew of their boast of holding to the ideals of the Star League. Almost three centuries ago, their commanders had refused to join the Exodus, claiming they would remain behind in hopes of keeping the traditions of the SLDF alive. To a Clan warrior, the Light Horse's decision not to join the Exodus was the height of treason. They had refused to follow their lawful commander out of the Inner Sphere in his effort to save humanity from itself. All of the Light Horse's high-sounding claims of adhering to the ways and traditions of the Star League were the gravest of insults to the Clans, and to the honored memory of the great Aleksandr Kerensky. To Mehta's mind, only the high-tech gladiators who fought and died for the amusement of the decadent crowds of Solaris VII were deserving of greater contempt.

If the Eridani Light Horse was truly present on Huntress, if this was not some sort of mistake or jump-induced hallucination, it could only mean one thing. The Inner Sphere had somehow managed to learn the route of the Exodus Road, and had committed the ultimate heresy. Under the banner of the Star League, an act of abomination in and of itself, a task force had made the long trek across the empty depths of space, and had attacked Huntress.

There was no denying the evidence before her. The calm-voiced message sent from the planet's surface to the Inner Sphere WarShip confidently keeping station at the system's zenith jump point confirmed what the ilKhan had said. Not only had the Inner Sphere located Huntress, they had attacked and captured the Smoke Jaguar homeworld, *her* homeworld.

The desire for revenge that had been festering in Mehta's heart ever since her beloved Delta Galaxy had been virtually destroyed by the Inner Sphere boiled over into a bloody rage.

Before she could speak another word, an excited shout rang from the primary sensor operator's station.

"Galaxy Commander, my instruments show an energy bloom in the engineering section of the enemy WarShip. I believe he is bringing his maneuvering engines on line. It also appears that he is powering up his weapons systems. Long-range scans have detected similar drive traces, probably belonging to other invader vessels. Sensors suggest that we may be facing as many as ten enemy vessels."

"Freebirth!" Mehta spat. "Star Captain," she snarled at Sumner Osis, her aide. "How many combat-worthy 'Mechs do we have aboard this fleet?"

Osis, a young man despite his thin, graying hair and cadaverous complexion, stepped into the holotank. A hand-sized scar on his right cheek showed where a blistered burn, earned in combat against the Davion Assault Guards had at last healed, leaving new, pink skin in its place.

"Galaxy Commander, we have the equivalent of two Galaxies aboard," Osis said, waving a command at the holotank operator. The hateful image of the FedCom War-Ship vanished, to be replaced by a laser-projected combat roster. "In all, I'd say we have no more than three hundred-forty combat-ready 'Mechs and Elemental Points at our disposal. That does not include aerospace fighters. Star Colonel Durant reports that he has less than fifty aerospace fighters ready for combat."

"It will have to be enough," Mehta said decisively. "Send to all transports. 'Detach all DropShips immediately.

DropShips are to begin a high-G burn for Huntress. Attack the enemy wherever he gathers.' To all WarShips, close with and engage the enemy fleet. If possible, destroy their transports. I do not want to leave the enemy even the remotest chance of escape.

"Technician Feike, patch me through to Star Colonel Paul Moon."

"Aff, Galaxy Commander," said Star Colonel Paul Moon. He folded his massive arms across his broad, muscular chest, watching the meter-high holographic image of the commander of this ad hoc Galaxy as though he were a predatory cat and Hang Mehta his prey.

Moon was perfectly at home on the bridge of the *Descending Storm*, an *Overlord-C* Class DropShip mated to the *Korat*'s number four docking collar. Many ground officers, Galaxy Commander Hang Mehta among them, seemed ill at ease while aboard space- or starships. Most lacked even a basic working knowledge of any military system outside of their own arena of combat. As a result, MechWarriors were uncomfortable aboard WarShips, just as ships' crews would be out of place in the cockpit of a BattleMech. Moon was not one of these. He recognized ships' crewmen as trained warriors and respected them for their abilities.

Moon was on the *Descending Storm*'s bridge when the *Korat* jumped into the Huntress system, carrying the DropShip with it. He had seen the tactical feeds coming into the DropShip's holotank from the cruiser's sensor systems. He knew that Mehta was not yet sufficiently recovered from her wounds to allow her to take personal command of a major ground action. As the most experienced battle commander remaining to the roughly reformed Galaxy, he knew that she must turn to him to lead the assault to reclaim the Jaguar homeworld.

Hang Mehta was well known to him as a skilled leader and a superb MechWarrior. But any admiration Moon might have felt for her was tempered by the knowledge that she had not taken part in Delta Galaxy's final, glorious battle.

"Humph." Mehta's snort gave nothing of her thoughts away. "I see you are standing again, Star Colonel Paul Moon. That is good. I do not believe, however, that the medtechs have as yet given you clearance to resume your duties as a battlefield commander."

Moon glared at the hologram, knowing full well that the small, laser-based camera built into the projector's base would capture his angry grimace and transmit it to the Galaxy Commander's ship. The heavy brace supporting his left leg was a constant reminder of the near mortal injury he'd suffered at the hands of a black-hearted traitor named Trent. A short-range missile from the traitor's *Cauldron-Born* had severed his leg at the knee, leaving him crippled and bleeding on the battlefield at Maldonado. Only the medical pack built into his armor's superstructure had saved Moon's life.

After the battle, Moon was picked up by his comrades and returned to Delta Galaxy's base on Hyner. Clan medical technicians immediately began the long, painful process of budding a new leg for him. In the nearly two years since his wounding, a new limb had grown almost to the same massive dimensions as the original. But, because the limb had been regenerated under medical stimulus, it was nowhere as strong as his real leg had been. It would have been quicker and easier for the Clan medical technicians to implant an advanced prosthesis. But, due to the sophisticated systems that controlled Elemental armor, Moon would have found it nearly impossible to use such a prosthetic and still remain a warrior. Because of his rank, and his record, Star Colonel Moon was granted the rare privilege of having his limb regrown.

Over the past two months, Moon had endured in proud and angry silence the torturous ministrations of medtechs as they guided him through the rehabilitation process. Throughout rehab Moon had driven himself hard, as eager to be away of the soft-handed lower-caste therapists as he was to reassume his place as a warrior. The blackened metal brace was a constant reminder of his nebulous status in the martial society of his Clan. Though born and bred a warrior, Moon knew that the measure of a Jaguar was his performance in battle. The interminable period of enforced inactivity had left him with a temper drawn to a very dangerous razor's edge.

Moon had defied the orders of the medical technicians once already. During a recharging stop in one of the unnamed star systems along the Exodus Road, Hang Mehta had declared a Trial of Position to appoint commanders for her ad hoc Galaxy. Paul Moon cuffed aside the medtechs who had tried to hinder him, strapped himself into a battered suit of powered armor, and reclaimed his rank of Star Colonel and his station as a Jaguar warrior.

"That is correct, Galaxy Commander," Moon hissed. "But that soon will change. We will be needing every warrior to drive these filthy *stravags* from our homeworld, and when we do so, I will be at the head of my Cluster, no matter what those freebirth medtechs try to say to the contrary."

Mehta laughed, a short, ugly sound.

"Very well, Star Colonel. You are given command of the counterinvasion. Plan it well, Paul Moon. You are to attack the enemy wherever he gathers. You are to destroy the invaders to the last man and the last machine.

"Not one of those cursed freebirth vermin who have *dared* to foul the soil of Huntress is to survive." Mehta's voice rose in pitch as she spoke, until at last it was the scream of an angry jaguar. "I want them all dead. I want their leaders' heads brought to me on pikes. I want their bodies burned and their ashes scattered to the four winds. I want them and their seed wiped out of the universe forever."

"Affirmative, Galaxy Commander." Moon half bowed in spite of the rigid brace immobilizing his left hip. "It shall be done."

Moon waved imperiously to a bridge tech, who severed the connection. Instantly Hang Mehta's grim visage winked out, to be replaced by a holographic image of the Clan battle fleet. Tiny aerospace fighters darted from the

WarShips' launch bays, streaking toward the Inner Sphere fleet.

Moon nodded in satisfaction. This would be his finest hour. He was to lead the counterstrike against the vile barbarians who dared to challenge the Jaguar in his very lair. When he had washed out that stain in the blood of his enemies, then he, Star Colonel Paul Moon, the savior of Huntress, would be remembered in the same breath with Franklin Osis, the first Khan of the Smoke Jaguars, and even with the Kerenskys themselves.

For the first time in many long months, Star Colonel Paul Moon smiled, and it was a terrible sight to behold.

6

Battle Cruiser SLS Invisible Truth
Zenith Jump Point, Huntress System
Kerensky Cluster, Clan Space
19 March 3060

"**H**elmsman, bring us about." Alain Beresick rapped out his commands calmly, one after another. "Weapons officer, power up the guns. Air Boss, what's the status on our CAP?"

"Commodore, we have eight fighters on Combat Air Patrol!" the *Invisible Truth*'s flight control officer shouted back. As "Air Boss," the man had primary responsibility for overseeing all aerospace fighter operations, including overall control of the fleet's Combat Air Patrol. "We are launching the 'ready fives.' *Antrim* and *Ranger* are doing likewise. Estimate the entire wing will be deployed in twenty minutes. Lead fighter elements should engage the enemy in fifteen."

"Good." Beresick was pleased. Though the eight aerospace fighters on Combat Air Patrol wouldn't do much damage to a target as big as a Clan cruiser, they could certainly clip the point of the enemy's attack. The "ready fives" fighters held on the catapults, fully armed and capable of being launched with five minutes' warning, would further dull the enemy's fighting edge.

The *Invisible Truth*'s crew had swung into action minutes after detecting the electromagnetic pulse of the incoming JumpShips. It had taken that long to confirm that the new arrivals were indeed Clanners, though they could have been no one else. As soon as the targets were positively identified as hostiles, it had taken just six minutes to clear for action. That was a full forty-five seconds less than the crew's best time to date.

"Communications," Beresick snapped. "Send a flash message to General Winston. 'Inbound enemy starships. *Invisible Truth* detects at least three WarShips and three transports. Sensor analysis suggests that the transports are fully loaded. We'll try to head 'em off. But suggest you get ready to welcome your uninvited guests. Will advise when able.' Got that?"

"Yessir."

"Good, send it."

As the commtech turned to his panel, Beresick sighed, his lips curling into a half smile. A vague feeling of *déjà vu* had settled over him. In that moment he found himself sympathizing with Star Colonel Gilmour Alonso, the now-marooned Ghost Bear ship captain who had opposed Beresick in Serpent's first action against the Clans. Though the battle had been fought only four months ago, to Beresick's mind it seemed like the first naval engagement between capital ships in nearly two centuries was now a matter of distant history.

"Communications, message to all transport commands."

"Ready."

"All transport commands, this is Courtyard," Beresick said, using the codename assigned to the *Invisible Truth*. "All transports, with their assigned fleet-defense Drop-Ships, are to power up and jump outsystem to predesignated rally point alpha. You will remain on station at RP alpha until you are either called for or until seventy-two hours have passed. If the specified time passes and you receive no word, the senior officer, designated by the chain of command, will take charge of the fleet.

"Good luck. Courtyard, out."

For a half-dozen heartbeats, Beresick gazed at the miniature vessels represented by the holographic images floating in the air before him. The largest Clan WarShip had been identified by the *Truth*'s powerful computer as a *Liberator* Class cruiser. The vessel was based on an old design, the *Avatar* Class. According to information brought back by ROM agents attached to Explorer Corps missions, the *Liberator* was essentially an upgraded *Avatar* with heavier, more efficient weapons and thicker, ferro-carbide armor. Though the Explorer ships had not been able to get a full technical readout of the class, Beresick knew the *Liberator* carried heavy naval guns capable of breaching even the *Truth*'s thick hide in just a few blasts. Her lighter weapons could savage incoming fighters and DropShips long before the smaller craft could get close enough to do any significant damage. The *Liberator* must be the *Truth*'s primary target.

The smaller enemy ships were also old designs. *Vincent Mk 42* Class corvettes were primarily patrol craft, often used in sudden raids and fast-strike missions against lightly defended targets. In a pitched battle against larger, more powerful WarShips, *Vincent*s stood no great chance of victory. Still, Beresick could not ignore the patrol ships completely. Though their punch was much lighter than the *Liberator*'s, the little corvettes could still inflict telling damage against an enemy foolish, or unwary enough, to think them no threat.

A plan formed in Beresick's head.

"To all combat commands, this is Courtyard. The fleet will split into two sections and take the enemy in turn. *Starlight, Emerald,* and *Fire Fang,* along with the *Truth,* will comprise the lead section. *Antrim, Haruna,* and *Ranger* the second." As Beresick spoke, the holotank operator, knowing both his job and his commander, manipulated the laser-based viewing system to display in graphic, three-dimensional images the plan Beresick was laying out.

"First section, having greater weight and firepower, is to engage the enemy at close range in an attempt to break his line. I needn't remind you gentlemen that the *Liberator* mounts very powerful weapons, especially in her broadsides. Stay under her bows or stern if possible.

"Second section is to hang back until we are ready to engage. Then you will swing out wide, on whichever flank the enemy leaves uncovered. You will drive in behind the enemy line of battle and attack his JumpShips. Your task will be to cripple the JumpShips and attempt to board and capture them. You are to destroy the transports only to prevent their escaping this system."

For a moment Beresick paused, allowing the other ship commanders to catch up with his rapid-fire string of orders. He was a bit hesitant to send the next batch of commands, but he knew it had to be done.

"If you cripple a transport, call upon it to surrender peaceably. If they refuse to strike their colors, you are authorized to send in a boarding party. If they do surrender, or if you are forced to take a vessel by storm, secure the target ship so as to prevent it from jumping outsystem. Once a ship has been secured, the prisoners, if any, are to be treated according to the Ares Conventions.

"Remember, gentlemen, we no longer have the DEST or Fox teams to conduct boarding operations. You will have to rely on your own marines.

"As we close with the enemy fleet, ship captains may launch fighters or combat DropShips at their discretion. The BARCAP fighters are to form a screen across our line of advance. All other fighters are to engage the enemy. DropShips will either stand ready to engage enemy vessels or deliver boarding parties, as dictated by the standing orders.

"That is all, gentlemen. I wish I had more time to refine this battle plan, but that's the best we can do with what we've got.

"Good luck. Courtyard out."

Before Beresick was finished speaking, the holotank displayed a dull red flare the size of a child's clenched fist, showing where the *Banbridge,* the Com Guard *Monolith* Class JumpShip, had jumped away from the Huntress system. Though the deep-space rally point existed only as a string of stellar coordinates in the *Banbridge*'s computer core, it was there that the big transport would rendezvous with the rest of the ships of the Inner Sphere fleet, relatively safe from capture by the arriving Smoke Jaguars.

"Galaxy Commander, I detect power spikes in the engineering sections of the Inner Sphere transport JumpShips. I believe they are trying to bring their Kearny-Fuchida drives on line, preparatory to jumping outsystem." The *Korat*'s senior sensor technician was an experienced hand who kept his voice calm, level, and professional.

"What about the WarShips?" Mehta demanded. To her warrior's mind the transports were of secondary importance to the combat vessels. She viewed troopships as something one rode in on the way to battle. WarShips were more fitting targets for one born and bred a warrior. Without combat vessels to protect them, the JumpShips could be run down and destroyed at her leisure.

"The WarShips show power spikes as well," the tech replied. "But not consistent with a K-F drive buildup. Sensors also detect drive flares from all of the enemy combat ships. Wait . . . Yes. Sensors confirm that all enemy WarShips are now rounding on us. It seems as though they mean to engage."

"Good." Mehta's voice dropped to a deep-throated growl. "Send to *Ripper* and *Azov.* They are to close with the enemy as quickly as possible. If any WarShip shows signs of powering up its jump drives, the corvettes are to stall it, cripple it if possible. I do not want a single enemy WarShip to escape."

Minutes passed as the two fleets closed the distance between them. In a few moments she would leave the bridge, turning control of the space battle over to Star Commodore Clarinda Stiles, while Mehta herself oversaw the ground forces set to retake Huntress from the Inner Sphere barbarians. From her station in the holotank, Mehta watched the spectacle of two war fleets moving ever closer to each other.

The Inner Sphere commander had separated his fleet into two sections, with the larger, leading group headed by a *Cameron* Class battle cruiser. Hang Mehta knew that the brick-like vessel was a powerful opponent, mounting deadly naval lasers and PPCs as well as massed missile batteries. The *Cameron*s had been intended as ship-killers, whereas the *Liberator* was designed as a fighter-defense platform. Still, the *Korat*'s heavy guns could inflict massive damage on a capital ship as well as destroy aerospace fighters.

The latter, smaller group was the one that intrigued Mehta the most. The *Korat*'s sensors determined the lead ship in that section to be one she had never encountered before, a *Kyushu* Class frigate. Built by the Draconis Combine, the *Kyushu* was one of the newest Inner Sphere designs. Destroying the Combine vessel, or better yet, capturing her would somewhat satisfy Mehta's thirst for revenge.

She passed an order to the crewmen standing just outside the holotank. The tank was her domain during a battle, and none dared oppose her on that point.

"Send to the *Ripper*. If at all possible, lay alongside the *Kyushu*. Cripple, but do not destroy her. I want to capture that ship."

The crewman saluted and darted away to pass her orders along.

"Galaxy Commander, *Azov* reports he is within missile

range of the lead enemy vessel," another messenger chimed in. "She is a Com Guard *Essex* Class destroyer."

"Aff." Grim satisfaction stained Mehta's voice like blood. "Message to *Azov*. Commence fire."

7

Battle Cruiser SLS **Invisible Truth**
Zenith Jump Point, Huntress System
Kerensky Cluster, Clan Space
19 March 3060

"**B**loody hell!"

The *Invisible Truth* rocked violently as a stream of high-explosive naval autocannon shells slammed into her starboard quarter. Cursing fluently, Alain Beresick grabbed the brass railing surrounding the holotank. That rail had, seconds before, driven the breath from his lungs when the *Invisible Truth* lurched under the assault of the enemy *Liberator.*

The *Truth* had taken only light damage as she ran past the *Vincent* Class corvettes. Using a battle cruiser to combat patrol ships would, in Beresick's mind, be like swatting at flies with a Gauss cannon. He left the corvettes to ships like the *Emerald* and the *Starlight,* his two Essex Class destroyers. The *Emerald* was even now engaged in a close-range slugging match with the leading Jaguar ship.

Though some might view the result of the engagement as a foregone conclusion, Beresick knew better than to trust in preconceptions. All too often, a brilliant, or simply lucky, commander would reach into thin air and pull out a stunning plan for victory. He had no intention of allowing the Smoke Jaguars such a triumph.

At Beresick's order, the *Starlight,* the *Emerald*'s sister ship, swung across the *Vincent*'s stern and loosed a devastating broadside. The blast ripped through the corvette's thin armor, tearing away the target's dorsal jump sail supports.

But the *Vincent* was not yet out of the fight. She swung through a tight forty-five-degree arc toward her larger assailant. So deft was the maneuver that Commodore Beresick almost found himself admiring the enemy helmsman's skill. Naval autocannon fire and invisible lances of laser energy flashed from the *Vincent*'s starboard gunports. The *Starlight*'s heavier armor cracked under the hammering shells and melted to glowing slag at the lasers' deadly touch.

Seconds later, a pair of blue-white flares leapt from the Clan corvette's nose.

"Missile launch!" a sensor technician bellowed above the low hum of voices and equipment blanketing the *Truth*'s bridge. "The missiles seem to have targeted the *Emerald*."

Like unseen wasps, visible only because of the fiery stingers they carried in their tails, the missiles flashed between the stricken *Vincent* and the *Emerald*. The Inner Sphere destroyer heeled to the starboard as her helmsman tried to bring her around to present the smallest possible target aspect to the incoming missiles. He failed.

The relatively lightweight Barracuda antiship missiles smashed into the *Emerald*'s starboard bow just abaft her number two naval autocannon mount. The comparatively small warheads inflicted little damage. In her effort to avoid being struck by the Barracudas, the *Emerald* turned her portside to the second *Vincent*.

The Clan corvette unleashed a broadside, which savaged the *Emerald* viciously. The destroyer had suffered a terrific pounding at the hands of the Huntress defense fleet when Task Force Serpent first arrived in the Jaguars' home system. Lacking port facilities, the ship's damage-control crew had been unable to make effective repairs to the battered Essex Class ship. In some cases, relatively thin armor plate was welded over gaping holes in the destroyer's hull where formerly there had been heavily protected weapon mounts.

The effect was incredible. The thin armor patches gave under the smashing impact of the Clanners' naval autocannons. The blue-white glow of her drives flickered out. Frozen vapor trailed from rents in her hull, showing where atmosphere was venting to space. There was little doubt to anyone on the *Invisible Truth*'s bridge that the *Emerald* was out of the fight, possibly for good.

Seemingly hot for revenge, the *Starlight* came about like a dog chasing its tail and loosed a second, close-range blast. Laser and PPC fire ate into the first *Vincent*'s ravaged stern, ripping through her engineering section, shattering bulkheads and vaporizing the fragile human beings their infernal beams touched.

The boxy little raider shuddered and half-pitched on her nose, a sure indication that control of the vessel had been lost. Her structure twisted sharply, bending like a short, rectangular bow. For a moment, she seemed to right herself. Beresick wondered if perhaps the damage inflicted on the little corvette wasn't as bad as he thought. Then a bright, silent flicker of fire appeared through the gaping rents in her hull. Thick sections of ferro-carbide armor sloughed off like dried mud from a soldier's boots. In seconds, the *Vincent* seemed to consume herself. Orange flames, fed by the atmosphere escaping into the cold of space, jetted from every opening in her hull. A string of soundless flashes, like silent firecrackers, strobed from her hull.

There go her magazines. Beresick was dumbstruck by how quickly the enemy ship died. One moment she was a proud fighting vessel; the next, a drifting piece of smoldering junk. Briefly, Beresick wondered if any of her crew had survived. Recovery operations would have to wait.

Aboard the *Simas Osis,* the surviving Jaguar *Vincent,* Star Captain Ruffo cursed the commander of the Inner

Sphere destroyer that had battered his sister ship into scrap. He knew that his corvette was not designed to combat heavy WarShips. Still, there was no shadow of turning within his heart. Ruffo, like every Jaguar warrior in the little refugee fleet, still burned with the shame of having been driven from the Inner Sphere by the barbarians they had recently conquered with ease.

"Helmsman, hard to starboard. Bring our port guns to bear on the *Essex.*"

"Aff, Star Captain." The burly helmsman grunted, twisting the control yoke as hard to the left as he could manage.

The *Simas Osis* heeled sharply as the little corvette lurched through the turn.

"Fire as your guns bear!" Ruffo's command was hardly necessary. The Jaguar gunners had already locked the *Vincent*'s powerful naval autocannons and relatively lightweight lasers onto the underslung prow of the enemy destroyer.

"Portside guns firing," a technician shouted from one corner of the bridge.

Again, the corvette's lighter weapons inflicted little damage on the enemy WarShip. When the *Essex* replied, it was with the ferocity of an enraged cat. Three naval autocannons and two missile launchers spoke, reducing the *Simas Osis*'s portside armor to a glowing ruin.

Ruffo looked up at the tiny insubstantial ships floating in the air above the bridge holotank. He had been hurled to the deck by the staggering impact of the *Essex*'s attack.

"Star Captain," an engineering technician called from his bridge station. "Our drives are out. We are dead in space."

"Aff," Ruffo acknowledged, hauling himself to his feet again. "Where is the *Essex? Freebirth!*"

Before any of the bridge crew could reply, Ruffo learned the answer himself from the holotank. The enemy destroyer was bearing down on them as inexorably as of fate.

"All back full!" The brick-like shape of the crippled *Vincent* loomed large in the *Starlight*'s main bridge viewscreen.

"Captain, the controls are locked."

"My God, we're gonna hit. Sound collision! Brace for impact!" Captain Stan O'Malley reached for an overhead grab bar.

Just as his fingers closed over the thick brass rod, the *Starlight*'s back-raked prow smashed into the Clan *Vincent*'s shot-riddled portside. The shattering impact tore the grab bar from O'Malley's desperately clutching fingers. Thick, reinforced steel frame members groaned and shrieked as they buckled and sheared under stresses they were never designed to withstand. A deep, rolling boom sounded throughout the ship, underscoring the juddering wail of two WarShips colliding.

That had to be the forward magazines. The thought jumped into O'Malley's mind as he fought to regain his feet on the twisted deck of the *Starlight*'s bridge.

"All back full," O'Malley snapped.

"Captain, she won't answer the helm."

O'Malley loosed a profanity. The *Starlight* had been damaged, though not as severely as her sister ship had been when the task force first jumped into Huntress. Many of the damaged systems had been repaired, but the destroyer's armor could only be patched. The Clanner's broadside, which in other circumstances would have aroused little reason for alarm, had ripped through his ship's already-battered armor. Hauling himself across the bridge along the edge of a wrecked control console, O'Malley peered closely at the Ship's Status Display. All helm and engine control had been lost, and the destroyer's forward three decks were imbedded deeply in the enemy vessel's side.

Another shiver ran through the stricken WarShip, accompanied this time by a series of loud, crackling bangs.

"Sir," the bridge damage control tech called. "We've got out-of-control fires in all forward decks. Hull integrity is down to about thirty-five percent. I recommend we abandon ship."

O'Malley glanced at the SSD again. More areas of the ship were beginning to report severe damage. Human casualties were also very high.

"Very well," O'Malley said with a sigh. "Abandon ship."

Before the order to abandon the dying *Starlight* could be passed, another explosion ripped through the battered vessel.

"Mother of God." Commodore Beresick never learned who breathed those words. He was too engrossed in the spectacle of two WarShips locked together by a freak collision being consumed by a silent white fireball. When the explosion faded, there was nothing left but glowing wreckage. The fires resulting from the wreck had touched off either ammunition or fuel, and the blast tore both ships apart.

Momentarily forgotten in the spellbinding death of the *Starlight* and her Jaguar opponent, the big *Liberator* cut across the *Truth*'s bow, unleashing a fiery tornado against the larger battle cruiser. The *Truth*'s thick armor barely held. Had more of the Clanner's broadside connected with its intended target, Beresick would be lucky to be alive to curse his bruised ribs.

"Where is he?"

"Commodore, the target is at zero-three-niner, mark forty-five, going to starboard."

Beresick quickly located the ghostly image of the Clan *Liberator*. The enemy vessel was crossing the *Truth*'s bows from left to right. She was slightly to the starboard and a bit "higher" than the battle cruiser.

"Helm, starboard, thirty degrees, up fifteen!" Beresick shouted. "Weapons officer, ready to fire as your guns bear."

In the center of the bridge, also known as the "control pit," a young woman shoved the *Truth*'s helm hard over to the right, pulling back on the heavy, airplane-like yoke at the same time. While the technology was certainly available to maneuver a WarShip by simply pressing buttons, it had been learned through long and bitter experience that a helmsman gripped by the excitement of battle might accidentally press the wrong control, turning the vessel the wrong way at a critical moment. Control yokes were far less likely to produce such an error. The ship's designers had built a computer-simulated resistance into the control yoke. The further you turned the yoke, the more the myomer-induced resistance mounted. In theory, a particularly strong and determined helmsman might turn the yoke as much as ninety degrees each way, but Beresick, in all his years as a black-ocean sailor, had yet to see a crewman capable of turning the wheel more then sixty or sixty-five degrees. At thirty, the helmsman was fighting the yoke to keep control of the ship.

The *Truth*'s Chief Petty Officer half-sat, half-knelt in a padded seat behind and to the right of the helm station. The gruff senior noncommissioned officer muttered words of profanity-laced encouragement, directed alternately at the Clans, his own officers, and the helmsman's parentage. Despite (or perhaps thanks to) the stream of vituperation, the young woman held the quivering helm steady on a right thirty-degree turn. A second indicator showed the nearly kilometer-long WarShip steadily rising on a fifteen-degree angle to her original plane of travel.

Her bow-mounted missile launchers blazed as they came to bear on the turning *Liberator*. Big, gray-painted missiles streaked across the narrowing gap to slam into the Clan vessel's hull. A pair of naval PPCs belched lightning in reply. The unbelievable energies generated by the NPPCs ripped into the *Truth*'s thick armored hide, shattering hull plates and blasting her right forward autocannon to junk.

"Number two NAC out of action," the executive officer called from his station near the helm console. "That PPC blast was a direct hit, right on the turret. Rescue crews on the way, but they don't have much hope of finding anyone alive in the turret. Damage control reports hull integrity holding, but not for long with the pounding we're taking."

Beresick left the holotank briefly. The *Invisible Truth*'s Ship Status Display was one function that he'd rather not call up either in the holotank or on one of the large bridge repeater monitors. He didn't want the whole crew knowing how gravely the battle cruiser had been hurt. Orange splotches smeared across the graphic line-drawing of the *Invisible Truth* showed places where the vessel had been savaged by the *Liberator*'s attack. Other damaged sections showed green or amber blots indicating lesser degrees of devastation. There were few areas of the ship that showed no color at all. Fortunately, there were no bright red areas, indicating a section that had been completely destroyed, either.

Beresick knew that the *Liberator* must be suffering damage almost as severe as that taken by the *Truth*. For nearly a quarter of an hour, the WarShips had circled around each other, trying in vain to bring their massive broadside batteries into play. Only twice in all that time did the *Truth*'s huge naval autocannons lash out at the Clanner. The *Liberator* managed to deliver three broadsides at the larger battle cruiser, which left the *Invisible Truth* wounded, but not critically so, at least not yet.

"Sir, he's reversing his turn!" came the excited shout from the sensor chief.

"Helm, hard to port! Engines all back full, now!"

The helmsman yanked the control yoke hard, twisting the heavy plastic control to the left. Immediately, the *Truth* began to reverse her ponderous swing to starboard. The deck shuddered beneath Beresick's feet as the huge engines drove the 859,000-ton vessel forward to override its momentum. Like a freight train suddenly flung into reverse, the *Truth* traveled forward for some distance before the struggling engines broke her inertia and brought her to a trembling halt. For a long, painful moment, Beresick wondered if the ship's ancient engines would stand the strain. The sudden reversing of thrust might place so great a demand on the drives, installed when the ship was laid down in 2672, that they might shred themselves under the strain. Then, slowly, painfully, she began to move backward, swinging to port as she went.

The sudden deceleration bled off the big WarShip's inertial gravity. Bridge crewmen "floated" out of their seats, held in place only by thickly padded harnesses. Beresick had to grab the holotank railing again, as his magnetic boots failed to completely counteract the sudden change in inertia.

"Broadside guns now bear on the enemy," the weapons officer called from his bridge station. The gamble had paid off.

Beresick's next order was almost unnecessary.

"Fire!"

Cannons, lasers, and PPCs licked out from the *Cameron*'s boxy flanks, smashing the *Liberator*'s aft starboard quarter. A similar, but smaller, blast flashed from the Clanner in reply.

"Commodore, we've got heavy damage to all starboard sections." The damage control officer's voice carried a note of fear. "Suggest we break off and make running repairs."

Beresick didn't immediately reply to the officer's suggestion. "Sensor ops," he bellowed instead. "How bad is the Clanner hurt?"

"Sensors indicate he's got severe damage to his starboard side. He may have lost a couple of his weapons, too." The technician paused. "Commodore, he's rolling."

Looking at the holographic representation of the Clan WarShip, Beresick saw the bulbous-nosed vessel revolving along her long axis. Such tactics were common in naval warfare. When a ship was badly damaged along one side, the captain would order a roll to present the vessel's undamaged side to the enemy. Since there was no up or down in space, the tactic made little difference to the ship's crew, other than, in the space of a few seconds, placing the enemy on the other side of the vessel.

"Okay," Beresick answered. "It looks like he means to stay and fight it out. So will we. Attitude control, give me a one-eighty degree roll. Engines all ahead full. If he wants to start all over again, we'll sure oblige him."

Slowly, the massive battle cruiser began a counterclockwise roll around her center axis. Beresick could feel the motion in the pit of his stomach and in his inner ear. At the same time, the feeling of gravity returned as the *Truth*'s huge Cassion Vassers maneuvering drives thrust her forward once again.

"He is still with us, Star Commodore Stiles," the lower casteman manning the *Korat*'s sensors shouted from his station against the bridge's port bulkhead. "He has executed a longitudinal roll and has begun moving forward again."

"Freebirth!" Clarinda Stiles hissed.

"It seems he is not so badly injured as we believed," her executive officer said mildly, in the face of Stiles' angry curse.

Despite the long months since the Jaguar fleet had jumped away from the rim of the Inner Sphere, Stiles had not let go of her shame and fury at the idea of having to pull back. Discovering an Inner Sphere fleet hanging at the nadir jump point of the Jaguars' home system heaped yet another insult upon her already raw and bleeding honor.

Galaxy Commander Hang Mehta, the fleet's nominal commander, had departed with the 'Mech-carrying DropShips to destroy the barbarian invaders on Huntress. She had left Stiles to destroy the Inner Sphere fleet in space. Though the task would be difficult, it was not impossible. All of her ship commanders were burning for revenge, and their fury would carry them through the fight. In the first few moments of the fight, the *Korat* had brushed by a charging *Essex* Class destroyer. The smaller WarShip bore scars in its armor, silent testimony to the ferocity of an earlier battle. A single broadside from the *Korat*'s guns ripped through the destroyer's angular bow armor, reducing the *Essex* to a drifting, shattered hulk, burning in the Clan cruiser's wake.

For Clarinda Stiles, the victory was doubly sweet. The *Essex* had borne not only the emblem of the hated Com Guards, but a Cameron Star as well. Destroying the Inner Sphere WarShip so handily expunged some of the shame of the Clans' loss at Tukayyid and gave her hope that the Smoke Jaguars would defeat the larger Inner Sphere war fleet. When the *Vincent Mk 42* Class corvette *Azov* was destroyed by another *Essex* Class destroyer, Stiles' opinion began to change.

Then, as she began the close-quarters dance with the Com Guard *Cameron,* Stiles' belief in the invincibility of her little fleet eroded. In the end, she decided that all she could do was acquit herself like a warrior and take as many of the enemy as she could with her into the abyss.

"Bring us around, under his stern!" Stiles yelled at the helmsman.

"I am trying, Star Colonel." The young man's voice was tight with strain and fear.

"Do not try!" Stiles bellowed. "Do it!"

Desperately, with a muscle-cracking effort, the youth hauled the *Korat's* control yoke as far to the left as he could. At the same time, he shoved it forward against its stop. The result was a ponderous, far-from-graceful twisting turn, which in an aerospace fighter might have been called a wingover. The cruiser's spaceframe creaked and groaned in protest as the helmsman forced her into a turn tighter than her designers had specified as the maximum. For a wonder, the badly damaged ship held together.

The enemy vessel, still trying to accelerate from the sudden, jolting stop that had brought her almost directly under the *Korat's* stern, tried to follow the maneuver, but didn't have enough momentum. The *Liberator* slid past the big battle cruiser's stern with only a few kilometers to spare.

"All starboard batteries, fire!" Stiles' order was the scream of a triumphant jaguar.

Unbelievable energies lashed out, ripping through the enemy's thick armor. The big Inner Sphere vessel staggered and pitched under the hammering assault. The *Cameron* fired a pair of hastily aimed missiles, followed by equally ill-directed PPC blasts in reply, but not one of the attacks connected with the battered *Korat*. Star Commodore Clarinda Stiles let out another yell of triumph. One more broadside, and the Com Guard ship would be destroyed.

Then, she was lying on her back, looking up at the overhead. Warm blood was running down her left arm, and her face felt as though she had thrust it into a wasp's nest.

"Star Commodore, are you . . ."

Stiles slapped away her executive officer's helping hands.

"I am all right," she snarled, getting to her feet. The left side of her uniform hung in shreds. Blood oozed from a dozen small wounds in her side, and flowed freely from a deep cut in her left biceps.

"Get me a bandage before I bleed to death," she yelled at the medical corpsman assigned to the bridge. As was fitting, the lower casteman leapt to obey. The bridge was in chaos. The only illumination came from the emergency lights above each of the exit hatches and lifeboat stations. Thin smoke drifted through the air from smoldering control circuits. A severed power conduit swung from the overhead, striking sparks every time it touched metal. Several large bundles that might have been debris, but weren't, lay on the deck, near now-empty bridge stations.

"What in Kerensky's name hit us?"

Her second in command pointed to a holographic image, which was bearing down on the *Korat*'s injured starboard side. There was no mistaking the flat, blunt, arrowhead shape of a *Whirlwind* Class destroyer. A large blotch of flat gray paint showed on her nose, where her crew had apparently painted out the emblem of her former owners. The image brought a ripple of disgust to Stiles' guts. The barbarians were no better than the bandit caste, stealing the property of others to serve their own ends. Even more repulsive were the insignias crudely painted over the obscuring gray—a black, fanged serpent coiled around a star—the Cameron Star itself, the emblem of the Star League.

Autocannon fire flared from the *Whirlwind*'s nose, coupled with the flat, colorless glare of a Gauss cannon being fired. The projectiles slammed into the cruiser's already shot-riddled starboard armor. The *Korat* shuddered again under the impact of heavy cannon shells, and a massive chunk of nickel-iron accelerated to transonic velocities.

"Star Commodore," the damage control officer gasped, holding his ribs. "All sections report major damage. All starboard weapons systems are out of action. Sick bay reports heavy casualties. Star Commodore, we must surrender or be destroyed."

"No! You stinking freebirth coward, no." Spittle flew from the corners of Stiles' mouth as she raged at the lower caste technician. "We will not surrender to these vermin. If we surrender, we will lose Huntress. I will not allow these *stravags* to seize our homeworld, not so long as there is breath in my body to oppose them."

"Star Commodore, we will lose this ship and our lives if . . ."

Stiles silenced the technician with a back-handed blow that sent him staggering into a control panel that was already slick with blood.

"If we die, then we die!" she screamed. "Now get back to your post, or *I* will kill you myself."

Turning away from the white-faced tech, Stiles stalked back into the holotank.

"All guns, fire at will. If we are to die, then let us take at least one of these Inner Sphere freebirths with us."

Seconds later, the *Korat* twisted and leaped like a gaffed fish as both Inner Sphere WarShips poured volley after volley into the stricken vessel. A fireball burst into the bridge from the ship's main liftshaft, and the force of the explosion pitched Stiles backward across the holotank. Her hurtling body struck the tank's steel railing and folded around it like a rag doll. Stiles actually heard the dull crunch of her spine snapping in two. For a long, painless second, she hung there, suspended above the deck, then she slid to the floor of the holotank. Dimly, through the shock of her injuries, she was aware that her body was twisted at an entirely unnatural angle.

I should be in pain, she marveled. *But I can't feel anything.*

Before she could reason out this tiny mystery through the deadening shock, a Gauss slug ripped through the hull just a few meters above her head. In that timeless void known almost exclusively to accident victims, where everything seems to be suspended between the ticks of the clock, Stiles actually saw the glittering ball of death smash through the bridge bulkhead, decapitating her executive officer as he raced to help his crippled commander.

As the headless corpse dropped to the deck, the universe exploded in her face.

Commodore Beresick watched in sick horror as the Clan *Liberator* literally folded in on itself. The combined firepower of the *Invisible Truth* and the destroyer *Fire Fang* had reduced the once-powerful vessel to burning junk. The suddenness of the destruction left him with the gut-churning certainty that few of the Clan ship's crew would survive.

"Commodore, a report from the *Ranger*. Captain Winslow reports two Clan JumpShips disabled and one destroyed. All three WarShips have been destroyed. *Starlight* is gone," the communication technician paused and shook his head. "Just plain gone. *Emerald*'s commander, Captain Kole, reports she is afire and has lost ninety-five percent of her hull integrity. He says that, given a dry dock and a couple of months, she might be put back into fighting condition, but he wouldn't bet on it. He's given the order to abandon ship. Our DropShips, *Honor* and *Integrity,* are standing by to take off *Emerald*'s crew.

"*Antrim* was detailed to run down the Clan DropShips. Captain DeSalas reports that he has taken heavy damage. He does not believe that his corvette can be repaired in the field. *Fire Fang* is still engaged with a couple of DropShips. Captain Jones reports it's just a matter of time. *Ranger* is damaged but still battle-ready. I haven't gotten status reports on the other WarShips yet. All of our JumpShips jumped out safely."

"Stop! Wait a minute." Beresick interrupted his executive officer's flow of words. "*Ranger* says three Clan JumpShips were destroyed or captured. What about the other two?"

"Captain Winslow says that the other two Clan JumpShips,

a *Star Lord* and a *Monolith,* jumped out immediately. They must have been fitted with lithium-fusion batteries."

"Dammit!" A chill ran along Beresick's spine. "We have no idea of where they went, and no way of finding out. There's a bloody good chance that they're going for help.

"Send to General Winston. Tell her we won the naval engagement. Casualty and damage reports to follow. Advise her that we were unable to stop all of the Clan Drop-Ships from heading in-system, and that she's going to have company pretty soon, and I don't think they're going to be all that happy about her urban renewal projects. And tell her that at least two Clan JumpShips made it out-system before we could stop them. The Jaguars could be bringing in some really serious reinforcements in as little as a week, and God help us then."

8

Ariana Winston sat on the top step leading to the Light Horse's mobile headquarters, staring up into the dark slate-blue of the early morning sky. It was about an hour until local sun-up, a time referred to in military parlance as BMNT, Beginning of Morning Nautical Twilight. There was just enough light in the sky to let you see things on the ground—not well, but enough to know they were there.

Her eyes scanned the heavens like search radars, looking for the first faint scarlet streaks of re-entering 'Mech drop pods. The thin crimson traceries would herald the arrival of the incoming Smoke Jaguar forces. Less than two dozen meters from the open door of the mobile HQ stood her *Cyclops*. The 'Mech had been repaired, and its magazines topped off, shortly after the initial fighting had subsided. Now it stood silently, its feet bathed in deep shadows, waiting, like an obedient war horse, for her hand to guide it into battle once again.

Those of Task Force Serpent now occupying Huntress

had no way of knowing when the Jags would arrive. The destruction of the main planetary sensor net by the pre-invasion DEST strike had crippled the Smoke Jaguars' ability to detect the incoming Inner Sphere forces. Now, the tactic had turned against those who'd employed it.

A network of interlinked search radars and thermal and magnetic scanners had made up the Huntress space defense systems. Before being destroyed, the system let the Jaguars detect and track incoming Jump- and DropShips. If the ships were hostile, the same sensors allowed the Jags to target the inbound vessels for destruction with the Reagan system's powerful weapons.

Immediately after the fighting died down, Winston had set her technicians and a few men scrounged from the Com Guards to repairing the Huntress sensor nets. Unfortunately, much of the equipment destroyed by the DEST strike could not be repaired. Whole new units would have to be constructed and installed, and the task force didn't have that kind of time. The systems that could be repaired were repaired, leaving the Inner Sphere occupation forces with extremely short-range sensors, capable of detecting a fighter-sized object entering Huntress' stormy upper atmosphere, and long-range EMP/tachyon sensors used to detect incoming JumpShips. The long- and medium-range sensors needed to track the incoming Jaguar DropShips defied all attempts to bring them on line.

It had been seven days since the message from Commodore Beresick had arrived, telling her that most of the incoming Smoke Jaguar war fleet had been destroyed by Task Force Serpent's combat vessels, and that the Clan DropShips were inbound to the planet. Two JumpShips had detached their DropShips and jumped out-system again, using lithium-fusion batteries to power their jump drives. It was those two escaping vessels that worried Winston the most. Where were they going? She had to assume they were running for help. In that case, how soon would they be back, and with what kind of reinforcements?

According to Beresick's estimate, the Jaguar relief force DropShips would be in position to deposit their loads of OmniMechs and Elementals right in her lap sometime today. *No, relief force is the wrong term,* Winston told herself. *They're refugees.*

It had taken several days to round up and interrogate the few Smoke Jaguars who had survived the battle at the jump point. According to the prisoners, the DropShips carried a hodgepodge of Jaguar units that had been driven from the Inner Sphere by Operation Bulldog.

Though battered and bloodied, the prisoners were angry and defiant. It had taken every trick that Lieutenant Tobin, Beresick's one-time ROM intelligence agent, could muster to wring the desired information out of his prisoners. Winston knew she'd have a difficult time with Paul Masters once the truth of the interrogations came out, but for now she had bigger problems to worry about. According to Tobin's best estimates, the Jaguar fleet carried the equivalent of two full Galaxies of troops. Tobin's report cautioned that his number was an estimate based on information extracted from the prisoners, filtered through an intelligence analyst's natural skepticism. Though the inbound units had been thrown together from the remnants of at least five Galaxies, and were made up of equal parts front-line and garrison Clusters, they'd had several months aboard their respective DropShips to heal up, repair their damaged equipment, and run simulated integration exercises.

That last was speculation on Tobin's part, but the conclusion seemed logical. Even if the Jaguars had not expected trouble upon reaching the Clan homeworlds, it made sense that their commanders would be pushing the surviving troops to restore the fighting edge blunted on Operation Bulldog's armor. It was what she would have done in their place.

On the other hand, though, Task Force Serpent had no way of replacing combat troops killed or crippled during the initial invasion of Huntress. The Explorer Corps speculated that all of the Clans had bases in the Deep Periphery. If so, perhaps the Smoke Jaguars had drawn on some reserve forces stationed along the Exodus Road or elsewhere in the Clan homeworlds, but she couldn't be certain. Inner Sphere intelligence about such matters was sketchy at best. Though the Inner Sphere troops would enjoy a numerical superiority over the Jags, the Clanners still held the technological advantage. That made the battle about even.

No, that gives them the edge, Winston corrected herself. *They're the Smoke Jaguars. They'll be on the offensive, which is where they excel. They're probably still smarting from being kicked out of the Inner Sphere, and they'll be fighting for their homeworld. For them, this will be payback, and that will give them the advantage of morale.*

During the short time she'd had to prepare to defend the prize her task force had won, Winston had shuttled her troops around as best she could. The tactic of divide and conquer had worked wonderfully, and she didn't want the Jaguars to use the same ploy against her. That was why she'd decided to draw up her forces into two large groups, rather than leaving them spread out across the planet's surface. The Com Guards and the Second St. Ives Lancers had been assigned to augment the Eridani Light Horse in Lootera. Mount Szabo, with its huge Smoke Jaguar symbol and its now-extinguished eternal laser, the Hall of the Hunters, and the genetic repository, were all sacred places to the Jags. It would undoubtedly be one of the first targets they would attack.

The second force, comprised of the Kathil Uhlans, the Northwind Highlanders, and the Knights of the Inner Sphere, under the command of Andrew Redburn, had been positioned near Lake Osis on the southwestern border of the main continent. Winston had confidence in Redburn. She knew he would give the Jaguars as good or better than he got, using every means at his disposal to stop them. But if things got too hot, the Dhuan Mountains, the Dhuan

Swamp, and the Shikari Jungle would give Redburn's division sufficient cover to fight a guerrilla campaign against the Jaguars.

The smaller units, the Fourth Drakøns, Kingston's Legionnaires, and the battered Lyran Guards, were transferred to a remote location in the Lunar Range on Continent Abysmal. From there, any or all of them could be brought in at a moment's notice to provide a relief force, should one be needed.

The DEST teams, their training and Major Ryan's protestations to the contrary, were ill-suited to the kind of pitched 'Mech-to-'Mech fighting Winston was anticipating. She ordered Ryan to hold his men in reserve until a target worthy of their special brand of attention manifested itself.

Only the Rabid Fox teams remained in place in the Eastern Mountains, watching Falcon Eyrie. Winston still did not trust Trent's assertion that the Jade Falcons would take no active part in what was essentially a Smoke Jaguar matter. She'd been a soldier far too long to rely so implicitly on the word of a spy.

To make matters worse for the men and women of Task Force Serpent, Commodore Beresick reported that both the *Starlight* and the *Emerald* had been destroyed by the incoming Jaguar force, and the *Fox* Class corvette *Antrim* had been damaged beyond the task force's ability to repair. That left Beresick with just four operational WarShips to defend the system. If the Clanners arrived in force to attack Task Force Serpent, Winston doubted if any of the combat vessels would survive.

In line with the mission orders to protect the fleet's vulnerable transport JumpShips, Beresick had ordered them out of the system to a predesignated rendezvous point. Because the question of more Jaguar troops arriving from the Inner Sphere was still open, the transports could not be recalled. Only the most extreme circumstances—the choice between recalling the JumpShips and losing the entire task force, for example—could justify bringing the lightly armored transports back into Huntress.

If need be, the WarShips could be used to evacuate the ground forces, but that presented new problems.

The *Invisible Truth,* a *Cameron* Class battle cruiser, and the *Congress* Class frigate *Ranger* mounted only two docking collars each. The *Kyushu* Class frigate *Haruna,* loaned to the task force by the Draconis Combine, boasted four of the heavy rings of machinery needed to mate a DropShip to a starfaring JumpShip. The captured *Whirlwind* Class destroyer that had been renamed *Fire Fang* by her new owners lacked docking collars altogether.

If the task force abandoned all of their BattleMechs, vehicles, weapons, and supplies, it might be possible to cram all personnel aboard Serpent's eight largest DropShips and ferry them to the waiting starships. Winston quailed at this idea for two reasons. It would leave the Jaguars with nearly six regiments worth of intact war machines and a small mountain of ammunition and spare parts. While the booty from Task Force Serpent would not be enough for the Jags to resume their invasion of the Inner Sphere, it might provide the Clanners with enough defense materiel until they could get their war industries back on track.

Even if her troops tried to destroy the equipment being left behind, experience had taught her that a skilled technician could assemble a BattleMech by scavenging parts from several wrecks. And the Smoke Jaguars' technician caste were known to be some of the most skillful and resourceful 'Mech mechanics in the known universe.

So, figure they'll be able to rebuild one in three 'Mechs, she calculated silently. *That'll give the Jags two combat regiments, or galaxies, or whatever they want to call them. The point is, if we're forced to withdraw, we can't leave anything behind for the Jags to find, salvage, and reuse.*

One other Inner Sphere force, the smallest on Huntress, had been recalled to Lootera. Using the secure, send-only pager, Winston had summoned the nekekami team back to the command post. So far, she had received no confirmation of their return.

Winston had one other option, of course—to recall her JumpShips and withdraw the task force from Huntress. The Jags had no WarShips left with which to oppose the evacuation, and most of the troops under her command had executed a forced withdrawal under fire before, many of them during the Clan invasion ten years earlier. Though such a withdrawal would be difficult, even dangerous, it wouldn't be impossible. Some of her commanders, the most vocal among them being Lyran Guard Commander Marshal Sharon Bryan and Colonel Regis Grandi of the Com Guards, had lobbied for just such an action. The vast majority of the Jaguars' heavy industry had been either destroyed or severely damaged, Grandi argued. Why not call the mission a success, and bug out?

Winston considered the idea and then discarded it on two grounds. First, by the time the Jaguar JumpShips returned, the task force's ground troops would be fully engaged. Second, and more important, the mission of Task Force Serpent, and its sister operation in the Inner Sphere, codenamed Bulldog, was to destroy an entire Clan, not *part* of it, not *most* of it, but *all* of it. The forces burning hard for Huntress represented not only a major portion of the Smoke Jaguars' fighting strength, but a big hunk of their ruling warrior caste. Pulling out now would leave the job only half done. Winston had never failed to complete a task, and she didn't intend to start now.

She scanned the lightening heavens once again and scowled. It had also been seven days since two of the transport-type JumpShips had escaped from Beresick's WarShips, jumping out of the Huntress system, bound for whatever unknown destination. By Beresick's estimation, the Jaguars could be back at Huntress in as little as a week with, in his own words, some really serious reinforcements.

On this point the prisoners had been absolutely no help. Every one of the Jaguars captured, warrior and lower caste alike, flatly refused to even speculate about where the JumpShips might be headed. Even Adept Tobin, with all his ROM-trained interrogator's skills, could not coax, trick, or wring that one bit of vital information out of the prisoners.

"General."

Winston leaped to her feet at the sound of the whispered call. Her hand dropped to the holstered Mauser automatic slung low on her right hip. She searched the gloom for the one who had spoken.

"General Winston," again came the sourceless voice. "I have a message for you. A friend said to tell you, 'Which if not victory, is yet revenge.' "

She stiffened at the line from Milton, one of the secret recognition codes Morgan had passed to her. Her hand moved from the grip of her weapon.

"Where are you?"

A patch of deep shadow at her *Cyclops'* feet rippled like a dark pool into which a pebble had been dropped. A black shape detached itself from the shadow and glided noiselessly across the space between her 'Mech and the mobile HQ. A cold shiver ran along Winston's spine. For a brief moment she felt almost as though it were Death himself coming for her.

"Ohayo gozaimas." The figure wished her good morning in Japanese, executing a formal bow as well. "I am Kasugai Hatsumi, leader of the nekekami team. I wanted to wait until you were alone before reporting in. It might be that our presence would not sit so well with some of your other commanders. We are standing ready for your orders."

Winston nodded her acknowledgment, still too stunned by the sudden appearance of the nekekami to speak.

"I also wish to thank you in person for clearing Julia Davis of Morgan-*sama*'s murder," Hatsumi continued in a voice that seemed pitched so that it would reach her ears and then stop. "As I am certain you have surmised, she is one of my agents."

"General Winston?" The call came from the mobile HQ's darkened interior.

"W - wait here," she instructed Hatsumi, finding her

voice at last. Then she turned to the command truck. "What is it?"

"General, search radars indicate a large body of ships headed in our direction. We have visual confirmation. They're all Clan DropShips. The ready five fighters have been launched, and the rest are awaiting your orders."

"All right, this is it." Winston felt her warrior's blood rising as she reeled off her orders. "Launch the fighters assigned as interceptors, but have them hold just outside the atmosphere until the Clan ships are within easy striking distance, then ram it down their throats. They are to kill as many of those Jaguar buggers as they can. Keep the attack ships on the ground and under cover. We know we won't be able to stop the Jags in space, but we can whittle them down some. I want to keep some of our airpower on call for ground strikes once the Clanners establish their planethead.

"Notify General Redburn, although I'm sure he knows by now that the Jags are inbound. Call the rest of the northern force commanders. I want a full tactical briefing in fifteen minutes. Now move."

The command post exploded into a flurry of activity as Winston turned and leapt back to the ground. Hatsumi was nowhere to be seen.

"Ariana-*sama*, my team is yours to command." Again the quiet voice sounded in her ears. "Summon us when you need us. We will be close." Then, there was silence.

"Blast," Winston muttered. "I wish he wouldn't do that."

Five kilometers away, outside the captured city of Lootera, an urgent, raucous horn sounded in the inflatable field shelter serving as a barracks for the aerospace pilots of the Eridani Light Horse. Men and women leapt to their feet, scattering cards, data readers, and coffee cups. Others scrambled from their bunks, fighting to disentangle themselves from the thin nyo-wool blankets in which they had wrapped themselves. All across the impromptu airfield, technicians were crawling under and over the wings of the unit's *Corsair, Transgressor,* and *Stuka* aerospace fighters. Vital systems were checked over, weapons armed, and fuel tanks topped off, as the pilots clambered swiftly up the steel ladders leading to their cockpits.

Unlike the BattleMech, ground armor, and infantry forces, the Light Horse's aerofighter contingent had come through the invasion relatively intact. What Smoke Jaguar fighters there had been on planet were thrown against the initial assault wave, and had been destroyed. A few surviving fighters attempted air strikes against the landing zones, only to be swept from the skies. A number of the Light Horse's light and medium fighters had been shot down, and some of the heavier craft damaged, but the bulk of their aerospace units remained intact.

As Warrant Officer Leonard Harpool swarmed up the ladder to the cockpit of his *SL-17R Shilone,* he paused for half a second to pat the rump of the cartoonish porcupine drawn with infinite care on the side of his manta-shaped fighter's cockpit. The "nose art" was, at first, a source of irritation for the young flyer. Contrary to popular opinion, most fighter pilots did not choose their own names, but rather were christened by the squadron leader and the more senior flyers. Most of the names given were rather uncomplimentary. Harpool was nicknamed "Hedgehog" because of his unruly mop of black, spiky hair. Eventually, he came to see the humor in the name and had asked his techs to paint one on his ship.

"Okay, Ted, gimme the dope," Harpool shouted to his plane technician as he strapped himself into the *Shilone*'s ejection seat.

"The inbounds are at one-nine-seven, four hundred kilometers. They haven't entered the atmosphere yet, but that's just a matter of time," the technician bellowed in reply. It was necessary for Sergeant Ted Melo to shout, even with the communicators built into both the ground crews' and the pilots' helmets. The sound of the powerful aerospace engines spooling up was enough to instantly deafen anyone lacking hearing protection. The ship, like all the Light Horse fighters, had been housed in impromptu revetments built up out of sandbags. That only served to confine and concentrate the ear-splitting whine of the engines. Even through helmet baffles, the noise level was incredible.

"Switch to button one for air traffic control. Your missile bins are full up, and you've got max fuel. Watch that portside medium laser. It's been heating up quick."

"Right!" Harpool yelled in acknowledgment.

Melo waved a salute at "his" pilot and dropped to the ground. Harpool touched a control that caused the ladder to retract into the *Shilone*'s hull with a clang. Looking through the cockpit canopy, he saw a technician standing next to Melo waving a fist full of red nylon ribbons at him and flashing a "thumbs-up." Each streamer represented a vital system that the technical crew had checked out and declared fit. Had a system not measured up, the ribbon would not have been detached and the fighter would not be allowed to launch. Harpool saluted and returned the ancient "good-luck, good-hunting" gesture.

Feeding power to the single Shinobi 260 power plant, the pilot moved his ship from sand-bagged revetment onto the taxiway. Moments later he was airborne, hurled into the sky by the big engine's massive thrust.

"Hedger, this is Wildman. Nice of you to join us." Lieutenant "Wild Steve" Timmons was Harpool's wing leader.

"Sorry, boss." Harpool grinned inside his closed helmet. "I was holding a full house. I just wanted to finish the hand. Problem was nobody else did."

"Yeah, what were they?" Timmons asked, the jest plain in his voice. He knew that Harpool's love for cards would never come between the young aeropilot and his even greater love of flying.

"Don't worry, Wildman. Jacks over fives."

"Good. You gotta watch those eights and aces."

Timmons was referring to the "dead man's hand," the cards some legendary hero was holding when he got shot in the back by a rival. Neither Timmons nor Harpool really believed that the "eights and aces" were unlucky, but fighter pilots were, by nature, a superstitious lot, and why tempt fate?

"Echo Flight, this is Ground. Your vector is one-six-niner true, angels base plus fifty. Your signal is buster."

"Echo Five and Six, acknowledge," Timmons answered for Harpool and himself. "You got that, Hedger?"

"Got it."

"Okay, then let's go to buster."

Buster, like so many of the traditions surrounding military aviation, was an ancient slang term. When a pilot was told his signal was "buster," it meant that he was allowed to open his engines up to full military power, instead of a more controlled cruising speed. The pilots also understood the ground-controller's cryptic instructions to mean that the inbound Clan ships were off to the flight's southeast. The altitude given in angels, or hundreds of meters above ground level, was expressed as the "base" plus or minus. The base was an altitude never expressed over the radio for fear of interception by the enemy. Today the base was twenty thousand meters. "Base plus fifty" put the enemy at twenty-five thousand meters AGL. That meant the Jags were already inside Huntress' atmosphere. They were really pushing the performance envelope on their fighters.

Harpool shoved his throttle forward past the maximum cruise setting and into the overthrust detent. The big engine, located just behind his narrow cockpit, bellowed as additional fuel was sprayed into its combustion chamber. A long orange and blue flame jetted from the exhaust nozzle, kicking the fighter forward. The ship rocked and buffeted as it crashed through the sound barrier, but settled down once again as it reached its top transonic speed. Moments later Hedgehog Harpool could see the gleam of stars through the thin upper atmosphere.

Now, wait a minute, those stars are moving!

"Tally-ho!" Harpool yelled into his communicator. "I got visual contact on the Clan inbounds." A quick scan of his cockpit sensor displays confirmed the sighting. "Many inbounds, bearing zero-one-five relative, angels base plus forty-five."

"I got 'em, Hedger," Timmons replied. "Pick yourself a nice fat DropShip and let's go get 'em."

"Roger, Wildman. I got a *Broadsword* at zero-one-seven, mark twenty, range thirty-five," Harpool shot back. "Looks like we're on his five. We should be able to swing in on his six easy."

"Roger, Hedger, but remember, nothing is ever *that* easy." Timmons' fighter leapt away, veering slightly to the right to drop onto the Clan DropShip's "six-o'clock" position, directly behind the brick-shaped vessel. Harpool followed in his wing leader's path.

"I got him." Timmons' voice had taken on a strange detached tone, almost as though he were reading stock quotes. "Missile lock. Missiles away."

Twenty long-range missiles streaked out from their launcher beneath the manta-shaped fighter's nose, followed by a trio of laser bolts, invisible against the darkness of Huntress' upper atmosphere, save where they intersected the smoke trails of the missiles.

Timmons rolled his ship to the right, losing a bit of altitude in the process and clearing the way for Harpool to add his own missile and laser fire to the destruction already wrought on the *Broadsword*'s tail section. Corkscrewing short-range missiles and stuttering pulses of laser energy lashed out in reply.

Most of the Clanner's missiles whipped past Hedgehog's canopy. Harpool would later maintain that the missiles passed so close by his canopy that he could read "Made on Huntress" stamped on the warheads. The blast from the Jaguar ship's pulse laser ripped steaming pits in the *Shilone*'s tough armor.

As Harpool pulled his fighter into a tight, looping turn, he loosed a hastily aimed volley of missiles from his aft-facing launcher. Though none of the missiles impacted against the *Broadsword*'s armored hull, they must have caused the Clan gunner to flinch. The stream of laserfire shifted away from the retreating fighter and quit as the gunner lost his weapons lock.

Straining against the G forces that narrowed his vision and threatened to push him into oblivion, Harpool wrestled the *Shilone* through the tight loop, bringing the powerful nose-mounted weapons once again into line with the already damaged *Broadsword*. Missiles and laser fire ripped the tattered armor into metallic shreds and clawed their way into the DropShip's engineering section. The Clan ship lurched to the left, but came back swinging as the after guns pumped out another volley of death. This time the Clanner's aim was better. Most of the volley-fired missiles hammered into Hedgehog's flat hull, gouging out chunks of reinforced steel. The strobing pulse laser slagged some of the relatively thin armor protecting the cockpit.

This time it was Harpool's turn to flinch. Slamming his stick forward and to the left, at the same time stomping hard on the left rudder pedal, Hedgehog threw his fighter into a twisting dive to the left, trying to break away from the Jaguar guns that were savaging his fighter. As he continued his downward barrel roll, Harpool saw a dark gray boomerang flash past his canopy at no more than fifty meters. The crazy-eyed, club-wielding figure painted on the ship's nose left no doubt in his mind as to the identity of the pilot.

"Wildman" Steve Timmons had circled back, dropping in on the *Broadsword*'s six. Timmons' gentle, sweeping turn had taken a second or so longer than Harpool's tight, high-G loop. Smoke and light blossomed from the *Shilone*'s nose and wings. Laser and missile fire tore into the *Broadsword*'s shattered armor, smashing vital systems. Smoke billowed from the rents in the DropShip's hull. One of Timmons' missiles must have found the main engines, for the massive ship's drive flares flickered and died.

The brick-like vessel seemed to struggle to get its nose up, clawing for altitude, but to no avail. Large, square gaps appeared in the ship's hull. Five OmniMechs, looking like gigantic parachutists, leapt from the crippled ship. Harpool knew that 'Mechs were often dropped from high altitude, but something told him that these warriors were simply abandoning the stricken vessel. As the ejecting 'Mechs dropped, Hedgehog watched as a pair of *Transit* medium fighters, bearing the emblem of the Ninth Recon Company, swept in to savage the enemy machines.

"Hedger, you okay?" Timmons' voice was tight with concern mixed with excitement.

"Okay, Wildman. A little chewed, but okay."

"Good, let's get back at 'em. We're still on the clock."

Standing behind a row of technicians whose flickering monitors tracked the progress of the massive air battle raging above, Ariana Winston watched as her fighter pilots strove to bring down the Clan DropShips. She knew that the odds were in the Jaguars' favor. The tough DropShips could bull their way through the interceptors and discharge their loads of combat troops before the lightly armed fighters could pound their way through the bigger ships' thick hides. Here and there, a red target trace flickered and went out as her air-troopers destroyed an inbound, but those were far too few. Most of the Jaguar DropShips flew on as though the fighters worrying their heels were no more than mosquitoes. Occasionally a blue tracking symbol went out as well, and Winston felt a small pang of grief as an Eridani Light Horse pilot lost his life.

"General, I'm getting incoming radio traffic," a communications technician called. "It's being broadcast in the clear. He says he's the Jaguar commander. He's asking for the commander of the Inner Sphere forces on Huntress."

"Put him on," Winston said, pointing to the mobile HQ's small holotable.

The air above the holotable shimmered for a moment as the HQ's computer system translated the incoming message of the laser-image generators built into the table. Then, the meter-high image of an angry, arrogant man flickered into existence. For a long moment, neither the Jaguar officer nor Ariana Winston spoke. They coldly surveyed each other.

The first thing Winston noted about the Jaguar officer was the total emptiness of his face. It was as though she were looking at the wax image of a man, rather than the man himself. His eyes were cold and dead, like a shark's. A contemptuous sneer curled his lip. The deeply etched lines around his mouth told her that it was his most common expression. The man's hair had been cropped close to his skull, as was common with many Jaguar warriors, revealing the dark blue-gray traceries of enhanced imaging neural implants. Intelligence sources told her that only the bravest, most reckless of warriors dared to be implanted with the direct neural interface between man and machine. Far too often the implants caused a form of psychosis, and could result in death from synaptic overload. This warrior would bear watching.

The man's gray uniform, with its scarlet Smoke Jaguar emblem and red and gold rank insignia, failed to disguise the fact that he was huge, perhaps as much as two full meters in height and massing probably more than one hundred forty kilos. There was no mistaking the enemy commander as anything other than an Elemental.

"I am Star Colonel Paul Moon." The Elemental's words seemed to drip with a tangible poison as he spoke, so deep was his malice toward the one he addressed. "I am commander of the forces of Clan Smoke Jaguar, come here to drive the Inner Sphere barbarians from our homeworld. Who are you? And by what right do you come bearing the sacred insignia of the Star League?"

"I am General Ariana Winston, of the Eridani Light Horse, commanding officer of Star League Task Force Serpent." Winston spoke her words carefully, selecting each one for its maximum effect. "We have come to this ugly little world not to capture it, but to destroy the blight upon humanity's name known as the Smoke Jaguars."

Moon gave a short, ugly laugh. "So it is to be a Trial of Annihilation, then? Good. I challenge you to meet me on the plains west of Lootera, with your entire force, and we shall see whom is annihilated."

"Bargained well and done, Star Colonel," Winston replied, using the formal words of a *batchall,* the Clan's version of pre-battle bidding for what forces would be used, where the battle would be fought, and what the winner's prize would be. It was one of the forms the entire operation, Bulldog and Serpent combined, had been staged to eliminate. Bidding with the lives of warriors reduced the ugly business of war to the status of a game, and Winston for one hated the very idea. "But, isn't it the right of the challenged to set the place of the battle?"

"This is no *batchall,*" Moon shot back, folding his arms across his chest. "I am trueborn of the Smoke Jaguars. You are nothing but an Inner Sphere freebirth. Between us there can be no *batchall*. You and your filthy lucrewarriors would never bargain honestly, nor honor the *batchall* once it was done.

"No, General, this is merely a challenge. Come and meet me strength to strength on the plain west of Lootera. It is fitting, do you not think, that you will die fighting on the very soil you have dared profane with your presence? At least you will have the cold comfort of knowing that your bones will be buried in a place far too good for them. I, on the other hand, will have the glory of destroying you and your *surats* in the shadow of Mount Szabo and the great stone Jaguar of my Clan."

Winston glanced across the command van to where her Regimental Colonels Sandra Barclay, Ed Amis, and Charles Antonescu were just ascending the short steps into the mobile HQ's interior. Behind them were Major Ryan, Colonel Regis Grandi of the Com Guard Second Division, and Major Marcus Poling, commander of the St. Ives detachment. From their identical expressions, she knew that they had heard Moon's proud, boastful words. Seeing no protest from her subordinates, she shrugged.

"Very well, Colonel Moon. The plains it is." She chuckled inwardly at the spasm of anger that crossed Moon's face as she purposely misstated his name and rank. It was proper among the Clans to use a person's full name and rank.

"May I ask what forces you intend to use to take this place from us?"

There was no reply. Moon had broken the connection.

"That's it. They're coming," she said, turning away from the now blank holotable. "We haven't much time."

"Colonel Grandi, your Com Guards are standing at, what, eighty percent?"

"Yes, General." Grandi nodded. "Most of my losses were to tankers and infantry. My 'Mech force is still pretty much intact."

"Okay. We'll form up on a rough east-west line. Colonel Grandi, you'll take the center." Winston waved her officers closer as she spoke. Under her direction, the holotable displayed a map showing the Lootera region. A blue rectangle bearing the insignia of the Com Guards flickered into being in the flatlands about five kilometers west of the city. "Ed, I want your 21st Striker Regiment drawn up on the Guards' right flank. Major Poling, your Lancers will form up on the left.

"Sandy, Charles, the 71st and the 151st will form up here, and here." Winston indicated an area just to the north of the main battle line. "You'll be about a klick behind the main line of battle, with Charles' 151st to the east and Sandy's 71st to the west. You're the reserve. I want you to send out flanking scouts, not too far, maybe a dozen kilometers or so. Just enough to give you ample warning if the Jags try to pull an end run. You're the reaction force, so stay alert. I want you both ready to launch a cavalry sweep around your covered flank if the opportunity presents itself, or to move up and reinforce the main line of battle if necessary. Position our artillery assets behind the lines, between the 151st and 71st. They'll be able to hit most of the enemy line from there, and still be able to bug out northeast or northwest if the fighting gets too close to their positions."

"General, what about my men?" Michael Ryan asked with a cold glint in his eye. "We could move out in advance of our line and lie in wait for the enemy. We could let him bypass us and then strike him from the rear, or move against his landing zone."

"Your offer is noted, but I'm sorry, Major, I can't let you do that." Winston shook her head, forestalling Ryan's protest. "You've got, what, eight dead and five wounded from your attack on the command center? That's forty-three percent casualties. You're down to seventeen effectives. I can't risk you now."

"*Tai-sho* Winston-*sama*," Ryan said, reverting to the stilted, Japanese-laced speech of the Draconis Combine. It was plain from the propriety in his voice and the expression on his face that he was about to lodge a formal protest concerning his orders. "You are right when you say that I have only seventeen effectives but . . ."

"No buts, Major. I can't risk losing one of my most useful forces in a suicide attack. I'll need you and your men, alive, if this thing breaks down into a guerrilla war. I want you and your teams to cover the Mount Szabo C3 facility. It was the first place we hit, and it's probably going to be the first place the Jags try to recapture. None of my men are trained for that kind of close, no mercy fighting. Your DEST teams are the best we've got for that duty."

Ryan straightened his spine, seeming to swell with pride. "*Hai. Wakarimas, Tai-sho* Winston-*sama*. We will carry out your orders. *Arigato*."

Winston smiled a little, congratulating herself that she'd found a way to present the orders that gave Ryan and his teams more sense of honor than if she'd simply laid down the law.

No wonder this all drove Morgan so crazy, she thought, rubbing her eyes. For an instant a deep, echoing gulf opened in her heart. This was the very moment Marshal Morgan Hasek-Davion had lived for. The desperate defense against overwhelming odds. This was the very situation in which he had so often shone, pulling a stunning victory out of defeat by some trick that no human opponent could have predicted.

Blast it, Morgan, why'd you have to go and get yourself killed? I really need you now.

"One last thing," she continued, forcing the mournful thought aside. "We're going to have to move fast, but I want all the wounded, Clan and Inner Sphere alike, moved into the genetic repository. It may get the Clanners good and honked off, but I don't care. They won't dare attack the repository directly, so the wounded will be safe from 'collateral damage.'

"Any questions? No? All right. Move like you got a purpose."

9

Lootera Plains
Huntress
Kerensky Cluster, Clan Space
26 March 3060

"**S**wiftly, you *surats*." Star Colonel Moon gritted the words between his teeth without opening a communication channel. Cursing Inner Sphere barbarians was one thing, but deriding his fellow Jaguars for what he deemed undue slowness in debarking from a DropShip was quite another. Not all of the warriors under his command were the remnants of broken garrison Clusters. Some were front-line troops, driven off the worlds for which they'd paid in blood and bought with glory. How it galled him that they, the pride of the Smoke Jaguars, had been pushed off worlds they had won by lawful conquest of an inferior enemy. Weak, spineless troops of the Inner Sphere. To make the insult more grievous, those stinking *surats* had the effrontery to claim they had attacked his Clan in the name of the renewed Star League.

The indignity and injustice of it all turned Moon's guts to liquid fire. Though his unhealed injuries had kept him from taking an active part in the fighting on Hyner when his Cluster, the 3rd Jaguar Cavaliers, was destroyed, he had escaped, carried along by the medtechs who were overseeing the budding of his new left leg. Through all the weeks of the painful budding process, and the long months of rehabilitation and physical therapy, Moon had continued to push his limits, exercising as much as the medtechs would allow, and as much as he could bully them into. The new leg was not as strong as the right, and occasionally sent a lance of pain through the left side of his body, but it was a good kind of pain, the kind that let a warrior know he was alive and that his enemies were dead.

Those mewling medtechs had tried to keep him out of the fight, saying that his leg was not yet strong enough to withstand the rigors of battle, but he had knocked them aside as a dominant jaguar male cuffs away a troublesome cub. His leg was as strong as ever, and no weak-hearted lower casteman was going to keep him out of the fight to retake his homeworld from the spineless Inner Sphere *surats*.

From his position in the shadow of the *Overlord-C* Class DropShip, he gestured impatiently at the misshapen *Stormcrow* OmniMech jigging back and forth just inside the 'Mech bay door. The bloody, old-fashioned straight-razor painted on the *Stormcrow*'s jutting cockpit proclaimed that the 'Mech belonged to one of the few surviving members of the 19th Striker Cluster. Moon knew that the pilot of the 55-ton machine was a relatively green replacement, ferried out from Huntress only eight months before the Inner Sphere began its treacherous bid to retake the Smoke Jaguar Occupation Zone.

It is a good thing we did not attempt a combat drop, Moon thought bitterly. *With such fools as these coming into our garrisons, it is small wonder that we lost the Occupation Zone.*

At last the pilot had his machine lined up with the bay door to his satisfaction. Once the balky machine stepped off the ramp, the rest of the offloading went quickly. Striding swiftly to the big, humanoid *Summoner* piloted by the ad hoc Galaxy's second in command, Moon clambered up the OmniMech's legs, catching hold of a handgrip that had been installed for the purpose of allowing Elementals to hitch a ride into battle on one of their larger cousins. Four more of the massive, genetically engineered armored infantrymen swarmed into the *Summoner*'s torso right after their leader. Moon arrogantly took his place, standing on the big machine's shoulder, between its off-center cockpit and the cylindrical missile launcher perched above its left pauldron.

"Now," Moon said, at last opening a communication channel. "Let us go and reclaim our homeworld. Galaxy, advance!"

At that, ninety-six BattleMechs moved out. Moon clung fiercely to the handgrip as his mind sorted through the scant data his reconnaissance forces had gathered. The Inner Sphere warriors had drawn up their line of battle a few kilometers west of Lootera in the relative flatlands between the Jaguar capital city and the rugged Jaguar's Fangs mountains to the west. The area was broken only by a scattering of low, rolling hills and thin clumps of scrubby trees.

The bulk of the force awaiting him was drawn from the Eridani Light Horse. Moon knew from his training that the Light Horse had fought against the Jade Falcons during the first years of the Crusade and again during the Jade Falcons' foolish attack on the Lyran Alliance world of Coventry. The Light Horse was considered to be among the best warriors the Inner Sphere had to offer, and even had the effrontery to claim to trace their heritage all the way back to the Star League.

Moon snorted in disgust at that idea. If the warriors who fought under the name of the Eridani Light Horse really *were* descended from that illustrious Star League unit, they could never have strayed so far from the true path of a warrior as to fight for money. To Moon's way of thinking, those warriors awaiting him who claimed the name of the Eridani Light Horse were just another lot of filthy freebirths making a claim too big for their puny strength to back up.

The rest of the troops awaiting his Galaxy's arrival were

drawn from the Com Guards and the St. Ives Compact. Moon knew from experience that the Com Guards were not only good warriors, but equipped with machines almost the equal of his. Still, their lack of the Jaguar's breeding and training programs left them at a disadvantage. The St. Ives troops were a mystery to him, though he scoffed at the notion that the small client state could produce any warriors worth fighting.

The *Summoner's* even, rolling gait ate up the distance between the Jaguar landing zone and the Inner Sphere positions in long, jolting strides. At this rate, they'd be within striking range of the enemy in a matter of minutes. Moon forced aside his disgust at the nature of the troops he'd be facing to concentrate on his battle plan.

His scouts told him that the enemy was drawn up in a broad line of battle, with two large units in reserve. Moon elected to take them head on, in the best tradition of his Clan. Words from *The Remembrance* leapt to his mind:

> *Remember Franklin Osis,*
> *Father of his Clan.*
> *Three strengths he gave us;*
> *The jaguar's spring that brings the enemy down,*
> *The jaguar's claws that rend the enemy's heart,*
> *The jaguar's taste for the enemy's hot blood.*

"Alpha Cluster," Moon said, opening a channel to his troops. "We will be the spearhead of this attack. We will be the leaping Jaguar that brings the enemy down. Bravo Cluster, you will be our claws. You will follow on our heels. Once we have broken the enemy's line, you will reach past us to tear the heart out of his reserves.

"There will be no mercy. The enemy is to be destroyed utterly, wiped from the face of this world, and trampled beneath our feet. Now, form battle lines. Attack!"

The ad hoc Galaxy swarmed forward, keeping close formation. Alpha Cluster had been drawn together from the remnants of a half-dozen shattered front-line units. They were equipped almost exclusively with OmniMechs, including several newer models, just fielded within the past year or so. Bravo Cluster had fewer OmniMechs, the bulk of its warriors piloting the less versatile, second-line 'Mechs typical of garrison Clusters. As they ran to the fight, their ranks gained speed and power, until it seemed to Paul Moon that they had become an unstoppable predator that would not rest until it had feasted on the enemy's heart.

"Contact," said a voice in his ears. "Alpha One-one has visual contact with the enemy. Alpha Star One is moving to engage the enemy."

Suddenly there came a hollow, shrieking howl.

"What is that?" Moon bellowed into his communicator.

None of his warriors answered him. None had to. The howl ended in a series of sharp, flat cracks. Large, dirty gray flowers blossomed where the artillery shells hit the muddy ground. The burning white phosphorus generated thick clouds of obscuring smoke, the billowing murk cutting off view of the enemy positions. No matter. Many of his OmniMechs were equipped with sophisticated sensor suites capable of locating an enemy even through the cowardly barrier of smoke.

"Switch over to active probes," Moon ordered. Instead of getting a series of acknowledgments, all that sounded in his helmet-mounted speakers was a high, thin, crackling hiss.

Another volley of smoke shells screamed in on the Jaguar positions, these dropping directly among the lead elements of Moon's forces. Something hard and unyielding smacked into his armor with a dull clank. For a moment, he thought he had been struck by a nearly spent bullet or shell fragment, but the projectile ricocheted off his Elemental suit's thick carapace and fell clattering to the steel decking beneath his armored feet. With difficulty, Moon bent over, still keeping his battle-clawed left hand locked around the hand grip, and snagged the small object with the muzzle of his anti-'Mech laser. The flat, metallic gray thing bore no markings and would just fit into a normal man's hand, but began to cloud Moon's helmet sensors the moment he touched it.

A jammer pod. Moon cursed to himself, flinging the object aside. *An artillery-dispensed jammer pod. Is there no advantage these cowardly surats will not seek to gain?*

"Second Willie Pete barrage on time, and on target, General," Kip Douglass reported from his back-seat position in Ariana Winston's *Cyclops.* Douglass' report carried with it a note of amused surprise. He had always maintained that the "cannon-cockers" couldn't put their first five rounds where they were supposed to, when they were supposed to, even if you promised each of them a case of beer and a week's R&R in the Magistracy of Canopus.

This time, the artillerists proved Kip's theory wrong. Two barrages of Improved Smoke shells had landed exactly on target. The burning white phosphorus, nicknamed Willie Pete, produced high, thick screens of dense, acrid smoke that clouded both visible light and thermal scanning systems. The I-Smokes had six electronic jammer pods crammed into each shell that would take care of more sophisticated systems like Beagle Active Probes and Artemis fire-control systems. Until the Clanners passed through the smoke screens, they were effectively blind.

"Good." Winston grinned inside her neurohelmet. "Get me the FIST team."

"FIST here, General," the Fire Integration Support Team leader answered a moment later.

"Captain Jones, the scouts say you're right on target." Winston knew that her chief artillerist had already heard the report, but believed that a word from her was warranted. "Switch over to ICM and fire for effect."

"Roger, General. Improved Conventional Munitions, and fire for effect." Winston could almost hear the artillery man's grin. "The stuff's on the way."

Again, the scream of incoming artillery shells reached Moon's ears as the *Summoner* he was riding stepped at last into the clear. The cowardly artillery smoke screen had slowed up his advance, but not as much as the Inner Sphere *surats* had hoped. His troops were warriors, and Smoke Jaguar warriors at that. They would not be deterred by a little bit of burning phosphorus.

Ugly black flowers bloomed a dozen meters in the air as the cannon shells burst. This time they did not carry a payload of small smoke charges and jammer pods. This time they carried a payload of death. The Improved Conventional Munitions warheads were set to burst high overhead, showering their targets with smaller submunitions. Dozens of the bomblets rained down on Moon's advancing troops.

One OmniMech, a *Mist Lynx* still bearing the markings of the now destroyed 6th Striker Cluster, pitched over on its face, both legs severed at the knee by the anti-armor charges. A pair of black puffs blossomed directly over one of his lead 'Mechs. An irregular series of sparks flashed from the *Warhawk*'s torso, showing where two artillery shells' worth of small bomblets had detonated against the OmniMech's tough armor. The big machine weathered the firestorm with only slight damage to its armor. For the Elementals riding the *Warhawk*'s thick-skinned carapace, the effect of the submunitions was devastating. Two were killed and their companions badly damaged by the slashing anti-armor bomblets. Other 'Mechs showed varying degrees of damage from the artillery barrage.

Moon howled with fury.

"Independent action!" he bellowed. "All units, break formation and close with the enemy before the cowards blast us to hell with their artillery. All units charge."

Like an enraged berserker, the *Summoner* surged forward.

Another barrage delivered its tiny packets of death and destruction into the midst of his troops. Another light OmniMech, this one a brand new *Kit Fox,* was wreathed in smoke and flame. When it emerged from the cocoon of destruction, its armor was rent and tattered, but for a miracle it still limped forward, its pilot obviously enraged at the cowardly long-distance attack. Other units were not so lucky. A *Viper* lay on its side, struggling to get back up on its one remaining leg. The bodies of slain Elementals lay all around, looking like empty and discarded seed pods.

"Hit 'em again!" Winston shouted into her helmet's boom-mounted microphone.

"This will have to be it, General," Captain Jones returned. "They're at 'danger-close' already."

"Just hit 'em."

"It's on the way."

From her position in the center of the 21st Striker Regiment's formation, Winston could not hear the thump and crack of the massed artillery batteries firing, but she could hear the high, thin whistle of the shells as they passed overhead. Down-range, she could see the moving black shapes of dozens of Clan 'Mechs closing rapidly on the Light Horse's defensive position.

The tone of the howling artillery shells suddenly changed pitch. Her heads-up display showed the projectiles' course as a thin red line that dropped sharply, slanting toward the Clanners' front line. Again the dark popcorn puffs of white smoke appeared above the enemy ranks as black powder-bursting charges exploded, showering the enemy with submunitions. Again the small bomblets cracked and rattled against the Clanners' armor, crippling light BattleMechs and killing Elementals.

Captain Jones certainly knew his business. Any closer and the shells would have dropped among the Light Horse's leading units.

Off to her left, she could just make out the camouflaged shapes of the Com Guard machines as they hunkered down in their prepared positions, awaiting the Jaguars' charge. Farther to the east, out of easy visual range, were the twenty-nine surviving 'Mechs of the St. Ives Lancers. And ahead of her were the charging Smoke Jaguars.

With a crash reminiscent of a boiler factory in full production, the Jaguars smashed into the Light Horse lines. In some cases, heavy Jag 'Mechs simply careened into lighter Inner Sphere machines, knocking them flat. Many times one of these overborne 'Mechs would rise again to loose its fire into the thinner back armor of a Clan war machine whose pilot had assumed that down meant out.

The Clanners seemed to be insane with rage. A huge *Man o' War-C* stepped up to a green and gray-painted *Centurion*. Barely pausing in its lumbering run, the Jaguar 'Mech blasted the Light Horse war machine with a long burst of heavy autocannon fire. The armor-piercing rounds ripped through the hardened steel armor protecting the smaller 'Mech's chest, detonating the autocannon shells and missiles stored there. As the CASE panels blew out, saving the pilot's life, the *Man o' War* swung its stubby right arm like a massive club, driving the crippled Light Horse machine to its knees. A blast of laser fire finished the job.

Enraged by the cold-blooded murder of her trooper, Winston shoved the *Cyclops'* control sticks forward with such force that the black metal and plastic devices should have sheared off in her hands. The ninety-ton machine covered the ground in a lumbering, sixty-five-kilometer-per-hour run. Before the Clanner could turn away from the burning mechanical corpse at its feet, Winston slammed a flight of missiles into its relatively thin dorsal armor. A glittering, basketball-sized Gauss slug added to the damage. The big OmniMech staggered, lurching forward involuntarily. Then, recovering its balance, the enemy machine turned to face its attacker.

Winston saw the hideous grin created by the rectangular armored ventilator covers set beneath the twin cockpit viewscreens, and enhanced with a fanged mouth, painted on by some Clan technician. The gaping maw of the heavy autocannon swung onto line with her 'Mech, belching smoke and fire. Tracers streamed past her machine's torso to detonate in the hard-packed clay of the plain. More shells slammed into her *Cyclops'* armored belly as the Jaguar warrior walked his fire into her 'Mech.

Winston fed the grinning abomination another helping of nickel-iron, following the Gauss rifle slug with a pair of laser blasts. The ugly gray monster shuddered only slightly under the incredible impact. Twin strokes of lightning savaged the big OmniMech. Behind her, a *Vindicator* and a *Zeus,* each bearing the markings of the 21st Striker Regiment, poured devastation into the ugly Clan machine. Trailing smoke from glowing rents in its armor, the *Man o' War* collapsed to the ground. Its pilot didn't eject.

That's it, Winston said to herself. *The Clan RoEs are right out the window.*

So long as the Inner Sphere forces kept the battle down to a grand series of one-on-one fights, the Clanners would hold to their rules of engagement, which forbade more than a single warrior to attack any one target at a time. As soon as two or more Inner Sphere 'Mechs or infantry platoons "ganged-up" on any one Clan 'Mech or Elemental Point, the battle became a free-for-all.

The battle became a nasty, close-quarters brawl, with no holds barred and no quarter asked or given. After her initial mad rush against the *Man o' War* Winston seemed to come back to herself. She withdrew from the main battle line, settling into a command post a few hundred meters to the rear. Kip Douglass kept her apprised of the situation all along the battlefront. The news was not good. The Jaguars had smashed into the combined Inner Sphere force's line, partially breaching it. Unit reserves were thrown into the fray, bringing the penetration to a halt.

But a second wave of Clan 'Mechs was forming just inside the artillery support units' final protective line. The Jaguars were too close for the artillery batteries to shell them without dropping their rounds into friendly lines. The Clanners must have known it, from the amount of time and care they were giving to dressing their lines for the final assault. However, Winston still had a pair of aces up her sleeve.

"Phantom, Gendarme, this is Dancer. Enemy second wave is forming for an assault. Swing around the flanks and plaster them."

"Gendarme, will comply," Colonel Charles Antonescu replied in his characteristic short, concise manner.

"Dancer? Phantom," came the voice of Sandra Barclay, the 71st's commander. "We're on the way." For all the lightness of Barclay's words, there was an underlying edge that Winston could not identify and that she didn't like. She had no time to analyze her subordinate's tone of voice. At that moment, a Jaguar *Mad Cat*, oily yellow-green coolant fluid dripping from a shattered heat sink, stepped up to her 'Mech and scoured nearly a ton of armor from the *Cyclops'* torso with a single laser blast.

Cursing, Winston dropped the scarlet HUD-generated targeting reticle over the battered Clan 'Mech's center of mass. Caressing the triggers, she sent a pair of laser lances into the odd, petal-like structure on the Clan OmniMech's torso. A chunk of nickel-iron, moving at hypersonic speed, slammed into the *Mad Cat*'s back-slanting thigh, smashing halfway through the heavy leg armor before ricocheting away.

For several minutes, the *Mad Cat* and the *Cyclops* danced around, each trying to gain some advantage over the other. Each dealt and took damage. Warning lights began to flicker into life as the Jag pilot's accurate fire threatened to breach Winston's armor. She also knew that he had to be near the end if she was. Taking a gamble, she feinted her bulky 'Mech to the left, then dodged right, coming to within striking distance of the hunched-over Clan war machine. Deep, soot-smeared gashes marred the OmniMech's armored flank. Two were deep enough for Winston to see the inner workings of the *Mad Cat* through the gaps. Pulling back the *Cyclops'* armored fist, she lashed out at the enemy 'Mech.

The balled steel fingers smashed fairly and squarely through the largest of the rents in the Jaguar's armor. Winston all but felt the jarring impact the *Cyclops'* shoulder and elbow joints had to absorb. Quickly, she opened and closed the steel fist. The metal hand trailed sparking power leads and gouting coolant conduits as she jerked it back out of the gaping wound. The *Mad Cat* shuddered once, violently, like a man battling with malaria, then settled on its suddenly weakened legs. The cockpit split open and the pilot ejected atop a pillar of smoke and flame as the seventy-five-ton OmniMech crashed to the ground.

When she looked around, Winston saw a field full of

broken and damaged machines and broken and dying men.
The Jaguars were pulling out, but her force was too battered to give chase.

"General!" Kip Douglass shouted from the back seat. All
through the battle, Douglass had kept feeding her tactical
data, which she assimilated while barely acknowledging
the young man's presence. "I have reports from all northern
force commanders. The enemy is withdrawing in disarray.
They seem to be falling back on their DropShips."

"All right, Kip," Winston said, the weariness of battle
warring with the exultation of having survived. As she
spoke, she switched her 'Mech's power plant to standby
and locked its leg joints. "Message to all commanders. Pull
back to your original positions. Get me the butcher's bills
as quickly as possible. Get the techs up to the line to reload
and make running repairs.

"Send to Colonel Barclay. Detach recon elements to follow the Jags at a distance. Do not engage unless necessary. I just want to keep tabs on what the Clanners are
doing.

"And Kip, try to find out what's happening on the southern front, will you?"

"Sure thing, General." Winston could hear the fatigue in
Douglass' voice. "Anything else?"

"Yeah, Kip." She turned to face him, lifting the heavy
neurohelmet from her aching shoulders. Sweat ran in streams
down her face, and stung her eyes. "Good job today."

For Star Colonel Paul Moon, the stillness that followed
the battle seemed to be the Trump of Doom to his Clan. He
lay in the shadow of a ruined and smashed *Hellbringer,*
watching his warriors retreat in disorder. To have been defeated by the filthy, cowardly *surats* of the Inner Sphere in
the shadow of Mount Szabo seemed like an omen. The Inner Sphere would be the ruin of his Clan.

At least I will not have to live to see it. Moon's bitter
laugh broke down into a series of racking coughs. When
the spasm subsided, he saw thin, blood-stained phlegm
running down the inside of his helmet visor. The armor's

built-in medical pack had run dry of pain-killers and stimu-
lants. The black wound sealant that had been pumped into
and over his injuries was barely adequate to the task.

An artillery shell had burst almost directly above the
Summoner he had been piloting. A single, armor-piercing
submunition struck him on the back of the right shoulder
and detonated. Many of the Elemental armor's vital components were destroyed or damaged by the tiny shaped
charge, among them the automatic medical pack and the
communications system.

Lying there, drifting in the shock-induced netherworld
between consciousness and oblivion, Moon could still feel
the high-velocity explosive jet ripping through the thick
muscles of his back, through his shoulder, and out the front
of his armor. His throat was still raw from the scream of
pain that had been ripped involuntarily from his lungs. The
suit's systems had performed as expected, administering
drugs to keep him from going into shock, and pouring out
the black, tarry substance that had once saved his life. But
the injuries were so severe that the suit's damaged systems
could not complete the treatment. Paul Moon knew he was
going to die. He could feel the blood drying on his face
from the automatically staunched wound in his cheek, but
blood still flowed from his shell-flayed back. He was going
to slowly bleed to death from unsealed wounds.

"Look, I think that one moved." To Moon's shock-
dimmed perception, the speaker seemed to be on the opposite end of a narrow metallic tunnel.

A helmeted head hove into view, leaning over Moon's
cracked and smeared visor. The green and brown camouflaged helmet and the olive-skinned face didn't belong to
any Clan warrior or technician. Neither did the flat, black-
finished Cameron Star pinned to the man's collar.

"Yeah, he's alive, but barely. Medic!" The man waved
to some unseen person, beckoning them closer.

"I will not accept your aid," Moon snarled, forcing his
awkwardly thick tongue to obey his will. Whatever had
opened the gash in his face had broken his jaw and dis-

placed most of his teeth. It was a struggle to make himself understood.

"You don't have to accept it, sonny," the infantryman told him. "But you're gonna get it anyway."

"No," Moon barked, trying to slash at the man with his suit's clawed hand. The soldier merely leaned out of the way of the weak blow. "I would rather die here than be beholden to any Inner Sphere *surats* for my life. I would rather die . . ."

Blackness collapsed in on Star Colonel Paul Moon.

"Is he . . ."

"Naw, Sarge, he's alive." The Com Guard medic fumbled with the latches securing the Elemental's scarred helmet. "Just passed out. He ain't gonna be alive much longer, we don't get him to a MASH unit."

"Hummph." The sergeant's reply was noncommittal. "Any ID on him?"

"Just a minute." The medic lifted the identity disk that hung around the Elemental's massive, but raw and bleeding neck.

"Moon," he read, squinting at the ID. "Star Colonel Paul Moon."

10

Battle Cruiser SLS Invisible Truth
Zenith Jump Point, Huntress System
Kerensky Cluster, Clan Space
26 March 3060

"**C**ommodore, look at this!" The startled shout rang across the *Invisible Truth*'s bridge like a cathedral bell.

Commodore Alain Beresick whipped around just in time to see a bright red flash fading from the battle cruiser's main view screen.

"What was that?" he snapped, a cold, leaden feeling settling in the pit of his stomach. "Play it back."

In replay, a small crimson dot appeared, this time on the sensor operator's secondary monitor. The dot grew until it reached the size of a large coin, increasing in brightness as it expanded. Then, in a eyeblink, it faded away.

"Was that . . ."

"Yes, Commodore, it was," the sensor operator answered Beresick's unspoken question. "The jump flare of an incoming JumpShip. Analysis says it's a big one. I'd say it's a WarShip, probably a cruiser or battleship."

Unbidden, the tech called up a graphic representation of the Huntress system. The original chart had come to the task force via Trent, and then been refined and augmented by Operation Serpent's own observations of the system. The chart placed the EMP flare on the outer edge of the second of the system's seven occupied orbits, just over one billion kilometers from the central star. That orbit was occupied by the planet Huntress.

"Mister Ng," Beresick called to his chief navigator. "Are our charts accurate enough to make a jump into a non-standard jump point?"

"You mean a 'pirate point,' sir?" The small oriental man chuckled. "Not a chance. Not even with the data we've gathered since we've been here. To do that you need a hyper-accurate map, plotting every piece of rock and debris in the system. Without it, you're inviting disaster."

"Dammit." Beresick smashed the heel of his fist into the metal console housing. "Sensor operator, turn your instruments in-system, maximum gain. I want to know what just jumped in. Mr. Ng, lay in a course for Huntress. Commo, get a message to General Winston. 'Unknown JumpShip, possible WarShip, entered the Huntress system at thirteen twenty-eight hours, via non-standard jump point. JumpShip is probable hostile. I say again, probable hostile. *Invisible Truth* is inbound Huntress to investigate and intercept. Take all possible precautions. Good luck.' Once you've sent that, alert the rest of the fleet, although I suspect they all know by now."

"Commodore, course plotted and locked in," Ng called from his station.

"Power up the maneuvering drives," Beresick hissed, fighting against the sick feeling in his guts. "Let's go."

On the bridge of the Black Lion Class battle cruiser *Streaking Mist* ilKhan Lincoln Osis stood at one of the ship's many viewports, glaring at the planet below. Though Huntress was his home, the storm-swept world had of late become a source of consternation. First were the disturbing reports about Russou Howell and his odd behavior concerning some freeborn warriors. Then there were the rumors that Howell had fallen victim to a malady virtually unheard of among warriors—addiction to alcohol. Either of these was unsettling enough in its own right. Finally came the panicked stories that the Inner Sphere had united under the banner of the Star League and was racing across his Clan's Occupation Zone, recapturing worlds that had fallen to his troops during the Crusade. The notion would have been laughable were it not for the steady stream of reports sadly proclaiming the loss of system after system to this "renewed Star League."

When these reports had first come in, Osis refused all aid from the rest of the Clans. He boasted that the Smoke Jaguars had taken those worlds during the Crusade, and they would retake them by their strength alone.

Then, two weeks ago, another desperate HPG message had crossed his desk, purporting to be a cry for help from none other than Russou Howell himself. The message claimed that Huntress was under attack by the forces of the Star League. At first, Osis refused to believe the reports, but when a second HPG message arrived, this one stating clearly that the Inner Sphere forces had indeed landed on Huntress, he could no longer deny the truth.

He had gone to the Grand Council, seeking the aid of the other Khans in retaking Huntress from the barbarians, but they had refused him. In a fit of anger, he had stormed from the council chamber, then spent the next few days gathering what military strength he could. His personal guard of five top-flight MechWarriors and ten superb Elementals would be augmented by the Smoke Jaguar Command Trinary. Named the Jaguar's Den, the unit consisted of fifteen elite MechWarriors, each equipped with the latest, most sophisticated OmniMechs his Clan had to offer. Ten Points of the finest Elementals available and ten aerospace fighters rounded out the Command Trinary's strength. The Shroud Keshik, Clan Smoke Jaguar's secondary Command Trinary, under saKhan Brandon Howell, added as many warriors again to his force.

He'd been able to scrape little else together. A few older warriors, not quite old enough to be considered solahma, but well past their fighting prime, had been rotated back to

Strana Mechty to act as trainers, design consultants, and liaison officers. Twenty-three of these had jumped at the chance to pilot a 'Mech into battle once again. For their courage and willingness to stand up and serve their Clan once again, Osis named them The Jaguar's Heart.

Thus, ilKhan Lincoln Osis jumped into Huntress to re-claim the Jaguar homeworld with just one hundred eighty-eight warriors at his command. The *Streaking Mist* was the ship that carried this mixed bag of warriors to the battle. For a long while he had considered turning the big ship's powerful weapons against the Inner Sphere forces occupy-ing his homeworld, but eventually discarded the idea. He had seen what the *Saber Cat,* a smaller, *Essex* Class de-stroyer had done to the city of Edo, on Turtle Bay, and he had no desire to see Huntress reduced to ashes at his hand. No, he and his ad hoc band of warriors would have to root out and destroy the invaders themselves.

"IlKhan," the *Mist*'s captain broke into Osis' thoughts. "We are in geostationary orbit above Lootera. It seemed for a while that there was fighting on the plain west of the city, but that seems to have subsided. Scans reveal a large pitched battle going on in the region of the Dhuan Moun-tains. Radio traffic indicates that some of our forces with-drawing from the occupation zone are engaged there with a large body of Inner Sphere troops, including the Kathil Uhlans and the Knights of the Inner Sphere.

"What are your orders, sir?"

Osis didn't answer immediately as he digested the naval officer's report. Then he spoke. "SaKhan Brandon Howell, the Shroud Keshik Command Trinary and The Jaguar's Heart will go to the Dhuan Mountains area. Have the war-riors of The Jaguar's Den stand to. We will make a high-G burn for Lootera and make sure that the *savashri* bar-barians there have been destroyed. Then I, Lincoln Osis, will have the glory of liberating our capital city from the enemy.

"You, Captain, will hold the *Streaking Mist* in geosyn-chronous orbit, and be prepared to deliver supporting fire if it becomes necessary."

Without another word, Osis spun on his heel, as much as the magnetic boots he was wearing would permit, and stalked off the battle cruiser's bridge.

"Blue Jay Six to Lion. General, they're coming again."

The shout yanked Andrew Redburn's attention away from the map box he'd been studying. The Uhlans, along with the Knights of the Inner Sphere and the Northwind Highlanders, had all faced stiff opposition before, but Redburn couldn't remember ever fighting warriors who seemed to be under the spell of suicidal rage. Three times the Clanners threw themselves against his rapidly weakening line, and three times they were driven back.

But, each time the Jaguars launched their assault on his position, the bloody, close-quarters fighting killed more of his men, burned up more of his ammunition, and destroyed more of his 'Mechs. Loss groupings had begun to take effect. Most of his light 'Mechs were gone, as were the lightest of his mediums. Redburn was forced to rely on larger, slower, medium-weight machines for reconnaissance. He had begun this affair with nearly three full regiments, but the vicious Clan attacks had whittled him down by almost fifty percent. Now his scouts told him that the Jaguars were massing for yet another attack.

Redburn felt a fire of frustration building in his chest. He didn't even know who he was facing. He knew they were Smoke Jaguars, sure, but not much more than that.

He'd tried to call General Winston for support, but she'd told him that her section had fought a major engagement of their own, and had suffered almost fifty percent casualties across the board. If he could get clear of the Jags for a couple of hours, Winston said she'd commit the 4th Drakøns to him as reinforcements, but he'd have to secure a Drop-Ship landing zone first. Few of the Drakøns were combat-drop rated, and many of their light, jump-capable 'Mechs were out of commission. So until Redburn could break away from the Clan forces pressing relentlessly against his front, he was on his own.

"How many, and where?" he asked the reconnaissance trooper.

"Hard to get an actual count, General," the scout replied. "They're movin' through the scrub woods northeast of your position, about eight klicks out. If I had to make a guess, I'd say about forty 'Mechs, and fifty, sixty Elementals. Hang on a minute."

Redburn held his breath, waiting for the scout to come back on the line. When he did, Redburn wished he hadn't.

"General, I'm looking at forty brand-new OmniMechs, all heavy or assault class, and about fifty Elementals, and ain't one of 'em got a scratch on their armor. Must be the reinforcements y'all picked up burnin' into the atmosphere. They've all got two different sets of markings. One ain't in the warbook—it's a smoke jaguar with a gold six-pointed star on its chest. The other set of insignias *is* in the warbook."

"Well, out with it, man," Redburn barked. He was too tired to play guessing games with his scouts.

"Yessir. The other set of markings is a smoke jaguar leaping out of a white mist." Redburn felt a sinking sensation in the pit of his stomach at the reconnaissance trooper's words. "General, I'm lookin' at the Shroud Keshik, the personal guard of saKhan Brandon Howell."

Redburn nodded sharply. "Understood. Blue Jay Six, keep track of them, and report all enemy movements. Lion, clear." He tapped a control that would change his communicator from the reconnaissance section's frequency to the command channel. Though he'd been piloting Morgan's *Daishi* since arriving on Huntress, it still took him a few seconds to locate the proper control. He was fully checked out on the combat systems of the assault OmniMech, but some of its other functions were not yet familiar. Occasionally it felt like Morgan was standing behind him in the cramped confines of the cockpit accessway, watching him with a critical but approving eye.

"Dundee, Paladin, this is Lion," Redburn called to Colonels MacLeod and Masters, respectively, once he located the proper radio control. "I just got a report from one of

the Uhlan advance scouts. He says we've got forty plus
heavy and assault OmniMechs, with heavy Elemental support, moving in on our positions from the northeast. That
means they'll hit my lines first, unless they change course.
The scouts say that the 'Mechs belong to the saKhan's personal guard."

"Say again, Lion?" Masters' voice was heavily overlaid
with disbelief.

"No mistake, Paladin. I trust my scouts. If they say it's
Brandon Howell, then it's Brandon Howell." Redburn
paused a moment, searching for the answer to the new
problem fate had dumped into his lap. He had no solid
idea of the strength the Smoke Jaguars could muster from
the Clan homeworlds, but he had to assume a worst-case
scenario.

"Okay, listen," he said at last. "If the saKhan really *has*
landed, we have to figure he's brought in at least a full
Galaxy of troops. We'll try to hold our current positions,
but if we have to bug out, you both know where the primary and secondary rally points are. If we have to, we'll
make a fighting withdrawal into the swamp and mount a
guerrilla campaign.

"I don't know how much time we've got until the
saKhan's troops are within striking distance, so here's
what I want you to do. Have your techs continue reloading
and making field repairs. If you've got any vibrabombs
left, now's the time to use them. Have your infantrymen
lay the mines about a thousand meters ahead of your lines.
Have your MechWarriors pile up whatever debris they can
find into revetments. Put all of your wounded who are able
to travel aboard your APCs right away. If we have to bug
out, your infantrymen can ride on top of the carriers if they
need to.

"I'm sorry, gentlemen, but given the sketchy nature of
my information, that's the best plan I can come up with."

"That's no problem, lad." MacLeod actually sounded
happy about the situation. "If there's one thing we Highlanders have learned, it's t' think on our feet."

*　*　*

Thirty minutes later, Brandon Howell launched his attack.

During that dreadfully short span of time, Redburn marshaled his forces into a rough line of battle. He deployed his Kathil Uhlans on the extreme northern flank of the Inner Sphere line, with the Knights of the Inner Sphere deployed to his right. On the extreme right, he stationed the Northwind Highlanders, anchored by the Royal Black Watch Company on their flank. There was little else he could do. There was no time to construct an elaborate plan of battle, and he hadn't Morgan's gift of somehow pulling wild, reckless, but unbelievably successful plans out of thin air.

The thought of Morgan's innate sense of how a battle should be run, brought back the empty, stinging chasm in Redburn's heart where his friend once stood. With effort, he pushed the memories aside. There would be time for grief and reminiscences later. Right now he had a battle to conduct. He had been with Morgan long enough that at least some part of the Marshal's tactical sense and battle savvy had rubbed off, and Redburn was determined that he would not bring dishonor on his friend's memory by failing in the coming battle.

The first thing Andrew Redburn saw of the Jaguar troops was a faint heat trace on his long-range scanners. Turning the instruments up to just short of the distortion point, he was able to pick out the moving thermal images of half a dozen OmniMechs. For once he was grateful for the superior technology the Clanners had at their disposal. Had he been sitting in the cockpit of his *War Dog* instead of Morgan's captured *Daishi,* he wouldn't have spotted the incoming 'Mechs for another hundred meters. Keying in a tight-beam communicator signal, Redburn quietly passed the word up and down his lines.

Minutes seemed to stretch into hours as the enemy machines crept closer. Redburn had ordered his men to dial back their 'Mech's power plants to minimum operating levels in hopes of evading detection by the Jaguars until the last moment. With luck, that would be after the Jags blundered into the thin minefield covering his unit's front.

"Lion, this is Paladin," came the voice of Paul Masters. Even through the built-in speakers of his neurohelmet, Redburn found the tight-beam communications difficult to understand. Masters was almost whispering, as though he were afraid the enemy might overhear him. "We have movement all along our front. It looks like saKhan Howell is trying to link up all forces for a concerted push."

"Roger, Paladin," Redburn answered. There wasn't much else to say. "Anything from MacLeod?"

"Negative, Lion. I haven't heard a peep out of *Dundee*." Masters stressed the code name in a gentle rebuke at Redburn's use of the Highlander commander's real name. There was virtually no chance of the encrypted, tight-beam, directional signal's being intercepted and decoded by the enemy. Only direct, hard-wired field telephones and lasercom signals were more secure. Still, there was no sense in taking chances, and Redburn was properly chastened.

"I'm out of position to get a direct link to Dundee," he said. "If he's not engaged, tell him to wait for my signal, and then swing in on the Clanners' flanks. Understood?"

"Roger, Lion. Understood."

Before Redburn could sign off, a deep, rolling boom sounded across the battlefield. A yellow-white flare lit the *Daishi*'s thermal imager. Redburn switched the instrument back to normal viewing just in time to see a *Puma* take one more step and collapse on its jutting face as the mine-damaged leg snapped off at the ankle. Four more mines went off in rapid succession, inflicting varying degrees of damage on the 'Mechs that triggered them.

The beauty of vibrabombs was also part of their problem. The explosives could be set to go off when a 'Mech of a certain weight moved over the mine's location. But a heavier 'Mech passing a few dozen meters away might also explode the weapon harmlessly.

Carefully, Redburn brought the orange targeting pipper generated by the *Daishi*'s heads-up display to rest on the chest of the nearest enemy 'Mech, a boxy-shouldered *Loki*. Patiently, he waited, watching the range counter scroll downward from nine hundred, to eight-fifty, to eight hundred. A few more steps, and the Clanner would be in range.

The range indicator flashed over to seven hundred-fifty meters, the maximum effective distance for the *Dashi*'s extended-range lasers. Redburn squeezed the trigger, unleashing a twin stream of impossibly concentrated light energy. Invisible in even the dim sun of the late afternoon, the laser beams snapped out of the *Daishi*'s right vambrace to savage the *Loki*'s chest and hips.

For a moment, the Jaguar 'Mech stood still, as though confused by the attack. Then, apparently spotting Redburn's suddenly powered-up 'Mech, it charged. They came in a rush. Forty Clan OmniMechs ran pell-mell across the wide, open meadow lying before the Inner Sphere's positions.

Without missing a step, the *Loki* pilot unleashed his PPC. The weapon's extended-range capabilities gave it a much longer reach than its Inner Sphere counterparts. An arc-white stroke of artificial lightning slashed into the *Daishi*'s legs, burning away paint and slagging armor. Redburn speared the charging machine again, feeling the waste heat generated by the powerful lasers wash over his already stuffy cockpit. The light beams bored deep, steaming holes into the *Loki*'s plastron, but still the enemy charged.

He waited patiently for the heat sinks to cycle and drain away the excess heat that could cripple or even shut down his 'Mech before reaching out again with the laser lances, this time adding a long, thundering burst of autocannon fire for good measure. Sweat broke out on his brow and ran into his eyes as the unbelievable energies he'd directed at the *Loki* carved another chunk of armor from the wildly advancing machine.

As more Clan 'Mechs came into range, the rest of the Uhlans opened fire, savaging the advancing enemy with missiles, PPC fire, laser bolts, and volley after volley of autocannon bursts. A deep-throated roar sounded to Redburn's right as a huge gun barrel spat heavy, high-explosive, armor-piercing shells into the *Loki*'s left knee. The Clan machine staggered at last, executing a curious hop-step-twist to keep its balance. The pilot at the OmniMech's controls must have been one of the most superbly trained warriors ever turned out by the Smoke Jaguars to execute that stunningly graceful, desperate maneuver, and still remain upright.

No sooner did the Clanner regain his balance than he leveled his 'Mech's boxy arms at the *Hunchback* that had come to Redburn's aid. Reckless of the heat generated by the assault, the Clanner let loose two streams of charged particles, which intersected on the lighter 'Mech's barrel chest. Already damaged in the previous Clan attacks against the Uhlans' position, the *Hunchback* sagged and dropped over onto its back, its gyro destroyed by the man-made lightning.

Redburn locked his weapons onto the *Loki,* noting as he did the waves of heat shimmering in the air around the Clanner's open heat sinks. He fired. The breath was driven from his lungs as his cockpit temperature spiked suddenly upward. Two heavy lasers backed up by a burst of auto-cannon fire lashed the Jaguar 'Mech, savaging the already weakened right leg and battle-scarred torso. The *Loki* staggered and fell, its right leg gone below the knee. Then the cockpit burst apart as the pilot punched out.

Redburn had no time to watch his enemy's lazy parachute descent. A *Masakari* and a *Gladiator* had stepped up to take their fallen companion's place. Both Clan machines leveled their weapon-bristling arms at Redburn's captured OmniMech.

Both of them? Somewhere along the line, one of my boys must have split his fire.

Redburn was not really surprised to have the pair ganging-up on him. Under the Clan rules of engagement an attack by two Clan 'Mechs against a single target was normally forbidden, unless an enemy attacked more than one target, or more than one enemy attacked a Clan machine. At that point the battle degenerated into a free-for-all.

In an attempt to strike the first blow against these new

enemies, Redburn turned the *Daishi*'s weapons on them, cutting slabs of armor from their thick hides, but to no avail. The pair of assault OmniMechs barely paused in their relentless approach. Missiles exploded all around his *Daishi,* at least half finding their mark. A Gauss slug drew a faint quicksilver streak from the *Gladiator*'s misshapen left arm to Redburn's torso. Armor splintered under the devastating impact.

Good God! Redburn's teeth ground together as he wrestled with the reeling *Dashi. Even this armored monster isn't going to take much more of this.*

Three more Uhlan 'Mechs collapsed under the Clanners' heavy fire. Another, an updated *Quickdraw,* disintegrated as its ammunition exploded, its magazines breached by the Jaguars' merciless gunfire.

"Pull back!" Redburn shouted into his communicator, sending the signal out on a wide-band carrier. "This is Lion. I say again, all Serpent units, pull back."

Without waiting for acknowledgment, he began to back the *Daishi* out of the shallow, hastily constructed revetment he'd been fighting from. Conserving his missiles and autocannon ammo, Redburn alternated blasts from the OmniMech's heavy lasers and the less powerful, but nonetheless effective medium pulse lasers. Were it not for the forward-leaning structure of his 'Mech, he was certain that his fighting withdrawal must surely resemble the right-left-right firing pattern of an old-West gunfighter in a holoshow.

How long he fought like that Andrew Redburn could never say for certain. It seemed like hours. He'd back up his 'Mech a few steps, let loose a couple of hastily aimed shots, and back up again. Eventually, the Clanners simply stopped advancing. He was never sure why. Perhaps the Jaguar 'Mechs, which had to be overheating, given the ferocity of their attack, had finally shut down, forcing them to abandon the pursuit.

As he cautiously backed his *Daishi* away from the battlefield, Redburn was torn between two emotions. His heart burned with the desire to reform his troops and launch a counter-attack against the Smoke Jaguars. He hated the notion that he'd been forced to withdraw from his positions, leaving the enemy in command of the field. His spirit raged against the enemy, and against the necessity of withdrawing to save his command.

And that was the second emotion filling his heart—a commander's love and concern for his troops. Redburn knew that if he ordered his withdrawing soldiers to turn about, re-form their ranks and charge again, the vast majority of them would obey, even if it meant their deaths in the fiery hell of close-quarters 'Mech combat. But he also knew that giving such an order would be tantamount to murder. *He* would be the one killing his men. The Smoke Jaguars would simply be holding the weapons.

No, as much as he hated being forced to pull back, Andrew Redburn knew that withdrawing was the only way of assuring that his troops would survive to fight again another day.

At the rally point, just inside the eastern edge of the Dhuan Swamp, Redburn learned the price his section had paid in the fighting withdrawal. Despite being heavily engaged, the Northwind Highlanders were more or less intact. MacLeod had arranged his regiment's sixty-five surviving BattleMechs in a rough semi-circle in front of the rally point, so as to provide a defensive perimeter.

When the Knights of the Inner Sphere came limping into the rally point, Redburn gasped in shock. All of the Knights' light 'Mechs had been destroyed, along with about half of their mediums. The sixty-five gold-trimmed white combat machines that remained operational enough to reach the rally point were covered in soot and mud. Many bore gaping rents in their armor, which let multi-colored wiring or drab gray myomer bundles show through. Yellow-green fluid leaking from shattered heat sinks and cooling lines completed the horrific picture. In all, the Knights of the Inner Sphere looked like nothing so much as their medieval namesakes returning home after a lost battle. As battered as they were, the Knights still carried themselves with an air of stubborn pride.

Redburn's own Kathil Uhlans had suffered the most grievously at the Jaguars' hands. Only forty-six shot-scarred 'Mechs had managed to break contact with the Clanners and limp into the rally point. The rest of their comrades, men and women with whom Andrew Redburn had trained and lived and fought ever since the unit was formed during the Fourth War, were either dead on the battlefield or had been taken prisoner by the Smoke Jaguars.

Redburn was horrified. The grief he felt after Morgan's death, the grief he had all but overcome came welling up once again. This time the sorrow was not for the loss of a single friend, but for the almost three-score men and women who were either dead or captured, and left on the battlefield. While less mind-numbing than the personal shock of losing his best friend to the hand of a cold, callous assassin, his sorrow over the virtual destruction of the Kathil Uhlans was no less real.

Redburn knew that a few of the missing warriors might have ejected from their disabled 'Mechs and managed to avoid capture. Given time, they might even find their way into the rally point. But he could not give them that time. The Jaguars had pressed his section so closely during the fighting that he feared they might resume their pursuit at any moment.

With a knot in his stomach that Alexander the Great's sword couldn't untie, he opened the command channel.

"Lion to all commands—" Redburn broke off, half-choking on the words. "All commands, move out. We're pulling back into the swamp."

Slowly, painfully, the shattered Inner Sphere Forces withdrew, pushing their limping column deep into the stinking fen called the Dhuan Swamp. Redburn hoped the Jaguars would be reluctant to pursue him into the tangled, overgrown marshes where their advantages of speed and superior weapon range would be all but negated.

As he sat, exhausted, in the cockpit of his battered *Daishi*, Redburn watched the staggering, shot-riddled 'Mechs of the Kathil Uhlans file past him, and prayed that he was right.

11

Outside Falcon Eyrie, Eastern Mountains
Huntress
Kerensky Cluster, Clan Space
26 March 3060

Captain Roger Montjar hitched his eye another centimeter above the rim of stone lining his concealed observation post among the crags of the Eastern Mountains. As uncomfortable as it was to crane your neck sideways so only part of your head and face was above the edge of the covering rocks, it was far more comfortable than the alternative. Especially when the alternative was a laser bolt through the brain.

For two weeks now, the Rabid Fox teams had been hunkering down in their uncomfortable, rocky holes, enduring cold, rain, and biting wind without detecting the least sign of movement from the Jade Falcons inside their mountain-top outpost of Falcon Eyrie. In fact the only shots any of his men had fired came when the Smoke Jaguars jumped Sergeant Kramer's section. Montjar fervently hoped that Henry and his men had made it out of the closing trap safely. His orders were to keep strict radio silence unless the Falcons seemed to be moving to support the Smoke Jaguars, or unless he was first contacted by task force

command. So far neither of those conditions had been ful-
filled. Montjar sometimes suspected that the rest of Task
Force Serpent had forgotten about him and his men.

Of course, he knew that wasn't the case. It only felt that
way on occasion. From the faint radio intercepts his team
was able to pick up from the task force's 'Mech units,
Montjar knew that the initial landing operations had gone
smoothly and that casualties were about what might have
been expected. He also knew that the task force had begun
to dismantle and destroy the Jaguars' war-making capability, thus fulfilling the second of the invasion's objectives. Then, something had gone wrong.

As best he could piece together from the sketchy radio
traffic, the Jaguars had brought in one, possibly two, relief
forces. Those forces had engaged the task force's heavy
maneuver elements, with mixed results. General Winston
seemed to have won a bloody victory somewhere around
Lootera, while Redburn had been forced to retreat into the
Dhuan Swamp.

Montjar silently cursed his luck. He and his own men
were some of the most highly trained warriors on Huntress, and so far what had they done? Nothing but sit in a
hole and watch a fence. If not for the unarmed, unarmored
men he and his troopers saw drilling inside of the Jade Falcon compound every day, he might have begun to wonder
if the installation was deserted.

But now, about an hour before sundown on the four-
teenth day of his surveillance, things were beginning to
change.

He'd been hunkered down in what passed for the Fox
Team command post, really nothing more than a wide,
deep hole in the rocky soil of the mountain, when a messenger came creeping into the hide. The number two observation post had spotted movement within Falcon Eyrie,
big movement. It had taken nearly ten minutes for Montjar
to crawl the hundred meters or so to the stony niche housing the surveillance team. When he finally arrived, all the
aches and fatigue that had accumulated in nearly two
weeks of living in the high, rocky mountains drained

away. A body of Jade Falcon troops seemed to be massing just inside the high chain-link fence closing off their compound from the rest of the world.

For a few minutes, Montjar remained in that uncomfortable position, his neck bent sideways, his left eye just above the edge of the boulder-fronted hide. Carefully, he counted all the enemy troops he could see. Then, to be certain, he counted them a second and a third time. Each tally produced the same result, ten armored Elementals and about fifty unarmored infantrymen in full field kit. If the Falcons were moving out to support the Smoke Jaguars, this was nothing more than a token force. While his fifteen commandos could not stop the Clan force, he could certainly slow it down some.

No, Montjar told himself. *You've got a more powerful weapon back at the command post.*

"Keep an eye on 'em, Private," Montjar said to the muscular, red-haired youth peering through the gathering gloom at the Falcon Troops.

"You got it, Boss." The private grinned but did not turn away from his objective. "I'll keep you posted on what the neighbors are up to."

The return trip took only a few minutes. This time Montjar was far more concerned with speed than a stealthy scrabble over the rocks. No sooner did he tumble onto the dug-out command post than he gestured for the radio headset.

"Dancer, Dancer, this is Rhino, FLASH, SITREP." Montjar spoke slowly and clearly, giving his emergency situation report exactly according to the book. "Rhino has detected movement from within target. We are currently tracking one-zero Echoes with approximately five-zero unarmored infantrymen in support. Targets have not yet passed the perimeter, but it looks like they might be intending to. Rhino will continue to observe. Request instructions."

Montjar knew that Ariana Winston would understand the somewhat cryptic message to mean that the Jade Falcons were moving their garrison force, consisting of ten armored Elementals and fifty infantry grunts around within the Eyrie. The Falcons hadn't yet made a move to leave their compound, but it appeared to Montjar that they were preparing to do just that.

"Stand by, Rhino," came a husky male voice. "Dancer is out of position. We are trying to establish a relay."

Seconds ticked by as Montjar sat staring daggers at the radio, wishing that the evil eye could be sent on an electronic carrier wave. Eventually the radio crackled to life again.

"Rhino, this is Dancer." The transmission was uneven and full of static, as though the radio link was being compromised somehow by electronic jamming. "Dancer is unable to send you any support. Both Dancer and Lion have fought major engagements this date. All reserve Bravo Mike forces are being committed to the main line of battle. Suggest you maintain your position and surveillance. If the Foxtrots leave target, act at your own discretion, but remember, do not fire unless fired upon. If the Foxtrots break out, attempt to determine their speed and heading. Over."

"Dancer, Rhino. Understood." Montjar was surprised at the bitterness in those three words. He did understand that all of the task force's BattleMech reserves had been thrown into the main line of battle and that the heavy 'Mech forces had been battered and bloodied in the conflict. That didn't make his job any easier. "Roger, Dancer. Rhino will comply. Rhino out."

"What'd she say, boss?" Corporal Richardson read the expression on his commander's face and flinched. "As bad as that?"

"Bad as that, Tim." Montjar shook his head ruefully. "'Remain in position and surveil,' and 'act at your discretion, but don't fire unless fired upon.'"

"Yeah."

Before either man could speak again, the evening air was split by the sharp crack-whoosh of a portable SRM launcher.

Montjar rolled to his knees, poking a cautious head above the rim of the command post hole. A few hundred meters to his right, and a like number south, he saw the bright streak of solid-fuel rockets as they arrowed out of the deep shadows of the jumbled landscape. The projectiles streaked toward the Jade Falcon troops, the rockets bursting a few meters short of the targeted Elementals, spraying the area with liquid fire.

Montjar knew that the incendiary inferno missiles were primarily anti-'Mech weapons. They were designed not to kill a 'Mech outright, but to force its pilot to choose between ejecting or being burned to death inside his cockpit. The effect on Elementals and unarmored infantry was somewhat more horrific. The burning napalm enveloped one Elemental and a handful of his unarmored counterparts, turning them into living torches. Montjar knew that the Elemental might well survive the liquid, sticky hellfire, but the infantrymen stood no such chance. They would have died in terrible agony had not another of his commandos mercifully cut them down with a burst of heavy machine gun fire.

Even before the dead infantrymen dropped to the rocky ground inside the Falcon compound, another Elemental stepped forward and began spraying the area before it with laser fire.

Still unbidden, Montjar's commandos reacted. More missiles flared out of the darkness to punch holes in the Elemental's hardened steel armor. The Clan warrior was knocked backward, his power suit deeply dented by shaped charges intended to bring down a BattleMech. The hairs on Montjar's neck stood up as he watched the massive Elemental clamber back to his feet, seeming none the worse for wear after being hit in the chest by an antiarmor missile. More Elementals joined the fray, returning fire even as they leapt over the broken, rocky terrain. The unarmored infantrymen, showing great discretion, if not great courage, went to ground behind whatever bits of cover they could find. Furiously they poured round after round of laser fire into the gloom. Montjar knew they probably couldn't see his concealed and camouflaged Rabid Foxes. The Falcon infantrymen were either firing blind or trying to target the muzzle flashes of the commandos' own guns.

Montjar swore. One of his men had broken discipline and fired without orders, and a general engagement with the Jade Falcons was shaping up.

A fusillade of heavy machine gun bullets stitched a line of broken rock splinters across the edge of the command hide. The commando leader instinctively ducked, knowing that the dodge was useless. If any of those steel-jacketed rounds had his name on it, he'd have been dead before he knew it. He had to get control of this battle.

Then, over the roar of gunfire, Montjar heard a sound he'd never expected to encounter. It was the amplified voice of the Falcon commander bellowing out the order to cease fire.

Not really knowing why, Montjar took up the cry.

"Cease fire, cease fire. All Rhinos, cease fire immediately."

Slowly, sporadically, the firing died away. For long minutes, the two sides stood there in the gathering night, staring at each other through the gloom. Then a faint metallic creak drifted across the stony battlefield to Montjar's ears. Searching for the source of the noise, his eyes lighted on the carapace of an Elemental who appeared to be no different than any of the others. The massive, genetically engineered warrior had opened the armor's visor, apparently in a gesture of trust.

Montjar could tell that the Elemental was a female only by her rich alto voice.

"I am Elemental Star Captain Gythia, of the Jade Falcons," she called in a loud, clear voice. "Who leads the warriors that attacked me?"

"I do," Montjar climbed out of the hole, feeling clumsy and misshapen next to the exquisite creature facing him. "I am Captain Roger Montjar, of Rabid Fox Team Three."

Gythia regarded him coldly.

"Why did you fire on my forces unprovoked and unchallenged?"

Montjar's mind spun. He had never heard of the Jade Falcons pulling back from a battle, nor even honoring a request for a cease fire. Something extraordinary was at work here.

"My trooper fired without orders," Montjar explained, unlocking and removing the helmet of his power suit as he spoke. "If he still lives, he will be disciplined."

"Aff," Gythia spat. The disgust, hatred, and barely controlled rage in her voice struck Montjar like a physical blow. "Khan Marthe Pryde has instructed me to avoid a conflict with your forces on Huntress at all costs. If engaged we were to defend ourselves but break off the action as soon as honorably possible.

"Perhaps your leaders feel they have sufficient reason to undertake this Trial of Annihilation against the Smoke Jaguars. But, understand, Captain Roger Montjar. I am a warrior of Clan Jade Falcon. I have obeyed the orders of my Khan. If you attack this base again, I will consider that you are expanding the scope of your Trial to include the Jade Falcons as well. I promise that you will not live to regret that decision."

Without another word, Gythia slammed her visor shut and stormed back into the compound.

Giving a silent, bewildered nod, Montjar gestured at his men, signaling them back into their hides.

"Sergeant Bosworth," he called to his senior noncom. "Who fired that inferno?"

"Private LeBelle, sir," Bosworth replied.

"Send him over to the command post. I want to talk to him."

"I can't, sir. He's dead." Bosworth sounded tired. "He got killed in the first exchange."

"You think the Falcons knew that?" Montjar was just as tired as Bosworth sounded.

"Sir?"

"Do you think the Falcons knew they killed LeBelle? Their Star Captain said she had to break off as soon as honor was satisfied. You think that was what she meant?

LeBelle killed a couple of their troops, and they killed him. I guess they figure the end result was even."

"Maybe, Captain." Bosworth removed his helmet, running his hand through his thick, graying hair. "I'll never understand these Clanners."

12

Eridani Light Horse Command Post
Mount Szabo, Lootera
Huntress
Kerensky Cluster, Clan Space
27 March 3060

In the distance, just over the horizon, General Winston could see the thinning pall of smoke rising above the Lootera Plains, visible only as a barely discernible smudge of gray against the darkening sky. There had been no rain to extinguish the grass fires, nor had there been any wind to disperse the smoke left from the day's battle. The fast-settling darkness concealed the terrible wreckage littering the broad, flat prairie, lying in the narrow triangle bounded on the northeast by the salty waters of the Dhundh Sea, the Black Shikari River to the south, and the jagged peaks of the Jaguar's Fangs mountains to the west.

Sitting alone on a camp chair, nursing a cup of coffee, Ariana Winston looked toward the faint glow in the western sky that marked the setting of Huntress' bright, yellow sun. The Jags had been forced from the plains, and were driven southeast away from Lootera. The St. Ives Lancers, backed up by the Light Horse's Sixth Recon Battalion, had given chase. They had hoped to drive the Clanners to the river and shoot them to pieces when they tried to cross. But the Jaguars' rear guard poured such a volume of fire into their pursuers' ranks that the Inner Sphere force had to give up the chase. The battle was over, the Light Horse and the Com Guards settled back into their original positions in and around Lootera. Winston and her staff returned to the brigade command post on the Field of Heroes, in the shadow of Mount Szabo.

Winston called the battle a victory for her side, since the planetary capital, its spaceport, and more importantly, Mount Szabo, the Jaguar's figurative heart, with its now smashed command control and communication center and the undamaged genetic repository, remained in the hands of the Inner Sphere forces.

The Eridani Light Horse had given a good account of itself during the day's fighting. The Com Guards and the Lancers had put up a valiant struggle as well, but the Light Horse had borne the brunt of the Jaguars' assault and the subsequent damage. Many of the wrecked and smashed BattleMechs that lay in tangled heaps of shattered wreckage had once belonged to her brigade. It gave her a certain sense of comfort and relief to know that most of the men and women who had piloted those now-destroyed machines had escaped with their lives. But those who didn't escape the destruction of their armored mounts weighed even more heavily on Winston's mind.

It was not regret or sorrow that painted a bleak hue over the canvas of her thoughts at that moment. That would come later. It was the loss of valuable BattleMechs and the deaths of the highly trained pilots who controlled them that concerned her. The Light Horse had been able to replace some of its losses by stripping out those 'Mechs that were still mobile but too badly damaged to continue the fight, or by salvaging Clan 'Mechs left on the field when the Jaguars pulled back. Still it wasn't going to be enough. Such replacements were never enough.

The Smoke Jaguars were in much the same shape, she knew. Their machines, while more durable, were as susceptible to internal damage as a similar Inner Sphere type, once the thick armor was breached, and the Clanners had started the battle with fewer 'Mechs in the first place. Scouts and after action reports told her that the Jags had suffered heavy losses. Several light and medium OmniMechs had been destroyed or critically damaged by the artillery barrages. More had been eliminated during the bloody, close-quarters brawl that resulted when they smashed into the Inner Sphere line. As a result, the odds remained what they had been in the beginning—about even.

"General," a soft voice called from behind her.

Instantly, battle-sharpened reflexes kicked in. Winston spun from her seat, dropping the coffee cup. It smashed on the cold gray stone of the Field of Heroes. The plastic camp stool made a dull, hollow clatter as it tumbled across the pavement. Dropping to one knee, she whipped out the heavy Mauser combat automatic she habitually wore slung low on her right hip while in the field. The weapon's gaping black maw centered on the forehead of a startled Trooper Elias Grau, a member of her Command Company's Security Lance.

"Trooper," she growled, holstering the big pistol. "Don't you know that's a bloody good way to get your head blown off?"

"Sorry, ma'am." Grau said. "Colonel Amis sent me to fetch you. Some of our scouts are reporting movement."

Before Grau completed his message, Winston had scrambled to her feet and darted off through the gathering night in the direction of the mobile headquarters van.

"Talk to me, Ed," she snapped, vaulting into the darkened vehicle's interior, with its faintly glowing holotable and humming data terminals.

Colonel Edwin Amis, the colorful leader of the 21st Striker Regiment, looked up at her arrival.

"Boss, we got a couple of scouts who've spotted what looks like a major striking force of Clan 'Mechs, headed this way," Amis answered, puffing on a thick, black cigar as he spoke. "From the feeds we're getting, looks like most of what survived today's fighting. I guess they're planning on launching a night attack."

Winston stepped up to the holotable, which was set to display a three-dimensional image of the area in which the contact had occurred. A tiny blue image of a Beagle light hovertank lay in a shallow depression between two low ridges, a dozen kilometers south of the Inner Sphere position. Several larger markers, these in the form of scarlet-glowing BattleMechs, were moving slowly toward the scout's hiding place. These represented the advancing Clan forces.

"Okay." Winston took a deep breath, then blew it out in a single explosive puff. The pause served to clear her mind. "Ed, go muster the brigade. We'll form a line of battle south of the city. The Light Horse is in the best shape, both logistically and numerically. Have Colonel Grandi move the Com Guards into the spaceport. If we get forced away from Lootera, he is to set fire to the port and withdraw. Likewise, I want the St. Ives Lancers to form up here on the Field of Heroes. They're in the worst shape of us all. I want them to stay back and form a tactical reserve. If the Jags slip by us somehow in the darkness, the Lancers may have to slow them up until the rest of the force gets straightened out. Tell Majors Ryan and Poling that they'll also be looking after our wounded, our techs, and support personnel.

"Now move, Ed."

Amis let out a short whoop of joy and dashed from the headquarters van. Winston smiled as she heard his baritone voice ringing through the darkness.

"Boots and saddles, people!" The ancient phrase caused an immediate stir in the Light Horse camp as her troopers responded to the sharp bellow. MechWarriors scrambled toward their steel mounts. Conversations ended in mid-word. Half-eaten plates of food were dropped to the ground and forgotten. One tank gunner, she learned later, had been caught in the latrine. He hauled up his trousers and vaulted into the turret of his Drillson without finishing what he was about.

Amis was an able and experienced field commander, and a shrewd tactician. Winston trusted him implicitly to deploy the Eridani Light Horse's three depleted regiments in a solid defensive position, which would take full advantage of the brigade's tactical flexibility.

Casting a final glance at the holotable, she tapped the technician in charge of the mobile HQ on the shoulder.

"Set up to run a tactical feed into my *Cyclops,*" she said.

Even before the tech could nod his reply, Winston was gone from the van.

Somewhere in the darkness, a machine gun rattled. It was followed by the deeper, more staccato yammer of an autocannon, and then silence. Winston sat in the cockpit of her big, humanoid *Cyclops,* glaring angrily at the tactical display monitor. Something strange was going on, and she could not determine what. Her scouts had tracked the advancing Smoke Jaguars almost to within striking distance of Lootera. Then, abruptly, all contact was lost with the reconnaissance units.

Winston moved a company of medium BattleMechs from her Sixth Recon Battalion, supported by a company of armored infantrymen, forward into the night, hoping to catch some signs of the suddenly elusive enemy. But no trace of the Jaguars could be found. The recon unit did however, find the burnt-out hulks of the four light hovertanks that had been tracking the Clanners.

"What the devil was that?" Winston hissed, cursing across the brigade command channel.

"Sorry, General," came the reply from Major Gary Ribic, one of Colonel Antonescu's battalion commanders. "One of my boys thought he saw a Clanner, but there was nothing there."

Blast it, we're getting really jumpy. Winston thought. She half turned in her command couch and ordered Kip Douglass to switch her over to the Com Guards' tactical frequency.

"Colonel Grandi, any movement on your front?"

"No, ma'am." Grandi answered, confusion in his voice. "We haven't had any word since your scouts lost the Jags.

I'm beginning to wonder if they weren't imagining things to begin with."

"If it wasn't for twelve dead troopers and four wrecked tanks," Winston replied with a nasty edge in her voice, "I might be inclined to agree with you, Colonel."

"Yes, ma'am." Grandi took the rebuke with good grace. "What're your orders?"

Winston thought for a moment, but, before she could answer him, Grandi spoke again, his voice full of surprise and anger.

"General, the Com Guards are under attack. I say again, we are under heavy assault. I estimate roughly one hundred enemy 'Mechs attacking my position. They're coming in hard. I think they mean to drive us away from the spaceport. I need backup, and I need it now."

"Blast," Winston cursed again. "All right Colonel. Hold as best you can. I'm sending you reinforcements. If you have to pull out, be prepared to destroy the spaceport."

Switching channels, Winston barked out orders to her brigade.

"Attention, all Light Horsemen, this is Dancer. The enemy has moved around our flank and is attacking the spaceport. The Com Guards are trying to hold, but the enemy is attacking in force. We're moving to support them.

"Magyar, move the 151st straight into the spaceport, and give the Com Guards some backup."

"Magyar acknowledges, General. We're on the way," came Colonel Antonescu's reply.

"Stonewall," Winston continued. "Your regiment will execute a right wheel, and swing in on the Jag's right flank. Sandy, I'm sorry to hit you with this, but you're going to have to extend your lines to cover the 21st Striker's position as well as your own. Can you handle it?"

"Yes, General."

Though there was no hesitation in Barclay's reply, Winston caught the hitch in her voice.

"All right," Winston barked, although she knew that all was not right. "Move out."

* * *

Galaxy Commander Hang Mehta spotted a flicker of movement off to her left. Pivoting her big, ungainly *Cauldron-Born-B,* she brought the PPC and pulse laser cannon mounted in place of the OmniMech's left hand to bear. A blue and gold humanoid 'Mech stepped from the cover of a corrugated metal shed, one of dozens gracing the Lootera spaceport's tarmac. Her warbook program identified the machine as a *Spartan,* an old Star League design, which had been rare three hundred years ago. The machine facing her must have been almost the last of its kind.

After her point units discovered and eliminated the puny hovertanks the invaders had sent to spy on her warriors, Mehta made a bold, somewhat unClanlike decision. Rather than charge at a forewarned and prepared enemy, she swung her column sharply to the south, crossing the shallow, sluggish Black Shikari River at a point well south of Lootera. A forced march through the darkness, and another crossing of the broad, 'Mech-hip deep river brought her troops out east of the city.

She had intended to drive straight toward Lootera. Reports given her by the lower castemen who had managed to escape from the Inner Sphere occupation force told her that the invaders had gone to a great deal of trouble to avoid fighting within the city limits. Others informed her that the barbarians, led by the contemptible lucrewarriors of the Eridani Light Horse, almost seemed to be under orders to avoid destroying anything other than military assets. How weak the barbarians were, to balk at destroying *any* of their enemy's possessions. She would certainly not hesitate to smash the invaders wherever they gathered.

In addition to her main assault on the barbarians holding Lootera, Galaxy Commander Hang Mehta had launched a second operation, one that would bring great glory to her and the troops under her command.

It will almost be a shame to destroy it, Mehta thought, gazing at the barrel-chested *Spartan. It is perhaps the last of its kind.* She angrily pushed the thought aside, berating herself for the weak and foolish notion. A Jaguar proverb held it that anyone who clung to the past belonged in the past, and she believed the aphorism with her whole heart.

Instantly her *Cauldron-Born*'s rangefinder declared that the enemy machine was well within the range of both her extended-range PPCs and large pulse lasers. Deftly, coolly, with an arrogance born of the knowledge that she was one of the finest warriors her Clan had ever produced, Mehta tweaked the aiming controls, trying to settle the targeting pipper over the enemy 'Mech's rounded head.

A cyan bolt of raw energy crackled from the Com Guard machine's left breast. The stream of charged particles tore into her *Cauldron-Born*'s left shin. Fiber-reinforced steel armor melted and shattered under the incredible thermal and kinetic energy of the bolt of charged particles produced by the enemy's PPC.

Mehta recovered quickly. A pair of azure streaks, followed by a volley of laser bolts, spat from her weapons.

The *Spartan* lurched, as the artificial lightning and amplified light tore into its thick hide. The Com Guard pilot recovered and came back for more. A blast of PPC fire lanced into Mehta's *Cauldron-Born,* paring more ferro-fiberous armor from the machine's thick carapace. She answered the barbarian with another one-two volley from her energy weapons. The particle stream slammed into the ridged metal of the storage hut behind which the *Spartan* had been sheltering. The pulse laser lashed the enemy's right leg, cutting deep into the heavy, reinforced steel protecting the vulnerable knee. A fresh wave of heat flooded into her cockpit as the *Cauldron-Born*'s heat sinks strove to keep the OmniMech's core temperature within normal operating limits.

Mehta knew that in a long-range duel such as this she held the advantage. The majority of her *Cauldron-Born*'s weapon load was designed to kill at distances reaching nearly seven hundred meters. The *Spartan*'s extended-range PPC could reach almost that far, but the balance of his weapons were designed for close-in combat. Apparently, the Com Guard MechWarrior knew it too.

Breaking from the rather tenuous cover of the shed, the

Spartan charged her *Cauldron-Born* in a flat-out run. Careless of the waste heat generated by such a massive discharge, Mehta fired both of her ER PPCs, following the incredible one-two punch with a volley of darts from both arm-mounted heavy pulse lasers. Sweat flooded across her face, and ran into her burning eyes.

All four weapon blasts found their mark. The *Spartan* doubled over at its articulated waist, like a man who had been kicked in the belly, as both PPC bolts and a stuttering laser shot tore into its torso. The other pulse laser slashed at the Com Guard's already damaged left knee. A rippling explosion tore the heart out of the big blue 'Mech as her particle streams ripped into and detonated the enemy's un-fired short-range missiles. Its pilot did not eject.

Though he did not realize its significance, Colonel Charles Antonescu saw the orange glare of the *Spartan*'s rather spectacular death even as he charged his regiment into the spaceport. A fragile-looking *Vulture* tried to bar his way, but a concentrated volley from his entire command lance reduced the Clan 'Mech to smoking rubble before the Jaguar warrior had time to fire his third shot.

More OmniMechs, supported by less versatile, but no-less dangerous second-line 'Mechs, moved to intercept him. With an angry wave of his *Hercules*' steel arms, and a disdainful shout of "Take them," Antonescu ordered his regiment into battle. Though the Dark Horses, as they were called, had been depleted by previous engagements, they were still a powerful fighting force. They ripped into the Jaguars, shattering Galaxy Commander Mehta's carefully planned attack the way a hammer smashes a porcelain vase.

The Clan warriors turned away from the Com Guards to face this new and potentially overwhelming threat slashing at their vulnerable flank. Antonescu sprayed a depleted Point of Elementals with a cloud of high-explosive submunitions from his dual-purpose autocannon, following up the vicious assault with a strobing blast of laser fire. When the smoke and dust cleared, two of the hulking armored infantrymen lay dead. Their companions rushed inexorably forward. Missiles reached out to hammer at the tough armor covering his *Hercules'* legs and torso.

A blast of charged particles reduced a third Elemental to a glowing heap of scrap metal and charred flesh. The remaining genetically engineered foot soldier bounded into the air, seemingly bent on self destruction. A dull clanging thud told Antonescu that the Elemental had managed to grapple one of the many projecting components of his seventy-ton 'Mech's outer surface. A flashing indicator on his 'Mech Status Display informed him that the Jaguar warrior, using his myomer-enhanced strength, was tearing at the relatively thin armor covering the *Hercules'* back.

Cold fear gripped Antonescu. He'd seen the amount of damage a single Elemental could do to a BattleMech by ripping off sheets of armor with its steel battle claw. Frantically, he triggered the paired, rearward-firing pulse lasers, which had been installed for the purpose of freeing the heavy 'Mech of "swarming" Elementals. The twin bursts of coherent light failed utterly to dislodge the Jaguar who was eating away his 'Mech's armored flesh like some steel-devouring parasitic insect.

"Hang on, Colonel," a voice rang from his headset.

Heat spiked into his cockpit, as intense white flame washed across the *Hercules'* back. A second wave of heat brought beads of sweat out on his face and back. The damage indicator flashed once more and held steady.

Turning the *Hercules* in place, Antonescu came almost cockpit-to-cockpit with Sergeant Maxy Houpt's *Vulcan*. Her incendiary 'Mech's right arm ended not in a hand, but in the flared muzzle of a flame gun, from which still trailed a line of oily black smoke. She had used the flamer to literally burn the attacking Elemental off his back.

"*Merci,* Sergeant," Antonescu gasped, drawing breath with difficulty against the sauna-like atmosphere of his cockpit.

"Not a problem, Colonel." Antonescu could almost hear Houpt grinning. "Sorry I had to scorch your 'Mech."

"Don't worry about it, Sergeant. You can repaint it after this business is over."

"I think it just about is." Houpt gestured with her *Vulcan*'s right arm. "Looks like the Jags are pulling out."

The Smoke Jaguars were indeed pulling out, only not as the enemy might have expected. The Com Guards had been pushed clear of the spaceport by the Jaguar assault. Then, caught between the southwestern edge of the city and the spaceport, the ComStar troops had dug in their heels and refused to be pushed any further.

When a regiment of the Eridani Light Horse slammed into the Clan force's left flank, the force of the impact was enough to shatter the Jaguar formation and drive the Clanners northward out of the spaceport. It angered Galaxy Commander Hang Mehta to see the warriors of her Clan withdraw before an enemy. But she was a warrior, and not one to give up easily. And there was the second string to her bow.

As the surviving warriors of Delta Galaxy drove toward the spaceport, one Trinary, made up of the Jaguars' remaining light and the fastest of its medium OmniMechs, split off, making for the symbolic heart of their Clan—Mount Szabo. It was an open festering sore to every warrior under her command to think of the filthy barbarians soiling the Hall of the Hunters and the Field of Heroes with their honorless presence. Retaking those places, and most especially the genetic repository that stood at the foot of the mountain, would help to expunge the shame and outrage that every Jaguar warrior felt at seeing the *savashri* on Huntress.

Mehta conceived the attack in haste as her forces were making their long, roundabout march crossing and recrossing the Black Shikari River. She had considered leading that attack herself. She would have exulted in the slaughter of the barbarians who had sullied her homeworld with their presence, but her sense of duty dictated that she command the attack on the barbarians' main line. Once the enemy's strongest warriors were dead, then she could drive on to Mount Szabo.

In response to this sweeping, flanking move, the battered St. Ives Lancers launched a counterattack. For a time, the Lancers, then down to only twenty-four battle-worn 'Mechs and a handful of conventional infantrymen, stopped the Jaguars cold, just west of the city. When the Jaguars' main body was driven back by the charge of the Eridani Light Horse, the Jaguars slammed, quite by accident, into the flank of the embattled Lancers. The Lancers, thrown into disorder by the sudden appearance on their flank of a larger, more powerful enemy force, broke and ran.

Then as so often happens in the heat and confusion of battle, the pell-mell retreat of the St. Ives Lancers triggered a general rout among the Inner Sphere forces. At first the Com Guards tried to stage a fighting withdrawal, but were soon driven into Lootera, where their tight formations were broken up. Once unit integrity was lost, their morale broke, and the elite ComStar troopers fell back. Even the Eridani Light Horse, for all their claims of elite status, were driven from the field in disarray. Pride swelled in Galaxy Commander Hang Mehta's heart as she considered what her battered, pieced-together Galaxy had accomplished.

Her warriors, hot for vengeance and thirsty for the blood of their enemies, began an almost berserk pursuit of the fleeing Inner Sphere troops. Mehta well knew that such a chase often turned in on itself, with the pursuers finding themselves trapped and set upon by a suddenly rallied quarry. In former times, she would have let her warriors go, allowing them to hunt the barbarians to a bloody death. In former times, she would have joined them in the chase and execution of those who had profaned her homeworld with their presence.

But, in the wake of the stunning defeat on Tukayyid, and now the shocking withdrawal of the Clan from the Occupation Zone, Hang Mehta had learned caution. The Inner Sphere freebirths could not be counted on to behave as honorable warriors, so she had come to count on them to behave as honorless brigands and assassins. She would not trust the *stravag* barbarians not to feign a panicked retreat before her advancing warriors just to lure them into some cowardly, killing trap.

Punching a key on her communications console, Mehta barked a command across the command channel.

"Attention, all Jaguars. Break off pursuit. I say again, break off pursuit." The words almost stuck in her throat as she spoke, but she knew in her guts they had to be said. "The enemy is in full retreat. We will allow him to withdraw. We have accomplished our goal for today. We have driven the barbarians from Lootera. Our capital city and the Hall of the Hunters is in our hands once again."

13

Eridani Light Horse Bivouac
Mount Szabo, Lootera
Huntress
Kerensky Cluster, Clan Space
27 March 3060

It had taken General Ariana Winston nearly an hour to rally her retreating troops. By that time, the Lancers were scattered to hell and gone across the Lootera Plains. The Com Guards were still filtering into the rally point north-west of the city. Only the Light Horse, by virtue of the fact that they had not been heavily engaged, remained some-what intact. But there were still two other groups that she was concerned about.

As the mercenaries pulled back from the fighting at the spaceport, Winston had passed command of the brigade to Colonel Amis.

"There's something I've gotta do, Ed," she said to her second in command. "And I don't want to do it over the radio. I'm taking the command company on a little side trip. Take the brigade to the rally point and wait for us there. If we're not back in a couple of hours, you're in command."

"Okay, General." Amis seemed to understand. "I'll see you when I see you."

The side trip took Winston and the ten 'Mechs and two hovertanks on a high-speed run around the western edge of the city to the Field of Heroes. When she got there, most of the task force's support troops were already gone. It spoke well for the technicians and other support staff that they were able to pack up and pull out with a minimum of warning and little equipment left behind.

She ignored the bits of forgotten gear and walked her ninety-ton mount straight across the Field, stopping only when she reached the low pyramidal structure housing the Smoke Jaguars' genetic repository. A dark, armored figure, visible only through her 'Mech's night vision gear, crouched in the narrow doorway, aiming a missile launcher at her *Cyclops*' head.

"Stand easy, soldier," she called over the assault 'Mech's loudspeaker. "It's General Winston."

For a moment, the nearly invisible trooper hesitated. The muzzle of the launcher never wavering from the circular sheet of high-strength armored polymer that made up the CP-11-C's faceplate. Then, waving his understanding, the warrior stood up and lowered the weapon. Lifting the visor of his Kage battle armor, he revealed himself to be none other than Major Michael Ryan of the Draconis Elite Strike Teams.

Winston locked the *Cyclops*' knees and threw the switch that would unreel the 'Mech's chain ladder. It seemed to eat up the little strength remaining to her to clamber down the nine meters to the ground.

"Major, what the devil are you still doing here?" she barked. "And why are *you* standing sentry duty?"

Ryan blinked at the suddenness of her words.

"Gomenasai." He bowed as far as the powered battle armor would allow. "I am sorry, Winston-*sama*. I misunderstood your orders. You instructed me to remain here and protect the wounded. That is what my men and I were doing. As for my standing guard duty, with so few men able to fight, we all have to share the burden. It is my turn."

Winston brought herself up short. With exquisite tact,

Ryan reminded her that he was following the last orders she had given him, unlike the rest of the northern army, which had retreated from battle.

"No, Major." She laughed dolefully, running a hand through her short, sweat-soaked hair. "I'm the one who should be apologizing. I shouldn't have barked at you."

"Shigataganai," Ryan answered. "It doesn't matter."

Winston nodded, ending that particular exchange.

"Major, I want you to pack up all your gear and whatever men who are fit to walk, and bug out for the rally point."

Ryan nodded and vanished within the darkened interior of the pyramid.

Once, the genetic repository had been an impressive structure, designed with the specific purpose of reminding anyone who set foot within its precincts that they had entered what was to the Clans sacred ground. The structure's cavernous interior had been carved out of living stone. The floors were flagged with black, gray, and white marble cunningly crafted to resemble running Jaguars. The walls were similarly tiled with black granite. Dozens of seals covered the polished stone walls in strictly regimented ranks and files. Each seal bore a name and a long alphanumeric string. Winston knew from Trent's intelligence report that each of these held in place a "giftake," the genetic material taken from some Bloodnamed Clan warrior. This was the heart and soul of the Clan Smoke Jaguar, and the wellspring of its genetic engineering and breeding program.

It was also the field hospital for the northern army.

Having been a soldier all her life, Ariana Winston had seen nearly every unpleasant form the essentially unpleasant business of war and killing could take, but the one sight that always brought her gorge rising into the back of her throat was that of a military field hospital.

Wounded and dying men lay on the cold stone floors, wrapped in blankets, with balled-up uniform jackets or rag-stuffed field packs for pillows. Some were blessedly unconscious, but others were awake. Of those who were conscious, some suffered the agonies of their wounds in silence. Others moaned softly in the back of their throat as morphine and other painkillers failed to wholly insinuate themselves between the soldier and the pain of his wounds. The air was heavy with a stench that can only be found in a military field hospital. The reek was made up of equal parts blood, antiseptic, and fear. The Jaguars had designed the chamber with subdued lighting to preserve the awesomeness of the place. The medical teams had brought in more powerful lighting systems, which replaced the solemn shadows with harsh, unrelenting glare.

The task force's medical personnel had cleared away the ceremonial, almost Levitical trappings from the repository's main chamber. Near the structure's main entrance, they had established a triage station. Blood spilled from many wounds had stained the beautifully laid marble a dull rust color. Winston thought that the hospital orderlies certainly must have tried to clean it up. Then she shuddered, remembering a tale from her childhood where the blood-stain left after a grisly murder kept coming back again and again despite the homeowner's best efforts to remove it.

"Doctor Fuehl!" she bellowed, summoning the Light Horse's chief surgeon.

"Dammit, keep it down," snapped a small, lean man wearing a blood-stained green smock over his camouflaged fatigues. "There are wounded men in here, and they need their rest."

"I'm sorry, Doctor, but I don't think they're going to get it." Winston moderated her volume, but not her tone. "We've been pushed out of the city. The Jags are headed this way. I want you to pack up everything and everyone that can be moved and bug out."

"No, ma'am." Fuehl rolled his head on his neck, trying to ease the burning muscles. "Some of these men cannot be moved, and I can't leave them behind. They're in my care, and I won't leave them."

The medic held up his right hand stopping Winston's reply. "You wouldn't leave a dismounted or wounded

MechWarrior behind, would you? I'm not going to leave any of my patients. That's final."

"For the love of God, Doctor . . ." Winston began.

"No, General, for the love of man," Fuehl countered. "Some of these men are going to die regardless of medical attention. All I can do is make them comfortable. Others might live if they get the proper treatment, and that doesn't mean being bounced around in an ambulance all across Hell's half-acre. If you order me to leave, I'll have to take those men with me. Those that are going to die anyway, will die, but only after hours of needless agony. Some of those that might have lived will die too. The rest will have to endure what is tantamount to torture if you drag them out of this hospital."

For long seconds she glared at the dark-haired, swarthy medic. Then, realizing that Fuehl was right, she grudgingly gave in.

"All right," she growled. "I think you're crazy, but all right.

"You know the Jags are likely to butcher the lot of you when they find out you've been using their genetic repository as a hospital, don't you?"

"I know that, General." Fuehl smiled sadly. "But I still can't leave my patients."

"General, I'd like to stay too." A tall stocky man with graying brown hair and a bushy mustache stepped up to join them. His fatigues were a bit cleaner than Fuehl's. A silver cross hung around his neck on a heavy rope chain. "Like Doctor Fuehl said, some of these men are going to die. My place is here with them. Maybe I can do them some good before they go."

Winston closed her eyes and nodded sadly. She knew better than to argue with Captain D. C. Stockdale once her brigade chaplain had made up his mind on such a matter. Her business, he once explained, was winning battles, his was winning souls. A man's deathbed was Stockdale's last battlefield.

"All right," she sighed. "You two can stay. Doctor, pick out enough people to help with the wounded who cannot be moved. We'll leave you as many supplies as we can. Everyone else is coming with me. Now."

Less than an hour later, the repository-turned-field hospital had been cleared of the Inner Sphere force's walking wounded. Only the severely injured were left behind, along with Fuehl, Stockdale, and a few medics. All of the Jaguar wounded were also left in the repository. The Clanners would be better able to treat them, and they wouldn't be a drain on the task force's limited medical resources.

Dropping wearily into her 'Mech's command couch, Winston stared at the tiny column of vehicles creeping west toward the rally point.

"General?" Kip Douglass called softly from the Communication and Sensor Operator's position in the big machine's second cockpit.

"I'm okay, Kip," she answered. "But I hope I didn't just sign their death warrants."

$$\equiv \mathbf{14} \equiv$$

Southern Army Command Post
Dhuan Swamp, Huntress
Kerensky Cluster, Clan Space
28 March 3060

For two days, the shattered remnants of the southern army slogged through the thick, stinking mud of the Dhuan Swamp. If Andrew Redburn had ever seen, or smelled, a more stomach-churning mess, he couldn't recall when or where. He remembered accounts from ancient history of how soldiers fighting a brush-fire war in Southeast Asia, during the late twentieth century, had to slog through deep, muddy swamps in hopes of rooting out enemy guerrillas. He had even seen films, converted to holovid, of young men in olive-drab uniforms, wading sometimes chest-deep in the polluted water, holding their rifles above their heads as they went.

As horrific as the accounts of those conditions sounded in the dry pages of a history book, Redburn was sure those swamps could not have been any worse than the putrid fen that seemed to close in around them the moment they withdrew from the battle line.

His heart ached within him. He'd been forced from the battlefield in the past. This was the first time in his long career as a soldier that Andrew Redburn had been forced to order his men to retreat. That knowledge burned inside him like white phosphorus, refusing to be extinguished.

All around him, the battered, shot-scarred 'Mechs of his sadly depleted army limped and slogged their way through the deep mud of the swamp. At first the retreat had been an orderly one. Combat units broke off one by one according to orders, moved a short distance away, and then turned to cover their buddies as they withdrew. But the Jags wouldn't let up. Taking advantage of their new, undamaged OmniMechs, the Clanners pressed the retreating Inner Sphere force closely. Two Stars of OmniFighters swung in low over the retreating lines to strafe the Inner Sphere units. That had been the signal for a general rout.

Redburn wasn't certain who first broke and ran. He didn't even know what unit they belonged to. All he knew was that a single BattleMech, a *Hermes II,* bolted and raced at top speed for the thick swamps. Then another warrior's nerve snapped, then a group of three. Soon the entire army was in a state of panic. Masters, MacLeod, and he had tried to stop the pell-mell rush, as did a number of their officers, but to no avail. The fleeing mass of troops simply carried them along.

By the time they were able to get control of the situation again, the army was broken, scattered to hell-and-gone in the fetid Dhuan Swamp. Some reports said that some of the Northwind Highlanders had managed to withdraw into the rocky Dhuan Mountains, south of Lake Osis. Redburn had his doubts as to the accuracy of the stories. The mountains lay more than two hundred kilometers to the southwest of the Highlanders' last solid position. It would be impossible for Inner Sphere forces to make that long trek and not be located and destroyed by the hard-pressing Jaguars.

As near as anyone could figure, nearly half of the southern army had been killed, crippled, or scattered during the rout. Redburn knew that he and he alone would have to bear the guilt of that humiliating defeat. A few 'Mechs sporadically trickled into the Inner Sphere lines as the withdrawing army pushed deeper into the swamps. At first the arrival of these stragglers gave Redburn's morale a tiny boost. Perhaps he hadn't lost as many men and machines as he'd feared. That optimism quickly died when, after a dozen lost warriors rejoined their units, the stragglers stopped coming in.

"Lion, this is Dundee," MacLeod called. There was a note of weariness and worry that the metallic effect of the helmet's speakers couldn't cover. "I think we may have a bit of a problem here."

"Dundee, this is Lion, go ahead." To Redburn's own ears, the exhaustion and dejection in his heart came out in his voice.

Blast, I hope I don't sound as bad as I think I do.

MacLeod seemed not to notice. "General, have a listen t' this."

The mercenary's voice was quickly replaced by a static-laden message, whose hollow, tinny sound led Redburn to decide that it was a recording.

"Dundee One, this is Prowler Six." The voice was young and full of fear. "I have movement, lots of it. We're at . . . ah . . ." The transmission ended there. When MacLeod came back on the line, he explained.

"General, that was one of my rearguards. His transmission got cut off at the source, and we cannot raise him again. If he was where he should have been, he was about two klicks southeast of my current position. I've got my regiments turned about, and formed up into something like a line of battle. If it was the Jags that caught up with Prowler, then they're on to us."

Star Colonel Wager cursed the thick, clinging mud that seemed to suck the energy out of him and his OmniMech with every water-splashing, muck-splattering step. He cursed the Inner Sphere troops for the cowardly freebirths they were. He even cursed saKhan Brandon Howell for ordering the older warriors of The Jaguar's Heart to pursue the enemy into the fetid Dhuan Swamp, while Howell and his personal guard stood watch on the firm, dry ground to the east.

Wager would have been content to allow the enemy to slip away into the marshes. They would have to come out eventually or starve to death. He knew that there were few plants and no animals fit to eat in the swamp. Most of the vegetation was either inedible or outright poisonous, and quite a number of the swamp-dwelling animals would try to eat you first if they could. The invaders would have to emerge eventually. But Howell didn't want to wait that long. He had ordered Wager to root out and destroy the enemy, and as a loyal Jaguar warrior, Wager was bound to obey.

Moving through the muddy swamps had been no easy feat. Every dozen meters or so, he had to pause while one of his Starmates levered himself free of the thick, sticky mud. Twice, his *Mad Dog* had gotten so badly mired it took a cooperative effort to free the sixty-ton machine. The interwoven swamp grass, vines, and mangroves made impenetrable barriers that had to be circumvented. Maintaining unit integrity in the marshes was a nightmare.

After they had followed the retreating Inner Sphere troops for the better part of a day, the trail had grown cold. The enemy commander seemed to have gotten control of his routed troops shortly after their headlong flight from the battle. Except for a few stragglers, the enemy had begun moving with some sense of discipline, making it difficult to track them.

Wager had deployed his scouts, hoping to find some trace of the barbarians' passing. For many long hours, the recon units had nothing to report. Then, just as he was about to abandon the search, a report came in.

"Star Colonel, this is Star Captain Rohana. We have made contact with the Northwind Highlanders." A string of numbers followed, placing the enemy a few kilometers due south of his position. Wager had nearly bypassed them.

"Well done, Star Captain," he told the scout. "All units converge. Key on Star Captain Rohana's position. Engage and destroy the enemy wherever you find him."

Without waiting to see if his Starmates were following him, Wager turned his ungainly 'Mech southward.

"Watch it, Ken, ye've got a Jag comin' in on yer nine."

Kensie Gray twisted the torso of his *THG-11E Thug* to the left, just in time to take a blast of autocannon fire in the chest. The stuttering explosions blew shallow divots out of the 'Mech's thick hide and obliterated the circular silver crest painted on its left shoulder. Bellowing a curse in Scots Gaelic, the young Highlander raked the enemy war machine with a bolt from his *Thug*'s left wrist-mounted PPC.

The man-made lightning punched into the *Blackhawk-B*'s rounded shoulder joint, melting armor and jerking the hunched-over OmniMech backward half a step. The little Clan machine recovered quickly and resumed its water-splashing charge.

Gray pumped yet another PPC blast into the advancing enemy 'Mech, and with a pang of regret, sent his last rack of short-range missiles corkscrewing across the tangled, flooded battlefield. The dull clank of the SRM launcher running through its reload cycle, but finding no fresh clip of missiles to feed into the tubes, sounded like a judge's gavel after the pronouncement of a death sentence.

In all the long, unpleasant retreat through the swamps, Private Kensie Gray and the Northwind Highlanders' Royal Black Watch Company had taken the rearguard position. Theirs had been one of the few units not swept away by the panicked rout that had ended the battle of the day before. The Black Watch and a few Knights of the Inner Sphere had stayed behind to delay the Jaguars for as long as they could. When at last the order to withdraw came, only three Black Watch 'Mechs remained. The rest had given their lives that others might live.

As they were the rearguard, it was the Black Watch that the pursuing Smoke Jaguars first encountered. Now, it fell to them and to the Highlanders to again sell themselves as dearly as might be, until the rest of the army got themselves organized. Gray laughed, broadcasting the bright, joyous sound across the enemy's communications channels.

"Come noo, m' *niowenchet,* ye useless li'l kitty," he taunted the Jaguars. "Come an' see how a true man lays his foes aboot."

The *Black Hawk* sprang like a leaping cat, its pilot obviously enraged by his foeman's rant.

Gray exulted in the joy of battle, and there was a feyness upon him that he'd never felt before. He savaged the Jaguar 'Mech with twin PPC blasts, the arc-bright particle streams ripping into the machine's spindly legs and underslung torso. Then the Clanner was upon him. The impact of the racing OmniMech made Gray's *Thug* stagger and fall. The Jaguar recovered more quickly and lashed out with one muddy foot. Gray brought his 'Mech's left arm up to ward his lightly armored cockpit, taking the blow in the elbow instead. Armor buckled and tore as the Clanner drove two more tooth-rattling kicks into the upraised arm. A third blow from the oddly bird-like, clawed foot shattered the arm's reinforced metal framework, snapping it off in mid-biceps, and sending the severed limb spinning away into the steaming fen.

"Now, you worthless freebirth," came the Smoke Jaguar pilot's mocking voice from Gray's communicator, "I shall show you how a true warrior lays his foes about."

The *Blackhawk* extended both of its heavily vambraced arms. Gray watched, feeling surprisingly calm as the gaping maw of a heavy laser and a rapid-fire autocannon lined up on his cockpit.

The death blow never fell.

A blast of laser fire ripped into the mud at the Clanner's feet, flashing the soggy earth to dirty steam. Gray roared like a demon and lashed out with his *Thug*'s heavy foot. The kick struck the *Blackhawk* squarely against one of the gaping wounds in its skinny left leg. Though lacking power, on account of his semi-prone position, Gray's attack was well-aimed. The squat OmniMech staggered and fell into the mud.

Fighting the controls, the slippery mud, and the lack of a

left arm, Gray rolled his 'Mech up to its knees. In a single powerful blow, he drove the *Thug*'s right fist, with its wrist-mounted PPC, into the enemy's cockpit. Plasteel shattered as the cockpit glazing gave. Deep in the rage that often follows a close call with death on the battlefield, Gray triggered the PPC.

Though the beam had no time to focus, it didn't matter. The appalling energy released by the weapon flooded into the devastated OmniMech. The *Blackhawk*'s cockpit glowed a dull red as the man-made lightning slagged everything in the tiny space. If the Clan pilot hadn't made his contribution to the Jaguars' breeding stock, Gray told himself, he never would. The Clanner's genetic material had been vaporized in the stinking air of the Dhuan Swamp.

Something loomed over Gray's 'Mech. He yanked his fist free of the burning wreckage. The slightly glowing muzzle of the PPC swung around, almost of its own accord, to line up on the barrel-chested shape of a *Huron Warrior*.

"Are ye finished, boyo?" Colonel MacLeod's voice seemed to come from a long way off.

"Aye, sir." Gray blinked, shaking his head convulsively, trying to clear away the red mist that had descended across his vision. "Aye, sir. I am."

"Good, laddie, 'cause you're not gonna kill anything with that." MacLeod's voice drifted a bit closer. It was cold and hard. "That's not good for anything now but a club."

Gray looked at his extended right hand. The PPC barrel was split down its entire length.

"You're bloody lucky the whole blessed thing didn't blow up in your face," MacLeod said. "Now get on your feet and cover our flank."

Two kilometers away, Andrew Redburn was struggling to get the battle sorted out. The Jaguars had apparently made contact with the Highlander rearguard and had moved in force against them. Ten minutes later, the northernmost units of the Kathil Uhlans reported that they were also under attack. Caught between two fires, Redburn turned the Uhlans toward the north in a desperate attempt to hold that flank. He put a call through to Colonel MacLeod, only to find that MacLeod had already thrown the survivors of his unit into the line against the enemy.

Redburn contacted the last of his commanders. "Colonel Masters, any movement in your area?"

"Lion, Paladin. Our area of operation is clear," Masters replied.

"I think we can dispense with the code names, Colonel. The Jags know who they're fighting," Redburn said irritably. "Move your outfit north and a little bit west. I want you in position to support either MacLeod or the Uhlans if the Jags force a breakthrough."

"Roger, General." Redburn decided that Masters didn't sound happy. He had probably offended the Knight's sense of propriety by suggesting that they drop the code names.

"Lion, this is Tiger Two. The Jags are moving out to our left, and we're gonna have to get some help soon or we're gonna lose the line." Tiger Two was the Captain in charge of the Uhlans' second battalion. After the death of Major Curtis during the initial invasion, his executive officer had stepped up to take his place.

"Hang in there, Tiger Two. I'm working on it." Redburn switched channels. "Colonel Masters, you'd better hurry, I'm about to lose the left flank."

All surliness was gone from Masters' voice when he acknowledged the order.

Redburn sat anxiously watching the battle unfold on the *Daishi*'s tactical display. As nearly as the small battle computer could figure, the Knights were about three kilometers south of the Uhlans' line of battle. Under ordinary circumstances the distance would be negligible. Even the heaviest 'Mechs could cover that much ground in five minutes. Given the treacherous ground the Knights would have to negotiate, Redburn estimated it would take them at least twice that to get into action, and ten minutes was a long time on the modern battlefield.

As he watched, the Jaguars kept pushing more 'Mechs

into the battle. The Uhlans threw in their tiny reserve, lengthening and strengthening their line, but it was not enough. Soon, the Jags had turned his left flank, and the army began folding back on itself.

"Command Lance, with me!" Redburn yelled over the Uhlans' tactical frequency. As he urged the *Daishi* into a lumbering, squelching run, he contacted Paul Masters once again.

"Masters, you'd better come quick. The Jags' have turned my flank."

"Two minutes, General." Masters' voice had the characteristic broken, jolting quality imparted by a BattleMech at a full run.

The man was mad, running a 'Mech through a flooded swamp. Well, *if he is insane,* Redburn thought, gritting his teeth and wrestling with his controls, *it's a good kind of crazy.*

A squat metallic shape loomed from out of the trees in front of him. Bringing the *Daishi* to a skidding, splashing halt, Redburn brought the targeting reticle into line with the camouflaged shape, but did not squeeze the triggers. The tall, skinny form belonged to a Kathil Uhlans *Quickdraw*.

"What's going on here?" Redburn demanded, stepping up next to the 'Mech.

"General, we're being pushed back, hard!" The Mech-Warrior fairly yelled his report. "The Jags came up and flanked us. We had to pull back to keep from getting surrounded."

"Where's the front line?" Redburn asked, having lost all faith in his tactical display.

"Sir, this *is* the front line."

Redburn looked away into the mist-shrouded swamp. To the north, he was just able to discern the outline of a battle-scarred *Axman*. To the south there was nothing.

"Listen up," he yelled into the *Daishi*'s communicator. "We're the flank. If the Jags circle out again, we'll be surrounded and destroyed in detail. Command Lance, form along this line. Give me a thirty-meter spread, and don't let any of the buggers get past you."

"Sir, here they come!" the *Quickdraw* pilot shouted.

Striding out of the mist came a single lance of Clan 'Mechs. Two were battered and patched OmniMechs. The rest were older, second-line models.

Redburn locked his *Daishi*'s guns onto the lead Omni, a tall, skinny-armed *Mad Cat*. For half a breath he held his fire, then unleashed a storm of death upon the enemy machine.

The *Mad Cat* shrugged off the damage as though Redburn had hit it with a handful of confetti. Missiles streaked from the twin cubical launchers set high on the Clan 'Mech's shoulders. Some of the high-explosive wasps slammed into the muddy ground at the *Daishi*'s feet, but most found their marks. Shaped-charge warheads tore through the remaining armor on the big assault OmniMech's side, leaving smoking gaps in its right leg and torso. With his thumb, Redburn tapped the switch, often called a "pickle," on the 'Mech's firing grips, and set the Ultra autocannons to their highest rate of fire.

Smoke and flame belched from the *Daishi*'s handless wrists. Tracers flashed orange-red in the dim, steaming air. Explosions rippled along the *Mad Cat*'s body and shoulder, some shells flying past the boxy missile launcher to detonate harmlessly in the swamp beyond. Redburn clamped down on the triggers again, running the autocannon magazines dry and savaging the Jaguar 'Mech once again.

The damage was enough. The *Mad Cat* had taken a heavy pounding in the previous day's battle. Its left arm snapped off at the shoulder and dropped into the muddy water below. Even before the severed limb began to sink, the *Mad Cat*'s CASE panels blew away. Redburn expected to see the Clan pilot riding his ejection seat to safety, but it didn't happen. The starred and broken canopy told the tale of a pilot dead at his controls.

A fin-backed shape hove into Redburn's peripheral vision. Pivoting the *Daishi,* he brought his weapons into line with the *Nobori-nin*'s center of mass. Again he hesitated.

He paused because he recognized the sword-rising-from-the-lake crest painted on the OmniMech's left shoulder as the insignia of the Knights of the Inner Sphere.

"Is this how you welcome your friends, General?" Paul Masters' laugh rang from the communicator.

"It's how I welcome my friends when they're piloting an enemy 'Mech," Redburn retorted. Masters had taken possession of the captured OmniMech after his own *Anvil* had been destroyed in the fighting at New Andery.

"You're one to talk, General."

"I guess you're right at that," Redburn said, chuckling softly. "Now, let's go surprise the Jaguars."

15

Eridani Light Horse Bivouac
Foothills, Jaguar's Fangs
Huntress
Kerensky Cluster, Clan Space
28 March 3060

Ariana Winston gently probed the swollen, painful lump on her forehead, the legacy of a Smoke Jaguar warrior who had mistaken her *Cyclops* for a punching bag. She leaned back in her camp chair with a heavy sigh, conscious of the approach of exhaustion. The Jaguars had tried another assault just before daybreak, and had been repulsed once again, with moderate losses on both sides. One Clanner piloting a *Hellhound* bearing the insignia of the Cloud Rangers of Delta Galaxy had jumped over the Light Horse front lines to attack the 'Mechs in the unit's reserve formation. Whether by design or by accident, Winston's *Cyclops* was the first 'Mech the Jaguar had engaged.

The bloody fool leveled his submachine gun-like laser at her stocky assault 'Mech and charged, spraying green darts of energy all over the landscape as he ran. Winston tried to halt the mad rush by pumping Gauss slugs and laser fire into the careening *Hellhound*, but the enemy seemed bent on closing with her, even if it meant his own destruction.

The Clan 'Mech bounded into the air, just as Winston was locking it up for what surely would have been a mortal hit from her Gauss rifle. With a shattering impact, the *Hellhound* crashed down again, striking the *Cyclops* in the left shoulder. Her 'Mech tumbled to the ground, as did the *Hellhound.* The Jaguar got to his feet first and delivered a stunning kick to the side of the *Cyclops'* head. Even as the Jaguar warrior was pulling back for another devastating blow, Regimental Sergeant Major Steven Young poured four blasts of laser fire into the Clan 'Mech's thin back armor. The *Hellhound's* missile ammunition cooked off, destroying the 'Mech and killing the brave, if foolish, warrior.

That's the way it's been ever since the Jag reinforcements arrived, she thought. *They hate us enough already, then we go and wreck their homeworld.* She sipped the hot, bitter coffee that came packaged in all battlefield rations. *No wonder they all seem crazy.*

In the aftermath of the abortive night assault, both sides had withdrawn from the battlefield. The Jaguars pulled back toward Lootera, while the Eridani Light Horse, the Com Guards, and the St. Ives Lancers fell back to the west. The northern army moved steadily westward throughout the day, and settled into bivouac just after nightfall, setting up a defensive position in the foothills of the Jaguar's Fangs, the peaks west of the planetary capital. In their evacuation of Lootera, most of the Inner Sphere's wounded were loaded onto armored personnel carriers, empty ammunition haulers, or commandeered civilian ground cars, and carried along with the retreating task force. Winston felt a spasm of guilt every time she thought about the sheer agony those wounded troopers must have endured, being dragged all over creation through some of the worst terrain she had ever seen.

She felt even worse when she thought of the critically injured men she had to leave behind. A few of the Light Horse's medical staff had volunteered to stay to care for the wounded, as did brigade Chaplain Stockdale. In the past, the Jaguars had treated injured men and their caretakers reasonably well, if not necessarily according to the Ares Conventions.

Under normal circumstances, leaving a badly wounded man behind was bad enough, even when you thought the enemy would honor the conventions of modern warfare to look after him. But this was different. The Inner Sphere had invaded the Jaguar homeworld. Worse yet, they had done it under the banner of the Star League, an idea the Clanners seemed to regard as blasphemy. Often, those kind of circumstances voided all rules of civilized conduct.

Winston counted it a minor miracle that the withdrawing Inner Sphere force saw no sign of the enemy during the long, exhausting, spirit-crushing retreat. Perhaps the Jags had been battered as badly as her troops had been. Unfortunately, she couldn't rest on that assumption.

Much of the Light Horse's light armor had been destroyed in opposing the Jaguars' initial landings on the Lootera Plains. What hovertanks remained to her, Winston sent out on a wide patrol sweep south and east toward Lootera. She had to know what the Jaguars were up to in enough time to formulate a response. It was nearly oh-three-hundred, local time. The patrols had been gone for nearly five hours, and yet there had been no word.

She swallowed the dregs of her coffee, then dropped the stainless steel cup onto her field desk. She chuckled ruefully at the idea that, no matter how bad things got in the field, her orderlies would always make sure her tent was set up and in order. At times she hated the perks that went along with being a commanding officer. To those under her command, even the small comforts of a roomy, self-inflating tent and an orderly to look after the small details must have seemed like a wasteful luxury. She herself had thought so when coming up through the ranks. Then, one day, her father had taken her aside and, in a rare moment of anger, had told her to shut her trap about the officers.

"Sure, they've got orderlies to look after them," he growled. "But they've also got all of you to look after.

What do you want them worrying about, getting a tent set up or drawing up a good battle plan that might just save your life?"

Ariana Winston never forgot that lesson. It had been one of the last her father ever taught her before he died.

Stepping out into the cold night air, she turned up the collar of her heavy green and gray field jacket. The Light Horse camp was eerily quiet. Gone were the friendly voices, the joking banter, the soldiers' songs. In their place were the crackle and snap of the small campfires built against the night chill and the low groans of the wounded. Those noises only served to intensify the silence rather than to relieve it. She'd never heard the camp so still.

"General?" A communication tech jogged up to her, out of breath. The tech was painfully young. Winston vaguely remembered seeing him marching proudly among the last graduating class of cadets on Kikuyu. That was a little over a year ago. It seemed an eternity. The youth skidded to a halt, his right hand beginning to come up, then he stopped, remembering that it was against regulations to salute in the field. One never knew when there might be snipers about.

"General, we've finally made contact with the scouts," the tech gasped, his breath fogging in the cool damp air. "We've got Scout Four on the horn right now."

Winston grunted her thanks and darted past the tech. The mobile headquarters van was twenty meters away. She covered the distance in seconds.

Leaping up the short flight of steps to the van's interior, she barked, "All right, people, what've we got?"

"General, we've got Scout Four on the line." The senior commtech pointed at an electronic map, which displayed the recon unit's position as a single bright dot against a darker green background.

"Let me talk to him. What's his code name?" Winston asked, grabbing a communication set and stretching it across her head.

"That'd be Cheyenne Four."

"Okay, patch me in." Winston waited for a nod from the

commtech, then said, "Cheyenne Four, this is Dancer. Give me a sitrep."

"Dancer, Cheyenne Four, wilco. Sitrep. Grid: Mike Alpha niner-five-four-seven." Winston glanced at the electronic map. The tracking dot was right on target, eleven kilometers east northeast of the northern army's bivouac. Cheyenne Four's transmission was thin and scratchy, but the scout spoke slowly and clearly to make sure he was understood. The message was being encrypted to evade interception by the enemy. "We're hull-down in a defilade about five hundred meters southeast of their position. It looks like the Sierra Jays have pulled up for the night in an abandoned metal processing plant. I count about one hundred-fifty Oscar Mikes and one hundred plus Echoes."

"Say again, all after 'processing plant.'" Winston wasn't sure she'd heard the scout correctly.

"I say again, I count about one hundred-fifty, that is one-five-zero OmniMechs and one-zero-zero plus Elementals. About half of the Oscar Mikes look like they just came off the assembly line, or out of a parade. They haven't got a scratch on them. Stand by."

In a moment, the reconnaissance trooper came on again. "General, I've got a positive ID on those new 'Mechs. The warbook says they're the Jaguar's Den Command Trinary, commanding officer, Khan Lincoln Osis."

"Dancer copies, Cheyenne Four. What are the Sierra Jays up to?" Winston had distracted the scout from his report by asking him to repeat himself. Now, she had to get him back on track.

"It looks like they're making running repairs on their damaged 'Mechs," he said. "They're bolting sheet metal over broken armor, trashing out their really shot-up 'Mechs to repair those less badly damaged, that sort of thing. If I had to make a guess, I'd say the Jags are really low on supplies and spares. I don't see much ammunition being loaded into their magazines, and the techs are swapping out pods wholesale, trying to mount lasers and PPCs rather than ballistic weapons. Again, it'd be a guess, but I'd say they're almost out of ammo.

"That's about all we can see from here, unless you want us to move in for a closer look?" The scout's voice betrayed reluctance to undertake a close reconnaissance of the Jaguar camp.

Winston thought a moment. "Negative, Cheyenne Four. Stay where you are as long as you aren't compromised. I want half-hourly updates on what the Jags are doing. If it looks like they're getting ready to move, I want you and your team to bug out, got it? No hero stuff. You understand?"

"Roger, Dancer. No fear there." The scout leader sounded amused and relieved at the same time. "Updates to follow at thirty minute intervals. Cheyenne Four, clear."

"Runner." Winston motioned to a young trooper standing by the command van's open door. "Go and fetch the Light Horse regimental commanders and Colonel Grandi and Major Poling. I want to see them right away."

The infantryman repeated the order back to her just to make sure he had gotten it straight, then darted off into the night.

As she awaited the arrival of her subordinates, Winston ran over her section's readiness figures. The initial invasion and the subsequent fighting had reduced the northern army, as it was now being called, to about sixty percent of its pre-invasion strength. The heaviest casualties had been among the light, fast BattleMechs and the unarmored infantry platoons. In addition, many of the Light Horse's fast hovertanks had been knocked out. Surprisingly, much of the armored infantry attached to the Com Guards and the Light Horse had come through the fighting relatively intact.

Ammunition was in good supply, a surprising fact when one took into account the heavy fighting in which the northern army, as individuals and as a whole, had been involved. On the other hand, expendables like satchel charges and food and medical supplies were running low. The shortages were not critical yet, but they could easily become so if the Jaguars forced the Inner Sphere units into a protracted campaign.

Another question that had nagged at her ever since the Jaguar reinforcements arrived became even more pressing with the scout's report that the newest arrivals were commanded by the Khan of the Smoke Jaguars. Two Clan JumpShips had escaped from the Huntress system, probably energizing their drives from a bank of lithium-fusion batteries. Where had they gone, and how long would it be before they came back with enough Clan 'Mechs and warriors to wipe Task Force Serpent out of existence?

If the Clanners did send reinforcements, would Serpent be able to recall their own JumpShips and escape, or would the Inner Sphere force be caught with no means of retreat and chopped to pieces by vengeful Jaguars? Should she even try to recall the transports, knowing that the task force's naval arm probably didn't have enough strength to protect the unarmed JumpShips? The battered ground forces might be able to evacuate Huntress aboard the Drop-Ships grounded on the Continent Abysmal if they left all of their heavy equipment behind, but she didn't like leaving any useful material behind for the Jags.

"What's up, General?" Edwin Amis took the steps into the command van in a single bound. For perhaps the third time since she'd known him, Winston realized that Amis had no cigar in his hands. Maybe he had finally run out.

"C'mon in, Ed. Take a seat. I only want to go over this once, so we'll wait until everybody's here."

Winston hadn't long to wait. Charles Antonescu, looking as dapper as ever, and a particularly haggard-looking Sandra Barclay slipped into the mobile HQ only seconds after Amis flopped into a lightly padded seat. Regis Grandi and Marcus Poling arrived moments later. Winston made a mental note to seek out the runner after the meeting and give him a personal word of thanks.

Quickly, not wasting words, she sketched out what her scouts had learned about the Smoke Jaguars' position and situation. Almost before she finished speaking, Colonel Regis Grandi was recommending that they launch an immediate attack.

"They're only about two hours east of us. If we move

now, it'll still be dark when we hit them. We should be able to catch them flat-footed."

"I agree with Colonel Grandi," Amis put in. "The Jags are low on ammunition, many of their 'Mechs are shot up, and most of their Elemental support is killed or crippled. If we jump them now, we got 'em cold."

"And what if we get hung up in transit?" Sandra Barclay put in. "What if we get turned around and it takes more than two hours to get there? This planet has an east-to-west rotation, doesn't it? If we launch our attack any later than oh-five-hundred, or oh-five-thirty at the latest, our guys will have the sun in their eyes before the battle is over."

Winston looked askance at Barclay, who seemed not to notice. Winston caught the momentary whitening of the young woman's knuckles as she spoke. Barclay had always been the safe middle ground between Amis' daring, almost reckless courage and Antonescu's cautious stubbornness. Something was eating away at her now. Winston had thought the problem resolved after the Light Horse's combat drop onto Huntress, in which the young Colonel acquitted herself quite well.

Apparently, it wasn't. Before the Coventry campaign, Winston had considered turning the Light Horse over to Barclay's command when she retired. After that bloody operation something seemed to change inside Barclay. Winston couldn't quite put a name to it, but the change was definite. Now, in light of the younger Colonel's reaction to the desperate situation they were facing, Winston began to wonder if she shouldn't reconsider her choice of successor. For a moment she lost track of the discussion while she debated how to handle this officer who might be losing her nerve.

She couldn't leave Barclay out of the fighting entirely. That would give the impression that Winston didn't trust her to command her troops under fire, and further exacerbate the problem. On the other hand, if Winston included Barclay's troops in the coming strike, Barclay might freeze up, or fall apart, leaving her regiment leaderless.

"Okay, here's what we'll do," Winston said at last. "Charles, you'll move the 151st out to the south. You're our screening force. The mountains will cover our left flank. Colonel Grandi, you and Colonel Amis will be the main striking force. You've got the greatest number of heavy 'Mechs still in operating condition. Sandy, the 71st will form up about three klicks behind the main striking column. I want you to stand ready to either make a flank strike, reinforce the main attack, or hold the door open for the 21st and the Guards if they have to bug out in a hurry. Major Poling, you're down to about a company and a half of medium and heavy 'Mechs, right? I want you to stay here and protect this encampment. Remember, Major, you'll be guarding our wounded and our supplies. Don't let me down, son."

"I won't, General." Poling smiled tiredly.

"This is going to be a fast raid-in-force," Winston continued. "No fancy stuff, just hit 'em, cause as much damage as you can, and get out.

"Now, remember, people, there have been a lot of times when we've been on the ragged edge, hanging on by our fingernails. That's when warriors put their heads down and fight the hardest. The Jags are pretty shot up out there, but the scouts say they've gotten a fresh influx of troops—elite guard troops. We can't afford to slack off on this one. We may beat them, but it won't be any kind of a walkover. In fact, unless we play this just right, we may get our heads handed to us.

"That's it, mount up."

An hour later, Winston was once again at the controls of her battered and dented *Cyclops*. Kip Douglass was strapped into his seat behind her, humming tunelessly as he watched his instruments through half-closed eyes. At times, Winston actually thought she heard his off-key warble fade into snores. Once she'd confronted her communication and sensor operator about sleeping in the cockpit. Douglass had grinned and rubbed the back of his head.

"Well, General," he said. "You got the hard part, driving

that beast. All I do is sit in back and listen to the radio. It gets boring after a while." The mischievous glint in Kip's eye told her that he was pulling her leg, but she wondered exactly how much.

But, in this case, Kip Douglass was right. There was little to see and less to hear. Winston had ordered her troops to move as quickly and as quietly as possible, navigating only by the light amplification systems built into their 'Mech cockpits. Strict radio silence was to be observed. The Jags had to have detected Cheyenne Four's transmissions, scrambled as they were. Even if they could not pin down his location, they had to know that an Inner Sphere scout had located their bivouac. A stray radio signal coming from the northern army could betray their intentions, and instead of attacking a sleeping camp, they'd be facing a prepared and angry defender.

It was another paradox of modern warfare. Ever since the development of reliable, practical night-vision equipment in the latter half of the twentieth century, most modern armies had the capability of waging war at night. Still, most armies, whether they had night operations capability or not, seemed to prefer fighting in the daylight. Now, with the refinement of available light amplification, so-called "starlight" systems, thermal viewers, ultrasound ranging and imaging gear, night and day were virtually the same to BattleMechs. But still, most battles were fought during the day, and in relatively good weather. Winston supposed it had something to do with man's primeval fear of the dark.

Well, be that as it may, she told herself as Kip's humming resumed once again. *Tonight we'll teach the Smoke Jaguars what kind of death lurks in the darkness.*

Galaxy Commander Hang Mehta couldn't sleep. The contact burns, caused by her left forearm carelessly brushing against the open mouth of a heat sink as she'd dismounted her *Cauldron-Born,* had come up in painful blisters. Every time she moved or turned over, the abused nerves in her wrist and arm sent a message of torture into her brain. Normally the pain would be a trifle to be ignored, but in her present state of mind it was just another insult she would have to bear.

With a disgusted snarl, Mehta threw off the thin blanket covering her field cot, and stalked out of her inflatable field tent. To the east lay the city of Lootera. On any normal night, Mehta might have been able to see the dull red glare of streetlights reflected from the bottom of the low-hanging rain clouds that often blanketed the sky. But not this night. The city's lights had been turned off by the barbarians, and left off by her forces. A lighted city was too visible to aerospace fighters, either as a navigation waypoint or as the target of an air strike.

After the long, grinding battle with the Inner Sphere forces and the spoiled night attack, Mehta had pulled her forces back north and east, across the rolling plains, to bivouac for the night at an old metal processing plant. Somewhere to the west the enemy had also drawn in for the night. Mehta's scouts hadn't located the Inner Sphere bivouac as yet, but she could make an educated guess where the barbarians were. In all probability, the *surats* were camped in the foothills of the Jaguar's Fangs, a dozen or so kilometers to the west. In the morning, she would send out her recon elements in force, locate the invaders, and smash them to dust.

It wasn't just the burns that kept sleep from her eyes. A sense of indignant anger burned in her heart. First the Inner Sphere *surats* had united under what they claimed to be the banner of the Star League. That was obscenity enough. Then, they had launched an all-out offensive, forcing the warriors of her Clan to pull back out of the Occupation Zone. But, was that the end of their effrontery? No. When she and the tattered remnants of her once-proud Clan arrived back in Clan space, what did they find but a fleet of Inner Sphere WarShips and a task force of barbarians attacking the Jaguar homeworld, also claiming to be acting under the aegis of the Star League. Her ragtag forces had dropped onto Huntress, straight into the wanton destruction the filthy freebirths were wreaking on the Jaguar homeworld.

When the Khans of the other Clans learned of the insults and injuries being heaped upon the Jaguar, *they had refused to act*! Never before had such a thing occurred in all the proud history of the Clans. Barbarians were seeking to annihilate one single Clan, and the others cravenly refused to give aid, forcing the ilKhan and saKhan Brandon Howell to commit the last two intact Trinaries belonging to the Smoke Jaguar to the retaking of their homeworld. Mehta swore by her bloodline that if the Jaguar survived this sore Trial, she would challenge each of those simpering cowards in turn to a Circle of Equals. She would start with that lying, *stravag* Marthe Pryde, and not rest until she had taught each one to write out the error of their ways with their own heart's blood.

A sudden cry went up from the center of the camp, jerking Hang Mehta out of her dreams of bloody revenge. A young MechWarrior ran up to her and skidded to a halt, saluting.

"What is happening?" she snarled.

"Galaxy Commander," he huffed out with relief. "There you are. You were not in your tent. The ilKhan sent me to find you." The youth drew himself to attention as he spoke. "Our scouts have detected a large body of Inner Sphere 'Mechs heading this way. The ilKhan believes they are a raiding force. He has ordered all warriors to their stations. We are to be ready to strike at his first command."

"Aff!" Mehta barked the word, returning the warrior's salute at last. She bolted across the bivouac area, drawing a straight line for her refitted *Cauldron-Born*. Her technicians had managed to scrape together enough spare parts to convert the graceful, birdlike 'Mech from its primary form to its Beta variant. While the *Cauldron-Born-B* lacked the Gauss rifle and missile launchers she had come to favor for their low waste-heat output, it was equipped with nothing but energy weapons, which freed her from ammunition concerns.

Snatching the cooling vest from the technician assigned to her, Mehta shrugged into the bulky garment, careless of the blisters obscenely decorating her arm. The rough fabric of the vest ripped many of the skin-bubbles open, allowing the straw-colored fluid within to leak down her arm. She barely noticed. She was a warrior, and once again the joy of battle rose in her to blot out all other sensations.

Quickly Hang Mehta swarmed up the narrow chain ladder that hung from a small compartment beneath her 'Mech's cockpit. Vaulting into the narrow control space, she yanked the lightweight neurohelmet from its ledge above and behind the command couch. Settling the bulky device over her head, she sent her fingers dancing across the controls, bringing the OmniMech to life.

"Pattern check," she barked into the helmet's integral microphone. "Galaxy Commander Hang Mehta."

"Voiceprint matches Galaxy Commander Hang Mehta," the 'Mech replied in a dry electronic voice. "Authentication."

"My teeth in the enemy's throat," Mehta growled, giving the code phrase that would release the *Cauldron-Born* to her control.

"Code accepted."

Before the computer's voice simulator unit clicked off, the cockpit blazed to life around her. Of primary interest to her at that moment were the tactical situation monitor and the 'Mech status display. According to the latter instrument, her technicians had done an excellent job of repairing the heavy OmniMech's armor, which had suffered moderate damage in the last battle with the invaders.

The tactical monitor showed tiny red icons approaching the Jaguar's bivouac. The nearest enemy was just over a kilometer away. Mehta knew from the discrete in the upper-left corner of the display that the image was being sent via a secure link from one of the light scout OmniMechs the ilKhan had stationed around the temporary base. Lincoln Osis had predicted that the Inner Sphere *surats* would attempt a night attack, and he was correct.

"Galaxy Command Star, form on me." she said, opening a communications channel.

Quickly three OmniMechs and one battered *Galahad* stepped into formation with her *Cauldron-Born*. Only one of the warriors now forming her personal unit had originally been a member of her Star. All the others lay dead on the battlefields of the Occupation Zone.

"Move out." As she barked out the command, Mehta shoved the control sticks forward, urging the Omni into a slow, loping run. Her warriors followed close on her heels.

"All Jaguars, this is Lincoln Osis." The ilKhan's deep voice carried well over the communication circuits. "Pick your targets carefully. Wait until I give the command to fire, then open up. Do not waste a single shot. Remember, you are fighting for more than glory today. You are fighting for the survival of our Clan."

Mehta tapped a single button, which brought the *Cauldron-Born-B*'s active probe on line. Though the device was intended to detect hidden or shut-down units rather than active and moving ones, Mehta disliked having any system idle when it could be working for her. In her HUD, she picked out the ghostly thermal image of a large Inner Sphere 'Mech. She locked her weapons onto the misshapen blob of color and keyed in an interlock. With a single brush of the right trigger, she could discharge both of the BattleMech's long-range PPCs. Such an attack would spike the temperature in the 'Mech's core to dangerous levels, but the *Cauldron-Born*'s high-efficiency heat sinks would bring the heat to a reasonable level in very short order.

Patiently, as patiently as a jaguar hunkering on a branch as it awaited its prey to pass below, Mehta sat, watching the insubstantial heat trace with an unblinking stare. Twice she deftly moved the controls, just a millimeter at a time, keeping the cross hairs locked onto the enemy's center of mass. Once, the image wavered. A set of identifying numbers popped into existence, revealing the target to be an *Orion,* one of the Inner Sphere's oldest designs.

"Come, and I shall feast on your heart," Mehta promised the enemy aloud.

Suddenly a flight of long-range missiles lit the cloudy night sky with their orange-red glare. Then another, and another, until there were at least a dozen volleys of rockets in the air, all of them out-going.

Mehta checked the HUD range-finder, and learned that the *Orion* was well within range of her PPCs. She stroked the trigger.

Heat flooded into her cockpit, as twin beams of coruscating energy snapped out from her massive primary weapons. For a brief moment it was difficult to breathe in the overheated air, then, somewhere beneath her feet, a pump kicked on, sending a fresh wave of coolant through the *Cauldron-Born*'s heat sinks and into her cooling vest. Her breathing eased a bit.

In her viewscreen, the *Orion* reeled under the thermal and kinetic impact of the twin particle streams. Though most Clan designers gave no thought to aesthetics when drawing up new 'Mech plans, Hang Mehta thought the Inner Sphere machine truly ugly in appearance. It had a box-shaped torso, a pair of gangly legs, and an off-center cockpit between high, hunched shoulders. The left arm boasted a cylindrical missile launcher, while the right ended in a laser's focusing head. From the *Orion*'s right side projected the muzzle of an autocannon, a weapon the enemy pilot was even now bringing in line with Mehta's cockpit.

The gun's muzzle seemed to catch fire. The stream of projectiles glowed slightly in her thermal-imager screen, illuminated by burning tracer rounds. The *Cauldron-Born* shuddered as the explosive slugs hammered into the 'Mech's torso. Mehta screamed in outrage and unleashed a one-two blast from her PPCs. Her controls suddenly became mushy as another suffocating wave of heat flooded into her cockpit. In her rage, she ignored the computer-voiced warning about shutdown temperature, and added the hellish caress of her heavy lasers to the appalling energies already savaging the enemy machine.

The *Orion* reeled, dropping to one knee like a boxer who'd just taken a particularly stunning blow. With an inarticulate shout of joy, Mehta rushed forward, wrestling with her balky controls. Eager for the kill, she closed the distance with the badly damaged enemy in a lumbering run. Off to her right, an explosion ripped the darkness as an ammunition magazine detonated, shredding a 'Mech from the inside out. Whether the devastated machine belonged to the Inner Sphere or the Smoke Jaguars, she didn't know, nor did she care, such was the battle lust that enveloped her.

In her sights, the *Orion* struggled back to its feet and lashed out at her *Cauldron-Born* with autocannon and laser fire. Warning lights flared on her 'Mech status display, telling of damaged armor, but Hang Mehta paid them no mind, the damage to her heavy OmniMech but trifling. For the Inner Sphere pilot, the payback was catastrophic. One stuttering stream of laser darts flew wide of the target, Mehta's aim a victim of the elevated heat levels affecting her targeting computer. But the blast from her left pulse laser ripped into the already cratered armor over the *Orion*'s left breast. A series of tiny explosions flashed and snapped from the shredded armor as the *Orion*'s supply of NARC pods detonated. The big machine tottered like a drunken man, then pitched over on its face.

Mehta roared her triumph and searched the battlefield for an unengaged opponent. There. A lone *Assassin* stood its ground over the fallen shape of a Jaguar *Viper*. Mehta locked her right PPC onto the enemy machine, waited a moment longer until the heat sinks brought the temperature under control, and fired.

The blast took the enemy in the leg, snapping the left shin like a rotten stick. The *Assassin* dropped like a poleaxed steer. The pilot must have been stunned by the fall, for the enemy machine did not try to rise again.

Three heavy blasts rocked the *Cauldron-Born*. Mehta whipped her Omni to face not a single opponent, but three. She screamed into her communicator, bellowing the ritual words that lifted the normal Clan rule of one-on-one engagements. Once again the *savashri* barbarians had violated the rules of civilized warfare.

Before she could bring her weapons into line with the cowardly trio, one of the enemy 'Mechs, a *Trebuchet* whose armor showed deep gashes from a previous fight, executed a clumsy, but rapid about-face and bolted from the field.

The second, and then the third of her opponents took to their heels, quickly disappearing into the night. All along the battle line it was the same. The Inner Sphere *surats* were retreating.

Disgust overtook rage. Hang Mehta slouched back forcefully in her sweat-slicked command couch. A snort of exasperation escaped her lips. The mewling cowards did not even have the nerve to finish the battle they had started. As the last few enemy 'Mechs faded into the darkness, Mehta swore a solemn oath. She promised the retreating foemen that she would hunt them down and make them pay for both their effrontery and their cowardice in blood.

16

Aerospace Fighter Flight Whiskey
Above the Dhuan Swamp, Huntress
Kerensky Cluster, Clan Space
29 March 3060

Warrant Officer Leonard "Hedgehog" Harpool glanced for perhaps the hundredth time at the circular sensor warning receiver display set into his *Shilone*'s control console, just above his right knee. The small LCD instrument revealed the presence of no sensor-emitting aircraft within its sixty-kilometer range, and only a few ground-based sensor-sources.

It was possible that there *were* other aircraft in the air, their pilots having switched off their active sensors, and now flying on sheer instinct and guts, listening intently with passive sensors only. In fact, Hedgehog *knew* this to be the case. Strung out before and behind him, in staggered formation, were five more fighters belonging to the Eridani Light Horse's depleted aerospace group. They were observing strict radio and sensor discipline in hopes of avoiding detection by their ground-bound prey.

Continuing the visual sweep with his instruments, Hedgehog flicked a glance at the center of three large multi-function displays gracing his control panel. A thin sable thread traced the preprogrammed course to his flight's designated target area. That area was an expanse of rolling hills east of the Dhuan Swamp, into which Redburn's southern army had been forced to withdraw. The Smoke Jaguars had already launched one devastating attack on those beleaguered troops. His flight's mission was to help break up another assault before it started. He knew that off to the north and west were five more flights, similar to his, all vectoring toward the Jaguars' temporary staging area. Each pilot had the same goal in mind—blast the Jags hard enough to forestall any more attacks on the southern army.

Like most of Task Force Serpent's aerospace assets, the Light Horse's Eighty-fifth Aerospace Fighter Company had been ordered to ground on the Continent Abysmal following the bitterly opposed landing by the Smoke Jaguar relief force. Twice since then they had been called back over the continent called Jaguar Prime. This current mission made three.

The first occasion was to oppose a second wave of Clan DropShips that arrived only a few hours after the first. Harpool later discovered that the ships he and his comrades had attacked without much success were carrying Lincoln Osis, Khan of the Smoke Jaguars, and his saKhan Brandon Howell. Despite the Inner Sphere fighters doing everything possible to down the incoming DropShips before they could drop their lethal cargo of front-line OmniMechs and highly skilled MechWarriors, the Jaguars got through.

That mission had been one of the most difficult Harpool had ever flown. The Jags seemed possessed by some demon of battle. They fought with a ferocity he'd never seen in all his time in the air. The Jaguar pilots drove each successive wave of Inner Sphere fighters away from the plummeting DropShips and then settled in around their charges once again. Harpool's flight leader, Captain Stacy Vorliss, even tried splitting her flight into two groups, one to draw off the fighters, and the other to attack the ships. The tactic met with some marginal success but cost four irreplaceable fighters and three equally valuable pilots. The fourth managed to eject from his burning ship and make his painful way into the southern army's lines.

The second mission had been a close air support strike against the Jaguars harrying General Redburn's force. The Light Horse fighters' bombs, missiles, and lasers had blunted, but not broken the Clanners' advance. Thus, they were called back again to "have another go at the Jags," as the wing commander put it.

Flying in Huntress' stormy skies was a real challenge. The *SL-17* was a graceful, responsive craft with broad wings and a powerful engine, but none of that mattered much in the unpredictable winds and rain of this planet's lower atmosphere. Ordinarily, on such a long mission Harpool could have set the fighter's autopilot and let the ship fly itself. But the sudden crosswinds, downdrafts, microbursts, and vicious turbulence forced the human pilot to stay alert for signs of trouble that the autopilot couldn't handle.

Looking down through the *Shilone*'s flat canopy, he saw a dark gray-green mass of vegetation. From up here, three thousand meters above ground level, the Dhuan Swamp looked like a cool, shady spot. Of course, Leonard Harpool knew better. He'd grown up in the coastal flats along Mogyorod's western ocean. There, the swamps and salt marshes were ugly, smelly, polluted wastes of mud, mosquitoes, and variform crocodiles. He couldn't imagine this one being any different.

Under his *Shilone*'s broad wings hung an array of ground-attack weapons. A powerful Arrow IV missile occupied two of the manta-shaped fighter's wing stations, while the center fuselage station was taken up by a long, narrow pod containing sophisticated Target Acquisition Gear. The Arrow IV air-to-ground missile was a slightly modified version of the heavy anti-armor weapon mounted on a number of BattleMechs and ground vehi-

cles. The missile was able to home in on a target designated by a TAG pod, delivering its high-explosive warhead with great accuracy. Set apart from an ordinary
bomb by its powerful, solid-fuel rocket motor, the Arrow
system gave an attacking aerospace fighter a capability
the craft had never enjoyed before—a stand-off weapon.
Given a successful destination of the target, Arrow missiles were capable of being fired at targets more than two
and a half kilometers away. Unfortunately, the designation gear had only a fraction of that range, requiring the
spotter to be within four hundred-fifty meters of the target. This limited range required at least one strike fighter
to be "on station" above the target while the rest delivered their lethal payloads from a relatively safe distance.

Harpool checked his moving map display. The narrow,
vee-shaped cursor that designated his position was almost
on top of the target waypoint. If the intelligence officers
who analyzed the information sent them by General Redburn's staff were right, the main body of the Smoke
Jaguars' southern force would be somewhere below him. A
flick of his left forefinger against a button set into the
throttle lever switched the *Shilone*'s sensor system to active, and selected the air-to-ground mode.

Instantly a wedge-shaped targeting grid popped up on
the fighter's right-side multi-function display. A dozen or
more bright green dots, indicating moving targets, pep-
pered the grid. Harpool brought the TAG system on line,
designating the closest dot as his first victim. A small
square discrete snapped on in his HUD, indicating the location of the target. A low hum in his earphones told him
that the TAG pod was active and searching for the selected
unit. Automatically, his *Shilone*'s IFF transponder interro-
gated the target, getting no response. The ground unit was
most likely an enemy. There was the slight possibility that
the target was a friendly unit whose Identify-Friend-or-Foe
transponder was damaged, or switched off, but most pilots
didn't like to think about such things.

"Whiskey Flight is on station." That was "Wildman"

Steve Timmons, today's flight leader and Harpool's wingman, breaking radio silence just long enough to let the rest of the flight know that they were on time and on target. "Stepping into attack."

Half a kilometer ahead of Harpool's *Shilone*, and a bit to the left, Timmons' fighter rolled sharply to the right, across Hedgehog's bow, and dropped an attack run. Harpool copied the maneuver perfectly, a second and a half later.

Even if the Clanners picked up the brief message, it didn't matter. Hedgehog's TAG pod was emitting enough electromagnetic energy to betray his position to every Jaguar Kerensky ever spawned.

Harpool steered toward the target indicator, waiting until the low hum in his ears became a shrill, rapid beeping. Tiny, deft adjustments to the stick, rudder pedals, and throttle, kept the illusory square in the center of the HUD.

Then, the TAG pod found and illuminated the target, and the lock-on tone tortured his ears. Taking half a breath, like a marksman about to fire his rifle, he squeezed the trigger.

The big Arrow IV missile dropped away from the *Shilone*'s number one weapon station, its solid fuel igniting a half second later. Streaking away from the wide-winged fighter, the missile accelerated to its maximum speed in less than a second. The seeker had locked onto the dot of reflected energy provided by the Target Acquisition Gear, homing in on it like the hand of fate.

Five seconds later, the missile arrived at its destination with devastating results. The warhead slammed into the left breast of a humanoid *Thor* OmniMech belonging to the Jaguar's Heart. The resulting explosion wasn't quite enough to breach the war machine's armor, but the incredible blast was sufficient to knock the big OmniMech off its feet.

In his cockpit, high above the Jaguar ranks, "Hedgehog" Harpool grinned behind his helmet's dark faceplate at what he perceived to be the destruction of the target.

Quickly, he selected another glowing dot, designated, acquired, and fired on another Smoke Jaguar 'Mech.

"Whiskey One-two is winchester AGM," he called as the last Arrow dropped free of his wing. With the heavy Air-to Ground Munitions gone, his *Shilone* would be much easier to maneuver, though for the next few seconds that maneuverability wouldn't do him any good. He would have to remain on a relatively constant course to keep the TAG beam locked on the target and so guide the Arrow to its prey. His track-while-scan sensors revealed that Timmons had already pulled out of his attack run, and was turning away to the north, out of the target area.

Scarlet bolts of laser fire pulsed upward past his port wing, followed by a brilliant white stroke of artificial lightning. The Jags had finally figured out what was happening and had started to return fire. The PPC blast ripped into the *Shilone*'s flat belly, vaporizing an empty weapon pylon, and cutting a deep gouge in the fighter's thick armor. The ship bucked and danced as Harpool struggled to keep the TAG beam where it belonged.

Just one more second, he told himself, gritting his teeth and fighting the impulse to throw the *Shilone* into a spinning climb away from the enemy guns.

More weapon fire reached up out of the thin, scrubby woods concealing his enemy to savage the attacking fighter. The *Shilone* rocked, pitched upward, and yawed to the left as something massive slammed into its nose. On the HUD, the target square winked out. Whether because the missile had impacted or the lock had been lost, Harpool didn't care. All he knew was the blessed release from that deadly straight-and-level course imposed by the Arrow IV system's targeting demands.

Hedgehog yanked back and right on the control stick, rammed the throttle fully forward, and kicked the right rudder pedal. Instantly the fighter responded, pulling itself through the climbing, rolling wing-over, sometimes called a Shandel turn. His vision dimmed as the high-G forces threatened to bludgeon him into unconsciousness. The pressure suit covering his legs and lower abdomen hissed and swelled as air rushed into its tubes and pockets, forcing the blood back up into his chest and head where it belonged.

When his gray-tinged sight cleared, the fighter was upside down, having rolled one-hundred eighty degrees even as it turned through ninety. In the grove beneath him, he could see a column of black greasy smoke where the missiles had done their deadly work.

The gunfire that had been tearing at his fighter stopped. The bright tracers and laser bolts lanced upward through empty air, a quarter-kilometer behind him. So abrupt was his turn that the Jag gunners had temporarily lost track of the target.

Off his left wing, a pair of big, white-painted *Stuka*s were beginning their attack run. Harpool rolled his fighter upright, and looked again at the attacking ships. The number two spot in the strike package was usually the most dangerous. The lead pair of ships often took the enemy by surprise. The third and subsequent pairs usually had time to locate and avoid any ground fire that survived the previous attack runs, but the second pair of ships in an air strike had no advantage.

The trailing fighter of the pair, piloted by warrant officer Harry Quint, a veteran of the Clan invasion, dove steadily, aiming for the center of the Clan formation. Quint's warload consisted of four "slicks," standard, general-purpose bombs that would rip big holes in anything they hit. Before he could release his cargo of destruction, a glittering chunk of nickel iron smashed into the *Stuka*'s belly. The big fighter shuddered under the terrific impact. Then a firecracker series of explosions lit the sky, and the *Stuka* was gone, save for bits of flaming debris spiraling toward the ground below. The enemy's Gauss slug must have penetrated the fuel tank or detonated one of the heavy bombs slung under the *Stuka*'s fuselage. Either way the ship, and Harry Quint, were gone.

Seemingly unaffected by the sudden and violent death of their friend, the remaining fighters swung in on their attack run. Hedgehog Harpool knew differently. He knew that the loss of a comrade was felt as deeply by a fighter pilot as by any other soldier. But there was no time in the midst of battle to grieve for a fallen buddy. The survivors of Whiskey Flight would have to wait to mourn their loss.

17

**Smoke Jaguar Bivouac
Lootera Plains, Huntress
Kerensky Cluster, Clan Space
29 March 3060**

Thin, wispy smoke was still trailing from the shattered wreckage of a dozen tangled heaps of steel that had once been BattleMechs as the weak pre-dawn light filtered through the thick gray clouds obscuring the sky. Lincoln Osis, ilKhan of the Clans, emerged from his temporary headquarters. The offices had once belonged to the now-abandoned mining facility the Smoke Jaguars were using as a fallback position. In breach of Clan tradition, Osis still held the rank of Jaguar Khan even though he had recently been elected ilKhan. There hadn't yet been a full meeting of the Jaguar Clan Council, which was required to appoint a new Khan. When the Council of bloodnamed warriors was convened, he would relinquish his former title, probably to saKhan Brandon Howell. But, until that time, the Jaguars needed a Khan and that was still Lincoln Osis.

Osis was tired. He had spent the previous twenty-four hours planning the offensive that would drive the Inner Sphere barbarians into their graves. But the weariness paled in comparison to the feeling of exaltation and pride

that warmed his warrior's heart. He himself had led the
loyal warriors of his Clan in a fierce night action against
the invaders, handing the enemy a stunning defeat and
forcing them to flee before his wrath like the cowardly
freebirths they were.

Beside him walked Galaxy Commander Hang Mehta, an
identical expression of pride on her broad, olive-skinned
features. Mehta's warriors had acquitted themselves
well—not perfectly—but well. A substantial number of
barbarians had been permitted to escape the battle area.
Osis would have preferred to see them all good and dead.
As things stood now, the invaders would have to be hunted
down and killed. But that was a plan for Galaxy Commander Hang Mehta to execute. Lincoln Osis had a more
important task to perform.

"Galaxy Commander," he began with no preamble, as
was his wont. "I am leaving within the hour. I will be returning to Lootera. I have been informed that the technicians who survived the shameless, cowardly attack on the
secondary command center in the city proper have reestab-
lished at least a portion of the command, control, and communication facilities to operational condition. From there, I
will assume command of the overall campaign to reclaim
our world from the barbarians. Here in the north, I charge
you, Hang Mehta, with the responsibility of locating and
eliminating the last vestiges of the enemy force. Do not fail
me, Galaxy Commander."

"No, ilKhan, I will not fail you," Mehta promised. "I
will run these *stravag* barbarians into the ground. I will
kill their leaders with my bare hands if necessary, and I
will bring you their hearts on a plate."

Osis merely nodded at his subordinate's snarled vows.

"The cowards have fled deep into the Jaguar's Fangs,"
Mehta continued, encouraged by the ilKhan's silent accep-
tance of her promises. "It will not be easy to locate them.
Many of our aerospace fighters were destroyed in the Occupation Zone. What few remained to us were wiped out
by the barbarians as we approached Huntress. I have already deployed several Stars of light reconnaissance

'Mechs to track down the enemy. Their commanders assure me that they will find those *surats* sometime today. Then, I will move up the main body of my warriors and crush out their miserable lives."

Again, Osis nodded.

"Do not fail me, Galaxy Commander," he repeated. He turned on his heel and strode off toward the salvaged groundcar that would carry him into Lootera.

In the Eridani Light House mobile HQ van, the mood was bleaker than the cloudy pre-dawn sky. Ariana Winston sat morosely nursing a cup of coffee. Wearing identical haggard expressions of shock, sorrow, and exhaustion, Major Marcus Poling and Colonel Regis Grandi slumped in chairs bolted to the floor next to the van's holotable. None of the commanders seemed willing to break the oppressive silence that pervaded the headquarters van.

On the holotable lay a hardcopy report summarizing the previous night's action. At the top of the document was a shockingly long casualty list.

"There's no getting around it, gentlemen," Winston said at last. "All three of our units are well below half strength, though saying we're at one-third strength might be more accurate. The Light Horse is down to ninety-six operational 'Mechs. A couple of my key officers, including Colonel Amis, of the 21st Striker, are dead, wounded, or missing. Major Ryan and the DEST teams took a beating in the withdrawal from Lootera. He's down to five effectives and eight walking wounded. The Com Guards have, what, fifty-three functional 'Mechs? Major Poling, how many St. Ives Lancers do you still have?"

"Twenty-one," Poling mumbled. "And about thirty infantrymen."

"Reports I've gotten from Andrew Redburn indicate that the southern army is in similar condition." Winston tapped the report as she spoke. "The Kathil Uhlans are in the best shape, with about fifty-six of the regiment's one hundred-forty 'Mechs still combat ready. The Highlanders and the Knights have taken somewhat heavier casualties, leaving

the entire southern army with just over a regiment's worth
of BattleMechs still able to fight."

Winston remembered the flat, emotionless tone in the
Davion officer's voice as he read her the after-action report on the Jaguar's latest attack on the southern army.

"We got smacked around a bit," Redburn told her.
"Somehow, the Sierra Jays managed to almost bypass our
position before we spotted them. To tell the truth, I think
they were as lost as we were."

"How're your supplies holding out?" Winston had asked
him the question she didn't want to ask, and Redburn didn't
want to answer.

"Not too bad." Redburn's reply was guarded. They still
didn't know if the Smoke Jaguars had figured out a way of
breaking the encryption on the task force's communications, but neither he nor Ariana Winston wanted to take
any chances. "There are still some things we could use,
and a few things we're running short of. I'd like a couple
of really thick, juicy steaks, fireworks, a couple of new ac-
tuators and two aspirin the size of a DropShip, but on the
whole we're doing okay."

Reading between the lines of Redburn's cheerfully
worded, but flat-toned report Winston was able to determine that the southern army was badly shot up, low on
food, ammunition, spare parts and medical supplies.

"One good thing," Redburn added. "Those fly-fly boys
you sent us seem to have really discouraged the Jags. Our
scouts say they've pulled back almost to the edge of the
Swamps. I think they're licking their wounds and trying to
decide what to do next."

"Our best intelligence guesses, which aren't all that
good, say that the Jags are in substantially better shape
than we are." Winston snapped back to her briefing, which
she had been continuing on autopilot as she recalled her
conversation with Redburn. "What we're probably facing
is two full Clusters of mixed front-line and second-line
'Mechs. According to our scouts and the after-action reports from last night's debacle, what we're facing is an ad

hoc Galaxy, tossed together from survivors of the Jaguar forces Victor drove out of the Inner Sphere."

Winston's voice was as bitter as her coffee as she spoke of the disastrous night raid against the Jaguar field repair facility. "We also have confirmation that last night we fought at least part of the ilKhan's personal guard. I have battle ROMs taken from the gun cameras of a Light Horse 'Mech that clearly show half a dozen brand-new heavy and assault class OmniMechs bearing the markings of The Jaguar's Den. We have to conclude that Khan Osis is on Huntress and that he's brought at least a full Galaxy of troops with him.

"Redburn hasn't been able to come up with an accurate intelligence estimate of what he's facing in the south. The marsh is so badly overgrown and tangled that it prevents effective reconnaissance. Most of the wrecked Battle-Mechs from yesterday's battle sank into the swamps before they could be salvaged or examined. He thinks the enemy on his front is scattered and suffering from the same kind of problems he is. He tells me they'll try to hold out as long as they can." She smiled grimly. "He says they'll throw rocks if they have to.

"So, gentlemen, let me have your opinions."

Grandi spoke first. "Well, General, the Com Guards have enough ammunition for one more good fight. After that, we're down to energy weapons only, and some of my 'Mechs aren't fitted out that way. Maybe we can prolong this affair by stripping out our badly damaged units, kinda consolidating our force. But we've still only got enough ammo for one battle.

"Win or lose, we're going to be forced onto the defensive, assuming your intelligence estimates are correct. We've already been forced back into the mountains. I suggest we take advantage of the situation."

"How do you mean, Colonel?"

"I mean we fall back deep into the mountains," Grandi said. "We find a secure landing zone and we bring in the Capellan and Rasalhague troops. We tell Redburn to do the same, and deploy the Lyran Guards. I know that all of those outfits were reduced to about half-strength during the initial invasion, but they've had a couple of weeks of relative peace and quiet for rest, refit, and repair."

"General Winston," Poling interjected. "I'm afraid that even with these reinforcements, we're going to be reduced to fighting a guerrilla campaign, and a defensive one at that. I'd suggest contacting the fleet. Bring a couple of WarShips in system and blast the Jags from space." He held up his hand, forestalling Winston's protest. "I know you don't want to think about orbital bombardment, but that might be the only way we're going to live through this thing."

"It isn't going to be that easy," Grandi put in. "We don't have any accurate coordinates on the fleet's location. Since we were driven away from Lootera, we don't even have accurate coordinates on our own position. We could broadband the message, but every Jag and his sibkin would hear it if we did that. Even if we can contact Commodore Beresick, about all he'll be able to do is bombard an area designated by coordinates. We don't have any spotting teams left. They all got trashed back at Lootera. I don't know if any of Redburn's teams survived or not. We could try to coordinate and direct the naval fire ourselves, but it's going to be pretty rocky. We may never be able to talk accurate fire onto a particular target. In fact, a minor error on our part, and we're liable to bring down fire on our own positions.

"No, all we have left is saturation bombardment."

For a long while Ariana Winston sat silently mulling over the situation. The silence in the command van made it seem difficult to breathe.

"Very well," she said at last, not liking the decision she had just been forced to make. "We'll deploy the last of the reserve as suggested.

"Colonel Grandi, call in the fleet. If you can contact Beresick, ask him to move the *Invisible Truth* and the *Fire Fang* in system. We can try calling in saturation fire on a small area if we have to, but I will not allow indiscriminate naval bombardment, even if it means losing the whole task force."

She said bitterly, "I doubt that the ships will get here in time to do much more than break up the Jags' victory celebrations if we can't defeat them on the ground."

"General," Grandi said solemnly. "If we can't defeat the Jags in the next fight, and if Redburn can't stop them in the south, we're going to *need* those ships in system, because the task force will have to evacuate Huntress."

"Colonel Grandi, do you know the dangers of making a forced withdrawal under fire?" Winston asked. An unpleasant fire burned behind her dark eyes. "I've been in that situation, and please God, I'll never be in it again.

"You start bringing in DropShips, every enemy warrior on this planet will key in on the landing zone. The DropShips will have to ground, and stay grounded until we move the wounded and the support personnel aboard. Then we can start loading the combat troops. In a worst-case scenario, the ships will be under fire the whole time. We'd be lucky if half of them made it off the ground again.

"We have no idea how many fighters the ilKhan brought in with him. We've taken heavy losses among our fighters. The screen for the DropShips is going to be pretty thin.

"The only thing in our favor is the losses we've taken. Remember, when the Clan reinforcements jumped in, we had our transports withdraw until sent for. Well, we can't send for them and expect them to arrive in time to bail us out. No, we're going to have to use the WarShips for evacuations. The only good thing about getting chopped down so badly is that the DropShips we've got collar space for will be able to handle the evacuating ground forces.

"No, gentlemen. If we don't win on the ground, Task Force Serpent is finished."

"General," a sensor technician called from the other side of the van. "I'm sorry to interrupt, but I think you should listen to this."

The tech punched a series of controls and a static-laden voice crackled from the van's overhead speakers.

". . . coln Osis orders you to move your force north and

west. It is believed the enemy forces may be trying to link up. Delta Galaxy will continue to drive the barbarians in the north."

"Where is that coming from?" Winston asked.

"General, as best we can figure, it's coming from Lootera." The tech shrugged. "I guess the Jags got their secondary C3 center back on line."

"All right, gentlemen, you have your orders," Winston snapped, drawing strange looks from her subordinates. She knew that ending the planning session so abruptly was out of character, but she had a new crisis to handle, and she needed privacy to do it.

Wearing identical expressions of confusion, Grandi and Poling saluted and left the command van. Winston immediately turned to the communications technicians and rapped out a series of orders.

"Send to Marshal Bryan. Tell her to deploy the Guards to reinforce the southern army. The 4th Drakøns and the Legionnaires are to move to support us here in the north. Try to locate the fleet, and tell Commodore Beresick to move his ships insystem. They are to stand ready either to provide support fire or to evacuate the task force."

She turned away and headed for the door.

Five minutes later a young man wearing the uniform of an Eridani Light Horse 'Mech tech ducked into her tent. Winston was not surprised to see Kasugai Hatsumi dressed in the green and gray jumpsuit. From all she'd heard of the mysterious nekekami, she wouldn't have turned a hair if he'd shown up wearing the jeweled mask and skin cloak of a Wolf Clan Khan.

"I have an assignment for you," she said quietly. "The Smoke Jaguars have at least partially repaired their secondary command, control, and communication center in Lootera. If they get it back on line, they may be able to send out HPG messages, and whistle up more reinforcements."

Though she knew that this man and the warriors he represented needed no explanations, having been trained to accept a mission with unquestioning obedience, even if it meant their deaths, she was too used to outlining the reasons for her orders. It was a well-known fact that human beings respond better to orders accompanied by an explanation than to orders alone. Winston had modeled her command style with that fact in mind.

"I want you to take your team into Lootera and destroy the facility. Tell me what you need and I'll try to get it for you."

"We have all we need," Kasugai Hatsumi said.

"There is one other thing. Our intelligence suggests that Lincoln Osis, Khan of the Smoke Jaguars, is on Huntress."

"And you wish him dead," Hatsumi said flatly.

"No I do not wish him dead," Winston's temper, shortened by exhaustion, flared briefly. "Understand this. I was merely apprising you of his presence and the heightened security that will mean. You may not, I repeat, *may not* go hunting for him. We are acting under the banner of the Star League. Assassinating an enemy's political leader will hardly serve to legitimize our claim among the other Clans. He is a warrior, and killing him in battle is one thing. Cold-blooded murder is another."

Hatsumi bowed stiffly.

"*Sumimasen,* Winston Ariana-*sama*. Please forgive me. I have mistaken your intentions. We will destroy the facility, as ordered."

Before Winston could respond, Hatsumi turned as fluidly as a striking cat and vanished through the door of her tent.

18

Eridani Light Horse Bivouac
Foothills, Jaguar's Fangs, Huntress
Kerensky Cluster, Clan Space
29 March 3060

Huge and ugly, its face distorted by a hideous rictus, the
Man o' War loomed up out of the thin fog that clouded
Sandra Barclay's viewscreen. Like a specter of death, the
Clan OmniMech leveled its misshapen right arm at her
Cerberus, unleashing a volley of laser fire that scoured
nearly a ton of armor off her 'Mech's torso. Feeling anger
rise like a fever, Barclay countered the big assault 'Mech's
attack with a blast from each of her wrist-mounted Gauss
rifles.

The massive chunks of nickel-iron, accelerated to transonic velocity by the series of powerful electromagnets
lining the rail guns' barrels, drew a faint silvery streak
through the thin, scrubby woods in front of her revetments.
Both smashed into the *Man o' War*'s chest, but so thick
was the OmniMech's armor that the heavy metal pellets
merely chipped the "dress-green" paint on the monster's
reinforced steel carapace.

The Clanners had besieged the Light Horse's hastily
constructed defensive positions for nearly two weeks.

Again and again they tried to bull their way through the Inner Sphere lines. Again and again they failed. But, each frustrated assault, each mad rush turned back cost the expeditionary force valuable men, 'Mechs, and ammunition. Every time the Clanners charged the increasingly thin picket line, morale level dropped among the defenders. Then came this last, suicidal charge of OmniMechs and Elementals, seemingly under a geas to annihilate the Eridani Light Horse.

Barclay's troops had performed beautifully, but they could no longer keep it up. All around her, the 71st Light Horse regiment was coming apart. Battered and torn 'Mechs fell under the unbelievable energies generated by the enemy's superior weapons. Infantrymen and tankers were being slaughtered wholesale, some before they'd fired their first shot. To Sandy Barclay, it seemed that only her command company was standing firm. The rest of her troops seemed to be on the verge of a general retreat.

Then the metal giant now opposing her had appeared. A series of blasts from its battery of extended-range lasers shredded the armor on Captain Daniel Umsont's *Warhammer,* sending the vintage-design machine crashing to the ground. As the dark-skinned warrior crawled out of his shattered and burning 'Mech, the Clanner detonated one of the explosive anti-personnel A-Pods mounted in the *Man o' War*'s left ankle. The storm of flechettes ripped Umsont to shreds, leaving his ragged, bloody corpse hanging half out of the *Warhammer*'s narrow cockpit, with red, oily flames beginning to lick at his ruined cooling vest.

Barclay screamed, rage mixing with horror at the cold, callous manner in which the Clan warrior murdered her exec. She leveled the *Cerberus'* Gauss rifles and slammed round after round into the grinning steel monster. The heavy slugs barely staggered the *Man o' War*. The ugly Clan 'Mech turned to face her.

For a moment the enemy paused, giving her enough time to realize the horror of the situation. Some Clan technician had painted the *Man o' War*'s face to resemble a hideous gargoyle, the mythical creature from which the

Clans derived *their* name for the eighty-ton assault Omni-Mech. The creature's mouth was drawn across the line of cooling vents around the lower half of the machine's head. Painted white fangs curled downward, dripping painted blood onto the 'Mech's chest. As she stared at it, the gargoyle's visage seemed to twist in rage and revulsion.

The *Man o' War* slowly extended its left arm. A thick, stubby gun barrel had replaced the OmniMech's hand. As the muzzle lifted to point at Barclay's face, she watched, frozen in place, as the weapon's gaping maw grew a set of blood-stained fangs of its own, then belched forth fire and death.

With a choked cry of fear, Sandra Barclay snapped awake, blinking uncertainly at the walls of her field tent. Outside the nylon canvas walls, she could hear the sounds of an encamped army. It gradually came to her that she was on Huntress, in the Eridani Light Horse bivouac, not on Coventry in the besieged city of Lietnerton. She was fighting the Smoke Jaguars, not the Jade Falcons.

A shuddering breath escaped her throat.

I'm coming apart. Barclay had heard of warriors cracking under sustained battle conditions. Over the years, doctors and psychiatrists had given it many names: shell shock, battle fatigue, operational exhaustion, and post-traumatic stress disorder.

Barclay had never spoken of the frightening visions that had been tearing at the edges of her sanity ever since the final, bloody battles outside Lietnerton on the Lyran Alliance world of Coventry. A Jade Falcon *Man o' War* had smashed its way through her unit's front line, seemingly under a compulsion to destroy her.

The Falcon warrior had tried to bring the assault 'Mech's left arm, with its massive autocannon, into play, but the limb twitched spastically, and refused to move. Before the Clanner could train the clustered lasers in his right arm on her *Cerberus,* Barclay smashed the *Man o' War* into useless junk with a combined volley of laser and Gauss rifle fire.

That should have been the end of the matter. But starting

a few days after her brush with the *Man o' War,* she'd begun reliving the short, brutal fight in the form of an unpleasant dream, replaying the event over and over in her mind like a grainy holoshow. But, as time went on, the dream turned into a nightmare, her subconscious mind adding to the true events, extrapolating what really happened into what *might* have happened, until now, nearly two years later, she was seeing the visions while awake, and the short, swift destruction of an already damaged Clan 'Mech had warped into the annihilation of Barclay's entire command company, herself included.

She'd been reluctant to speak of the visions, at first because thinking about them made her uncomfortable. Then as they developed and grew more intense, she was afraid that the regimental surgeons would place her on permanent sick call, or have her transferred to the training command if she mentioned the nightmares. Recently, since the Task Force entered Clan space, the visions had come during the day, when she was awake, and they had become more intense, until she could almost see the horribly grinning *Man o' War* every time she closed her eyes. The memory of the actual events could not lay to rest the fear of what might have happened.

It can't be that I'm a coward, Barclay thought. *I've never run away from a fight in my life.*

Then, in the sleep-fogged, nightmare chilled corners of her mind a new thought began to form.

I'm going to die. I'm going to die here on this ugly rock, and there's nothing I can do about it. On the heels of that thought came a sharp self-rebuke. *Stop it, Barclay. You're a professional soldier. You're paid to fight, not indulge yourself in stupid fantasies. Now straighten up.*

Sandra Barclay sat bolt upright in her narrow bunk. She knew that both voices in her head had been her own, but there was something odd in the quality of the second, a strange mocking tone. She was afraid her sanity was being torn from her by a battle that had happened on a backwater planet, nearly two years ago.

With the little sleep she had gotten shattered by the

nightmare, Barclay tossed back the thin blanket of olive drab nylon wool and swung her long legs off the bunk. She pulled on her boots, snatched up her field jacket, and walked unsteadily out of the tent. The sun was just coming up.

Maybe a walk and some cool fresh air will clear my head, she told herself.

By the time the dim Huntress sun had climbed to its highest point in the sky, it was no longer visible. Thin gray clouds had gathered, building into a heavy overcast, now more black than gray in places.

Barclay pulled her field jacket tighter around her. The temperature, which had hovered around thirteen degrees Centigrade for a daily high, had dropped at least six degrees in the past half hour. The ugly day matched her mood perfectly.

Last night's raid on the Jaguar repair facility and bivouac had been a complete disaster. Somehow, the Jags had known they were coming and were waiting for them. Using their superior targeting systems and weapons, the Clanners had attacked the Inner Sphere force long before any of her comrades could have hoped to reply. Several Light Horse 'Mechs were put out of action within the first few minutes of the fight. Though her regiment had been assigned to act as rearguard, remaining several kilometers behind the actual line of battle, she could still remember the burning BattleMech set afire by the merciless Clan assault.

Worse than that, Ed Amis was missing in action. His exec, Major Eveline Eicher, had seen his *Orion* going toe to toe with a Jaguar *Cauldron-Born*. Eicher claimed she saw Amis crawl out of the cockpit of his crippled machine after the *Cauldron-Born* moved on to another victim. But she didn't know if the Colonel had survived the battle.

With Ed Amis gone, only Charles Antonescu and Ariana Winston remained of the Light Horse's experienced regimental commanders. Despite her baptism of fire on Coventry, Barclay could not bring herself to include her name on that list. Her hands began to shake every time she got into the cockpit of a BattleMech, even if it were something so routine as updating the security system.

Again the premonition of death floated across her mind like a ghost. If she ever entered battle again, Sandra Barclay *knew* she was going to die. The walk had not helped to drive away her waking nightmare.

"Here they come!"

"Colonel Barclay." An aide rushed up to her, panting. "We've got a big enemy formation moving in on our front. General Winston has ordered all units into the line. It looks like this is it."

"What about the pickets? Why didn't we get any warning?" she barked at the junior officer.

"I don't know, Colonel," the youngster shrugged. "I guess they might have gotten overrun before they got a report out. The first warning we had was the sounds of the Jags moving in on our perimeter."

Barclay felt the blood drain out of her face. To cover her overwhelming fear, she saluted, then turned and bolted for her 'Mech. Fighting the certainty of her impending death, she swarmed up the chain ladder dangling from her 'Mech's chest. Vaulting into the cramped cockpit, Barclay skinned off her uniform and struggled into the bulky cooling vest.

Thin spatters of rain rattled off her *Cerberus'* armor as she slammed and dogged the hatch. Through the thick plasteel glazing of her cockpit viewscreen, Barclay saw the hunched gray shapes of Clan OmniMechs approaching the Light Horse positions. Her stomach bucked and squirmed. For one awful moment she was afraid she was going to be sick. Despite the fear that threatened to suck her down into despair, she had to go on. She was still the commanding Colonel of the 71st Light Horse regiment, and she would not allow her troopers—her comrades, her friends—to go into battle without her.

Steeling her nerve, she struggled into the command couch, snatching up her neurohelmet and settling it over her head even before she was fully seated. One of the enemy machines blossomed flame. Seconds later a flight of short-range missiles rocked her 'Mech. The dull roar of the exploding warheads was lost in the crack of thunder as natural lightning split the sky overhead, seeming to mock the comparatively feeble man-made discharges of PPCs lancing across the rocky battlefield.

Cursing the slowness of the 'Mech's central computer, Barclay ran her machine through the start-up procedure. Twice more the big *Cerberus* shuddered under the impact of enemy missiles. Then her tormentor stepped in close. It was a tall, elegant *Grendel,* one of the Jaguars' newest designs. Without taking time to aim, Barclay snapped the *Cerberus'* arms into line with the smaller 'Mech's chest and jerked the triggers. Heavy, solid slugs from her paired Gauss rifles smashed into the *Grendel*'s chest. Armor fragmented, sending shards of fiber-reinforced steel cascading into the rain-pocked soil. Four pulsing blasts of laser energy lashed out of the *Cerberus'* torso. The *Grendel* staggered, gaping wounds showing where the pulse lasers had tracked across the OmniMech's right leg, side, and shoulder.

Undeterred, the Jaguar replied to Barclay's hasty but luck-guided volley. Lasers slagged the top layer of her 'Mech's tough hide, but inflicted little real damage. Barclay flinched away from the intense beams of light, then came back with a laser blast of her own. Internal structure showed through the faintly glowing rents in the Clan 'Mech's chest. Rain water flowing down the torso armor evaporated into steam wherever it touched the hot, ripped metal.

Waste heat began to build in Barclay's cockpit as the two 'Mechs began to circle, trading shots, each looking for an advantage. The Clanner fired a volley of short-range missiles from his chest-mounted launcher. The radar-guided chain-gun of Barclay's anti-missile system clawed half of the flight from the air before they could inflict any damage. A heavy Gauss slug from the *Cerberus* splintered the remaining armor on the *Grendel*'s right arm, snapping the endo-steel bone beneath. The partially severed limb hung useless by a few strands of unbroken myomer. Yellow-green coolant fluid, spread and diluted by the sheets of cold rain lashing the combatants, flowed from the arm-stump like discolored blood.

The Clanner tried to fight on, but only succeeded in delaying his own end for a few more seconds. Barclay dispatched the *Grendel* with a pulse laser blast that destroyed the Clan 'Mech's gyroscope. As the ejecting pilot dropped to the rain-softened ground, a burst of heavy machine gun fire cut him in half. Barclay was never certain where that stream of heavy bullets came from. She hoped it was stray fire and not some act of battle-induced savagery on the part of one of her warriors.

The rain fell in thick sheets the color of old lead, lashing Jaguar and Light Horse alike. Men fought, killed, and died, the sound of their weapons echoing in the rumble and crack of the thunder and lightning.

Gradually, the Eridani Light Horse was forced to give ground. All along the battle front, they fired and fell back. The unit's artillery batteries fired the last of their smoke rounds, hoping to cut the Jaguars' line of sight to the retreating 'Mechs. Rain and wind ripped the obscuring gray curtains to shreds. Command frequencies were jammed with requests for fire or air support that never came. Calls for reinforcements went out, but no additional troops were available.

Despair began to overcome Sandra Barclay. Once again her troops were dying around her. The 71st Light Horse Regiment was being slaughtered by a relentless, implacable foe, and she could do nothing to stop it. It was almost as though her nightmare had become a reality. She released her 'Mech's controls and sat still, staring out the narrow viewscreen at the advancing Smoke Jaguar 'Mechs, waiting, almost praying for death.

Suddenly, a tall stocky shape loomed up out of the sheet of rain. Horror lanced through her, bringing a physical pain to her heart. A *Man o' War*. The same class of Omni-Mech that had almost ended her life on Coventry. The assault 'Mech's humanoid form and empty, grinning skull-face gave it the appearance of the grim specter whose presence she had been awaiting.

Something snapped inside her. In place of that dull, dreadful emptiness, a hot, angry fire burned. The Clan machine seemed to her to be the banshee that announced death, and in that moment Sandy Barclay decided that she wanted to live. For that to happen the banshee had to die. Screaming her rage, Barclay brought up both Gauss rifles, firing them point-blank into the *Man o' War*. The Clan 'Mech seemed not to have noticed the attack. It brought up its stubby arms and unleashed a tempest of fire and steel, rivaling the thunder and rain of the storm.

Barclay cursed the Clanner, consigning him to the deepest, hottest fires of Hell, then did her best to send him there, savaging the *Man o' War* with every weapon in her complement. Heat spiked into the cockpit, sucking the breath from her lungs. Warning indicators flared orange and red on the control console and 'Mech status display. Barclay didn't notice them. All of her berserk rage was focused on the *Man o' War,* which had come to represent death to her, cast in steel and fire.

Autocannon shells ripped across the *Cerberus'* head, leaving behind a spider web of cracks in the viewscreen. Barclay's ears rang from the deafening sound of hollow-charge warheads detonating against the relatively thin cockpit armor.

Furious at the attack that had come so close to killing her, Barclay screamed incoherently in rage. Blindly, she charged the enemy machine. It tried to sideslip to avoid her insane rush. A split second before her hurtling, ninety-five ton 'Mech would have plowed into the Clanner, Barclay jerked the steel beast to a skidding stop. The *Cerberus'* thick, handless wrists flashed up and came crashing down. The heavy armored vambraces smashed into the *Man o' War*'s shoulders. With the screech of bent and tortured metal, the big OmniMech staggered, its pilot desperately trying to keep the machine on its feet. He tightened down on the firing grips, loosing a wild blast of gunfire.

Autocannon bursts blew the last, thin armor from the *Cerberus*' right leg, exposing and splintering the heavy metal structure that supported the assault 'Mech's artificial muscle and armored skin. Barclay paid the damage no mind.

Again the armored limbs lashed out. The impact of metal on metal jarred Barclay as heavily as if she'd struck the blow with her own fists. Ferro-fibrous armor shattered, internal structures bent and broke, and soft, living tissue was reduced to a liquid pulp of blood and bones as one massive, handless steel wrist found its way through the lighter armor protecting the Clanner's cockpit. The *Man o' War* collapsed with a crash.

Dazed, panting for breath, Barclay failed to notice the boxy, hunched-over shadow that had slipped around her right side. Heavy lasers ripped into the *Cerberus*' armored ribs. The big machine reeled. Barclay fought for control. Autocannon fire ate through the thigh bone exposed by the *Man o' War*'s attacks. It snapped.

Barclay's hands flashed downward, grasping the yellow and black ejection handle between her knees. Flame, heat, and a roar louder than a thousand jet engines boiled up all around her. It felt as though an invisible giant had kicked her hard at the base of the spine. Then, she was airborne, tumbling heels over head through the air. A rattling snap jolted her as the parachute built into her command couch deployed. Briefly an image of the *Grendel*'s pilot, cut down by a stray burst of machine gun fire, crossed her mind.

The ground rushed up to meet her. Pain rocketed up her spine as her swaying ejection pod slammed into the ground at an awkward angle. For a long moment, Sandra Barclay lay on the muddy ground, the cold rain washing the sweat from her body. Then she pushed herself into a sitting position. A spasm of pain ripped through her back muscles. With steady hands, she reached up and undid the parachute latches.

The Jaguar *Masakari-A* that had destroyed her *Cerberus* turned away to seek another victim.

Wincing, Barclay levered herself to her feet, and limped toward the rear. The peace and calm she felt made her wonder if the death-curse was broken at last.

Smoke Jaguar Secondary Command Center
Lootera, Huntress
Kerensky Cluster, Clan Space
29 March 3060

"IlKhan, I have a message from Galaxy Commander Hang Mehta," a technician called from across the recently restored communication center.

Lincoln Osis looked around the room as though he hadn't heard. The chamber still bore the signs of the attack that had destroyed or crippled much of its equipment. Smoke and soot stained the once light gray walls into a dirty black-green color. Deep gouges marred the plaster where metal fragments blasted loose from control and monitoring consoles had impacted the thick plaster. Everywhere was the lingering stink of burning. Even the windows, opened to admit a breeze that carried the clean, fresh scent of the evening rain, did little to relieve the smell.

Against the far wall, all traces of his purported madness and alcoholism gone, Osis saw Galaxy Commander Russou Howell. On the very evening that Osis had led his troops in their devastating counterattack against the Inner Sphere's assault column, Howell and what had remained of his command swept in from the Shikari Jungle from whence they had been conducting a series of raids against the invaders. The sudden and violent rush of Howell's troops against the barbarians' flank had turned an orderly fighting withdrawal into a rout.

As displeased as he was at Howell's loss of the Jaguar homeworld to the Inner Sphere, Lincoln Osis also had to give the man the credit he was due. When the call of battle was sounded over Huntress, Howell had responded instantly, snapping out of his madness to put up the best fight possible in the face of overwhelming odds.

Lincoln Osis curled his lip in disgust as he stalked across the control room floor. His passage stirred up a new wave of the dry, burnt smell that pervaded the room. If there was one odor he could not abide, it was the stench of a structure fire, the combined reek of seared metal, charred wood, burned paper, and liquefied plastics.

"Let me hear it." Osis felt a deep pang of anger against the Inner Sphere vandals who had wrought so much damage against the Jaguar homeworld. Among their crimes was the destruction of the secondary command center's holographic generators. Thus he was limited to voice only-communications from his officers in the field.

"Greetings, ilKhan." Hang Mehta's voice was heavily colored by exhaustion. "I bring you mixed news. Three hours ago, the forces under my command attacked the remnants of the Inner Sphere army infesting the Jaguar's Fangs. We drove them before us. Much of their artillery and supply train fell into our hands, as did most of their wounded. We killed many of their warriors and destroyed no fewer than twenty medium, heavy, and assault type BattleMechs, most of which belonged to the Seventy-First Light Horse Regiment. The invaders are once again on the run. Unfortunately, we lost as many 'Mechs ourselves, and were beaten back.

"I am certain that the invaders are down to their last reserves of food, medicines, and spare parts. Many of their 'Mechs did not fire their ballistic weapons in today's battle. Most were not even repaired from last night's action. It will only be necessary to push them a bit harder and we will be able to wipe them from the face of our homeworld, but we must have reinforcements of our own in order to push them."

"Galaxy Commander," Osis replied with a hiss. "I have no more troops to send you. I have given you my whole command Trinary and have you been able to bring these barbarians to heel? No, you come whining to me, asking for more warriors, warriors I do not have to send.

"Star Captain Gareth, second in command of The Jaguar's Heart, tells me that Star Commander Wager is dead. Killed by the Kathil Uhlans. He is begging me for more troops to help root out the last of the barbarians hiding in the swamps.

"What is worse, though you may not yet know it, is that our sensors have detected two groups of Inner Sphere DropShips that were apparently hidden on the Continent Abysmal. They have lifted off and are even now inbound to Jaguar Prime. Course projections indicate that they are headed for the Dhuan Swamp and the Jaguar's Fangs.

"The only thing left for me to do is to return to Strana Mechty. I will demand that the rest of the Khans intervene on our behalf. Perhaps with my first-hand testimony I may be able to sway some of them, but I doubt it. In the meantime, Galaxy Commander, I will remind you of your duty to the Jaguar and to the Clans. Find and destroy these Inner Sphere barbarians, or die in the attempt. For I assure you, Hang Mehta, that if you have done neither by the time I return, you will answer for your failure."

With an angry wave of his hand, Osis signaled the technician to close the channel.

"What will you do, ilKhan?" Star Captain Maddox, leader of the ilKhan's personal guard, asked boldly.

"I will do as I said." Osis shook his head and blew out his breath. The short huffing noise sounded like the growl of a hunting jaguar. "I will return to Strata Mechty and try to summon what aid I can. Come, Maddox, let us go."

Several floors below, another man's actions recalled those of a hunting cat.

Kasugai Hatsumi and his team of nekekami had slipped unseen into the city under cover of the driving rainstorm that stung exposed flesh and chased casual passersby indoors. Hatsumi and his team were familiar with the city, having ventured into its heart once before to wreak havoc within the Jaguar command center. The Jaguars had subsequently moved to a backup location, which had also been damaged when General Winston called for destruction of the Jaguars' military capabilities.

Perhaps he and his team had been far too conservative in their initial efforts. In the attempt to follow General Winston's orders to keep civilian, so-called collateral casualties to a minimum, the saboteurs had merely destroyed key pieces of equipment instead of wiping out the entire building, as Keiji Sendai would have liked. This time would be different. This time he and his team would follow their training rather than the desires of a line soldier who knew nothing about Hatsumi's kind of war.

The unarmored sentry at the facility's only door died easily, painlessly. Rumiko Fox sent a single thin wire dart from a short blowpipe into the man's eye. The concentrated shellfish toxin killed him before he felt the sting. Had there been anyone around to witness the event, they might have sworn that a quartet of dark, hunch-backed ghosts killed the guard and then flitted into the building.

The hump-backed profile of the shadowy figures was created by the large rucksack each wore. The heavy packs were not part of the team's original inventory of deadly gadgets. They had been looted unseen from the Eridani Light Horse's engineer company. Each ruck was stuffed with ten one-kilo blocks of pentaglycerine.

The nekekami slipped quietly into the building, down a short corridor and into a soot-blackened stairway. Treading lightly, so as not to make any noise that might echo up the concrete-walled shaft, they descended into the basement service area. One by one they slipped into the subterranean chamber.

"Hey, what do you think . . . urk!" A laborer casteman who had been at work in the service room noticed the ghostly team's entry. He was just beginning to protest their presence when a heavy steel shuriken took him in the throat.

Sparing the rapidly stiffening corpse not even a second glance, the agents went to work. Under Keiji Sendai's expert direction, they salted the contents of the rucksacks throughout the large basement room. To Hatsumi, the locations appeared to be no different than any other part of the basement, but to the trained eye of his demolitions expert the spots were key points in the building's structure.

Working quickly, Sendai pulled a large coil of dark green cord from the kit bag he wore slung over his left shoulder. The stuff looked like an exceptionally dirty coil of green clothes rope, but Hatsumi knew that it was high-grade detonation cord. He set about running the rope-like detonator from charge to charge, humming to himself an off-key happy tune. To Hatsumi, Sendai's actions and attitude looked more like those of some ordinary *henin* roping off a section of his yard for a vegetable garden than a trained assassin. In less than five minutes, Sendai had finished his deadly work. Each of the large satchel charges was connected by the det-cord to a single initiator. When the triggering device was activated, the team would have a predetermined, but very short time to get clear of the building and the immediate area before the powerful charges went off.

"Ready," Sendai said at last. "I wish we had the time to do this job right, or at least to tamp the charges, but . . ." He shrugged. "How long of a delay do you want?"

"Five minutes," Hatsumi said after a moment's consideration. "Any more and they might find the charges, any less and we may not be able to get clear."

"*Hai*, five minutes." Sendai fiddled with the initiator and looked up.

Hatsumi gave a single, quick nod, and Sendai pulled a small plastic pin from the side of the initiator.

Moving quickly, the nekekami team sprinted as quietly as they could up the stairs, with Kasugai Hatsumi in the lead. He cautiously peeked through the stairwell door's single, mesh-reinforced window, head cocked to one side, listening intently for the sounds of an enemy's presence. Little of the corridor was visible, but what he could see was dark and still. Slowly opening the door, he slipped into the corridor. The others followed him.

A clunk, then a sharp hiss echoed through the corridor like a missile leaving its launch tube. Every one of the nekekami spun in place, each dropping immediately into a defensive stance. Five men strode arrogantly out of the building's main elevator. Instantly the assassins recognized the huge, dark-skinned Elemental trailing behind the rest of the group as Lincoln Osis.

Hatsumi acted first. A sharp steel throwing star seemed to materialize out of the air, already in spinning, deadly flight. It struck the closest Jaguar warrior in the chest. The *shuriken*'s short, wedge-shaped points were in no way long enough to reach the enemy's vital organs. But the concentrated neurotoxin coating the weapon's six blades was powerful enough to stop the man's heart almost before he had time to gasp in pain.

Three more deadly projectiles spun, whistled down the hallway, each finding its mark in throat, chest, or belly. Each man struck by one of those deadly missiles collapsed without a protest.

A flicker of motion at the edge of his peripheral vision caught Hatsumi's eyes. With a graceful, sinuous motion, he caught Rumiko Fox's right wrist before she could send the toxin-coated *shuriken* spinning into the Jaguar Khan's unprotected throat.

"*Ie,*" Hatsumi barked. "No!"

"That was foolish, little man," Osis growled, a smile of puzzled amusement curling his lips. "You should have let her kill me."

"You will die, Lincoln Osis." Hatsumi spoke softly, in the formal tone he might have used before the *jonin,* his nekekami Clan leader. "But you will die according to your own law. I am Kasugai Hatsumi, spirit cat of the Amber Crags nekekami. I challenge you, Khan of the Smoke Jaguars, to a Trial of Grievance over your actions against the Draconis Combine. I call upon you to meet me in a Circle of Equals."

Osis laughed cruelly. "You expect me, Lincoln Osis, to meet you, an honorless murderer and spy, in a Circle of Equals? No, little man, I will not afford you the honor of dying at my hands."

"Is Lincoln Osis afraid of one man?" Hatsumi used his voice as he'd been taught, finding the right blend of pitch and intonation to achieve the maximum effect on his enemy. "Can the rumors be true? Can it be that the Khan of the Smoke Jaguars rose to power not through honorable combat, but through murder, bribery, and boot-licking?" Hatsumi could see in Osis' face that his use of *dosha,* the technique of tempting a short-tempered enemy into doing something rash, was working. "Perhaps it *is* so. The Khan of the Smoke Jaguars is a coward."

"Very well, you freebirth *surat,*" Osis bellowed in rage. "If you wish to die at my hand, what is that to me? I will forego my right to choose the weapons for this Trial. Choose, filth. Choose to your best advantage. I care not, for in the end only death awaits you."

"Do you not know, Lincoln Osis, that we of the nekekami are already dead?"

Reaching back over his right shoulder, Hatsumi slipped his *shinobi-gatana* from its wooden *saya.* The steel sword was shorter than the vibrokatana carried by the DEST troopers, and had a straight, relatively stiff blade. The chemically blackened blade reflected no light, save from the narrow band of bright steel that accentuated the cutting edge. Unlike a samurai's *katana,* the nekekami's sword was not razor-sharp, having instead an edge similar to a brush-cutting machete. Often the sword's wide, square guard was used as a climbing hook. A finely honed edge would leave a nekekami minus his fingertips if he tried scaling a wall with such a weapon.

Hatsumi glanced at Honda Tan, and gave a short jerk of his head. The other man nodded once. Tan slipped his own sword, still in its protective wooden scabbard, from his shoulder. Tossing the weapon to Osis, Tan stepped back, dropping once again into a defensive stance.

"Honda, you and the others return to General Winston. I will join you when I can."

For a moment, Hatsumi felt Tan preparing to protest the order, but the moment passed.

"Hai." Tan inclined his head again, bowing to Hatsumi's wishes. With a wave of his hand, Tan led Fox and Keiji Sendai away into the night.

"And what is to be our Circle of Equals, little man?" Contempt fairly dripped from Osis' words as he drew Tan's sword, dropping its scabbard to the tile floor of the hallway.

"Right here will do," Hatsumi replied. Wasting no more words, he dropped into a *seigan no kame* stance. With his feet shoulder-width apart, the right somewhat in front of the left, and the sword held at his waist, blade outward, he was in the best position to attack or defend.

Osis demonstrated that he was not unfamiliar with swordplay as he smoothly mirrored Hatsumi's posture.

For several heartbeats they remained like that, a few bare meters separating them as they gazed into one another's eyes. Hatsumi carefully kept his masked face in a neutral expression, so his eyes would not betray his thoughts. Osis, on the other hand, had no mask to hide his features. Such a veil would have done nothing to conceal the raw anger and hatred burning in his eyes.

Hatsumi struck first. In a short, snapping motion, he beat Osis' borrowed sword upward, and out of the way. Crossing his wrists, Hatsumi cut at the Khan's exposed right knee. Osis whipped his own blade down in a sharp half circle. Steel rang on steel as he caught Hatsumi's attack on the sword's reinforced spine, sidestepping to the right at the same time. With a brutal, inelegant motion, Osis twisted his body, slashing at his opponent's groin.

Hatsumi glided back, out of the reach of the dully gleaming blade, deflecting it with a light tap from his own. He brought the *shinobi-gatana* around in a whistling arc that would end with its chisel-shaped point buried in Osis' muscular chest. Osis parried high and replied with a cut of his own at Hatsumi's head.

Sword blades sang a high, chiming tune as Hatsumi parried the blow, and was in turn parried when he struck at Osis' head.

Stepping in close, Hatsumi smashed his weapon's steel pommel into the ilKhan's vulnerable jaw. A dull, grinding crunch told him that he'd broken some of his enemy's teeth. Osis, half-stunned by the blow, replied with a rockhard fist driven forcefully into Hatsumi's face. Colored lights danced in Hatsumi's vision as the Jaguar leader's knuckles fractured his left cheekbone.

Briefly, both men backed off, shaking their heads, trying to regain their poise and balance. Osis recovered first, and announced the fact with a fierce, drawing cut at Hatsumi's chest. Hatsumi twisted away from the blow. What the movement lacked in grace, it more than made up for in effect. Instead of having his chest laid open to the backbone, Hatsumi took a deep gash in the left biceps.

Osis pressed his attack, raining a pitiless series of blows onto his reeling opponent. Acting on instinct alone, Hatsumi managed to parry each of the deadly attacks amid the ring and grate of steel on steel. More sensing than seeing an opportunity, Hatsumi lashed out with his sword. The brutal point just missed Osis' eyes, cutting instead through the thin skin of his forehead. The strike half-stunned him. Blood flowed across his dark face, into his eyes. He reeled under the ugly, intimate sensation of sharp, killing metal invading his flesh. Hatsumi did not let up. He pursued the staggering Osis, throwing just enough blows to keep the big man off balance, to tire him, to force him to make the one tiny mistake that would prove fatal.

He made that mistake.

In a superhuman effort to deflect a powerful slash that would have left his head rolling in the dust and debris of the command center, Osis whipped his sword upward, deflecting Hatsumi's weapon, striking a thin shower of pale sparks from the hardened steel blade. But, in so doing, he left his legs wide open to attack. It was all the opening a superbly trained nekekami would ever need.

The *shinobi-gatana*'s edge flashed in the dim light of the ruined building as it descended like the unalterable hand of fate to bite deep into Osis' exposed left thigh.

The man's scream of agony all but blanketed the hollow, meaty sound of the narrow blade striking his femur and severing it as efficiently as a butcher's cleaver could have done. Hatsumi twisted his blade as he yanked it free, widening the gash.

Osis dropped Tan's sword as he fell. He wrapped his hands around the gaping wound in a desperate attempt to staunch the bleeding. The limb had been all but severed by the hatchet-edged sword. Only the thick layers of muscle of the quadriceps held it to his body. Hatsumi couldn't see past the blood-slicked hands squeezing tightly over the ugly gash, but he wondered if he had gotten the femoral artery.

Probably not, or he wouldn't still be conscious.

Silently, Hatsumi stepped forward, his blade running with Osis' blood. Words at this point would be trite. Wasted. Foolish.

Lifting his sword, Hatsumi drew the weapon back for the powerful slash that would, both literally and figuratively, separate the Jaguar's head from his body. Before he could commit the blow, Osis released his crippled leg and rolled away from the decapitating strike.

Hatsumi missed what should have been an easy stroke when, against all belief, Osis twisted out of the sword's deadly arc. In one short, gliding step, he followed his prey, lifting the weapon's point for the final blow. It didn't matter to Hatsumi that he'd be stabbing Osis in the back. Most of the men he'd killed had died that way. But, before he could deliver the thrust, Osis twisted around to face him. Like a striking snake, the Jaguar's arm uncoiled, carrying with it a single, blackened steel fang.

Tan's sword struck a rib, tearing a long bloody furrow in Hatsumi's side before the angled point skipped off the bone and through the narrow gap between it and its neighbor. An odd feeling, like a narrow spear of ice, invaded Hatsumi's chest. His breath caught in his throat as the blade sliced through his lungs.

With an animal growl and a savagery born of hatred and pain, Osis twisted the blade in the wound, eliciting a tortured gasp from the man impaled on his sword.

Hatsumi felt the edge cut into his heart. Suddenly, the finely honed strength left his limbs, leaving only a heavy weariness. The sword dangling loosely in his right hand, a thing no heavier than a kilo, suddenly seemed to be a great weight anchoring him to the earth. He coughed once and collapsed to the floor. A gray mist closed in from the edges of his vision, then blackness.

Lincoln Osis released the blood-slicked grip of the sword, allowing the assassin's body to slump gracelessly to the floor. For a moment he swayed drunkenly, fighting for consciousness. Steeling himself against the siren-call of blissful oblivion evidenced in the eyes of his would-be killer, he slashed a long strip from the hem of his uniform tunic, using the blade of the dead man's sword. His own was still lodged in the assassin's body, and he hadn't the strength to pull it forth.

Wrapping the makeshift bandage tightly around his ruined leg seemed to drain away the last of his vitality. Osis leaned against the wall, panting heavily. Twice he tried to lever himself to his feet, using the strong sword blade as a steel crutch, but to no avail. Each time he failed, dropping heavily to the debris-cluttered floor.

Is this how I die? Sitting helpless among the wreckage of my homeworld, the bodies of my warriors strewn about me? Is this the fate of the Jaguar? Is this the fate of the Clans? To be destroyed at the hands of filthy freebirth lucrewarriors and paid assassins? Is all truly lost?

Osis' eyelids fluttered as the orbs beneath them rolled back in his head. Unconscious, he slumped sideways, his head less than a meter from that of the man who had come to end his life.

"IlKhan!" The panic-edged shout echoed along the shattered corridor like a trumpet call.

Five pairs of heavily armored feet pounded down the corridor as a security Star of Elementals ran to help their leader.

"Is he . . ."

"He is alive," the Point commander grunted. "But he will not remain so if we do not get him to the hospital. Gaspar, see if you can find a medical kit. Rankin, find out if any of the ground cars outside still run. We must get the ilKhan to the hospital."

Cradled in the Elemental's massive, steel-skinned arms, Lincoln Osis opened his eyes, pain and shock clearly written in the gray irises.

"Rest, my Khan. I am here," the Elemental said. "I am Point Commander Jagadis. We will look after your wounds."

"How—" Osis broke off, coughing. "How did you know?"

"We did not, ilKhan," the Elemental said. "We are merely the security Star for this facility. Finding you here was a stroke of luck."

Osis sighed, a deep, painful sound, and lapsed once gain into unconsciousness. Cold fear shook the hulking Elemental standing over him. This was the ilKhan he was tending. If the life beneath his hands should ebb away before he could act to save it, what would become of the Smoke Jaguars? What would become of the Clans?

"Point Commander, I have a vehicle waiting out front. A military transport." The Elemental had taken a few extra moments to shed his armor, thus permitting him to drive the heavy hovertruck. Point Commander Jagadis scooped the ilKhan up in his arms as gently as he could and carried the bleeding man out into the street. Carefully, he placed the ilKhan into the open back of the vehicle. The truck sagged on its cushion of air as he then vaulted in next to his Khan.

The unarmored trooper leapt into the driver's seat and stomped on the accelerator. Fans howled as the hovertruck shot away from the curb.

"Hold on, my Khan, we are on our way to the hospital," Jagadis said. "Just hold on."

Minutes later, a hollow roar shattered the night. There were no secondary explosions, no after fire, nothing. Just that one, great, shattering bellow, then an eerie, ringing silence. Standing in the shadow of an ugly gray building only a few blocks away, Honda Tan looked back impassively in the direction of the now ruined command center. Keiji Sendai knew his business, and there was no doubt in Tan's mind that the control center was now just a hollow shell filled with smoking rubble. He was as equally certain that the body of his leader and his friend lay somewhere inside that ruined pile of concrete and brick.

Tan wasted no energy on tears, grief, or any other display of emotion. Kasugai Hatsumi was a nekekami, a spirit cat. He had lived with death in his pocket all of his adult life. What Hatsumi said to Lincoln Osis was true. Nekekami counted themselves as dead from the time they completed their training. Some even had funeral services held, attending the ceremonies themselves. To a nekekami, death was a welcome friend.

With a slight nod of his head Tan signaled Rumiko Fox to take the lead, and the ghostly trio slipped silently out of Lootera.

20

Northern Army Operational Area
Jaguar's Fangs, Huntress
Kerensky Cluster, Clan Space
29 March 3060

A patch of sunlight illuminated a meter-square portion of
the drab gray rock behind which Major Michael Ryan lay,
carefully concealed both by his position and by the
mimetic electronic camouflage built into the skin of his
Kage battle armor. A break in the clouds admitted the narrow beam of sunlight, a rare occurrence on the normally
overcast world. In similar hiding places and similarly concealed lay the last four members of the Draconis Elite
Strike Teams that had accompanied Task Force Serpent to
Huntress. Ryan felt a momentary flicker of sorrow and
loss. He had come to this ugly, blood-soaked world with
thirty warriors under his command. Now, he was down to
five, including himself. Four more were alive and relatively well, back at the task force's bivouac a few kilometers deeper into the Jaguar's Fangs than his present
position. Those men had been wounded, but not so severely that they were relegated to the northern army's field
hospital.

That was doubly lucky for them. First, because given

the conditions under which the Inner Sphere invasion force now found itself, a badly wounded man would be likely to die as a result of the rough handling he'd get being moved from place to place as the task force was forced to withdraw, reestablish a base camp, and fight the Jaguars again. Second, because those unfortunate souls who *had* been confined to the field hospital were now in Jaguar hands. Following the early morning attack by the pursuing Smoke Jaguars, much of the northern army's supply train, artillery assets, and worst of all, medical personnel and equipment had been captured by the enemy. That didn't include the number of seriously wounded and dying soldiers the Inner Sphere units had to leave behind when they evacuated Lootera only two days earlier. Ryan feared that the Jaguars, enraged by the Inner Sphere invasion of their homeworld, would summarily execute the wounded soldiers and the medical personnel caring for them.

The rest of his men were dead. They had died as they had lived, serving the greater interests of the Dragon—the Draconis Combine and its Coordinator, Theodore Kurita. That would be a source of pride and comfort to the friends and comrades they had left behind.

Most of his dead warriors still lay where they fell, unless the Smoke Jaguars had begun telling off burial details. Ryan knew that many DEST commandos had no family. It was not a requirement for entry into the program, it just seemed to work out that way. With no children or nieces or nephews, there would be few to grieve the loss of his brave warriors. For most of his men, there would be no one to mourn, no one to offer prayers and incense for their loved one. He knew that the majority of the Combine would never learn the names of the brave men and women who fought and bled and died on faraway Huntress that the Combine might continue to live. Ryan harbored no bitterness in his heart. This was the way of *giri,* the way of duty to the Combine and to one's liege lord. But *Sho-sa* Michael Ryan would remember every one of them. He knew their names, and had etched their faces to his mind. So long as he lived, his people would have someone to keep their memories alive.

Against what she called "her better judgment," General Ariana Winston had allowed the DEST troopers to establish what Ryan called a listening and observation post along the narrow mountain pass through which the northern army had been driven following the debacle of that morning. Ryan argued that his commandos' unique talents were being wasted by forcing them to remain with the noncombatants while the BattleMech, armor, and conventional infantry assets marched off to fight the Clanners.

When she at last gave in, Ryan outlined his plans for the General.

"We'll move out about five klicks and establish a series of overwatch positions along the road. We know the Jaguars have got to follow it. There is no other way through these mountains, at least none any of the scouts could find, *neh*?"

He tapped his right forefinger against the faintly glowing display screen of Winston's mapbox. "If we site them properly, we should be able to see the enemy a long time before he is able to see us."

"Uh, hmm," Winston agreed. "Given the terrain and the average speed of a 'Mech moving over bad ground, that would give us about thirty minutes' warning."

"It would give far more than that, General," Ryan countered. "My unit has two intact and functioning TAG designators. I know your Eridani Light Horse has at least three 'Mechs equipped with Arrow IV launchers, as well as a pair of Chaparral missile tanks fitted with the same weapon. I suspect that the Com Guards have at least a few similarly armed units. And, I understand the one type of ammunition that is still in relatively good supply is Arrow IV guided missiles. I suggest that my men and I could designate targets for your Arrow IVs.

"It is well known that the Clans regard artillery and indirect missile fire as cowardly, and are slow to use it themselves. But it is also a well known principle in warfare that troops subjected to artillery fire, who have no means of counter-battery fire, tend to suffer injury to their morale as well as their machines and their bodies."

Winston considered Ryan's words carefully. Watching her, he could see her mind weighing the potentials for gain and loss. Ryan had weighed them himself.

If the venture worked, the Jaguars would find their attack broken up before it could develop. They would lose valuable men and machines to the horribly precise guided munitions. The Jaguars would expend time and their dwindling store of spare parts in repairing the damage the missiles would inflict on the 'Mechs that survived. Such occurrences placed a terrific drain on the enemy's combat readiness, and an even greater stress on his morale.

On the other hand, the Clanners always regarded long-range artillery fire as a coward's way of fighting a battle. If the task force suddenly showered an advancing Jaguar force with guided projectiles, there was a good chance that the Jags would simply lower their heads and charge. If that happened, Ryan and his men would find their position overrun by enraged Clan warriors. It would not be too likely that any of the DEST commandos would survive the engagement.

This was potentially the most difficult job of a commanding officer, weighing the potential benefits of a combat tactic against the potential losses, particularly in the form of warriors killed in action.

"All right, Major," Winston said at last. "Go ahead and deploy your men. Take your TAG designators along, but do not attempt to engage the Jags, either with Target Acquisition Gear or with your own weapons unless you get clearance from army command. Got it?"

"Hai, Winston-*sama. Wakarimas,"* Ryan answered with a bow of respect. "I understand."

"Good," Winston nodded. "Now, if your unit is in danger of being discovered or overrun, then all bets are off. You do whatever you think is necessary to ensure the safety and survival of your command."

"Hai," Ryan repeated, with another bow. He knew that Winston understood that commandos as a breed were possessed of a high degree of independence and initiative, and were thus frequently given to altering battle plans on their own, without approval from a higher authority. Ryan's strict devotion to bushido would not allow him to violate her orders once they were given and acknowledged. But, he also knew that she was too good a commander to hamstring his ability to react to a fluid situation, and a pitched battle was always a fluid situation.

Almost as quickly as it appeared the bright patch faded. The gray, unremittingly gloomy skies had become a solid mass of clouds once more.

Watching a narrow strip of empty mountain road on a dismal, rainy planet is perhaps the most tedious assignment a warrior could face. The flat, uninspiring gray and black of the vista tends to grind away at one's attentiveness until a full regimental parade with band music could march past the observation post unnoticed. To combat the onset of this dangerous condition, Ryan rotated his men through the observation post at fifteen-minute intervals, not sparing himself from the dull round of staring at the narrow mountain pass.

Something moved just at the edge of his vision, where the steep, rocky road doubled back on itself in one of the many hair-pin turns that broke its upward climb. Ryan punched up the magnification on his Kage suit's visor to maximum. Scanning the area, he searched every rock, every shadow, every shallow puddle of rainwater until he found the cause of the movement. A large black bird twice the size of a crow had landed on a boulder, and was hammering away at what seemed to be a large nut or snail.

As relief flooded into his keyed-up mind, he realized that the bird was the first indigenous life form he'd seen since his team arrived on Huntress. He was certain he'd seen other forms of life, but he hadn't really noticed them.

Ryan dropped the visor's magnification back down

to the four-power setting he'd been using to scan the road. As he did, the field of view widened to include more of the rocks, embankments, and muddy ground he'd been observing before the bird caught his attention. And, in the center of his suddenly widened viewing area, was a gray and black mottled *Ryoken*. The ugly OmniMech had stepped into his target area while he was looking at a cursed bird. Behind the *Ryoken* were several more 'Mechs.

Keying his helmet-mounted communications set, Ryan alerted the men of his command, then established a link with the army command post and General Winston.

"Dancer, this is Cobra Leader," he called. "Cobra is in contact with the enemy. At least one Star of medium Oscar Mikes is moving up the road toward my position. They are approximately five-zero-zero meters west-northwest of my position. I can make out no unit markings at this time. The enemy force consists solely of Oscar Mikes. No Echoes in evidence at this time. Cobra Leader requests instructions."

"Cobra Leader, this is Eagle. Dancer is out of position." Colonel Regis Grandi of the Com Guards answered Ryan's situation report. "Stand by. I will relay your report and get Dancer on-line ASAP. Meanwhile, continue to observe and report."

"*Hai,* Eagle, *wakarimas.* Observe and report. Cobra standing by."

By the time Ryan completed the exchange with the command post, Talon Sergeant Raiko had dropped into the shallow, rocky hole beside him. The rest of his badly short-handed team had moved into their prepared positions as well. Normally each DEST trooper carried a light anti-personnel type weapon in his suit's metal hands. For this mission, his team was equipped with more powerful 'Mech-killing weapons, like the small laser mated to his suit's right forearm. Most of the commandos had heavy satchel charges prepared and lying close at hand. If an enemy 'Mech got close enough, the prepackaged bombs could be jammed into the machine's vulnerable knee or ankle joints. The resulting explosion would be enough to cripple or even sever the leg. Private Jinjiro Mitsugi, the last survivor of Team Four, was armed with a heavy man-portable short-range missile launcher and an adequate supply of incendiary Inferno missiles. Talon Sergeant Raiko, on the other hand, carried perhaps the most deadly weapon the DEST teams had brought with them to Huntress—a portable TAG designator.

Raiko, a seasoned veteran, didn't waste words. Instead, he leveled the heavy designation unit that had replaced his suit's primary weapon at the nearest enemy machine. Having received no orders to do so, and not wishing to risk giving his position away unnecessarily, he did not activate the TAG unit.

Ryan watched as the *Ryoken* walked cautiously up the road. The Jaguar pilot swung the machine's torso back and forth, rotating it on its wide hips. The pilot seemed to be wary, almost as though he were expecting a trap.

Perhaps these Clanners are learning something at last, Ryan thought. *I hope they haven't learned too much too fast, or we may be in serious trouble.*

"Cobra Leader, this is Dancer." Winston came on the line at last. "Say your tacsit, over."

"Dancer, Cobra Leader. Tactical situation is unchanged. Cobra is observing at least one Star of medium Oscar Mikes. I see no Echoes." Ryan repeated his earlier report, stating that he was facing at least five medium OmniMechs, with no Elementals in support. "The enemy seems to be unaware of our presence. My assessment is that this is a reconnaissance Star. I suggest that we leave them alone unless they spot my team. If we engage them now, the rest of the Jaguars will either come in hot, or circumvent my position and look for another way into the mountains."

"Dancer concurs, Cobra Leader," Winston replied after a few seconds. "Allow the recon element to pass unharmed. Wait for the bigger fish."

"Acknowledged, Dancer. Cobra Leader out."

"What did she say?" Raiko asked.

"She said, 'wait for the bigger fish,'" Ryan answered with a half chuckle. He would never completely get used to the rather cavalier manner in which non-Combine officers phrased their orders.

"So ka," Raiko answered. "That is how it is to be."

Ryan nodded. He just hoped that the electronic camouflage built into the skin of his team's Kage suits would protect them from the enemy long enough for "bigger fish" to swim into his net.

Ryan hadn't long to wait. Just over ten minutes after the reconnaissance Star made its slow, careful way past his concealed position, another 'Mech appeared at the bottom of the winding road. This one had a definitely humanoid look to it, with a low, centered cockpit, and a boxy missile launcher perched on its right shoulder, balanced by the blank lens of a searchlight mounted on the left. It took only a few seconds for Ryan to identify the OmniMech as a *Loki.* Behind the newcomer were even more and larger war machines. Most appeared to be Omni-Mechs, but a few were Clan second-line machines. Small dark figures, looking like demonic insects, either clung to hand-holds welded to the OmniMechs' armored surface or darted and bounded along between the feet of their larger cousins.

"Dancer, this is Cobra Leader. The big fish are approaching the net. Estimate upwards of thirty, that is, three-zero Oscar Mikes. This time they have Echoes in support."

"Roger, Cobra Leader," Winston replied immediately. "Can you assess their condition?"

"Affirmative, Dancer. Most of the 'Mechs look to be in good condition. Some have unpainted patches on their armor, suggesting that they have been repaired."

"Very well, Cobra." Winston paused for a few moments. "How long until the enemy is in range of your designators?"

Ryan passed the question to his Talon Sergeant.

"The leading elements are inside maximum range now,"

Raiko answered. Ryan relayed the information to the General.

"All right, Cobra. Pick out a nice fat Clanner and get ready to start the music," Winston said. "I'm handing you off to the fire direction team."

Within moments, Ryan heard a long tearing sound made by the first big Arrow IV missile as it ripped through the air. He could almost see the massive projectile as it homed inexorably on the tiny spot of laser energy reflected off the breastplate of the leading Jaguar 'Mech. A bright explosion bloomed on the *Loki*'s chest. The big OmniMech staggered and dropped to one knee as the explosive warhead blasted more than a ton of reinforced steel away from the supporting internal structure. A second missile crashed into another Clan machine, slamming the *Vulture* into the rocky cliff-face.

Before the Jaguars could recover, two more missiles dropped into their positions, one exploding harmlessly in the muddy, rocky soil next to the road, the other hammering the *Loki*'s already damaged torso into a mass of twisted wreckage. Ryan was shocked at the sheer destructive power of the Arrow IV missiles. Just two of the big warheads had disabled a heavy OmniMech. Beside him, Raiko shifted slightly, tracking the TAG designator across the narrow mountain road to locate and illuminate another victim.

A burst of autocannon fire raked across the rocky slope a few meters in front of Ryan's position. He looked up to see the *Vulture,* a blackened crater in its left breast, striding quickly up the hill. Behind it, a second *Loki* stood, gesturing.

Probably a command 'Mech, he realized.

"Lock up that *Loki*," he shouted to Raiko, who was shifting the heavy designator to the gesticulating OmniMech without being told.

"Target designated," Ryan heard his subordinate say to the fire direction control center. "Fire for effect."

* * *

Two and a half kilometers west of Ryan's position a Light Horse Captain relayed the firing data to a cluster of 'Mechs and vehicles gathered a few dozen meters away from his converted APC. Originally designed to carry a squad of conventional infantrymen, the tracked armored personnel carrier, had been modified to serve as a mobile fire-direction center. It was the last one remaining to the northern army. The rest had been captured, along with all of the tube artillery units, following the calamitous night action in the foothills of the Jaguar's Fangs.

Almost immediately two of the five *Catapult* heavy BattleMechs comprising the battery released a single Arrow IV missile each. A Chaparral tracked missile tank belonging to the Eridani Light Horse fired a half second later. Three massive surface-to-surface guided missiles streaked away into the cloud-choked sky.

Ryan ducked below the rim of his shallow foxhole, desperately trying to dig himself deeper into the sheltering earth, while a storm of laser and autocannon fire blew the ground around his position into a slashing cloud of shell fragments and rock splinters. Shrapnel ripped into Raiko's armor. The Talon Sergeant staggered. Over his communicator, he heard the noncom grunt in pain as at least one of the metal or rock shards found its way through the heavy armor into the flesh inside. Without a sound, Raiko regained his balance, fighting the inertia of the heavy Target Acquisition Gear pack, and re-leveled the designator beam on the *Loki*'s chest.

Ryan leapt back to his feet. Extending his right arm, he brought his Kage suit's anti-Mech laser up to point at the center of a Jaguar machine's dark gray mass. When the targeting cross hairs projected onto his visor flashed gold, he triggered the weapon, sending an intense beam of invisible light burning into the enemy 'Mech.

The Clan machine, a *Mad Cat,* absorbed the attack as though Ryan had hit it with a bean bag. Twice more the small laser ripped into the big hunched-over 'Mech's leg and torso. The *Mad Cat,* seeming to have located its tormentor at last, stretched out its left arm. To Ryan the hand-less hexagonal vambrace, with its over-and-under laser mounts, seemed to be pointed straight at his head. If the Clanner fired now, nothing in the world would save him.

Again, Ryan heard the harsh, ripping-sailcloth sound of a heavy Arrow IV missile arriving over its target. Three of the missiles smashed into the *Loki* that seemed to be di-recting the battle. Two more tore the right leg off a fin-backed *Nobori-nin*. Both OmniMechs fell and did not get back up.

The quintuple blast must have momentarily distracted the *Mad Cat*'s pilot. Ryan seized the Clanner's moment of inattention and flattened himself against the bottom of the shallow foxhole. Heat and light, more intense than the hottest fires Ryan could imagine, washed over the hole. Fiercely, he clawed at the armored legs of Talon Sergeant Raiko's Kage suit, trying to drag him into the safety of the hole. Only the man's legs and hips tumbled into the rocky shelter. Everything above the waist was gone, vaporized by the *Mad Cat*'s main gun.

Ryan shoved the blackened remains of what had once been his friend away from him with a convulsive jerk. He was sickened by the sight of what a heavy laser could do to a human being. What a Clan laser could do to his friend.

Major Michael Ryan surged out of the foxhole, burning for revenge. He sprayed the enemy 'Mech with laser fire as he ran and dodged. Trailing from his Kage suit's left hand was a green canvas bag. Twin streams of orange-glowing tracers reached out from the OmniMech's torso, seeking to end his life. The heavy slugs tore up the ground around and behind him, but none scored a hit. A pulse laser lashed out at him, flashing the rain-soaked ground to dirty steam. The explosion threw Ryan off his feet, sending him into an undignified rolling sprawl. He felt, and all but heard, the gruesome, rasping pop as something in his left knee tore.

He cursed the Clansman, and clambered to his feet again. Anger and adrenaline slammed a barrier between

Ryan's mind and the pain of his injured knee. He broke into a staggering run, gathered himself, and leapt. The tiny stub wings mated to the Kage suit's back unfolded in an instant, stabilizing his short, jump-pack powered flight. With a crash that rattled his bones, Ryan slammed into the *Mad Cat*'s left leg.

Hooking his right elbow around the seventy-five ton OmniMech's steel thigh, and bracing his feet against the odd, spur-like projection that jutted out from the 'Mech's canted knee joint, Ryan jammed the four-kilo satchel charge into the gap between the upper and lower legs. Grasping the short nylon cord attached to a standard M-12A igniter, he released his hold on the *Mad Cat*'s thigh and dropped to the ground. As he fell, the lanyard jerked the release pin out of the igniter. Now nothing could stop the satchel charge from exploding.

As he hit the ground, agony lanced through Ryan's injured leg, then up his spine to the base of his neck. He fought down the waves of nausea and hollow blackness that threatened to engulf him, ignited his jump pack again, and bounded away from the sabotaged OmniMech. At that moment, life was far more important to Major Ryan than the condition of his knee. When he landed, his injured leg gave way completely, and he fell heavily to the ground.

Behind him, he heard a sharp bang. Biting off a curse of pain, he saw the *Mad Cat* settle strangely on its left leg. The Clan machine tried to turn to follow its minuscule tormentor, but something was wrong. As it stepped out with its right leg, it tottered, and with the ear-rending shriek of tearing metal, the left leg came part at the knee. The *Mad Cat* crashed to the ground.

Ryan lay on his back in the middle of the stone-choked muddy battle field, fighting for consciousness.

Below him, on the rocky mountain road, three Omni-Mechs were down. One trailed thick black smoke from gaping holes in its armor. The rest of the Jaguar force was passing by, paying no attention to their wrecked and broken comrades.

"This is Cobra Leader to any Cobra," he gasped into his communicator. "I'm down, but alive. Somebody give me a sitrep."

There was no answering message.

21

Northern Army Operational Area
Jaguar's Fangs, Huntress
Kerensky Cluster, Clan Space
29 March 3060

"This is Cobra Leader to any Cobra. I'm down, but alive, somebody give me a sitrep."

Ariana Winston looked up from the mapbox, meeting Colonel Regis Grandi's eyes. Neither officer spoke as Major Ryan's voice crackled from the field communication set.

"Any Cobra, this is Cobra Leader. Give me a sitrep."

Again, there was no answer.

"Dancer, this is Cobra leader. General, I am ashamed to report that Cobra was unable to stop the enemy. I am watching at least thirty, that is three-zero Oscar Mikes, with many Echoes. They are bypassing my position, and are moving along the road toward our position." Ryan paused briefly. "General, it is also my sad duty to report that Cobra has been wiped out. I believe that I am the only survivor. I will continue to send you reports for as long as I can."

Winston's face, now worn and creased by the cares and

stresses of a long campaign gone bad, hardened into a mask of stone.

"Understood, Cobra," she said. *"Arigato. Sayonara."*

"That's it?" Grandi barked. "Thank you and good bye? You're not going to send a med-evac for him? Some of his men might still be alive. Aren't you even going to try to help him?"

"Colonel Grandi," Winston said between clenched teeth. "Don't you think I want to go get him? I've had to leave friends and comrades behind throughout this campaign. Do you think I haven't agonized over every one? That's the price of being a soldier, and the price of being in command."

"I'm sorry, General. I didn't . . ."

"Of course you didn't," Winston cut him off, her flash of temper gone as quickly as it had come. "What do you say we turn our attention to the Jags, eh?"

Winston looked down at the holographic representation of the Jaguar's Fangs. As accurate as Agent Trent's information was about Lootera, Pahn City, Bagera, and other major urban areas, his data on the remote sections of Huntress were sketchy at best. Task Force Serpent had been forced to rely on such maps as might be found in an atlas, rather than accurate military maps.

The Inner Sphere's engineers and intelligence officers had tried to make up, at least in part, for the lack of good charts by taking surveys of their operational areas. Orbital, high, and low altitude images both holographic and photographic were made by the Task Force's space and aerospace assets. The data was dumped wholesale into cartographic computer systems enabling them to generate large scale maps. Unfortunately, even with the new data, the best scale the Task Force could come up with was about one to fifty thousand. With one centimeter representing half a kilometer, that made the charts better than most civilian road maps, but not as good as the average one to twenty-four thousand scale military map. The trouble with the home-grown maps was their lack of detail. More than once a road or stream or building had been found where the maps claimed none existed. Then, during the retreat into the Jaguar's Fangs, the northern army was confronted by a wide chasm, spanned by a narrow steel and timber, truss-type bridge. The ravine itself was over one hundred-fifty meters deep, with sheer sides that defied even the most experienced climber to attempt them. Winston had to halt the column for several hours while her combat engineers checked the span.

Their report was not encouraging. The span was intact, but old. The chief combat engineer told her that the bridge would support most of the army's armored fighting vehicles, trucks, and armored personnel carriers as long as they only crossed one at a time. He doubted if it would hold any but the lightest of their BattleMechs. At first the assessment seemed a little off-kilter. Then Winston realized that most of her light and medium 'Mechs, those in the same weight range as her conventional vehicles, had been destroyed or crippled and abandoned during the bloody fighting at the Lootera spaceport and the confused night attack on the Jaguars' repair point.

She called a quick conference with her commanders to hammer out a plan. Jump-capable 'Mechs could vault the canyon and establish a defensive perimeter on the other side. The heaviest combat machines would go back the way they had come to form a defensive line in case the Smoke Jaguars caught up with the retreating column. The wounded, medical staff and support units would cross the bridge first, followed by the tanks and APCs. Then the defending 'Mechs would cross in increasing weight ranges. Winston's *Cyclops* at ninety tons would be one of the last across.

For a wonder the ancient span held. Winston knew she would never forget how the bridge swayed and groaned under her 'Mech's steel feet as she reached its center.

In a bid to stop the Clan pursuers once and for all, Winston ordered her engineers to mine the bridge, an operation which used up the last of her army's heavy demolition charges. But she felt it would be worth it. The explosives were tied into a series of initiators, including a sophisticated vibration sensor and a good, old-fashioned pull-release detonator. All were arranged to explode the demolition packs when the first enemy 'Mech to cross the bridge was in the middle of the span.

An hour after leaving the rickety old bridge behind, the army's rearguard elements informed her that they had heard the sound of an explosion echoing faintly through the mountain passes. Winston was pleased by the report. If the Clanners had detonated the bombs, that meant that one more enemy had gone to the Kerenskys, and the bridge was nothing but rubble at the bottom of the gorge. As far as she knew, the only avenue of pursuit open to the Jaguars had been cut.

Unfortunately, the Jags must have known of another path, because three hours after the bridge was destroyed, Major Ryan's command had been wiped out. How many more trails through the mountains were there that didn't show on her maps?

"Ryan's men were five klicks out," Winston said, indicating a point on the holographic map by tapping a control set into the table's edge. The small, crossed arrows icon representing the DEST unit's location winked on about ten centimeters from the marker indicating the northern army's HQ.

"Colonel Antonescu has what's left of the Light Horse—that's about sixty medium, heavy, and assault types—drawn up in a defensive position across the road about here." Another icon, this one representing a heavy 'Mech force popped up about two kilometers northeast of the headquarters marker. "Given the average speed of a 'Mech over rough ground, he's got about ten minutes before the Jags hit his line.

"Major Poling is down to about two lances of 'Mechs, so we'll hold the St. Ives Lancers back to defend the camp. How many Com Guards are operational?"

"Thirty-one," Grandi answered. "That includes everything, 'Mechs that have sheet metal tack welded in places where we couldn't fix the armor, 'Mechs whose primary weapons are autocannons or missile launchers, but are out of ammunition. That's it, thirty-one."

"Okay," Winston said after a moment's thought. "Leave your out-of-ammo 'Mechs here with Major Poling. How many will that give us?"

"Nineteen."

"All right. You and I will move the rest of the Com Guards forward to back up the Light Horse. I don't anticipate needing a reserve, but nothing has worked out the way we planned it since we landed on this god-forsaken rock. Be ready in case we need you. There isn't much space to pull fancy flanking maneuvers. This is going to be a straight slugging match. If the Jags come up in force, we may have to fall back on your position. If that happens, try not to shoot any Light Horsemen, huh?"

Grandi smiled thinly and nodded.

Winston motioned to the technician manning the mobile HQ's communication console.

"Inform Colonel Antonescu that the Jaguars have gotten past Cobra. Tell him he can expect them to arrive at his position in about ten minutes, and that Colonel Grandi and I are on our way."

"Understood, comm center," Colonel Charles Antonescu replied. "Inform General Winston that I have deployed my pickets, and will turn the Jaguars back if possible."

"Roger, Magyar," the communication tech replied, using Antonescu's codename. "I will relay your message to Dancer."

Antonescu switched his communicator to stand by. The steep, rocky mountains created dead zones and pockets of poor radio reception and transmission that made communication difficult. Antonescu's battlefield command post had been sited specifically because of its line-of-sight to the northern army's mobile headquarters van. The fact that the communications center would have to relay his message to the General suggested that she was on the move, and out of position for a direct radio link-up.

His force had been deployed two kilometers northeast of the army's bivouac, in a position to intercept the Smoke Jaguars as the Clanners continued their relentless pursuit of the retreating Inner Sphere troops. With nearly sixty 'Mechs at his command, he had deployed his force in a shallow arc across the mountain road. Understanding the need for unit integrity, Antonescu had positioned his warriors according to lance and company. He kept the existing force structure wherever possible, allowing the survivors of depleted lances to remain with their comrades. Single warriors were assigned to reinforce depleted units.

The survivors of the Fifth Recon Company were posted half a kilometer down the road to act as pickets and provide an advance warning should the Jags approach his line. So far there was no sign of the enemy.

Antonescu glanced at the instruments cluttering his BattleMech's cockpit. There was still no trace of the enemy. His pickets were deployed about five hundred meters in front of his main line of battle, and so far they had reported nothing. The Colonel knew that the Jaguars had managed to bypass one obstacle by going around the demolished bridge. He was beginning to wonder if the Clan warriors hadn't again veered off onto some unknown trail to strike at the northern army's rear area.

"Magyar to Knave One, any movement in your area?"

"Negative, Magyar," Lieutenant Joseph Miele, the commander of the pickets, codenamed Knave Group, answered. "No movement anywhere along our front. Want us to push out a bit further, see if we can make contact?"

"Negative, Knave One," Antonescu shot back. "Remain in your present position. I'm certain the Jaguars will find you soon enough."

Colonel Antonescu heard the last report from Major Ryan's ambush team. He knew that the Jaguars had gotten past the DEST position with only slight losses. They should have approached the Knave Group pickets before this. Something was wrong.

Exercising what General Winston called "command

initiative," he contacted another of his reconnaissance company commanders.

"Gale One, I want you to pull your company out of line and head back toward the bivouac area," Antonescu ordered. "Pay special attention to anything that looks like it might be a trail. I don't care if it's only big enough for a mountain goat to use. If you find one, I want to know about it. I have a horrible feeling that the Jaguars are flanking again."

"Magyar, Gale One, acknowledged," said Jack Gray, commander of the Gray Gales, as the Eighth Recon Battalion's Sixth Recon Company was called. "Move back toward the bivouac, and look for possible flanking routes. Gale Company will comply." Eight battered 'Mechs, led by a patched-up *Nightsky* pulled out of the Light Horse's main line of battle and moved slowly toward the rear.

No sooner was the reconnaissance detachment out of sight than a hollow boom rolled up the narrow mountain pass, followed a few seconds later by the *pom-pom-pom* of a firing autocannon.

"Magyar, Magyar! This is Knave One." Miele's voice was a breathless shriek. "Knave Group is in contact with enemy 'Mechs, estimate twenty or more, that is two-zero plus. No Elementals in sight. We are engaging."

Antonescu acknowledged the recon officer's shouted report. The Light Horse Colonel looked intently at his 'Mech's tactical display. The device was just beginning to draw a score of tiny red triangles on its LCD screen. The small, but powerful computer which generated the images gathered and collated data from the tactical feeds coming in from each of Antonescu's troopers. Each scarlet icon represented an enemy 'Mech. Open blue circles marked the location of friendly units. So far, the blue circles outnumbered the red triangles by about three to one. He knew the numerical superiority of his force would not guarantee victory. The Clanners enjoyed a technological edge over the Inner Sphere troops. The Smoke Jaguars were on the offensive, at which they excelled, and they were fighting for their homeworld. All things considered, the odds were even.

One thing in our favor, Antonescu thought. *They will be attacking uphill, and our greater weight of fire should help.*

For long minutes the muted snap and rattle of gunfire to his front continued. Then, as the Jaguars' tactical superiority began to tell, the noise dropped in volume and intensity. Lieutenant Miele was performing as instructed. The pickets were not emplaced to stop the Jaguars, merely to blunt the force of their attack. Once the fighting got too hot for Miele's troopers, they were to withdraw and rejoin the Light Horse's main battle line. The tiny blue dots trickling across his tactical display told Antonescu that was precisely what was happening.

"Magyar to all Light Horse commands," he said calmly. "Be prepared, the Jaguars are on their way. Be careful that you do not engage our pickets as they rejoin our ranks."

He switched his communicator from the tactical frequency designated for the day's operations to the command channel.

"Magyar to Dancer. The enemy has engaged my pickets. The pickets are withdrawing back into the main line of battle." Antonescu quickly ran down his tactical situation for General Winston.

Her voice came over the line. "Very well, Magyar. Dancer and Eagle are on the way, with some reserves. Do you need immediate reinforcement?"

"Negative, Dancer," Antonescu said. Looking through his cockpit viewscreen, he could see the picket 'Mechs filtering into the forward edge of his own formation. "But it would be nice to have some reserves at my back."

"Affirmative, Magyar," Winston's voice sounded uneven and out of breath, as though she was running. He knew the shaking was due to the long, jolting stride of a BattleMech moving at flank speed. "We're on our way."

Then, from his position in the center of the Light Horse formation, Colonel Antonescu saw the leading elements of the Smoke Jaguar column. An ungainly looking *Hunchback IIC,* with its twin, boxy autocannons perched high on its shoulders stepped around a bend in the road. Immediately a volley of laser bolts lashed out to perforate the Clan adaptation of an Inner Sphere design. The barrel-chested machine rocked back on its heels, like a boxer dealt a stunning blow. Also like a boxer, the machine caught itself and hit back.

At a bit over three hundred meters, the Inner Sphere line was just inside the maximum effective range of the *Hunchback*'s massive autocannons. In a rapid one-two attack, the Clanner fired first his right then his left gun, sending a murderous barrage of high-explosive armor-piercing shells into the Light Horse formation. At first, Antonescu thought the Clanner leveled his quickly aimed attack simply to keep his enemy's heads down. Then he saw a Light Horse 'Mech, a *Quickdraw,* topple into the rocky soil. The double stream of autocannon shells had blown away the heavy 'Mech's right leg, and laid its torso open. The pilot had either been killed or stunned by the fall, because he made no attempt to extricate himself.

Then, more Clan 'Mechs were swarming around the bend, charging headlong into the Light Horse formation. There was no hint of the enemy's adherence to his own strict rules of engagement. The Inner Sphere laser volley, which had savaged, but not destroyed the *Hunchback IIC,* had violated the Clan rule that one warrior should attack one opponent, and that they should be allowed to fight without interference until one was defeated. Any multiple attack on a single Clan unit always released the enemy from that rule, and triggered a general melee.

Antonescu picked out the biggest Clan machine he could see, a hunched over *Masakari.* The OmniMech's thickened left vambrace, and the single gun barrel extending from the right, told him that the assault 'Mech was configured as a variant of the primary design. Carefully manipulating the targeting joysticks set into the *Hercules'* arm rests, he dropped the holographic scarlet circle that served as the 'Mech's Lead Computing Optical Sight across the Omni-Mech's boxy carapace. An "In Range" discrete flashed on his heads up Display, and Antonescu squeezed the trigger.

A jagged blast of charged particles lanced out from the extended-range PPC mounted high on the *Hercules'* right torso. The argent flash ripped into the flat projection overhanging the enemy machine's cockpit. The impact and searing heat tore away nearly a ton of armor.

Sliding the "coolie hat" switch on his right joystick forward, Antonescu selected another weapon and sent a ripping burst of heavy autocannon fire into the Clan 'Mech. Armor-piercing shells stitched a line of craters in the big OmniMech's torso.

The *Masakari* lurched backward and to the right as the explosive shells and charged particles took their toll on its thick armor. The Clanner recovered his balance easily and turned to face Antonescu's lighter 'Mech. Two powerful lances of coherent light stabbed out of the *Masakari's* left vambrace, followed by a short burst of autocannon fire from the single LB 10-X dual-purpose gun built into its right arm. The thick ferro-fibrous armor covering the *Hercules'* legs and belly failed to completely absorb the incredible destructive energy of the Clanners' triple assault on the heavy 'Mech. The armor shattered and starred, but thanks to the woven fiber reinforcements, it did not spall away as ordinary hardened steel would have done.

The mercenary officer aimed again, settling the targeting cursor over the blackened furrow left by his PPC discharge. A stroke on the trigger produced a coruscating beam of energy that savaged the *Masakari's* torso. More autocannon shells drew a tracer-accentuated line across the battlefield, slamming into the OmniMech's backward-acting knee. A Light Horse *Grasshopper* added to the destruction, spearing the Omni with a trio of laser bolts. Thin vapor clouded the air around the *Masakari* as metal was flashed from its solid to gaseous state in an instant by the intense energy of the Light Horse lasers.

The Clanner tried to reply to the brutal, and by his lights, dishonorable concerted attack. A laser lance flashed past Antonescu's cockpit, while a burst from the Omni's right hand autocannon pocked the *Grasshopper*'s thick carapace. Before the Clan warrior could adjust his aim, a third Light Horse machine, a battered *Champion,* slammed a flight of missiles into the badly damaged *Masakari* and followed them up with a burst from his autocannon and twin darts of laser fire. The big OmniMech reeled, then collapsed onto its left side. Black smoke and oily green fluid leaked from rents in its armor. Antonescu watched the pilot wriggle out of the narrow hatch in the machine's dorsal surface and hunker down in the shelter of his wrecked machine.

In that moment's respite, Antonescu glanced at his tactical display. He saw icons representing around twenty Clan 'Mechs still active enough to assault the Inner Sphere line. But there were no Elementals to be seen, either as electronic blips on the screen, or through the tough, armored viewscreen. Where were the rest of the Omnis? And where was their Elemental support?

22

Delta Galaxy Command Trinary
Jaguar's Fangs, Huntress
Kerensky Cluster, Clan Space
29 March 3060

Galaxy Commander Hang Mehta silently cursed the noise her depleted trinary was making as it slipped along the narrow pass that paralleled the main road through the Jaguar's Fangs. Loose gravel crunched under the feet of her 'Mechs and Elementals. Armor scraped and thudded off the sheer rock faces as the uneven treacherous ground shifted beneath them, making one war machine stumble into the cliffs that lined the narrow pass. Occasionally, a large rock or two would be dislodged, causing a loud clatter as they tumbled down the escarpment. Though she knew the enemy was not likely to hear the racket, Hang Mehta was not one to take unnecessary chances.

Though the scouts she had detailed to keep track of the Inner Sphere forces she was pursuing assured her that the barbarians were all clustered together in one of the few high mountain valleys that dotted the rough, craggy range, she did not wish to risk having the *surats* discover her force by accident.

She smiled grimly within the mask of her neurohelmet.

Though some might consider the action unClanlike, she had devised a plan whereby she could pin the barbarians in place with the bulk of her sadly weakened Galaxy, while she pushed ahead and struck them where they were weakest, their rear area. Hang Mehta had noticed that all during the invasion force's cowardly retreat from Lootera, and then during their veritable rout from the foothills of the mountains in which they now sought to hide, the Inner Sphere warriors had displayed a strange tendency to risk the lives of their warriors and machines to protect their wounded, their technicians, and other noncombatants.

To Mehta, this was a sign of ultimate weakness. Only the injured warriors were deserving of care. They at least might heal enough to fight another day. Technicians, cooks, and other such "rear echelon" personnel were lower castemen, and therefore not worthy of a warrior's concern or respect. For a warrior to sell his own blood in exchange for one who had neither breeding, nor skill, nor the inclination to fight was foolishness. That foolishness might bring the Inner Sphere to its knees.

To that end, the bulk of her force was launched in a major attack against the Inner Sphere's line, forcing them to use up their 'Mechs and the lives of their warriors at the same time diverting their attention from the main line of battle. While the invaders were so diverted, she with her smaller attack force would strike where the enemy was weakest, his baggage train. She would capture their technicians, staff, and medical personnel. The *surats'* store of spare parts, food, ammunition, and medicine could be seized or put to the torch. More important to her warrior's mind was the capture or destruction of the enemy's depleted, yet still dangerous artillery assets. In capturing or killing those noncombatants, Mehta knew she would sap the enemy's strength, shatter his morale, and destroy his will to carry on a protracted campaign.

There would be warriors left behind to guard the train, that was certain. Even her own Clan did that. To the Jaguars, those security troops were usually *solahma,* warriors not fit for the field of honorable battle. In the case of the Inner Sphere barbarians, experience had taught her that the rear-area guards were either green warriors who had not yet been blooded in combat, or troops specially trained for the task. Given how badly the enemy's ranks were depleted, she believed that the guards were likely the invaders' "walking wounded," too badly injured to fight on the main line of battle, but not so severely injured that they were hospitalized. In either case, the force protecting the enemy's baggage train was not likely to pose much of a threat to her attacking troops.

"Galaxy Commander, this is Point Commander Arita," a voice said in her ear. Arita, the leader of her advance scout unit was under orders not to break radio silence until she reached her objective. "I have reached the end of the pass. I have the enemy encampment in sight. I count nineteen BattleMechs and a few infantrymen. The 'Mechs bear the markings of the St. Ives Lancers. All of the 'Mechs are of the heavy class, and they show some battle damage. They exhibit no sign that they are aware of my presence. It is my assessment that we should be able to sweep in and destroy these *surats* with little difficulty."

"Thank you Point Commander," Mehta responded. "Hold your position and observe. Do not engage the enemy until the rest of the force is in position."

"Aff, Galaxy Commander."

Mehta considered Arita's report. The enemy had nineteen heavy BattleMechs guarding their train. She had ten heavy OmniMechs and two points of Elementals. If Arita's assessment was correct, she also had the element of surprise. In a few moments, Galaxy Commander Hang Mehta would learn if her bold plan of dividing her force in the face of the enemy would work.

Her *Cauldron-Born* lurched as the bird-like machine's left foot slipped in the loose, rocky soil. She recovered her balance with a curse. Another step, and the tactical display set into her main console lit up. Small icons representing enemy and friendly 'Mechs dotted the pale green field, which was delineated by darker green contour lines.

"Attention, all warriors," she said into her helmet mike.

"We have reached our objective. Check your tactical displays. You can see the enemy's disposition. We will be coming in on the south side of his camp. When we exit this defile, the Command Star will break to the left. Bravo Star will break to the right. We must overwhelm the enemy as quickly as possible. Destroy his BattleMechs and kill his infantry. If we can capture his baggage train and haul it off, so much the better. If not, it is to be destroyed. That is all."

Mehta shoved her controls forward, and the big 'Mech responded instantly, striding out of the narrow pass at nearly fifty kilometers per hour. A Lancers' *JagerMech* seemed to spot her. Its barrel-shaped torso twisted as the pilot brought the long, stiff arms with their piggy-backed autocannons up to point at her 'Mech. The barbarian fired the light Class two weapons, filling the air with their alto bark. He didn't fire the heavier Class five ultra weapons that comprised the *JagerMech*'s main armament, even though she was well within their six-hundred meter maximum range. The lightweight slugs spent their impotent fury on the thick armor covering her 'Mech's body and left arm.

He did not fire his Class five main guns. Perhaps they are as short on ammunition as we are, she thought, taking three more steps before replying to the barbarian's attack.

The *Cauldron-Born* had been refitted following the confused night action against the barbarians at the Jaguars' field repair station on the Lootera Plains. Ammunition had been running low for all ballistic weapons, and following that battle, they were out of some kinds. Thus, she ordered her technicians to reconfigure the sixty-five-ton machine into its Beta variant, which carried nothing but energy weapons.

Twin extended-range PPCs spat and thundered, sending a double stroke of artificial lightning across the rock-strewn battlefield to slash into the *JagerMech*'s body and leg. Armor melted and shattered under the thermal and kinetic impact of the PPC bolts. The massive particle discharge from her right arm had flayed the armor from the *JagerMech*'s left shin, peeling back the fiber-reinforced metal hide to expose muscle and bone beneath. Strands of severed myomer cable whipped around like snakes, as the last vestiges of the PPC's electrical energy caused the broken artificial muscles to flail wildly.

The barbarian replied with another lightweight burst from each of his small-caliber autocannons, adding a volley of laser darts from the matched pulse lasers set in its cylindrical torso. For all its fury, the attack signified nothing. The *Cauldron-Born*'s thick armor absorbed the damage without strain.

Mehta glanced at her heat indicator, which showed that the 'Mech's heat sinks were easily dissipating the high temperatures generated by firing her primary weapons, but she had no wish to overheat the *Cauldron-Born* so early in the fight. She toggled up her heavy pulse lasers, allowing the higher-heat-producing PPCs to cool and recharge. Two stuttering bursts of unimaginably intense light clawed at the enemy machine. More heavy armor was reduced to slag, and another gaping wound appeared in the *Jager-Mech*, this one in its left breast.

A secondary sensor, a thermograph, built into the *Cauldron-Born*'s cockpit flared a bit brighter. One of her shots must have holed the barbarian's engine housing. The *JagerMech*'s image on the thermographic display grew brighter as waste heat poured out of the enemy machine. A thin trickle of sweat escaped the absorbent cloth lining of her neurohelmet and ran into her right eye. The heat was beginning to rise in her own 'Mech as well. But, given an intact engine housing and more efficient heat sinks, hers was nothing compared to the temperature the Lancers pilot was facing.

The big enemy 'Mech fired again. More small-caliber slugs danced and sang off her *Cauldron-Born* armor.

Time to end this, Mehta told herself. Keying in an interlock, she fired both PPCs with the same press of a trigger. The ungainly *JagerMech*'s right arm took the brunt of the impact from one PPC blast, all but severing it. The other tore into the ragged hole in the 'Mech's torso. More heat cascaded from the wound as the fiery touch of the charged particle stream reduced half of the remaining engine housing to slag. Panels in the *JagerMech*'s back blew out, as what little ammunition remained detonated, either from the elevated heat levels or the blowtorch fire of her PPC.

A smaller explosion, barely worthy of the name next to the report that tore out the barbarian's CASE panels, sparked from the *JagerMech*'s low-set cockpit. Strapped firmly into his command couch, the Inner Sphere pilot rocketed free of his dying machine.

Mehta turned away, seeking new prey. A brown and green camouflaged *Black Knight* stepped around the fallen, burning *JagerMech* and leveled its PPC at her *Cauldron-Born*. The actinic stream of highly charged particles tore into the OmniMech's side, just forward of the active probe radome. The sophisticated electronics lining her cockpit blinked as the powerful electrical charge delivered by the PPC bolt threatened to overload their circuits. It quickly dissipated. A beam of amplified light lanced out of the tall, gangly 'Mech's chest to turn some of the armor on her left leg into a thick molten stream that dripped, hissing to the ground.

Mehta knew the *Black Knight* would be a tougher opponent than the *JagerMech* had been. It outweighed her sixty-five-ton *Cauldron-Born* by ten tons. Its armor was considerably heavier, and its weapon load far more effective. Though the *JagerMech* hadn't been able to inflict much damage upon her *Cauldron-Born,* she hadn't walked away untouched. The fire-support and air-defense 'Mech had inflicted light damage to her legs and torso. The accumulated damage inflicted first by the *JagerMech* and now by the *Knight* was beginning to tell.

Careless of the heat build-up, she spiked the *Knight*'s chest with her HUD's scarlet targeting cursor, squeezed the trigger, selected another system and fired again. Two streams of charged particles lashed out from her 'Mech's handless arms. The blasts glowed in the dim sunlight. A fusillade of laser fire flashed and stuttered from the *Cauldron-Born*'s wrists.

The *Black Knight* reeled as both PPC blasts dug into its

chest, turning armor to flying gobbets of liquid metal. The heavy pulse lasers savaged the enemy's arms. The *Cauldron-Born*'s controls suddenly lost their sharp responsiveness, as waste heat began to build in the Omni-Mech's core.

For several minutes, the pair maneuvered and circled, each seeking an advantage, but finding none. Laser and PPC bolts were traded with the rapidity and devastating effect of a karate champion's kicks and blows. But the superiority of Clan weapon technology made the fight a foregone conclusion. A slashing volley of laser fire ripped across the *Knight*'s faceplate. Coherent light, too intense for the relatively thin cockpit armor to keep out cut through the hardened steel, flashing more than half a ton of armor into vapor. When the mist cleared, the *Knight*'s head was missing from the neck mounting ring.

For a moment the big machine remained upright, looking like an empty suit of armor fastened over a stand in a museum, then toppled backward, crashing heavily into the stony ground. Mehta hadn't seen an escape pod or ejection seat. For all she knew, the pilot had been vaporized, flashed into pink-tinged steam by the megajoule touch of her heavy pulse lasers. Whether the barbarian had escaped or died in his cockpit didn't matter to her. He had been an enemy of her Clan and now he was no longer capable of threatening her. If he lived, he'd be made a bondsman. If he was dead, it didn't matter.

"Galaxy Commander, this is Star Commander Morrison. We have taken possession of the baggage train," a warrior called, his voice crackling from her helmet communicator. "What are your orders?"

"Very good, Star Commander. Stand by for instructions." Mehta switched channels.

"Star Captain Devlin, this is Galaxy Commander Hang Mehta. What is your status?"

Devlin, one of the warriors who had arrived with her from the Inner Sphere, had been given the honor of leading the frontal assault on the Inner Sphere lines.

"Galaxy Commander," Devlin replied, slightly out of breath, "we are pressing the enemy hard, but they are being very stubborn. We have lost three OmniMechs and three second-line units. If we press a bit harder, I believe we can break their line."

"Wait five minutes," Mehta instructed, "then press them as hard as you can. Break their line and set them running. Kill as many as you can. Do not worry about *isorla* or bondsmen. Destroy as many of the freebirth scum as possible."

Even as Devlin acknowledged her orders she returned her communicator to its original setting.

Star Commander Morrison answered her call immediately.

"Star Commander," she said, "seize whatever supplies you can and destroy the rest. Those enemy personnel who may be useful to us are to be taken as bondsmen. The rest are to be executed."

"Aff, Galaxy Commander."

Hang Mehta knew that executing prisoners was often a two-edged sword. It could turn the enemy into a broken, defeated mob or forge him into an avenging army. She cared not for the risks. If the enemy's morale collapsed, she would have little difficulty in defeating them utterly when they came at last to the final battle. If the deaths of their noncombatants renewed the *stravags*' will to fight, her ultimate victory would be all the more glorious.

23

Eridani Light Horse Bivouac Area
Jaguar's Fangs, Huntress
Kerensky Cluster, Clan Space
30 March 3060

Ariana Winston was exhausted—physically, mentally, and emotionally drained. She barely had the strength to hold her head erect as she forced herself to focus on the faintly glowing map box before her. It had been nearly sixteen hours since the Smoke Jaguars had launched their last, unexpected attack on the northern army. The Light Horse and the Com Guards had beaten back the attackers, but at a heavy cost. The Jaguars, in violation of conventional military wisdom, and of what General Winston knew about the Clan version of tactical doctrine, had divided their strength in the face of the enemy.

The bulk of the Jaguar force launched an all-out attack on the Inner Sphere position, slowed only slightly by the last of the task force's long-range guided Arrow IV missiles. While this force pinned the numerically superior but technologically inferior Inner Sphere troops in place, a smaller body of OmniMechs and Elementals bypassed the task force's lines, using narrow mountain trails that did not appear on the Inner Sphere's sketchy maps, and struck at the rear echelon. There, they all but wiped out the already-decimated St. Ives Lancers. What personnel, materiel, and equipment the Clanners could not carry off they destroyed.

Once their murderous task was completed, the raiders pulled out, again moving by paths unknown to the Inner Sphere. In their wake they left a ruin of men and machines. At almost the same time, the Jaguar force engaged with the northern army's main strength broke off and withdrew.

Winston recalled with horror the sight that greeted her troops as they returned to their ravaged bivouac. Burnt-out hulks of BattleMechs stood or lay in heaps of still-smoldering wreckage in the narrow valley that had been the Inner Sphere camp. Supplies that the Jaguars could either not use or were unable to carry away had been stacked in piles and set ablaze. The fires were still burning when the stunned, exhausted warriors straggled back from the battle line. Tents, crew shelters, cook houses—all had been flattened and burned.

The big mobile headquarters truck was gone. It had apparently been deemed a valuable prize by the Jaguar commander, who had driven it away.

Worse still were the dead. They lay where they fell, in untidy heaps. Some had their eyes open, staring with a flat, unwavering gaze at the ugly, gray skies above. Others looked as if they had fallen asleep. Some had terrible wounds, their flesh torn by shrapnel or heavy-caliber machine gun or autocannon slugs. The looks of horror, shock, and pain on some of the faces showed that they had not died quickly or easily. Others were barely recognizable as human. They had died under the ghastly hand of flamer, laser, or PPC fire, which reduced their bodies to lumps of twisted carbon.

Worst of all was the stench. The thick, humid air was heavy with the acrid smell of expended ammonia-based propellant, petroleum-based flamer fuel, scorched metal, burnt plastics, and, above all else, the sickening-sweet smell of death.

Among the dead was Major Marcus Poling. Witnesses said Major Poling had tried to organize his devastated

Lancers in order to protect the army's baggage train, but the Jaguar attack had been too sudden and too determined. The rearguard had been overwhelmed. Major Poling was forced to eject from his burning *Caesar* or else be incinerated in his cockpit. An Elemental spotted Poling as he drifted to earth in his escape parachute. Three thirteen-millimeter slugs from the Elemental's anti-'Mech machine gun ripped through Poling's body, nearly cutting him in half. He was still alive when the northern army's main force returned to their ruined camp, but died an hour later without regaining consciousness.

Some hours after the fighting ended, the only positive event of the day occurred. Major Michael Ryan and one of his DEST commandos limped into the shattered bivouac area. They had been injured when the Jaguars overran their artillery spotting post. Ryan and his lone warrior were the last survivors of the three Draconis Elite Strike Teams that had been assigned to Task Force Serpent.

Winston had no choice but to order the northern army deeper into the Jaguar's Fangs. It was well after midnight when they moved through a narrow mountain pass and came to a relatively large, flat plateau beyond. There the exhausted warriors made camp.

Winston looked around the small bivouac area. The battles with the Jaguars had been costly. The price could easily be seen in the battered 'Mechs and exhausted soldiers drawn up into the temporary camp. Perhaps the most awful reminder of the viciousness of the fighting was a sadly battered *Victor* standing in one corner of the camp, the sole functioning BattleMech remaining to the St. Ives Lancers. The handful of dismounted MechWarriors from that unit still able to fight had been pressed into service as infantrymen.

How long the northern army would be able to hold out was uncertain, but Winston knew it wouldn't be long. They were almost out of ammunition for their missile launchers and autocannons. What spare parts they'd brought with them to Huntress were already used up, and many of their still functional BattleMechs had at least one battle-damaged system the Inner Sphere techs could not repair.

It was a source of some small comfort to know that her beloved Eridani Light Horse had fared better than most of the other units. About half of their 'Mechs were still in combat-ready condition. But that comfort was tempered by the knowledge that two of her regimental commanders were out of the fighting. Colonel Edwin Amis had been reported missing in action following the spoiled early morning raid on the Jaguar bivouac. In that same engagement, Sandra Barclay had sprained her back when her *Cerberus* was shot out from under her. Predictably, Charles Antonescu had stepped into the vacuum, and was in the field even now, organizing what was left of the Light Horse.

Short, broken radio messages led Winston to believe that Andrew Redburn's southern army was holding its own against the Jaguars. Both armies had been reinforced during the early morning hours. The Fourth Drakøns and Kingston's Legionnaires had landed unopposed on the northwest edge of the Dhuan Swamp, then linked up with Redburn's battered troops and withdrawn into the tangled Shikari Jungle.

"With luck," Redburn stated in his last report, now over seven hours old, "the Jags will waste their time hunting for us in the swamp. We'll make a forced march, and try to link up with your northern army. I don't think there's much hope, but we can still sell our lives dearly enough to remind the Clans that war isn't a game. That *is* part of why we came here, win or lose."

The Light Horse had been reinforced, just before dawn, by the remnants of the Eleventh Lyran Guards. Despite her broken arm, Marshal Sharon Bryan had insisted on leading the Guards herself.

"If this task force is to be destroyed," she said to Winston on her arrival at the army's headquarters tent, "then my place is with my troops, not in some rear-area aid station."

The Guards' arrival gave Winston's force a boost in morale. Fresh supplies of spare parts, food, ammunition, and medical supplies also arrived aboard the Guards' Drop-Ships. If the Clanners gave them enough time, Winston knew that they could make up for some of the appalling losses their force had suffered over the past few days.

As heavily as those losses weighed on her mind, there were other casualties that caused her even more distress. When the support train was overrun, most of the remaining medical staff, and all of their wounded, had been killed or captured. It was this last that caused her the greatest sorrow. She, like every Light Horse trooper, had been raised with the tradition of taking care of your own, of looking after the sick, the wounded, and the helpless. It was a tradition she had failed to uphold.

Winston made a conscious, almost physical effort to shake off the guilt and sorrow. She was not denying her responsibility to those she had to leave behind, only putting aside the emotions for another day. Right now, she had a job to do.

A small temporary command post had been set up beneath a rock overhang. A dark green waterproof tarp covered the small field communication unit set up in the corner of the post. A couple of folding camp chairs and a collapsible metal table completed the spartan facilities. A few lightly wounded infantrymen had been assigned to her as messengers.

Forcing herself to concentrate, she looked closely at the map box. She hadn't realized how useful the mobile HQ van's holotable was until it was captured along with the rest of her support staff.

Blast it, stop that! she told herself. *Put it away until you finish this business. Then, you can engage in all the guilt and self-recrimination you like. But for now, pay attention to the job at hand.*

Winston looked again at the notebook-sized electronic unit, which displayed a flat, topographic map of the mountains known as the Jaguar's Fangs. A distant corner of her mind was amazed at the sheer volume of information brought back by Trent, the Clansman-turned-spy. One entire file had been devoted to nothing but maps gleaned from military and commercial sources. The majority of the planet was represented in the charts Trent had supplied.

According to the maps, the northern army had been driven almost the whole length and breadth of the Jaguar's Fangs. A few score kilometers south of their position lay the northern shores of the Liberation Sea, the largest of Huntress' inland lakes. Beyond that was the tangled, continent-spanning expanse of the Shikari Jungle. If they could make the long trek through open country, around the Liberation Sea, the sadly depleted task force could easily lose itself in the dense forest.

For a time, she toyed with the idea of recalling the DropShips that had delivered the reinforcements, and then moving the entire task force to the Continent Abysmal. The Jags would waste their energy searching for troops that weren't on the same continent.

"General." Kip Douglass' voice broke into her thoughts. Her young communication and sensor operator had hardly left his cockpit station in over twenty-four hours. With the loss of the mobile headquarters truck, the *Cyclops*' powerful Olmstead 840 communications system, with its satnav uplink capability, provided the only link between the ground units and the task force's naval assets orbiting high above.

"General," Douglass repeated, finally getting her attention. "I have Commodore Beresick on the horn. He sounds really excited. He wants to talk to you."

Winston adjusted the field communication unit headset she had taken to wearing. If Douglass wouldn't leave the cockpit, the least she could do was wear the uncomfortable communication set and stay in touch with the young Warrant Officer.

"Okay, Kip, put him through."

The radio patch was weak, and the signal kept fading in and out. The *Cyclops*' communications gear, however good it was, was never intended to serve in the place of the more powerful units boasted by the mobile HQ.

"Dancer, this is Courtyard." The worry in Beresick's voice cut plainly through the hiss and pop of the poor communications link. "We have just detected multiple electro-magnetic pulses at the system's zenith jump point. According to our long-range scanners, we have multiple inbounds, possibly as many as twenty."

For a moment the line went silent, causing Winston to wonder if the communications link had been interrupted. Then Beresick came back on the line.

"We are unable to reach the *Ranger* or any of the other WarShips we left at the jump point. We don't know if they simply haven't received the message yet, or if they are unable to receive or reply. I'm not even sure they're still in-system. I left Captain Winslow in command when we detached the *Invisible Truth* and the *Fire Fang* to move in-system to provide fire support or evacuation should you need it. Her orders were to jump the fleet out of here if she was attacked by an overwhelming force. I'd say twenty ships might constitute an overwhelming force.

"I will continue trying to establish contact with the *Ranger* and her group. Meanwhile, I will begin moving the *Truth* and the *Fire Fang* into position to intercept the ships. We may not be able to stop them, but we'll certainly whittle them down some. I'll report when I have more information.

"Good luck, Ariana. Beresick out."

A cold, empty feeling settled over Ariana Winston as the line went dead.

"Kip, you still on the line?" she asked hollowly.

"I'm still here, General."

"Good, stay on. Let me know the minute you hear anything, good or bad. Got it?"

"I got it, General." Douglass' voice was flat and emotionless. Winston wondered if it was some effect of the communication system, or if the news of a massive, unknown fleet arriving in the Huntress system had finally killed the CSO's seemingly eternal cheerfulness.

Winston swung the boom mike away from her lips and summoned a runner.

"Go get the unit commanders," she told the young Com Guard infantryman. "And tell them to expedite."

Even before the runner had turned away on his mission, Winston picked up the map box again. For several seconds she stared at the device, struggling to formulate a battle plan that would allow the task force to continue fighting against the numbers that such a fleet could carry. All of the experience, knowledge, and battle savvy she had built up during her long years as a military officer had left her. In their place was nothing but dull, aching despair.

The other commanders arrived to find her staring vacantly at the mapbox.

"General Winston, are you ill?" Charles Antonescu took the electronic chart display from her hands, peering closely at her empty, expressionless face.

"No. No, Charles, I'm all right," she said, a little life returning to her voice. "I just got a call from Commodore Beresick. He says he's tracking a large fleet of inbound JumpShips. He can't raise the *Ranger*, but he'll slow them up as best he can.

"Now, it's up to us to decide what to do down here. We can't give up and we can't withdraw. I need ideas, people, and I need them now."

Before anyone could speak, Kip Douglass' voice crackled in her ear again.

"General, I just got word from our pickets." Winston could tell from his voice that exhaustion and despair had finally taken their toll. "There is a large body of Jaguar troops coming our way. The pickets will try to slow them up, but they won't be able to hold for long."

"All right." Winston's face, which had sagged at Douglass' report, hardened into a visage carved in black marble. "Muster whatever troops you can. We're going out to meet them. I'm tired of running. Today, it's going to be them or us."

She turned to the communications technician.

"See if you can raise General Redburn. Advise him of our situation. He is not to attempt a link-up unless he hears from me first. If we can't hold the Jags here, there may not be anything left of us to link up with."

As the technician began to relay the general's message,

she darted from the command tent. Just a few meters away stood her *Cyclops*. Careless of any modesty, she stripped off her camouflage jacket, pants, and fatigue shirt and stepped into her combat suit. All around her the army's surviving MechWarriors were preparing for battle. As she sealed the jumpsuit's collar around her neck, the weariness seemed to leave her. In its place arose a grim determination.

If the Jaguars want to die here in these mountains, she thought, *then I'll do everything I can to oblige them.*

She swarmed up the chain ladder hanging from her 'Mech's right torso, and swung into the cockpit through the open hatch.

"General, we're all powered up," Kip Douglass reported as she belted herself into the command couch. "You've got a full Gauss magazine, but your LRMs are down to ten racks, so remember to take it easy on the missiles."

"Got it," she said, pulling on her neurohelmet. Her fingers danced across the controls that would unlock the *Cyclops*' legs and give her control of the ninety-ton behemoth. "Where are the Jags now?"

"About five klicks out," Douglass replied. "So far they haven't engaged the pickets, but are just kind of sniping at them. Sounds to me like they're trying to feel out our strength before they commit to the battle."

"They want to know our strength," Winston growled. "Let's show it to them."

24

Ten minutes later, Winston brought her *Cyclops* to a halt just below the mountain pass her army had passed through the night before. In the short time it took the bulk of her force to mount up and move the short distance between the bivouac and the pickets, the Jaguars had committed to the attack. Her sentry 'Mechs had been driven back into the narrow defile, where they took shelter behind the rocky outcroppings and large boulders that choked the pass. The Jaguars, meanwhile, could not move against the Inner Sphere without exposing themselves to enemy fire. But, expose themselves they did. One OmniMech after another launched itself against the improvised fortifications of the defile. The Jaguar warriors fought as if they were mad with the smell of blood.

Despite their reinforced position, the Inner Sphere pickets, two battered 'Mechs belonging to the Com Guards, died under the determined enemy assault. Triumphantly, the lead Jaguar 'Mech, a *Nobori-nin* bearing the markings of the Jaguars' Den, stepped into the gap. The Clanner's victory was short lived. A Light Horse *Hercules* stepped into the opposite end of the gap, and blasted the *Nobori-nin* with PPC and laser fire, reducing the already damaged machine to scrap.

The *Hercules* and its lancemates then rushed into the pass, taking up the same positions as the downed Com Guard 'Mechs. The Light Horsemen poured heavy fire down into the Jaguars' ranks, forcing them to withdraw once more. But two of the Light Horse 'Mechs were felled in turn by devastating counter-fire from the longer-ranged and more powerful Clan weapons. Even before the shattered machines came to rest on the rocky floor of the pass, two more, a Com Guard and the shot-riddled *Victor* belonging to the St. Ives Lancers, stepped into their place.

Minutes seemed to stretch into hours, as one 'Mech after another was ground into scrap by the murderous fighting in the pass.

Though most of the machines engaged in the bloody, close-quarters fighting were heavy or assault class, both the Inner Sphere and the Smoke Jaguars had suffered heavy damage in earlier battles, damage that had yet to be repaired. As a result, 'Mechs that should have been able to withstand a storm of enemy fire were felled as quickly as light or medium machines might have been.

A bright explosion lit the gap as a *Stalker*, its missile bins breached by enemy fire, was consumed in a massive explosion. A remote portion of Winston's mind noted that the pilot did not eject—another dead man on her conscience.

Something inside her snapped at that moment. Shoving the *Cyclops'* control sticks forward, she shouldered aside the Light Horse *Grasshopper* that had been moving to take its place in the gap. With a bellow of inarticulate rage, she brought her HUD's targeting reticle to rest on the torso of a scarred and battered Jaguar *Thor*. Clamping down on the triggers, she sent a flight of ten missiles corkscrewing through the smoke-filled air to rip armor from the Clanner's torso and legs.

A glittering slug from her Gauss rifle widened the rents

her missiles had opened in the *Thor*'s chest. The Jaguar pilot replied with a blast of PPC fire that slagged the armor protecting her 'Mech's right breast. The *Cyclops* staggered as the sudden loss of almost a ton of hardened steel threatened to upset its balance. The Clanner seemed to sense Winston's distress, and launched his *Thor* into a headlong charge.

Heedless of Douglass' warning about conserving ammunition, Winston battered the *Thor* with yet another flight of missiles. Much of the volley went wild, scattering broken bits of rock around the narrow mountain road. A few shards impacted the Clan machine's left hip, but the Jaguar still came on. Winston struggled with the controls, bringing her reeling mount back on balance just in time to feed the Clanner another round from her Gauss rifle. The nickel-iron slug ripped into the *Thor*'s arm, smashing armor and severing the thick myomer strands beneath. A bright flurry of sparks told of a destroyed actuator package.

Undaunted by the damage inflicted on his already abused 'Mech, the Clanner back-handed Winston's *Cyclops,* smashing it into the wall of the pass. The backpack-like satnav communication module was crushed between the 'Mech's falling body and the unyielding rock.

Inside her helmet, Winston's teeth clicked together from the force of the Clan warrior's blow. The coppery taste of blood filled her mouth as she realized that she had bitten her tongue. In her HUD, she saw the Jaguar lining up his PPC with her 'Mech's cockpit. Screaming in anger, she thrust her *Cyclops*' hands forward, unleashing the medium lasers mounted in each wrist. Another Gauss slug added to the devastation she wrought on the Clanner's torso.

The *Thor* reeled under her assault. Winston tried to wrestle the *Cyclops* to its feet, but the machine's controls seemed to balk under her fingers. *I don't think I'm gonna make it,* she thought, surprised at her own calm. At that instant the *Thor* pilot fired.

Colonel Charles Antonescu stepped his *Hercules* into the gap just in time to see a battle-scarred *Thor* savage a green and gray *Cyclops* with a blast of azure PPC fire. For a long moment he froze, gasping in shock and pain, as though a knife of poisoned ice had just been driven into his heart.

Then a deadly coldness settled over him. His vision took on a blood-red tint. He locked his 'Mech's PPC over the *Thor*'s heart and squeezed the trigger. The bolt of man-made lightning hit home with a vengeance. Armor melted and broke under the deadly caress of the PPC bolt's incredible energy. The big OmniMech toppled, but Antonescu wasn't done with the Clanner. He continued to rake the fallen Jaguar war machine with laser and PPC fire until the gray and black *Thor* was nothing more than a pile of glowing scrap metal.

"Colonel! Charles!" A voice seeming to come from far off hissed in his ears. "Charles, what the hell do you think you're doing?"

Antonescu spun his *Hercules* to face the *Penetrator* piloted by Major Gray Ribic, of the 8th Recon Battalion. For a moment, Antonescu trembled on the edge of firing on his subordinate, so great was the battle rage that was upon him. He blinked a few times, trying to clear away the red haze from his eyes. There wasn't a single active enemy 'Mech to be seen. Those that hadn't been destroyed were withdrawing in disorder.

Then the killing-fever broke, leaving him feeling weak and sick.

"Major Ribic," Antonescu said, his own voice sounding distant and hollow in his ears. "Pass the word to the brigade. General Winston is dead."

Before Ribic could reply, a new voice broke from Antonescu's helmet-mounted earphones.

"Dancer, this is the com center. Dancer, this is the com center, come in please."

"Com center, this is Magyar," Antonescu broke in. "General Winston is dead. I am assuming command. What is your message?"

There was no immediate reply. Antonescu knew that his simple statement of Ariana Winston's death would seem cruel and heartless to some, but on a battlefield there was little room for emotion. That would have to come later.

"Com center, this is Magyar," Antonescu repeated. "What is your message?"

"Colonel, I have Commodore Beresick on the line. He is asking to speak to General Winston."

"I will take it." A shiver ran along Antonescu's spine. He knew that Commodore Beresick had detected an incoming fleet of unidentified JumpShips. He had been in the command post when Beresick had promised to advise Winston when he learned the identity of the new arrivals. To Colonel Charles Antonescu, Beresick's call sounded like a death knell for Task Force Serpent.

"Courtyard, this is Magyar," he said finally, his voice an emotionless monotone. "I am in command of the northern army. What is your report?"

After a moment's hesitation, Beresick came on line. "Colonel, this is Beresick." There was an odd note in the Commodore's voice. It sounded to Antonescu like equal parts of joy and relief.

"The inbounds are Task Force Bulldog," Beresick said. "I am in contact with Prince Victor Steiner-Davion and the Precentor Martial. They said to tell you, 'Well done and prepare to stand down.' They'll take over from here."

Antonescu stared open-mouthed at the communication set. "Clear the net," he barked. "Say again, Courtyard."

Beresick repeated his message.

Antonescu sighed and hung his head. Unlooked for and against all hope, Task Force Bulldog had made the long trip from the Inner Sphere, somehow arriving at Huntress just as the embattled Task Force Serpent seemed to have run out of options. It was almost too good to be true, a rescue straight out of some adventure holovid. Except that this was real life, and they had not arrived in time to save Ariana Winston.

"Message to Prince Victor. Magyar understands and will comply. Magyar out."

With trembling hands, Antonescu unlocked and removed his heavy neurohelmet. The crimson stain had finally cleared from his sight, but his vision was by no means clear. He looked up the narrow, bloodstained mountain pass to the broken hulk of what had once been the command 'Mech for the entire Light Horse brigade.

"I'm sorry, Ariana," he whispered. "I'm sorry I wasn't able to help you. I'm sorry . . ." The halting words were cut off by the first shallow gasp of sorrow, and tears welled up in Antonescu's eyes.

Ten days later, the battle of Huntress was over.

With the arrival of relatively fresh combat troops, the Smoke Jaguars were faced with two choices, surrender or die a glorious death in battle. Only a few elected to lay down their arms. Most held true to their stubborn Clan pride and sold themselves as dearly as they could. The newly arrived Inner Sphere troops quickly overwhelmed the Jaguars, taking only light casualties in the process.

As he stood in the shadows of the wrecked statues that had once proclaimed the Smoke Jaguars' triumph across the Field of Heroes, Andrew Redburn wished he could say the same for Task Force Serpent.

Of the eight regiments that had landed on that blood-soaked world, only a fraction remained. Hundreds of men and women who had put aside all thought of self to make the long trek through unknown space to war on a distant planet were now buried in the red-stained soil of the world they had given their lives to take and hold. Thousands more were horribly wounded, their flesh and bones torn and burned on the altar of war. Others bore wounds that no one could see—broken spirits and tormented minds, sanity sacrificed, and to what?

Redburn knew that many people would ask that question in the years and decades to come. What had Operation Serpent accomplished?

Gazing out across the broken Field of Heroes, he looked south across Lootera. The city was almost untouched by the terrible conflict that had raged near the north end of its gray buildings and straight, narrow streets. Only a few structures, those with some military value, had been damaged or destroyed. In the heart of Lootera stood a gutted shell, the ruins of the secondary Smoke Jaguar command center.

Almost as though she'd foreseen her own death, Winston had left a package of instructions for Redburn, just as Morgan had done for her. In those instructions, he learned of the last, and smallest, contingent of warriors attached to Task Force Serpent. No one had received an after-action report from the nekekami. Redburn knew that the ruined C3 building in Lootera meant that the team had succeeded in their final mission, but had any of the shadow agents survived? He might never know.

Prisoners taken when the newly arrived Inner Sphere troops moved into Lootera had revealed that Lincoln Osis had been badly wounded in an honor duel with an Inner Sphere warrior who had faced him with a sword. The Inner Sphere warrior was dead and Osis had returned to Strana Mechty. According to the prisoners' testimony, his ship had jumped out of the Huntress system less than five hours before Task Force Bulldog arrived.

The prisoners also told their captors that Galaxy Commander Hang Mehta was dead. She had apparently exercised a little-used rite in Clan culture, the rite of bondsref. Instead of having to submit to the indignity of becoming a bondsman to those she considered foul barbarians, Mehta had one of her subordinates shoot her through the head, in a form of ritual suicide or murder. In fact, few Clan officers above the rank of Star Captain had been made bondsmen. Most fought until they themselves were killed or chose the rite of bondsref over capture.

The garrison's original Galaxy Commander, Russou Howell, was missing. Supposedly he had been in the command center when it was destroyed, but his body had yet to be recovered. Some civilians claimed to have seen the Jaguar officer leave the building moments before it was torn apart by a massive explosion. Redburn snorted in half-amusement at the mystery. Were this the Inner Sphere, they'd be receiving "Howell-sightings" for the next twenty years.

For the Eridani Light Horse, there was a single bright spot in the grim aftermath of the campaign. The missing Colonel Edwin Amis had been found in the prison ward of a Clan military hospital. After being forced to eject from his wrecked *Orion,* Amis had tried to evade capture by the Clan forces overrunning the battlefield. When cornered by a Star of Elementals, he tried to fight his way free using only his reckless courage and a laser pistol. One of the hulking warriors clubbed him to the ground, claiming the mercenary officer as a bondsman.

When they learned that Amis was alive, Charles Antonescu and Sandra Barclay, who was still suffering from an injured back, commandeered a FedCom hoverjeep to go to his side. When they arrived, they discovered their comrade sitting up in a hospital bed, a thick bandage wrapped around his head, and, in open defiance of the hospital prohibition, a thin black cigar clenched in his teeth.

For a moment the Light Horse officers stared in disbelief at Amis. Sandra Barclay recovered first.

"Blast your hide, Ed," she growled between clenched teeth. "We thought you were dead. There we were, up to our armpits in blood and Clanners, and where were you? Sitting here in this nice clean hospital, smoking a bloody cigar. I ought to shoot you myself."

"Now, Sandy," Amis said, smiling. "Who would replace me if you did that? Another one like Charles here? C'mon, just think how dull things would be without me."

"Bah," Barclay snorted and turned away, allowing Antonescu to take his turn.

Since her vicious close-quarters duel with the Jaguar *Man o' War,* something had changed in Sandra Barclay. The furtive glances, the white knuckles, the shaking hands were all gone, leaving in their place a quiet confidence. She knew she was not quite the solid, steady officer she had been before Coventry, but she was well on the road to recovery.

Barclay shivered, feeling the emptiness where General Winston should have been. She looked toward the ceiling of the hospital ward and quietly said, "Don't worry about me, General. I'm just fine now."

In a corner of her mind, she imagined Winston's reply.

"Yes, Colonel, I know."

Gazing out over the ruins of a shattered world, Andrew Redburn suddenly became aware that he was not alone. He turned to see a trio of men keeping a respectful distance.

"I'm sorry, Andrew, we didn't mean to disturb you," Prince Victor Ian Steiner-Davion said.

Redburn quickly came to attention and saluted. "No, Highness, it's all right. I was just thinking."

"You were thinking of all those who are not here to share in this moment, were you not?" Anastasius Focht said quietly. "And you were thinking of all those who you wish could have been here to share in it."

"Yes, Precentor Martial, there have been so many along the way who worked and fought and bled to bring about this moment. Some are buried right out there." Redburn pointed to the long rows of white-painted steel markers where burial details had interred the dead of Clan Smoke Jaguar and Task Force Serpent alike. "Others have been buried on countless worlds after countless battles for nearly three hundred years. And now, it looks like a lot more good men and women have gone the same way."

"Yes, Redburn-*san*." The third man, Hohiro Kurita, spoke at last. "They will be buried here on Huntress, but they have not truly died, not so long as the dream for which they gave their lives still stands. So long as men and women seek to live in peace and freedom, those who died here will live in our memories as patriots and martyrs to that noble cause."

A sudden pang of regret pierced Redburn's heart.

"Your Highness, I'm sorry. I should have said something sooner, Morgan . . ."

"Is dead," Prince Victor said, completing his thought. "I

figured that out when I was told you were in command of the task force. I'm sorry we didn't get here sooner."

Redburn stared at him. "I never knew you would come at all."

"Blast," Victor swore. "Maybe if we'd gotten here sooner, Morgan would still be alive."

"Hasn't anyone told you?" Redburn asked.

"Told me what?" Victor obviously knew nothing.

"You don't understand, Highness." Redburn's voice cracked as he struggled for control. "Morgan wasn't killed in battle. He was murdered in his bed aboard the *Invisible Truth* long before we got to Huntress."

As Redburn laid out the details surrounding Morgan's death and the subsequent events, Victor Davion's face grew pale, then flushed with anger. Sadness and rage warred in his eyes. For a moment, Redburn was afraid he had said too much all at once. Then, the Prince of the Federated Commonwealth's face cleared once again. Only his clear blue eyes showed any trace of the latest sorrow that fate had heaped upon him.

"Revenge will have to wait for another day," Victor said. "This business *still* isn't over. Lincoln Osis escaped, as did a number of his warriors. We still have to hunt them down and destroy them."

For a long while the four of them stood silently, each keeping to his own thoughts, looking out over the ruined statues, the bodies being prepared for burial, and the pall of smoke rising above the city of Lootera.

This is the true horror of war, Redburn told himself. *The human cost.*

The keening wail of a pair of hovercars shattered the grim spell that held them. The vehicles pulled to a stop, discharging Charles Antonescu, Sandra Barclay, Paul Masters, and the rest of the unit commanders who had led the campaign on Huntress. Victor Davion, Hohiro Kurita, and the Precentor Martial had words of congratulations, gratitude, and solace for each of them.

"I was going to ask you for a full commanders' debriefing," Victor said, expanding his gaze to include all of the officers of Task Force Serpent. "But I think that can wait until tomorrow or even the next day."

Davion turned to Charles Antonescu. "Colonel, I'm truly sorry. I understand that if we had arrived a few hours sooner . . ." He broke off, realizing how futile were the words. "Anyway, I want you to know we'll be taking General Winston's body back to the Inner Sphere with us. She'll be given a state funeral with full military honors, right along with Morgan."

"No, your Highness." Antonescu shook his head. "Thank you very much, but no. It is the tradition with the Eridani Light Horse to bury its dead in the soil for which they fought. We will bury General Winston alongside her troops, in the soil of Huntress. I can think of no more fitting place than this, the place we have all sanctified with our blood."

Victor nodded his understanding. The traditions of the Eridani Light Horse stretched back to the Star League. He would not ask Antonescu to break them now.

"Ah, your Highness," Colonel MacLeod said to the Prince with a gleam in his eye. "I'm sure you know that the Eridani Light Horse was once a Star League unit and that the Northwind Highlanders had exceptionally close ties to the SLDF."

"Of course I know that, Colonel," Victor answered warily. "That's why they were selected for this task force. Where are you going with this?"

MacLeod's craggy face split into a mischievous grin. "Well, Your Highness," he said. "I was just wantin' to discuss the small matter of three hundred years' back pay."

Epilogue

Captured Military Hospital
Lootera, Huntress
Kerensky Cluster, Clan Space
09 April 3060

Awareness returned slowly to Star Colonel Paul Moon. He had no idea how long he had been unconscious. All he knew was that he was lying uncomfortably on his stomach, his left arm stretched stiffly at his side. He could feel the pull of elastic butterfly closures where they stretched across a deep, jagged gash on his face and forehead. His back throbbed dully through the haze of pain-killers he knew the medical technicians must have pumped into his body after the battle outside Lootera. Oddly, his right arm seemed to be asleep. He could feel the strange pins-and-needles sensation of blood beginning to flow through it again. He tried to flex the arm, but nothing happened. In his sleep and drug-fogged mind he thought he must have been lying on the rm for quite some time if it refused to obey his will.

Moon lifted his head a few painful centimeters from the thin hospital pillow and saw the truth. His right arm and shoulder, along with much of the muscle from his chest, and, by the feel of it, his upper back, were simply gone.

Then he remembered the black rain of submunitions that had broken his charge against the *stravag* invaders. One of those small bomblets had struck him in the back, slicing his arm from his body, leaving a ragged, bloody wound behind.

Moon dropped his head to the pillow and closed his eyes.

Why was I not allowed to die? What trick of perverse fate would allow me to live as a cripple?

He knew that his chances of being allowed to undergo the budding process again, this time to grow a new arm, were nonexistent. He knew that the Smoke Jaguars would look upon a warrior who had been twice wounded so grievously as inherently flawed, and would not waste the precious scientific resources needed to bud a new limb a second time.

"Good afternoon, Star Colonel." The voice was familiar, but Moon could not immediately place it. He opened his eyes.

"You!"

"Me," the horribly scarred man dressed in the olive drab field uniform of a Star League MechWarrior said quietly.

"I do not know what devil's trick you used to escape your death, traitor, or by what foul magic you now stand before me wearing the uniform of the Star League," Moon rasped out. "Well, it was that I named you traitor. Would that you had died." His voice sounded as though he was speaking through broken glass. "Have you come here to gloat?"

"Gloat, Star Colonel Paul Moon?" Trent echoed. "Some say it is the right of the victor to gloat over the vanquished. But no, I have not come here to gloat over the fall of Huntress. Nor have I come to rejoice in the fall of my Clan. Seeing our homeworld reduced to smoking ruin gives me no pleasure. But I must admit that it is rather gratifying to see the man who destroyed me as a Smoke Jaguar brought low."

Trent shook his head sadly before speaking again. "Why did you hate me so? Was it because I was among those who fought at Tukayyid and yet lived? Was it because you believed that I failed my Clan? Well, Star Colonel, think on this. You are one of those who lost Huntress to the Inner Sphere and yet you live. You failed your Clan far more grievously than ever I did. Worse, you are to be a bondsman to the very Inner Sphere 'barbarians' who invaded and wrecked your homeworld and who have exterminated your Clan."

"You *savashri* freebirth traitor," Moon cursed, knowing what Trent said to be true. "If you have one drop of trueborn Smoke Jaguar blood in your filthy honorless veins, you will grant me bondsref. I ask you to release me from my shame. Kill me."

Trent threw back his head and laughed.

"Bondsref? Kill you? Oh no, Star Colonel Paul Moon. Why should I grant you the release you seek, when I will have to live with my own shame? No, I believe that you should live a long and useless and miserable life, wallowing in the bitter poison of the knowledge that you failed as a warrior.

"And know this, Paul Moon." Trent's voice rose in volume as he stabbed a single scarred and bony finger directly into Moon's defiant face. "You are the very smith who forged the instrument of your own destruction.

"Do you wonder who it was that revealed the Exodus Road to the Inner Sphere? It was I. And how did I acquire that secret? I mapped it out during the long voyage to Huntress to which you condemned me. Were it not for your blind, stupid hatred of me, and all of my generation, Huntress would still be untouched and the Smoke Jaguars would yet be the proudest and strongest of all the Clans. You, Paul Moon, caused your own destruction, and that of your Clan."

Trent turned then and walked away.

Watching him, the man he had hated for so long, Paul Moon felt the defiance and pride drain out of him, making him feel like a broken thing.

What Trent had said was true.

About the Author

Thomas S. Gressman lives with his wife, Brenda, and an assault lance of house cats in the foothills of western Pennsylvania. When not busily engaged in fighting wars in the thirty-first century, he divides his time between leathercrafting, living history reenactment, and a worship music ministry, all of which tends to leave him seriously, and permanently, time-lagged. *Shadows of War* is his third BattleTech™ novel. Previously published are *The Hunters* and *Sword and Fire,* also part of the Twilight of the Clans series.

Cyclops

Cauldron-Born

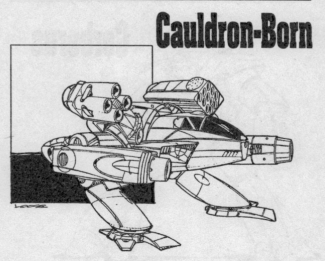

Thor

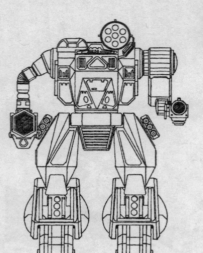

Cerberus

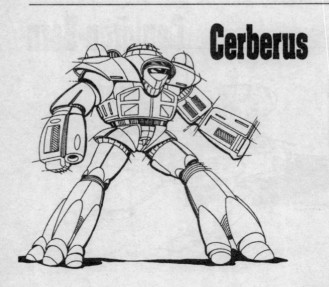

Shilone

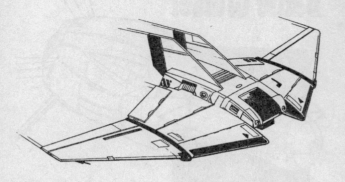

Elemental

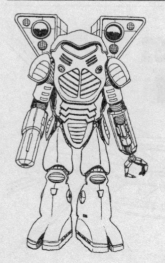

Black Lion Class
Battle Cruiser

Cameron Class
Battle Cruiser

Don't miss the next thrilling book in the
Twilight of the Clans series!

PRINCE OF HAVOC
by Michael A. Stackpole

Trained to be one of the best warriors in the
Inner Sphere, Prince Victor Steiner-Davion has
only known one enemy on the field of battle:
the Clans. A year earlier he led a massive
counterstrike against them, shattering the
Smoke Jaguars, sending them in a headlong
retreat to their homeworld, and he followed.
From there he travels to Strana Mechty, to face
all of the Clans in one last battle that will forever alter the future of the Inner Sphere.

But for such a man of war, can there ever be
real peace? And how will he react when he dis-
covers that the realm he left behind has been
swept away, and he is now a hero without a
home.

Coming from Roc in December 1998!